DHANAPATIR CHAR

ADVANCE PRAISE FOR THE BOOK

'Amar Mitra, an accomplished fiction writer in contemporary Bengali literature, has conceptualized *Dhanapatir Char* with rare originality and insight. Time weighs down on readers like an ambiguous and mysterious dream. We slip through the closely woven layers of the gradually unfolding narrative and feel as if we are approaching the edges of our earthly abode. None can escape the significance of the temporal yet multipolar existence unfolded by Dhanapati, Dhaneshwari, Yamuna, Batasi, Kunti, Sabitri, Pedru, Nabadwip Malakar et al. Throughout, reality mingles with timeless collective memory on the one hand, and, on the other, the guiles of scheming power are thwarted by the magic of the infinite. It appears that the author has led us through a maze and we have no other option except walking around. The reader realizes that worldly existence is nothing but a metaphor. Dhanapati and his meta-world symbolize predestined collapse of habitations and possibilities. The novel has been brilliantly conceived and brings the reader under a hypnotic spell, with its surreal expositions and exuberant storytelling. *Dhanapatir Char* is both alluring and outlandish, yet none can escape its deep socio-philosophical message'—Tapodhir Bhattacharjee, eminent poet, critic, literary theorist and editor of *Shatakratu*

DHANAPATIR CHAR

Whatever Happened to Pedru's Island?

AMAR MITRA

Translated from the Bengali by
JHIMLI MUKHERJEE PANDEY

VINTAGE
An imprint of Penguin Random House

VINTAGE

USA | Canada | UK | Ireland | Australia
New Zealand | India | South Africa | China

Vintage is part of the Penguin Random House group of companies
whose addresses can be found at global.penguinrandomhouse.com

Published by Penguin Random House India Pvt. Ltd
4th Floor, Capital Tower 1, MG Road,
Gurugram 122 002, Haryana, India

First published in Vintage by Penguin Random House India 2022

ISBN 9780670095223

Typeset in Adobe Garamond Pro by MAP Systems, Bengaluru, India
Printed at Replika Press Pvt. Ltd, India

www.penguin.co.in

Jhimli worked very hard on this book, but she never ever ignored her better half (Ramesh) and her son (Vaibhav). More than journalism, she always got a thrill in completing a book. She would always tell me that anybody and everybody nowadays can become a journalist, but they can't become an author. Vaibhav and I are very proud of her achievements. She has never left us, as we feel her presence in our lives every day.

—Ramesh Pandey

Part I

One

And so, the isle rose above the water, says Dhanapati,
The rivers merged into the sea around it.

Six and a half leagues away from Ghoradal, at the estuary of the Bay of Bengal, the island of Dhanapati rose above the waters like the back of a tortoise. People believed it to be a real giant of a tortoise that had been sleeping there for thousands of years. Just like the tortoise avatar of Vishnu, deep in slumber by the bay. As time passed, silt collected on its stagnant back and, gradually, the island was born. For a period of six months each year, as the waters receded somewhat, the island rose to become home for those who came to live and work there. Six months later they would return to Ghoradal, only to come back in another six.

No one at Ghoradal knew who had actually measured the distance of the island to Ghoradal. Those who went to live on the island temporarily didn't know it either. Some people, like the old Dhanapati Sardar, who might be as ancient as the tortoise itself, say that what used to be six and a half leagues during the time of the European pirates is now not less than ten leagues. After all, the island of Dhanapati is not stable! Every day, it is inching towards the sea. Even in its slumber, the ancient tortoise avatar is instinctively preparing for a sea voyage towards Lisbon—the land of the Portuguese pirate. One fine day, in the month of Ashwin just after Durga Puja, boats carrying settlers from Ghoradal to the island will not be able to locate it anymore. The tortoise avatar will vanish, leaving behind only frothy waves all around.

There are rivers—never-ending and deep, just like the sea—on three sides of the island except the southern side. Old Dhanapati says, this six-months-a-year world will not remain forever. It cannot. And perhaps, the death of the island would mark the awakening of the tortoise avatar. The engulfing high tides during the peak monsoon of the Bhadra month shake him up and make him move forward. He will carry coconut, betel nut, mango, balsam, ebony and other trees that grow well in the marshy coastal environs of the place on his wooded back, and move away from one water to the next. The truth is that the island of Dhanapati will not stay forever.

For that matter, is anything permanent in this world? People of Ghoradal and those who set up their six-monthly home on the island say that, perhaps, the tortoise avatar—the chieftain of all tortoises in the world—and the earth are the only things that are forever. At least they've lived on for thousands of years. These southern lands have seen so many generations of foreign pirates and looters. They've come and gone and their tales are mostly forgotten now, but the world they left behind stays on. Ghoradal remains and so does the tortoise chief. That, of course, doesn't mean that they will stay on forever. Dhanapati Sardar knows that it often takes one, maybe two, or sometimes even seven days to cross the distance of ten or thirty leagues from Ghoradal, but still, the island of Dhanapati will not be found. The ancient chief of the tortoises will either move towards foreign shores or go down under, within the depths of the sea. The abyss of the sea is difficult to fathom. So, the deeper he goes, the further it seems to deepen.

The island will simply vanish, not leaving so much as a speck on the water underneath the canopy of the sky. The sea will become one with the rivers in the north, east and west directions; the sea will engulf them. You will not be able to differentiate between rivers from their colour anymore. The island might even carry a river with it too. It's possible that the Kalnagini river, to the north of the island, would move along with it and raise its crocodile-like head in the land of the pirates. The Kalnagini river is infested with crocodiles; the greedy creatures prey on living beings in Ghoradal and on the island too. To reach the island of Dhanapati from Ghoradal, you have to sail on the Kalnagini. The river, true to its name, flows in never-ending, serpentine twists and turns; gets lost in other rivers; and ultimately finds its way back, wriggling and slithering along, till it reaches the island of Dhanapati.

The island comes alive only for six months. For the remaining six—from Baishakh to Ashwin—old Dhanapati says, is the time when the tortoise chief wakes up from sleep. After goddess Durga returns home, he goes back to his slumber and that is when people choose to come to the island.

Though old Dhanapati believes that the island will vanish one day, the fortune seekers—the fisherwomen who come to the island for six months—say the old man is wrong.

'You are mistaken, chief. The island will exist as long as the sun and the moon will.'

Old Dhanapati asks, 'So how long will your sun and moon exist?'

'As long as the sky holds the stars, the sun and the moon will exist.'

The old man waves his stick and asks, 'For how long will the sky and the stars be around?'

The girls snap back readily, 'For as long as the island lives.' And then they wave the loose end of their saree impatiently to shut the old man up.

In Ashwin, after goddess Durga leaves, the fishermen are reminded of the island and of the fisherwomen they meet there, as is the case every year. Leaving their homes, wives and children back in Ghoradal, they set out for the island. Over the next six months, they will fish, dry the catch and send out the dried fish via Ghoradal to unknown shores. The fisherwomen come to Ghoradal from everywhere and are one of the many reasons why the men come here, year after year, unfailingly. It's an island of desire too. The whole island is like a sensuous woman who begins to spread her charm from the month of Ashwin. Men and women are enamoured by that call alike. The fisherwomen literally starve between Baishakh and Ashwin, feeding on grass and leaves. It is during their six-monthly stay on the island from the end of Ashwin to Chaitra that they eat . . . eat and live . . . happy and less starved, even sexually. You see them alive and feel their rhythm as they join the annual puja of the tortoise chief, dancing to the tune that was coined to celebrate life on the island, 'So long as the moon and the sun live . . .'

On the full moon night of Kartik, the fishermen and women worship the tortoise chief underneath a Malabar ebony tree, towards the southern side of the island. They take the whole day to build a massive clay tortoise with a trunk and shells for eyes. The clay image has its trunk outside the shell, just like when thunderous clouds gather and the sky is overcast, it is said. They build the entire image with great care, down to the trunk. There are some women who are experts in modelling the face and the trunk. Some even thought the trunk looked like a man's manhood. They would joke with the maker and say, 'Batashi, what a perfect trunk and why not? After all, you have known it better than anyone else, isn't it?' While making the back of the tortoise, men help out and there is no mistaking its likeness to a woman's bosom! Women notice this invariably and try to hide behind their veils. The tortoise chief takes on male and female attributes and creates an aura of fantasy as it is worshipped underneath the ebony tree on the island. The preparations for the puja are elaborate. All the time, the women imagine that one day, old Dhanapati would tell them that the tortoise chief has gone to sleep, and will not wake up in a short while. It would go off to sleep with the island on its back, not to move an inch for a hundred thousand years.

'How long is a hundred thousand years, old man?'

'Ones, tens, hundreds, thousands, ten thousand, hundred thousand . . . many, many years.'

'Shall we live for a hundred thousand years?'

'You women are just incorrigible!'

The puja of the tortoise chief is unique to the island; you will not find it anywhere else on earth. Batashi had lived an absolutely wretched life for the last six months. She landed up in Kolkata and spent the torrential rains of Shravan on the pavements there; got soaked to the skin yet again in Bhadra and spent sleepless nights; then took shelter in the scraggy hut of a rickshaw puller only to get kicked out and roamed about aimlessly, all skin and bone. As soon as the sky turned azure blue, she headed towards Ghoradal. Here, she got a saree at the donation camp during the pujas. Covering herself as best as she could with it, she moved to the island the moment Ma Durga was immersed in the water. She reached and prayed, 'May the island live as long as the sun and the moon shall . . .'

A month after she came to the island, Batashi has started filling out and is looking rosier. She is the most enthusiastic about the worship of the tortoise chief. She has brought her mate for six months to the celebrations underneath the Malabar ebony. The other fishermen have also returned from the mouth of the sea to join in with their women in tow; their mates for six months. Together, they are rejoicing and celebrating, praying for the long life of the tortoise chief. The annual event has become so popular that even traders have landed up on the island from Ghoradal. Each one present at the venue has come with some desire, some wish to be fulfilled.

It's Kartik Purnima today. The moon looks like a ball of gold in the sky, almost like the smooth underbelly of a golden tortoise. You can see the shadow of the fisherwomen's bosom on the moon, the smoothness reminding you of their shapely bellies. The tortoise chief is worshipped in silence. He is lovingly lulled to sleep by the fisherwomen. No one blows the conch shell, rings the customary bell or beats the drum.

Batashi hums a lullaby, 'Sleep, chief, sleep. We offer you water, milk, bananas, sweets, bread and biscuits. We offer you a hatchling of a killer crocodile.' She asks others to join in the hymns.

Jamuna and Kunti follow her. 'Sleep, sleep. We are keeping you warm by lighting a fire nearby. We are spreading a blanket over you. Here's jaggery and date juice. Go on and sleep like a baby as we keep watch.'

Batashi whispers, 'On the dark Kartik night, the full moon shines bright. Her light washes the bay and quiet our good chief lay . . . O lord of the tortoises, sleep . . .

The fisherwomen keep murmuring, 'O lord of the tortoises, you sleep underneath the sea. O lord of the tortoises, you hold the world's key. Millions of years ago, when all was water and there was no land . . .'

Jamuna doesn't remember who told her this story. She has been coming to the island for ten years now. She must have heard it in the course of these ten years from one of these fishermen, from a trader or perhaps from old Dhanapati himself. One night, the old man sat up telling Jamuna the story of Anna Bibi and while on that story, he went on to another. The other story happened much before old Dhanapati or Anna Bibi's time. Jamuna could have been as young as Batashi then. She too had Batashi's youth and vitality at one time. She was fertile and full of youthful desires. Her youth would dry and shrivel up for six months but Ashwin came with the promise of food. And even before Kartik was out, her body filled out again, like the full moon. She had spent one season with old Dhanapati. He would look at her and say, 'You remind me of Anna, have you heard of her?'

Look at old Dhanapati sitting there on his red plastic chair. He has brought these chairs from Ghoradal. When big people come visiting the island, they invariably visit old Dhanapati's shack and even spend the night there. So, he makes arrangements for such occasions. Jamuna turned towards Dhanapati and said, '. . . that was the time when there was water all around and the tortoise chief was alone. There was no island here, no world as we know it today. The world was born later.'

Everyone knew this story. The year before last, Jamuna had told it to Batashi. Others have also heard it from Jamuna. This is the only story that she knows well. The story of the tortoise chief that she had heard once was the only story she lived and loved. She didn't think that there could be any story beyond it. She kept looking at old Dhanapati as she went about her story. The tortoise chief floated in and, with him, came a lotus leaf. The chief received the leaf on his back and kept floating. Earthworms started depositing mud on the lotus leaf.

Batashi took the baton from Jamuna and continued the story. The day the back of the tortoise chief was filled with clay and mud was the full moon of Kartik. 'The night of Kartik full moon, darkness awash . . . teem with youth and life, this island lush. Then came Dhanapati, not the one you see, another Dhanapati.'

Old Dhanapati does not agree with this theory. 'No one but me. I am the only Dhanapati here.'

'The first man to set foot on the island was Dhanapati. This happens every time. There were Dhanapatis before you and there will be Dhanapatis hereafter. On a full moon Kartik night . . . the face of Dhanapati came in sight.'

Dhanapati is very old. This year, he is wielding a lathi. Till last year, it wasn't like this. He could walk straight in his six-foot-tall frame. After all, he is a descendant of European pirates. No one knows this and no one talks about it, but Dhanapati knows for certain that he belongs to Lisbon and that his ancestor was the fierce pirate, Pedru. Once upon a time, the rivers and the seas had been under the control of the pirates. The blood of these pirates runs in Dhanapati's veins, making him the rightful owner of the island and the rivers that flow around it.

Batashi hums her favourite lines, 'Dhanapati, Dhanapati sails on his boat . . . which route, how long did he stay afloat?' Old Dhanapati snapped at her. 'Sing the litany of the tortoise chief, girl! Old Dhanapati is as old as your great-grandfather, you don't have to think about him.'

Batashi pulled her veil over her face to hide a giggle. One month on the island has magically filled out her body. She knelt before the clay idol of the tortoise with her hands folded. You can clearly see her heavy and shapely hips; you can feel her heavy, rounded breasts and her comely thighs . . . a perfect female figure. Old Dhanapati's words fell on deaf ears.

'The real Dhanapati is the tortoise chief, the master of the island. So, I sing,'

> Golden Dhanapati, tortoise chief,
> Here's milk and rice to expand your fief.

> This full moon night, we won't fall asleep,
> Welcome Dhanapati, our promise we keep.

Old Dhanapati agreed. Indeed, one was golden when one was young. 'Those who knew me in my youth, would vouch for that!'

The middle-aged Jamuna looked at him. She smiled through her eyes. 'Why pine for your youth, handsome . . . the tortoise master is forever lissome.'

A forty-year-old man came and stood behind old Dhanapati. He wore jeans and a red jacket and was a redhead. Beside him stood a cop dressed in khakis. 'Stop, stop Batashi. Enough. Mangal Babu government has himself come with this gentleman. Sir, when did you come to the island?'

The constable of Ghoradal police station, Mangal Midde said, 'This is Dasharath Singh. He hails from Purulia. It is there that we met. I was posted there before I was transferred to Ghoradal. He had heard of the island from me and has hence come here for business.'

Two fishermen pulled up two plastic chairs. Mangal Midde and Dasharath Singh sat down. Batashi started humming again. Soon Jamuna and the sixteen- or seventeen-year-old Kunti joined in. Not long thereafter, three more young fisherwomen, two old fisherwomen and two young girls were added to the group.

> The night of the Kartik full moon is awash with light
> For Dhanapati's attention, the damsels fight.
> One chief Dhanapati slumbers in the deep,
> The other on top has an island to keep.
> Both Dhanapatis are wakeful throughout,
> The sly crocodile thieves, fish that sprout.

Batashi stopped to catch her breath. 'We don't just talk about the tortoise chief, we talk of all Dhanapatis. But we will now keep quiet, let the tortoise sleep now. As long as he is asleep, we are safe. He had said before going off to sleep that he would sleep for a hundred thousand years . . . master, how long is a hundred thousand years?'

Two

Lulled in night waters, Dhanapati sleeps,
Moon-soaked coil, his slumber keeps.

The night is dark; it ticks on and minds old Dhanapati's sleep. The prayers sound like a lullaby. The verses have been taught by Dhanapati Sardar. And why not? He is the one who discovered the island. He has been coming to the island year after year after year and now, he is old. Dhanapati the tortoise, on whose back the island rests, is ageless. No one has kept count of his age. The fisherwomen know that he too is Dhanapati. They say that he is much older than Dhanapati Sardar, the owner of the island. There was another Dhanapati before this chief and another before that and yet another before him. Whoever owns the island is called Dhanapati. The tortoise chief, however, sleeps on, with the island on his back, oblivious of time.

The fisherwomen hummed their lullaby. They will watch the night cross over as they sing their lilting tune. The men will leave one by one, only the women will stay on under the ebony tree. These are childless women. There is no system of childbearing and birthing in this world that comes alive for six months. For the remaining six months, they live on the streets, leading the lives of beggars and surviving somehow. That too is an unwelcome world for bringing in another life. So, it is in singing their lullaby and lulling and cradling Dhanapati to sleep that they quench their thirst for motherhood.

Who sleeps? Dhanapati, the tortoise. Who remains awake? Batashi, Yamuna, Kunti and Sabitri. Who sleeps? The treasure that they guard with their bosom.

'Who's that woman?' the trader asked in a low tone.

'A fisherwoman,' said Mangal Midde.

'Very beautiful for a fisherwoman,' the trader continued in his low voice.

'Pretty, yes, but don't ignore the fishy smell in her body and mouth. You can smell that from a distance! They live here for six months and then wander here and there for the remaining six.'

'What's the name of the fisherwoman?' the trader asked.

'Batashi, she's Ganesh fisherman's wife,' Midde said.

'There's no denying that she raises my urge, constable bro,' the trader said.

'Rest that for now, they are putting their tortoise god to sleep,' Midde said in a low voice.

'Six months on the island and six months as a vagabond . . . so where's the trouble, constable sir?! That woman arouses me every time I look at her. Look at the way she thumps her thigh and how her bosom heaves. Look at her hips. I just cannot wait!'

'Wait, wait . . . don't rush! Where's the hurry? They are all within my control!'

Their humming fills the air. 'Don't talk, government sahib. The old tortoise chief will sleep now. He is old and lacks proper sleep these days,' old Dhanapati said. '. . . even whispers and small noises can break his slumber. Then he remains awake for the rest of the night. What if he wants to toss and turn? Will that be good for us?'

Batashi mumbled her lines,

'Kartik full moon is a wakeful night,
Deep beneath, sleeps Dhanapati tight.
The moon-washed night keeps all awake,
Comely Dhanapati, our slumber you take.'

'Tortoise worship? You get tortoises here?' the trader asked.

'Will tell you later . . .' Mangal Midde said in a low voice.

'It's winter and tortoise meat is particularly juicy now . . .'

'Aah! Stop talking!'

Trader Dasharath Singh was quiet for a few moments, but he was talkative and couldn't stay quiet for long. 'Does she sing?'

'Don't you hear that she is singing a lullaby?'

'Look at her buxom body, who can sleep after having seen that? Look at how aroused I am!'

Chief Dhanapati turned around and looked at them, signalling them to be quiet. He indicated that the tortoise chief was about to fall asleep below the waters. Dasharath continued to whisper. It reached Jamuna's ears now. She stopped humming suddenly and snapped, 'Stop talking! Who's this man? Why does he talk so much?

'Okay, okay. He won't talk anymore,' Mangal Midde stepped in.

'I heard him. Why does he talk like that?!'

'Okay, okay . . . what he said was wrong.'

'If you talk, the tortoise chief will wake up. He holds the island on his back. In the deep, he is the one who saves men from the storms, the white pirates and their demons, the magical breezes and illusions . . . there are death traps everywhere!'

'But he is asleep!' Dasharath reasons.

'He is asleep here but awake there. There's an island in the big waters which is home to the eggs of these tortoises. They lay their eggs there and get into the water of the ocean, the menfolk have told us.'

'Kartik full moon silent and deep,

Sunken chief goes to sleep, to sleep.

Dhanapati, Dhanapati slumbering chief,

Water-coiled moonlight washes the reef.

Only after the night graduates will he sleep.'

'Constable sir, I want that fisherwoman . . . none other than Batashi.'

'Totally up to you,' replied Mangal Midde.

'You will help me with getting her?'

'She's already got a man for these six months. Try next year.'

Dasharath heaves. The moon has crossed over to the west, lighting up Batashi's face and breasts. The earthen lamp under the ebony tree has blown out. The kerosene lamp too is flickering, perhaps the oil has burnt off. Dasharath tries his best to attract Batashi's gaze but it slides each time. She stops humming and tells Jamuna to offer prasad to the men and see them off before the women start to sing again.

'No, no, please go on singing . . . let my heart go pit-a-pat,' the trader requests.

Batashi laughs and starts to hum. Pulling her saree to cover her waist, she sings,

> In the Kartik full moon night, all sleep but one,
> His eyes are on one and settle for none.

'Shut up! The trader's not a good guy,' scolded Jamuna.

'What does he sell?'

'Warm clothes, wrappers, soap and scented oil, I think.'

'What else does he sell?'

'Perhaps creams, powders, vermilion, lipstick and nail polish.'

'He's a bad guy . . . that trader,' Jamuna Di.

'Bad? He's evil, no less. Only if you heard what he was saying . . .' Jamuna said.

'His body . . . his loins . . . his mind, both are lustfully aroused,' Batashi laughed aloud.

'You heard it all?!'

'She stays here for six months and roams the other six . . . one look at her and I cannot control myself . . .' Batashi repeated what the trader had been whispering to Mangal Midde.

'What a woman you are! You think you can put the tortoise chief to sleep with your song?'

'Six months on the island and six months in his rooms, what say, Didi?'

'No, no . . . not possible! Shut up, dear!' Jamuna said helplessly.

'Wish he was a man who sails on the water, Didi!'

'I implore you to be quiet. This island has its own rules and its own traditions, girl.'

'I know, I know. I was just joking. As if I care for him! On this full moon night in Kartik, come bring the food offerings for the tortoise chief. He'll have it when he wakes up.'

Jamuna shook her head from side to side. 'The tortoise chief won't wake up so soon,' she said.

'Then let's distribute it among the others. Where's your man?'

'Not here. Must be drinking somewhere . . . Where's your Ganesh?'

'He was here, a while ago. There are so many babus who have come from Ghoradal, he must be sitting with them somewhere and drinking too!'

'They didn't even stay to listen to our songs.'

'So what if they aren't here?'

> Kartick full moon night, we all keep watch
> Years ago, this place did Dhanapati touch.

Humming her song, Batashi ladled out portions of the prasad and called out to the others. 'Come here and take your prasad. Okay, wait . . . Jamuna |Didi will come over and hand them to you. Sit there.'

Small bowls of sal leaf filled with prasad were distributed among those present.

'This will cause acidity,' Dasharath, the trader, told the constable.

'Yes, I suffer from acidity too. But since that happens anyway, I will have the prasad.'

'Yes, I too will have it. After all, it's my fisherwoman who has prepared it.'

The constable didn't want to hear it. He felt sleepy. He could see on his quartz watch that it was past one. Old Dhanapati stood up and the others joined him too, excepting the women who would remain awake and sing all night.

It was getting colder. The girls didn't shiver though. Batashi and Jamuna shared one blanket, Kunti and Sabitri shared another. Some of the girls had left so there were twenty girls in all. Those who remained sang sleepily. Dasharath shoved a hundred rupee note into the constable's hand.

'Call the fisherwoman.'

'This won't do. Moreover, it's the night when women remain awake for the puja. Get up.'

The constable held Dasharath's wrist as if cuffing a criminal and tried to lead him away. 'Don't create trouble here. These women are dangerous. It cannot be done like this. Don't worry, everything is within my control here.'

Batashi raised her voice from the midst of the women. 'Getting up to go, government? Is that all you came here for today?'

'Yes . . . you girls go on singing,' the constable replied, a little irritated.

'You come and join us.'

'Call that woman . . .' the trader said in a low voice.

'You call her if you want to,' the constable replied, exasperated.

'Will she come if I call her?'

'See for yourself. I have lots of work. I will sleep now. Tomorrow morning, I will go around collecting money so that I can go by the afternoon ferry. This time, each one will have to pay at least fifty rupees more. The officer in charge of the police station has clearly told me that.'

'To hell with your money. I will give you what you want. Just call her.'

'Ok, let me see. You go and wait there underneath the neem tree. How much more do you have in your pocket?'

'I have already given you a hundred-rupee note.'

The constable made a rude gesture, shook his body and spit on the ground. 'That hundred was for allowing you to listen to the song. You think you could enjoy it for free?'

'How much should I pay you? I need to talk to you about this . . . I need a few women.'

'Who will you supply to? First give me five hundred rupees. The constable's eyes shone with greed. The trader's lust was writ large all over him. He was aroused but did not have the courage to make his first move without Midde's help. This was Midde's time to make as much money as possible by squeezing his prey. He brought the trader to the island after much coaxing and cajoling and with utter reverence. Already, he was addressing the trader with utter irreverence. He was a veteran of fifty years and knew exactly how things had to be said. He had come to collect money from the island of Dhanapati. The six-monthly island had come to life exactly a month ago, on the full moon night of Kojagori Lakshmi puja. The officer in charge of his police station has asked him to collect one-sixth of the total income of the island. It was an old rule.

One-sixth of the total produce is always given as tax by the subjects. On this island, fish is the only produce. Who will keep track of how much fish is hauled up? But Midde will have to return with a hefty collection. The officer before this one didn't have demands of this kind. He was happy with whatever Midde collected and gave him. The earlier one had worked himself up from the grassroots through subsequent promotions. This one was young and had got himself the position through exams. Naturally, his demand was high as was his temper. He had killed an accused by beating him mercilessly in the lock-up of the police station where he was last posted. That case was still on.

'Come on . . . pay up,' Mangal Midde rushed the trader.

'I paid you already.'

'Cough up a thousand rupees first and then talk. We charge a higher rate for supplying women.'

'You don't need to worry about that. A good woman will get you good money.'

In the shadows of the asper tree, away from the moonlight, the two men haggled over Batashi. The fisherwoman was half asleep as she went on humming her soul song for the tortoise lord, stopping once in a while to talk to Jamuna.

'If the six-monthly home turned into a twelve-month arrangement, Didi, would I have wavered? I too would have had a home, a frontage, a cowshed with cows and calves, a field full of ripe paddy and a barn to hold the rice after harvest. Ma Lakshmi would be blessing my home too. This is that time of the year when the harvest is complete and the barn is full; new clothes have come for the women of the household, ornaments and packs of *alta* and vermilion have been bought . . .'

'Not in this life,' sighed Jamuna. 'We will not have a twelve-month family life this time . . .'

'Life in Kolkata is so tough and scary. At Sonarpur, in a single night, three men pounced on me. Anyone else would have died.'

'See! You have survived! Women don't die so easily; they need to be killed. They say that women's lives can be compared to that of the carp (koi), the toughest breed to kill,' Jamuna said.

'In Kolkata, I met Irfan Ali from Bhangar. He is my uncle's brother-in-law. One day, he beat me so hard . . .'

'Forget it, dear. Our six months on the island are our only reality.'

'I try hard, Didi . . . but I yearn for a twelve-month family life.'

'Not possible. Men forget the island for the other half of the year.'

'I cannot forget . . .'

'Neither can I,' Jamuna whispered before humming again.

> One Dhanapati sleeps underneath,
> the other Dhanapati one floats with.

Batashi hums along. 'So many Dhanapatis, so many of them . . .'

She saw the constable coming towards her. 'Batashi, come and see me tomorrow morning. I will be in old Dhanapati's rooms . . .'

Batashi stared at him in surprise. Then suddenly, she turned to Jamuna and asked, 'Where's my man, Didi? He drinks so much that I just cannot stop him.'

'You give yourself to him properly. Only then will he stop drinking.'

'He is very headstrong, Didi. He keeps saying that he drinks only for the six months that he is on the island.'

Jamuna swayed from side to side, slowly. 'What if we choose to stay back on the island for twelve months?'

'We? You mean the women? Where will the men be?'

'Yes . . . we will wait for them to return after six months, assuming that they have gone out to work. We must remember that they have their wives and families back there, so they won't come and stay here for the remaining six months. Am I right?'

'Yes, you are.'

'So, let them leave us back here and let them come back after six months. We will stay here with our children and cattle. Once we have a home, do we really need them?'

Batashi was listening to Jamuna intently and then she saw that the 'constable' was coming back again.

Three

I'll give you fragrant oil, give you soap,
Bring on my night, that's all I hope.

Families, villages, markets, temples and mosques define a human as do banyans, peepals, creeks, brooks and rivers. They are rooted to these. Along with these come other tags like someone's daughter, someone's wife, someone's niece, someone's daughter-in-law, backed by paternal and maternal genealogies. The women who come to the island of Dhanapati leave these definitions behind. They uproot themselves to come and live here for six months. In their struggle to stay alive outside the island for six months, they willingly give up their roots, paternal and maternal identities and even caste and religion. On the island, between mid-Ashwin and mid-Chaitra, new roots grow. This life of six months on the island is like entering a new life, year after year.

Who is Batashi the fisherwoman? What place has she come from? Is she married or is she a widow? Has her husband left her or has he died? The constable of Ghoradal police station, Mangal Midde, wasn't able to trace her history and it made him bolder. It was not flesh but money that he was after. He knew that money could get him everything, even women . . . as many as he wanted.

Trader Dasharath Singh had been hounding him for that fisherwoman. He was willing to pay two thousand rupees for her. No one knows the details of the negotiation and Midde had said that it would take time. He was trying to kill time till the end of the Chaitra month. It would not be difficult to send Batashi with the

17

trader after Chaitra. He didn't want to break the rules and traditions of the island, since that might have made it difficult for him to collect the money. At the end of the six months, in Chaitra, the shanties of the fishermen are set alight. When everything turns to ashes, they get into their boats and leave the island. The lonely home of old Dhanapati is the only one that remains intact.

Mangal Midde's and the trader's interests did not match. Buying and selling was a matter of habit for the trader and he was not willing to wait for six months. He caught hold of Midde and got him to shadow the fisherwoman, both during the day and in the darkness of the night. Soon, they were discovered by Batashi. She knew that not one but two people were trailing here. She could make out that one pair of feet moved around her shanty while another kept watch. Batashi's man was in the waters then. They only came when the fishermen were out in the sea.

One day, she came out of her hut and asked, 'Why do you come here? Why?'

'He will give you a home for twelve months,' the constable replied.

'Who? Who is it?'

'Look underneath the kewra tree. He's standing there, the trader.'

'But I am Ganesh the fisherman's wife!'

'That's a six-monthly arrangement. This one will be for the whole year!'

'Who's there? Come here, let me see you!'

The huge man—lust evident all over him—came out of the shadows. He held out fragrant oil, soap and cream for Batashi. Take these and have that fishy smell off you,' he said.

'Why are you giving these to me?'

'To take you with me . . .'

'Wait till Chaitra.'

'That's a long time from now! It's just Agrahayan!'

'Only a few months . . . let the winter pass.'

'How will I stay alone this winter?'

'Get hold of a woman. Ask government to help you. He will bring you someone from Ghoradal.' Batashi laughed.

It was the new-moon phase and the evening was pitch dark. Batashi knew how to adjust her eyes to the darkness. She could clearly see even in the dark. It's all a matter of habit. She couldn't afford a torch. Who would pay for the batteries? She had lived in the darkness for so long that she was friends with it. Unless it was absolutely necessary, she avoided lighting the small open kerosene lamp. Kerosene was precious. It came from Ghoradal and was sold at a premium. Only if she could save his money would she get the fisherman's love and attention!

'On days when Ganesh is out, you can stay with the trader,' Midde suggested to Batashi.

'Some such women have come here, but I am not one of them,' she replied.

'How can you be different? You are living with the fisherman!'

'I'm his wife!'

'Don't joke! A wife of six months?'

Batashi didn't want to continue the conversation. She went inside her shanty. Why did the man come with the 'government police'? She was scared of the police. No one on the island liked Mangal Midde. He just came there to extort money. Batashi thought that the man had brought the police to force her to sleep with him. Why should she? She had a safe home for six months and didn't need to sleep with another man. For the remaining six months from Baishakh to Ashwin, she had no choice! She felt naked in those months, without a roof over a head and no windows or doors to hide her modesty. The saree, blouse and petticoat didn't seem enough. But the six months on the island gave her that much-needed security and shielded her modesty. Her ramshackle shanty was made of jute sticks, but gave her shelter. It managed to give her greater relief than what a pucca house might. She went in and sat there like a stone.

Will he come in? she thought to herself.

Batashi came out again. She was scared that the policeman would send the man in and stand guard at the door. *What would she do then?* The moment she came out, the constable focused his five-battery-powered torch on her body and roved it all over. She cringed.

'Don't do this. Go away or I will scream.'

'Don't you know what's good for you?'

'No, I don't. You two go away.'

'Okay, we're going . . . but this won't be good,' the cop said in a menacing tone.

'Have I said anything wrong?' Batashi hissed.

'Tell me which village you belong to . . . where's your family?' the constable asked.

'I don't know.'

'Give me your paternal details.'

'I don't know.'

'Were you married when on land?'

Batashi was quiet.

'What is your caste? Religion?'

Batashi wanted to run away in the dark. Not only the fishing colony but the entire island was silent. The fishermen would come back at dawn. During the evenings, lamps would be lit and people would chit-chat with each other. Everything would feel normal. The constable had taken advantage of the lonely night. It was still an hour before moonrise. When the moon shone on them, they would get rid of their malaise, Batashi thought. Darkness made them bold, but these creatures were scared of light. Batashi was getting ready to run. These two did not know the map of the island the way she did. She would take advantage of the dark cover and hide in a way that her tormentors would not be able to seek her out even if they went past her.

'You don't have to sleep with me immediately. Get rid of your fishy smell first. It's revolting and might make me vomit. With the constable babu by my side, we have nothing to fear . . .' the trader came forward and said.

Batashi spat in the dark, spewing out the anger that was building up inside. That bastard of a constable had brought this man. He behaved as if he was a benefactor, but Batashi knew that she would have to take the constable too. God alone knew if he had brought some more men who were waiting in the dark. The whole island lusted after her beauty and sex appeal.

'For me, six months is as good as a year. Just let me stay with my man and lead a family life for these six months,' she appealed.

'You carry on, who's denying you that?' The constable now focused the beam on her breasts. 'Why do you go on wearing the same saree and blouse, you beggar?'

'It's enough for me.'

'Dasharathji, give her a saree and a petticoat. These fisherwomen wear neither blouses nor petticoats. Of course, that makes the job easier.'

'Are you blind?'

'How will I know that having a blouse also means having a petticoat?' the constable jeered. 'Give her a petticoat of a modern cut and a brassiere too. Do you have one?'

Batashi felt like she was being disrobed. She started walking in the darkness. The torch beam was on her again.

'You slut, where are you off to? Wait or else I will set your shanty on fire.'

Batashi froze. The constable changed his tone now. 'Why are you going away? The trader has taken a fancy to you. Why should you leave him in the lurch and walk away? Is he a beast who will eat you up?'

'I am someone's wife.'

'To hell with that, you are his keep.'

'No. On this island, you are allowed to have only a half-yearly married life, else I would have been his wife for all seasons. Leave me alone, government uncle.'

'Have I held you that you are seeking release? Anyway, Dasharathji, it's your call. I am leaving now.'

The constable melted into the darkness. The man he left behind looked like a pirate. After the constable went out of sight, Batashi turned towards the trader.

'You leave now. I will not talk to you any further.'

'You should not talk to the police in this manner,' the trader advised.

'So how does one talk to them?'

'You should be scared of them. They are above all else.'

'I am indeed scared of them.'

'They can do anything. Don't you know that?'

'Do what?'

The trader lit a cigarette. A strong, manly scent filled the air. Ganesh smoked a hubble-bubble and bidis. Batashi often told him that she liked the fragrance of cigarettes. Ganesh would tell her that it's was all in the mind and that cigarettes made him cough.

The trader released some smoke and spoke again. 'Why don't you give me a mat to sit on? I will sit a league away from you. Do you know what a league means?'

'I don't.'

'Should be three miles. That's the distance I'd like to keep from that fishy smell of yours.'

'Fisherwomen smell exactly like this. Sit if you like.'

She went inside her shanty, brought out a mat and threw it at him.

'Sit at a distance.'

'It's cold outside and you might catch a cold in the mist. Go sit inside.'

'No.'

She pulled out a cloth from inside the hut and wrapped herself from head to toe.

'I must confess that you have aroused me since the time I first saw you. Anyway, you must listen to the advice of policemen.'

'Who said that?'

'Everyone. After all, they are the caretakers of the law of the land. I have travelled all over and seen how those who have defied the police have eventually suffered.'

'Are you his counsel?'

'In our village, a man used to drink to drink himself silly. When the police warned him, he spat on them. The police simply picked him up and returned him maimed.'

'Who told you this?'

'No one. I saw it myself. Then there was another incident where a group of dacoits who would routinely loot buses and give half the collected amount to the local police station cheated twice. The police found out how much the amount was in no time.'

'How?'

They just inquired and when it was proved that the dacoits were cheating, the leader was nabbed and his eyes were gouged out.'

'What have I done that has brought the police to me?'

Nothing. But there's no reason why they cannot come, isn't it?'

'I haven't called the police.'

'You haven't, but he's still come . . . just to ensure that the law is not being violated. In my area, when a new OC or new police boss of the thana comes, he beats up a few people immediately after joining office.'

'What for?'

'They do this to set an example . . . so that no one dares to break the rules, you see.'

'Are you a policeman? How do you know so much?'

'I know. My elder brother is a police officer as is my younger brother and several of my uncles. I too joined the police but left it and started doing business. I think it's more fun to be in business. Being in the police service calls for a lot of hard work.'

'Go now.'

'I am going. If I bring a saree, warm blouse, brassiere and petticoat for you, will you wear them? Will you use the soap and the fragrant oil, Batashi?

'I don't want these. Go away. I am Ganesh Sardar's wife . . . hey Allah!'

'Why are you calling out to Allah? Are you a Muslim?'

'When did I say Allah? I am calling God! I have worshipped Shiva earnestly on Shivaratri. Where has my lord gone?'

'It doesn't matter whether a woman is Hindu or Muslim, Batashi. I won't tell anyone. But you should be scared of the police. That will do you good. Don't forget to use the soap daily.' The trader got up to go.

Four

Six months of roaming and six months home,
That's how our years go and come.

The trader came back after a few days. His tone had changed then. 'No matter how much you show off your Shiv puja, I know that you are a Muslim. What will happen to you now?'

Batashi could read the cunning on Dasharath's face. These were her six months of living a family life with her fisherman. The men had their families at Ghoradal, Firingitala, Firinginagar, Kultali, Kakdwip and Namkhana. They came to the island alone, leaving their wives, kids and parents on the shore. All they looked for here were women who would cook for them and keep them warm on winter nights. Fishermen did not have the time to look for their women's religious backgrounds. It was easier to look for the familial histories of men but not so for women.

'Does your man know that you are a Muslim?'

'Why?'

'Remember, he worships Ganga and Lakshmi as his deities.'

'I offer flowers and sweets to them.'

'Now I know why you are so dirty. You neither bathe properly nor use soap and fragrant hair oil. You are handling dirt and fish all the time. You eat burnt fish and that's what you smell of!'

'So stay off me! My man likes this smell and that is all that should bother me, trader! We live by fishing. What else should I smell of? Perfume?

The trader paced up and down, looking at Batashi on the sly. Batashi could make out that he was lusting after her.

'O Mother Ganga, O Goddess of the woods, O tortoise chief, O Kapilmuni, why have you given me such sex appeal? Why don't you give me food and a safe home instead? Turn me into an old hag. By tomorrow morning, O God of the seas, turn me into an old woman so that the police government stops looking at me and the trader stops lusting after me and wanting to buy my freedom.'

Batashi sat there looking miserable, her chin resting on her knees.

'Hai Allah, Khuda Meherban, O Bhangarshah Pir, O Pir of Ghutiyari, please turn Batashi into an old woman. Take her youth away while she is asleep. After that, she will have nothing to fear. The trader won't come.'

'Why are you so quiet?'

'That's the best, I feel.'

'That won't do, dear. Which village are you from?'

'I belong to the island of Dhanapati.'

'I won't have that for an answer, Batashi. Is this a village? Where are your parents?'

'I don't know.'

'That won't do, what is your identity?'

'What do you mean?'

'Give me your parents' names.'

'Why do you need that?'

'You will tell all to government. I haven't bought you for nothing!'

'Hai Allah!' A deep sigh escaped her lips again. The trader knew already and Batashi didn't care to hide any more. Why should remembering Allah cause trouble, she thought.

'Isn't he the real saviour? Her man, fisherman Ganesh too prayed to the Pir of the seas. He prays to God in trouble. God is supposed to save one in trouble. Allah will certainly save Batashi.'

'Let the constable come back. I will tell him that he has misled me to a woman who is a Muslim. I will be kicked out of my community!'

'So, go away! Who has asked you to come to me? I am fisherman Ganesh's wife. Let me look after my home.

'The trader was cunning. He had paid for Batashi to the constable and was behaving like her owner. He was just waiting for the right moment to leave the island with her. She just had to clean herself with soap and fragrant oil to get rid of her fishy smell. Most of the women on the island were bastards and no one cared for their lives. No one kept count of them . . . so no one would bother if one went missing. The trader had paid for her, so he had the right to take her away. He just had to put her on the motorboat. Thereafter, Batashi would be taken to Kolkata . . . Howrah . . . and then by train to some part of India. If she were younger, she would have been sent to some Arab country. With these thoughts running through his mind, he mumbled, '. . . two-and-a-half-thousand rupees . . . had I known earlier, I wouldn't have paid so much.'

'Get lost,' Batashi said.

'Muslim women cost much less . . .' the trader laughed.

'Good for you. Now get lost.'

'Women can be given any job. Suppose I take you to serve a sadhu? If he hears that you are a cow- eating Muslim, will he keep you?'

'Will you leave or shall I bring out the broom?'

'How will I leave now, Batashi? I have already invested in you. What are the names of your parents?'

'I didn't have parents.'

'Were you born out of thin air?'

'Yes.'

'Are you a Bangladeshi?'

'What does that mean?'

'Have you come from across the border?'

'No, I am from this side,' Batashi replied nervously.

'So where are your parents?'

'Why should I tell you?'

'I have bought you.'

'Why should I accept what you say? I am not aware of any buying or selling!'

'You're just a woman . . . Why should you know?! Just give me your parents' names.'

'I won't.'

'Then you are a Bangladeshi. An illegal migrant.'

'Will you leave, trader?!' Batashi screamed aloud in a hoarse voice. I don't know anything about your government. I belong to the island of Dhanapati.'

The trader knew that he had nailed the woman. She could be a Bangladeshi. Borders didn't matter for such vagabonds who looked for food from place to place. He lit a cigarette and took a long drag. Turning his gaze towards Batashi, he saw that she had finished screaming and stood panting, leaning on the neem tree in front of her shanty. Her heavy bosom heaved, breasts shivering like a scared pigeon. The trader relished it. Her body invited him from underneath her torn and dirty saree. He was aroused.

'I just cannot wait . . .' he whispered under his breath and looked out into the horizon.

Some more land eroded into the water. The trader took a step towards her.

'If you say you belong to the island, the government will take you to be a Bangladeshi.'

'Let them say what they want,' Batashi gasped.

'They will handcuff you and put you behind bars.'

'Let them do what they want.'

'Then they will kick you over the border.'

'Let them.'

'On the other side, they will call you an Indian and kick you back.'

'What will happen then?' Batashi seemed to come back to her senses.

'You'll not find an inch of space in either country!'

'Where will I go then?'

To a brothel, the trader thought to himself. 'Come with me . . . you'll have no trouble. I am close to the government . . . the constable's my pet and so is the government. All my brothers work in the police force. It is safe to be with me.'

Tears came out of Batashi's eyes. The man was determined to take her. He had bought her from the constable.

'Please save me, Allah, Khuda. Save me, Pir of the Seas. I am in deep trouble; the dark waters of exile beckon me. O Mother of the Woods, save me. O Mother Ganga, I implore you.'

'Have you followed what I just said?' the trader asked.

Batashi shook her head from side to side.

'You are a cursed woman. You don't have to understand, just follow me.'

'You leave, else I am bringing out the knife I use to clean fish.'

The trader became serious. He wanted his women to be bold. It was fun to tame such women. It was as challenging as taming a wild horse.

She will finally cool down when I take her to her new master, the trader thought. That did not mean that he would not touch her. He knew from experience that the women he chose got sold at a premium. He knew that Batashi would fetch good money. He just had to take her out of the island and enjoy her before handing her over.

He had a garment business but that was an eyewash. He traded in women and that was his real business. It was thriving. He sent women not just to Delhi, Agra and Patna but also to Balia and Ayodhya districts these days. It was like sending flowers everywhere. This was one of the most profitable businesses in the country.

'Does Dhanapati Sardar know that you are a Bangladeshi?'

Batashi cringed.

This man was hell-bent on proving that she was from across the border. Batashi knew that when people crossed over from Bangladesh, they hid their identity. Batashi and the other women on the island had erased their identity and come to the island and the men on the island had done that too. Here they chose their partners among Jamuna, Batashi and other women and started their six-monthly lives. It was not uncommon to meet men from Bangladesh during the six-month stay on land. Once Batashi had lived with Jobbar Molla, a man from Faridpur, who had come to try his luck in Kolkata. For him, Kolkata was the island of Dhanapati. He would come in Chaitra and return in Bhadra. The man would be out all day and return in the evening, just like the fishermen on the island. The thought of Jobbar Molla made her nostalgic. He had promised to return the next year. He must have, but they did not meet. There were many like him from Bagura, Rajshahi, Khulna, Faridpur and Bagerhat who came to Kolkata every year from across the border. This is what Molla had told her. In winter, he chose to stay home but at the slightest hint of summer, he would pick up his umbrella and cross the border under its shade, to reach Kolkata.

'Where is Faridpur?'

'So you are from Bangladesh, aren't you?'

'I knew someone from Faridpur; I lived with him for six months in Kolkata.'

'I'll give you a twelve-month arrangement now. Does your fisherman mate know that you are from Bangladesh?'

'Who told you that I am a Bangladeshi?'

'You did.'

'No, I didn't.'

'You said it just now and now you are denying it! Never mind. I will keep it a secret,' the trader laughed.

'You are lying, trader. I did not tell you that. I don't know anything about Jobbar Molla's village except for the name.'

'Who is he? A Bangladeshi spy?'

'Why should he be a spy? He comes to repair umbrellas in Kolkata. I have heard of Faridpur from him. Faridpur, Khulna, Jessore, Bagerhat, Satkhira . . .'

The trader listened to her. He was trying to scare her into a confession but now, he was somehow convinced that she was from Bangladesh. He needed a healthy woman and she fit the bill. It didn't matter to him if she was from Bangladesh. It was an added advantage, actually. No one would come looking for her. It would also be easier to tame her.

'Either obey me or land up in prison. Let the police officers and constables take turns with you then. I hope you can handle the pain then.'

The moment the trader said this, Batashi looked scared. Taking the police officers and constables daily? She shuddered at the thought.

'Will you manage? You will die in pain. They'll clean you up and send you to even more senior officers. Can you imagine that? This will continue till you become old. If you contract diseases in between, they might let you go. But remember, living with these diseases can bring such suffering that you will pray for death. Did you run away from your village?'

Batashi was sinking in fear but decided to resist it. She was bold and that is why she had survived. She was ready to fight in order to live, so that she could come back to the island again and again.

'Go and bring your government police. If they say that I am a Bangladeshi, thought I haven't seen Bangladesh ever, I will say that I have a husband, Jobbar, with whom I live for six months and he is from Bangladesh. For the remaining six months, I live with my fisherman husband, Ganesh, on the island. Did you follow?'

The trader was startled by this reply. He couldn't fathom the answer.

'You have two husbands? Can any woman keep two men?'

'What else do I do for the six months outside the island?'

'So, you must be a Muslim.'

'I don't know that. My mother was called Panchi Bibi. Whether she was Hindu or Muslim, I am not sure.'

'What about your father?'

'I don't know who he was. My mother told me that the bastard left her when she conceived me. He was apparently a rich man.'

'Will you be able to prove this?'

'Prove what?'

'That Panchi Bibi is your mother?'

'I will once again have to enter her womb to get to know that.' Batashi laughed. 'You go away, trader. I will not go with you, even if you have bought me. This island is my country for six months. The remaining six, I will spend with Jobbar Molla, if I find him. At that time, Kolkata, Barasat or the slums along Kestopur canal are my countries.'

'Where does Panchi Bibi live?'

'I don't know.'

'Must be Faridpur?'

'If you wish, say so. All her life she was just crushed by men. In her youth, she was hounded by those dogs. Then they left her to die. I don't know when her end came.'

'Didn't you bury her?'

'I don't know whether she was buried or cremated.'

'When did she die?'

'I don't know.'

'Here or across the border?' the trader changed his question.

'Say Ghoradal or Dhanapati's Island . . . say in a graveyard or a crematorium . . . Jobbar Molla would say, the poor have no country.'

The trader was not happy. He realized that the conversation was going nowhere. He needed that woman. The conversation had to be steered towards that.

'You are a glib talker. You are a Bangladeshi. If you have to live, you will have to listen to what I say. When the policeman puts his stick into you, you will realize whether the poor have a country or not. I have bought many Bangladeshi women in the past.'

'I have never been to Bangladesh. I belong here.'

The trader realized that Batashi was scared. He tried to make the best use of her discomfiture.

'You can keep explaining to the police whether you have been there or not. Let them decide.'

Batashi became quiet. Jobbar Molla would always tell her not to talk much. The dumb have very few enemies. He would never talk to outsiders except when he was trying to negotiate with his customers. He knew that he spoke the Bangladeshi dialect and would get caught easily. He could never master the local way of speaking Bengali. He even got caught once, but the man who found out chose not to spill. Instead, he started chatting with Jobbar about his forefathers who had also come from Bangladesh. Coincidentally, his forefathers had also been from Faridpur. It was from Jobbar that Batashi had heard the name Faridpur for the first time. So Batashi always thought that she had one husband from Faridpur and another one from the island of Dhanapati. She always compared the island with the never-seen Faridpur. Was that also an island like this? Batashi travelled mentally between her two men. Her year was divided. Where was the space and time for the trader? Her reverie broke when she saw that the trader had started to walk away. She was taken from autumn to spring and then from summer to autumn again. How would the trader negotiate that?

Five

Aunts and sisters, they come to tell,
Go for the gold and all will be well.

Something's wrong with Batashi. In these winter months, she is never reminded of Jobbar Molla. At this time of the year, she is a fisherwoman on the island of Dhanapati. Where is the umbrella man now? At this time of the year, his face is a haze, buried underneath the dust of time. Batashi removed her wrapper. Has the chill vanished? Is it a clouded winter day? Is winter over? The cold northerly breeze didn't cross the dark water and reach the island via Ghoradal. There was a cloud over the island and the sea was sending in the warmer southerly breeze instead. Winter was over! The frozen coconut oil had melted. With the passing of winter, the island too would soon cease to exist. How far was Chaitra? It's arrived. The first hint of the southerly breeze on the island would shove the men towards Ghoradal. The breeze from Ghoradal carried the smell of home. The men yearned for their wives and children, forgetting the women of the island. They would call the women of the island and say, 'Now leave. It's time to say goodbye. Hope you are happy with the accounts. Don't come anywhere near us now. The season has changed and our homes beckon us. Let us start the next lap of our lives, at Ghoradal.'

'Go back to Ghoradal. We know it's Chaitra and you won't stay any longer. We will go back too.'

'Go, my man, go for now,' Batashi said to herself. 'My other man will start from Faridpur and reach India soon. I too will leave the island.'

The warm southerly breeze had a strange impact on everyone. Batashi felt her attachment for the island ebbing away. Her thoughts were full of the canal-side shanties of Keshtopur and Beliaghata and the unfinished construction sites of Dumdum Park. She had once lived with her umbrella man at one such site. During these months, Kolkata felt like the island. She had to search for Jobbar Molla. If she found him, her six months were secured.

'Batashi!' Was it the trader she heard?

'I have bought you, so all twelve months are mine,' a voice seemed to come out of the darkness. 'You will have to go where I send you. I can sell you anywhere. You will have to accept the master who buys you from me.'

'That cannot be! My umbrella man, Jobbar, will look for me. He comes for me every year. I will live with him in Kolkata.'

'You'll never be able to find him,' the trader said. 'Does he come every year? Unless it's extremely pressing, does anyone leave their country?

'That is not true. He will not be able to stay home once Chaitra knocks on his door. He will then leave home and head towards Dhaka, Chatgaon, Khulna, Bagerhat or Kolkata. He finds Dhaka and Kolkata better than the rest because he earns well here. In Kolkata, he has lived with his Batashi Bibi and found it worthwhile.'

Chaitra is the nonchalant harbinger of poverty and drags everyone to the streets. He loses interest in his home and family as the warm winds start blowing. He heads to Kolkata to set up his home with his Batashi Bibi, his door to another world. Can his family keep him back?

'Did he come last year?' asked the trader.

'No.'

'The year before?'

'No, trader.'

'Then he won't come. Rest assured.'

'That cannot be. He must have been coming, but we couldn't meet. All the canal-side shanties have been evacuated. Keshtopur,

Beliaghata, Garia, Naktala, Bansdroni . . . it's the same everywhere. That unfinished construction at Dumdum Park is now a liveable building and people have moved in. That is why Jobbar Molla has not been able to trace me. I have not been able to find him either. But Chaitra will bring him to Kolkata. He comes for his Batashi Bibi.'

'Forget all that. You don't have to live in a shanty anymore. You will stay in big hotels, with moneyed men, or in big houses with courtyards.'

'No, I don't need anyone else. Jobbar is one half of me and Ganesh is the other half.'

'You will have to go. There are barbed wires at the border that will make it impossible for Jobbar to cross over. His is a different country.'

'I don't find any difference.'

'He is a Muslim and a Bangladeshi. If he gets caught, you too will be behind bars. They'll release you only after you turn into an old hag.'

'He doesn't know that Faridpur and Kolkata are different countries.'

'He certainly does . . . even a newborn knows it.'

'He lives on the footpath and in shanties in Dhaka. It's the same in Kolkata. Where's the difference?'

'There's a lot of difference. Now listen, don't tell anyone that you are a Muslim.'

'I don't know whether I am a Hindu or Muslim.'

'Stop taking Allah's name from now on.'

'Hai Allah! Is that possible?'

'Say Ishwar, Ishwar . . . Thakur Thakur. Like the Hindus do.'

'It's a matter of habit, trader.'

'Get rid of your habit then. I've bought you. Now, I will have to remodel you. If they get to know that you are a Muslim, it will cause trouble. People will start spying.'

'Hai Allah! What have I done that they will spy on me? Trader, are there clouds in the sky?'

'I cannot make out in the dark,' the trader said.

'Are there stars in the sky?'

'Which star?'

'The stars of the north . . . the ones that can be seen from Ghoradal.'

'Which stars can be seen from Ghoradal,' the trader laughed.

'I had heard that there are such stars.'

'No one knows which star can be seen from where,' the trader said.

'The stars that rise in the sky . . .'

'Ghoradal is not a sky!'

'The sky that caps Ghoradal. Trader, tell me. Can you see that star in the north?'

'Come and see for yourself.'

'Unless that star is seen, my husband will not return from sea.'

'Let him be . . . you come with me.'

'Unless that star is seen from Ghoradal, even you will not be able to go, trader.'

'Oh, I will. Don't worry. I'll go in the daytime.'

Batashi kept quiet. The darkness seemed clouded. It seemed to rise from the island and reach for the sky. What if those clouds bring a storm with them? She shivered.

'Hey Allah, Hey Má Ganga, Hey Dariya Pir, Hey Kapilmuni, may all the gods listen to my prayers and take the clouds away. May the stars come back to the sky. Take the clouds and the trader away. Let him not shadow me saying that he has bought me.'

She heard the sounds of boots outside. Along came the strong smell of a cigarette. The boots were treading on the soft, sandy soil but why did they feel like footsteps on paved roads? Batashi cringed. The sound was similar to what she would hear in Kolkata. It was similar to the knock of the lathi of the watchman outside her shanty in Beliaghata. The watchman would come with the police officer in tow. They would look for women picking up polythene covers at the entrance of the shanties. Why could she hear that sound here? Did the sandy soil turn into a metaled road?

'The sound of boots is a must when you have to accomplish something big,' the trader remarked.

'What are you out to achieve?'

'I'll have to take you with me. They are sitting with the money on the riverbank.'

'Who's waiting?'

'Yamraj.'

'He doesn't like me. I've come back from the jaws of death so many times. Is this even a life? Think for yourself.'

The trader had no time to think. He was a fixer and loved to make and execute plans. Thinking was not his cup of tea.

'Come with me and put an end to your troubles.'

'Who told you that I am in trouble?'

'You are in pain, aren't you?'

'No, I am not.'

'Money?'

'I am happy with what my husband gives. The rest, I earn for myself. I don't want money.'

'How much can your fish gathering and drying pay you? You are meant to earn a lot of money. Think of the things you can buy with all that money.'

'I don't want to buy anything. I don't know even know all the many things that I can buy.'

The trader paced up and down in the dark. Batashi could not make out the movements clearly. It seemed that he was pacing up and down all the time . . . 'just like the river flows continuously into the sea. The sails of the boat were up and it was laden with goods. Some of them smelt so good! The boat then reached the shore and offloaded everything to make space for women. The trader loaded the boat with women after the cargo was emptied on the island.' Once, Dhanapati, the owner of the island, had told this story about his ancestors, the pirates. Their boats were filled with shackled women who had been captured. The trader seemed to be like those pirates. Batashi shuddered.

'You'll get good clothes, salwar . . . jeans . . . and whatnot! Rich women wear these.'

'I don't need them, trader.'

'Till the time you are youthful, enjoy life. Come with me and I'll show you the path to a happy life.'

'I am happy, trader.'

'I'll bring you pleasure.'

'I have that too.'

The trader got angry then and barked. Batashi could almost see the fire in those eyes through the darkness.

'No, you don't know what pleasure is.'

'I know, sir, I know.'

'No, you don't!'

'I do.'

The trader screamed. 'You don't. Only I know how to pleasure you, you slut! I shall give it to you in full measure.'

'I don't want that.'

'Say yes, you slut.'

Batashi shut her eyes and waited. The trader was also silent for a while. He had had to return again and again, failing to convince her. Batashi rejected his advances, again and again. She felt lonely on this island that she knew so well. The waves lashed against the shore and the sky melted into the water, adding to the overpowering loneliness that took over her. The trader matched his rhythm to her loneliness by constantly going and coming. Every time he came back, he brought a new story from his collection.

'Batashi, Batashi . . .' the trader called.

'Batashi stayed quiet. But she couldn't deny the shadow of Jobbar Molla that the trader brought with him.'

'Go, Batashi, go . . . go have a life!'

'Who are you?'

'I care for you, Batashi.'

'Are you Jobbar Miyan?'

'Perhaps him . . . if you say so.'

'Come in front. Let me take a look at you.'

The footsteps melted away in the darkness. She couldn't make out if it was really Jobbar. Who was it again? Was it Panchi Bibi? Who was calling out in that strained nasal tone?

'Go Batashi . . . I am your mother and I am telling you to do this. I brought you into this world, I know what is best for you,' the nasal voice stated.

'I don't want what is best for me. Who are you?'

'I told you . . . I am your mother.'

'She's underneath now.'

'The trader brought me up from the grave. This man is good. He gave me food and some money. Aah . . . money! It felt so good to count all that money!'

'You cannot be my mother. You are in the grave . . . rotting.'

The footsteps retreated into the dark. Some more came, one after the other. Jamuna Di, Sabitri, Kunti and then the elderly aunts. They came one by one and urged her to go.

'Come, Batashi, come,' the trader called again. 'I will give you a nose pin, anklets, a chain, a crown, a blouse, a petticoat, panties, many sarees, ghaghras, jeans and brassiere.'

'Can you give me one thing?'

'You just have to tell me . . .'

'Give me a knife. First, I'll shove it into you and then kill myself too. Malati from Sonarpur died like that. Can you give me a knife?'

'You whore . . . the police will stick a bayonet into your hole. Aren't you scared?'

Batashi did not reply. The island lay lonely by the sea in the dark stillness of the night.

Six

Tell me, O Jamuna Di, a way out of this,
Am I doomed if I give him a miss?

Winter days were short. The sand cooled fast. The nights on the island were long and cold. Batashi spoke to Jamuna under the ebony tree in the afternoon . . . the same place where they lulled Dhanapati the tortoise to sleep that night. You could see the sea at an angle from there. The water was blue, but it would soon turn black as darkness took over.

'Jamuna Di . . . I need to talk to you . . .'

'What is it?'

'You are never alone. There's always someone or the other with you. But I need to talk to you alone . . .'

'Why are you so breathless?'

'Can the police do everything?'

'What do you mean?'

'What if I don't listen to him?'

'Who? That Mangal bastard?'

'Will I be doomed?'

'Who told you that?'

'What will I do now, Jamuna Di?'

'About what?'

'If they ask me to go north, should I do so?

'Why should you? What happened?'

'If they ask me to go south, should I?'

'I really don't follow. Let's sit down on that raised ground. Police here means that constable. But he's gone!'

'Are the police the Almighty?'

'Who told you that?'

Batashi kept quiet, wondering how much she could share with Jamuna. She had to confide in someone . . . but what if that backfired?

'I am doomed, Jamuna Di. That trader has told me something that you cannot imagine. He's told me about a town . . . Jamuna Di, have you heard of that town?'

Jamuna listened to Batashi in wide-eyed wonder.

'The town was called Gopalgunj or perhaps Krishnagunj or Layalgunj or Chandan Piri. There was a wife who lived there. Not one but two. One was called Batashi, the other, Ahalya.'

'Never heard of such a place! Where is it?'

'I don't know where, but they didn't listen to the police. So, the police shoved their bayonet up their hole and . . . and there was a baby in the tummy that twisted horribly inside. Hai Allah! I have not stopped shivering since I heard this . . .'

Jamuna seemed to coil in like a worm. What was Batashi saying? Chandan Piri was where her aunt lived. Was it the same place that she was referring to? Jamuna had never been there. She had not seen her aunt since she got married. Jamuna's parents had died, then her husband had died and she was left with no immediate family. So she hadn't kept in touch with her relatives. The police stuck the bayonet up Batashi and Ahalya. They were pregnant. The police had warned them against going to the field. But how could they obey that? The field was full of ripe paddy. Their husbands were in the field. The police had said that the paddy had to be given up to the landlord's accountant.

'I don't have land nor crop. What do I need to listen to this story?' Jamuna asked.

'Neither do I, Jamuna Di. I neither have land nor paddy . . . not even a permanent husband. I am not pregnant and will never be. What do I fear?'

What if one day, old Dhanapati said that the tortoise won't move and the island would stay in place the whole year? These women would then have land, homes, husbands and kids. What if the police came and shoved the bayonet in still? Did the paddy belong to the police that they wanted to loot it?

'Mangal Midde's a bastard. But he just collects money and leaves. He is not armed. No question of using the bayonet on us,' Jamuna said.

'What is a bayonet, Didi?'

Jamuna explained it to Batashi. It seemed that she had seen it once. It was sharp and shone dangerously . . . like the harpoon to kill fish. Batashi thought she was familiar with the bayonet. Those three men who pounced on her at Sonarpur, weren't their members like bayonets? Could she ever forget that pain? From evening till end of night, she lay there in the field, soaked in blood. Were they the police? Batashi didn't know it then. The police stuck up the bayonet and brought the baby out. Batashi shivered. The trader told her the story of Ahalya and another Batashi. She lay there as they shoved in the bayonet to bring the baby out . . .

'He was trying to scare you,' Jamuna said.

'Is it okay not to listen to the police?'

'No. You have to listen to them if they ask you to do something. The police have the power to get you arrested and sent behind bars. There they can beat you to death.'

'I feel so scared, Jamuna Di.'

'Why should you be? Have you disobeyed them?'

Batashi was quiet for a while but her bosom heaved and she shivered inwardly.

'Be careful, Batashi. There are many eyes that hound you, because of your youth and beauty. These two are your worst enemies.'

'What should I do?'

'The faster your youth forsakes you, the better it is for you. Every year, you come to the island looking like a beggar. The island takes such good care of you that you plump up and become pink with health.'

'Is that my fault?'

'No, it isn't. This is both a gift and a curse from God. Tell me what has happened, girl.'

Batashi was confused. The trader had asked her not to open her mouth. You couldn't blame the police for anything. It was always considered an affront. If such rumours spread on the island, Batashi would be in trouble. The police were merciless. They could put the rifle to her private parts and blow them up. That had happened in some country. There were seven shots that not only killed the girl but destroyed that part. Batashi tried her best to hide her modesty between her thighs. She had heard of an incident where a girl lay flat on her back as the police emptied the gun into her stomach. Batashi's insides revolted. She desperately wanted to hide her female parts within her female parts. Knowing all this, Batashi didn't dare open her mouth. The trader's elder and younger brothers were cops, as were his uncles. Mangal, the constable, was his ally. The trader, while giving her clothes, had told him that she had to obey the police. That would help to keep peace, he had said.

'What will happen to me, Didi? Shall I tell old Dhanapati?'

'The old tortoise chief? He is asleep.'

'No, not him. The chief of the island.'

'Dhanapati, Dhanapati, old and wise, knows it all in his guise,' Jamuna hummed. 'Yes, let's go to him. 'But tell me . . . where is all this fragrance coming from? What oil have you used in your hair?'

'I don't know, Didi, but it is indeed a fragrant oil.'

Jamuna started studying Batashi's face. 'Have you used cream on your face?'

'Yes, my face becomes very dry in winter,' Batashi said, lowering her eyes.

'Is it your face or your heart? Did Ganesh give you these?'

Batashi stayed quiet. Jamuna grew suspicious. 'Which shop sells these on the island?'

'I don't know, Didi.'

Jamuna grabbed Batashi's hand. 'Is it that trader? The one who had come with Mangal constable on that full moon night and shamelessly lusted after you?'

'If I say that I am doomed, they tell me that if I don't use this oil, I'll be making it quicker.'

'What have they told you?'

'Just that the police are capable of everything.'

Jamuna walked with Batashi slowly. Batashi's fear and the cold outside made her slower.

'Does Ganesh know?'

'I don't know.'

'If that is your answer to everything I ask, why have you come to me?'

'I don't know that, Didi. But I just wanted to ask how much of the ways of the police do you know about.'

'I had to fall at their feet once to save my brother's life, Batashi.'

'Your brother! Do you have one?'

'Not anymore.'

'Why? What happened to him?'

'I don't know what happened to him thereafter, Batashi?'

'Why don't you know?'

Jamuna started walking faster. She almost ran. Batashi found it difficult to keep pace with her.

'I had a brother and a sister. I don't know what happened to them.'

'Why don't you know?'

'I know, but cannot tell. It won't bring them back.'

Batashi kept running after Jamuna. 'Please tell me more . . .'

'My brother begs at Bhangar. The big police officer broke his leg. He has been maimed for life. I had gone there during the fair and saw him limping on his stick. He was wearing the white dhoti that boys wear when parents die.'

'When did your parents die?'

'When we were kids . . .' Jamuna wiped a tear.

'Why did he wear that attire?'

'So that people take pity and give him more alms.'

'I went up to him and asked, "Aren't you my brother? Aren't you Haju?"'

'Did he recognize you?'

'Yes, he did. He asked, "Where were you, all these days?"'

'How happy you must have been!'

'My brother is a lame beggar. I am his elder sister but I can do nothing for him. I spend six months here and six months roaming the streets. What will I do for my poor brother? We just sat by each other and cried helplessly for our parents.'

'Did your mother die before your father?'

'Yes. I don't know when my father died.'

'Didn't your brother tell you?'

'He too didn't know. He heard from somewhere that our father was no more. God knows why people come, why they die and where they go?'

'Hai Allah,' Batashi cried.

'Does your husband know?'

'Yes, he knows all.'

'Does he know about the oil and the cream?'

'I don't know. I cannot tell him. I will be maimed by the police. What will be left of me then?'

Old Dhanapati sat like his namesake—the ancient tortoise—silent and still on his red chair. His was the only pucca house on the island. It had mud walls and thatched roofs. A young woman sat in the clearing. She was short, had a stub of a nose, a head full of hair and a coppery complexion.

The woman came up to the two women. 'What happened? Is there some kind of bad news? Has there been a shipwreck or sighting of pirates?'

'Have you even seen a ship once to be asking this?' Jamuna snubbed her.

'It is to see ships that I come to the island every year, Didi,' Kunti smiled. She then showed off her new glass bangles. 'My old man bought these for me from the hawker.'

Seven

May sleep befall my two eyes,
Let dreams take over, even if they are lies.

Old Dhanapati looked at the two women. From one to the other and back to the first. When he looked at Batashi, he forgot Jamuna and then came back to Jamuna again, leaving Batashi alone. He let his eyes fill his heart.

'Kunti, bring me some water,' he called out.

Kunti went to the western part of the verandah to fill water. Till she came back, old Dhanapati moved his eyes all over Batashi. 'Women never cease to surprise me. You can never have enough of them. Even at my age, my throat dries up when I see you, Batashi.'

At other times, she would have laughed and joked with the old bloke. Jamuna would have also joined in. But right then, both of them kept quiet. Their hearts seemed heavy like lead. Darkness engulfed them, ready to envelope everything around. Kunti brought water and gave it to the old man. He gulped it down and asked, 'Is it colder than usual today?'

'Master, it's because of your age that you feel cold.'

'Who told you that?'

'My father used to say that.'

'How could he be old, if you are just sixteen-seventeen?'

Kunti took the glass away. 'My first memories of him were as an old man. My mother, his third wife, was young.'

Dhanapati sat in silence. Batashi and Jamuna sat on their haunches in front of him. They wondered how to start the conversation.

46

Old Dhanapati kept looking from one to the other. 'Both of you are beautiful . . . and so is Kunti.'

Jamuna cleared her throat. 'Master, is that government Mangal gone?'

Kunti turned her head and Dhanapati looked at the two women suspiciously. 'Why do you need to know about the police constable?'

'We need to know. Where is he?'

'The police come here to take and not to give. He took and left!'

'When did he leave?'

'It's been two days.'

'He has left the trader here.'

'So what? Let him be.'

'He is here on this island.'

'If he were here, he would be seen. He cannot be thin air. Can he, Batashi? You are too beautiful! What a balm to my eyes you are!'

'Will the police come back again,' Batashi asked.

'They keep coming.'

'What kind of a man is the police?'

'He is an extortionist and has all the qualities of a man.'

Batashi fell silent, not knowing how to take the conversation forward. She didn't want to tell them more about the trader. That had to be kept under wraps. The trader had warned her. But her fragrant hair oil, the Himani cream and blouse were a dead giveaway. Jamuna had not seen her blouse underneath the wrapper. She kept pulling at it to make sure her front and back were covered well.

'Have you seen many cops in your life?' Jamuna asked.

'What do you mean by that?'

'How many kinds of policemen have you seen?'

Dhanapati looked at Jamuna with surprise. 'Let's change the topic now. Such discussions are not good.'

'Are you scared?' Jamuna asked.

'Not really, but I have had a lot of experiences and not all of them were beautiful.'

The tension, both in his voice and in the air around them, was palpable. Darkness crept in slowly and silently. Dhanapati wrapped his head with a wrapper. Kunti sat down to light the kerosene lamp. The old man stayed silent for some time and then said, 'It is good to listen to the police or else one should be ready to suffer.'

'What happens?'

'I know someone who remained behind bars for more than twenty years. He didn't know what he had done and the police didn't care to tell him.'

Batashi shivered. 'What happened next?'

'I know someone who vomited blood and died.'

'How did that happen?'

'I don't know. Police can do anything. They can shoot an invisible arrow at you or even kill the plants in your garden.'

'I never heard of such things,' Jamuna said.

'How will you know? Did I ever tell you? Once a man cheated a cop, and his wife went away with someone else.'

'Are they so powerful?' Kunti asked wide-eyed.

'Once, a ship capsized in the waters, about a league away from here. Police said that it was laden with smuggled goods. No one found any signs of that ship again.'

'How can you say that the police had a hand in that?'

'Sometimes they don't do anything. Things just happen.' The old man looked at them with eyes as sharp as pincers. 'Why are you asking about them? They come and go.'

Jamuna and Batashi fell silent. Kunti lit the lamp and came near them. 'Why are you talking of such evil things in this darkness? Don't you have other things to talk about?'

'Yes, at the start of the evening, one shouldn't talk about such things,' Jamuna agreed. 'One man simply became mad and another lay on the railway tracks and got mowed down by the train . . . all because of them.'

'Have you seen that for yourself?' Dhanapati got angry suddenly.

'I heard. How will I see?'

'Don't say what you have not seen.'

'Have you seen what you told us, master?'

'Why should I clarify that to you?'

'Did you go to collect things from the sunken ship?' asked Kunti.

'Am I a beggar like you women to go collect things from the ship? I did not leave the island.'

'They still talk about that shipwreck. They also say that one day, a ship laden with gold will sink similarly.' Batashi was irritated with everything that Kunti was saying. Those were tales that everyone on the island was familiar with. Kunti was moving away from the topic. She had to bring the conversation back to the police and from there to the trader. He was visiting her shanty now and then . . . even during the night when the fishermen were away in the waters. Was the trader lying just to scare her and get her to do his bidding? How could she avoid the trader? If only she could reveal everything . . . she would be at peace.

'Master, please tell me if I am beautiful?' Kunti changed the subject.

Batashi was irritated. 'Master, do police wear plain clothes?'

'Possible.'

'Are there some such cops on the island?'

'You would have known if they were there, Batashi.'

'Can I stay here for the night, master?'

'Why? Did Ganesh turn you out?'

'I am scared, master. What if I cough up blood and die? My husband, Ganesh, is out fishing. He will return tomorrow.

'Wait, let me give you some medicine.'

'If they shoot their invisible arrow at me? What then?'

'Why should they, Batashi?' Jamuna was surprised.

'What if I die of fear? There are no rail lines here, but I can hang myself.'

'Stop your banter, Batashi. The ghosts of the Portuguese pirates roam the island in the dark. They will hear you.'

'Am I safe?'

'As far as I know, you are . . . as long as you are on the island.'

'I don't think so.'

'Why?'

'Didn't Punnime die after soaking herself in kerosene and setting herself alight?'

Dhanapati kept quiet. Batashi had poured water on the fire. 'Who told you about Punnime? That was long ago,' said Jamuna.

'She was a mad woman . . . burnt herself alive.'

'I am scared that I too will go mad.'

They all fell silent. A night bird screamed through the silence of the night behind Dhanapati's home. An owl flew away, on the lookout for a mouse on the island.

'I know a mad woman who lives on the platform of a station,' Kunti said. 'Her stomach plumps up often. She looks beautiful then.'

'Shut up,' Dhanapati shouted. 'Go and sit there.'

'Shall I go off to sleep, master?'

'Yes, do that. What else will you do?'

'The moment I sleep, someone wakes me up. I can't make out who it is, in the dark. I tried to feel him but he vanished. Who was it, master?' Kunti asked.

'Please stop weaving tales. Those are your dreams.'

'No, it's not a dream. I know him but cannot talk about him.'

'Never mind. Go and sleep now.'

'I have seen him, but he has asked me not to tell anyone,' Kunti said.

'Who is it?' Batashi asked.

'He has been coming since the time my mother was alive. I have remained silent all these years.'

'You women are the cause of all trouble.' Dhanapati got up with his lathi. He hobbled forward. 'If you are so scared, why do you come to the island?'

Suddenly a beam of light pierced through the darkness. Batashi and Jamuna sprang up. Dhanapati turned around. 'Who's there?'

'Are you there, Dhanapati Babu?'

'Who is it?'

'I am Dasharath Singh. Can you please spare a few minutes?'

Dhanapati recognized him as the trader who had come with constable Mangal.

'Yes, yes, sure, do come in. Kunti, get him a chair.'

The trader came in. Batashi retreated as far back into the darkness as possible. Jamuna trailed her. The moment she moved, the beam fell on her and then went off.

'Don't go away . . .' Dasharath addressed Jamuna. 'I will leave soon.'

'No, let them go,' Dhanapati said.

Jamuna walked into the darkness and found Batashi there.

'I was waiting for you.'

'Wasn't he the trader?'

'Which trader? I didn't see properly.'

'Why did he come?'

'He knows best, Didi. Can anyone sell what is not his?'

Jamuna walked along with Batashi in the dark. She wondered what Batashi was hinting at. If she got into trouble, did that matter to Ganesh? This was a six-month world. Everything got erased after that. Someone else could easily replace Batashi. She too would cook, clean and feed Ganesh and keep his accounts. Just like Batashi, she too would dry the fish that Ganesh brought in. Even in a permanent world of twelve months, men replaced sickly wives. It was common to have a wife at home and a keep elsewhere. Men were not so emotionally attached to their women, were they?

'Batashi, why are you quiet?'

'Nothing, Didi.'

'Why did you ask that?'

'If your father had a piece of land where he grew crops, can someone else sell it? Can someone else take possession of that land?'

'Don't think so much, Batashi. We are rootless people; with no land or village to go back to. Don't you know that?'

Eight

Not a single shop, nor market in the dead Kans grass,
The month of Ashwin, brought us in a mass.

Using jute sticks and straw, mud huts were built for six months. By the time these six months got over, fishing ended and it was time to leave after setting the shanties alight. This was a part of the tradition of the island. The fishermen and women would come back again, afresh. Their old huts, the land on which they built them . . . nothing remained on the island to welcome them back. The monsoons and high tides of Bhadra wiped out every memory of a settlement. The slate was always clean when they came back again. Only the dried Kans grass welcomed them every time. These were cleaned up when it was time for the new settlement of six months. The settlers would not be able to identify where their old hut was built the last time. The only structure that remained as a marker was Dhanapati—the island chief's—pucca house. He would reach ahead of the others and wait for the rest. His house would be repaired and readied before the fishermen came in. They never knew when the old man reached the island; whether he came before the Durga puja or during the five days of the puja to get his house in order. He had to reopen the lock after six months, get the walls repaired, get the roof re-laid, chase out the snakes and get the overgrowth cleaned. After he got his act together, he would either wait at the waterfront or in his house for others to come in. It would seem that he had never gone away during the months between Baishakh and Chaitra. He would greet everyone by saying, 'How have you been?'

'Was that any life we went back to?' That was the reply that he got, invariably.

'Chief, will it be a good fishing year? This year's harvest has been good, chief. Can you gauge the breeze?'

'A good mango harvest brings good paddy with it. Good paddy means good fish too, Ganesh. It's going to be a good year for us.'

'How was the mango crop on the island, chief?'

'The birds ate them up, they know better.'

'How was your paddy harvest this time, chief?'

'I just have a bigha of land. I am a sharecropper and depend on my farmers. I am only bothered about this island, Ganesh.'

That was how the first day started every time. They would ask about weather predictions, cyclones and other vagaries.

'It seems calm as of now, but no one knows about the moods of the demon of the big waters. Even the weather office fails to foresee his movements.'

'What will happen to the island if a cyclone comes, chief?'

'All cyclones bypass the island and head straight for the deep waters. Old people know that. Storms happen outside the island; they cannot come here. The goddess of the island, Anna Bibi, protects it. This island also belonged to Pedru Dhanapati. If you trace his ancestry, you will see that he was a Portuguese pirate of the high seas. He belonged to Lisboan (colloquial for Lisbon). They came from the deep waters of the oceans and seas up to the bay here and took control over Kalnagini, Hogal, Kartal, Gomar, Vidya, Beula, Bartola and Mani rivers. Their souls still roam here and it is their spirits that save the island, every time a cyclone strikes.'

'Chief, are you a *firang*, a white man?'

'Of course I am! Isn't it written all over me? I belong to the bloodline of Pedru.'

'Do white men look like you?'

'Yes.'

'You aren't as fair as them!'

'The saline water and the heat have taken away my colour. I have been living here for ages . . . at least three hundred and fifty years!'

'What is three hundred and fifty?'

'Many, many years. If you come to my village, I will show you the graves of my firang ancestors. There are seven of them. One of those is my grandfather's, the rest were his ancestors.'

Each year, the fisherfolk came back with gifts for Dhanapati. It was mandatory. Money, sweets, fruits, rice, etc. were offered to him as entry fee to the island. Those who didn't bring these items brought eggs and chicken. Some brought a sack of puffed rice and some came with a new lungi and enquired who else Dhanapati had got along with him that year.

Kunti peered from inside. 'Here I am. Thank god, you people have come now! He came during the pujas. What a man your chief is, deciding to come during the pujas to a barren island that has no pujas, drumbeats and blowing of the conch shells on puja days!'

'That's the tradition of the place,' one fisherman said. He is the owner of the island, naturally he comes ahead of us. This huge island is his; some say that the waters around the island right up to the sea belong to him.'

'He is somewhat strange, doesn't talk much. I feel bored. I cook, clean, eat and sleep. The first few days go in making up for lost sleep. But how much do I sleep? At night, I remain awake and see that the master too is sitting in the verandah, wide awake. It scares me.'

'No, no, don't be scared. He's our chief, much revered and far above all of us. He guides us and that is why he comes much before we do.'

'One night, it seemed to me that the person sitting on his chair was someone else,' Kunti said.

'Who was that?'

'He told me that it was Pedru pirate. The master was at the spot where we pray to the old tortoise underneath the ebony tree. It was the dead of the night and I was alone here. This place is so unfamiliar to me. There are no fields, no shops or bazaars.'

'When did this happen?' a fisherwoman asked.

'On the night that we reached here, the island was almost a forest with overgrowth and dried up Kans grass. The labourers whom the master had brought along to clear up the island were sleeping behind the house. I woke up at night and came out of the room to see the firang pirate sitting on the chair. I thought it was the master and called out to him, but no one replied.'

Old Dhanapati nodded in assent. 'From Baishakh to Ashwin, the spirits are in charge of the island. They hand over charge after I reach and return to the waters.'

'Night wasn't over yet but it was almost dawn because there was a blue tinge in the sky,' Kunti said. 'Dewdrops could be seen. The pirate got up from his chair, walked towards the water and then vanished. I was so scared. This is such a big island and I was there with just the old master for company. If he were young, I would not have felt this scared. He is old and frail and will fall if someone pushes him. What will I do then? There's no shop or bazaar or cinema hall here. No one will come to my rescue.'

The first day was both happy and sad. Old Dhanapati, while welcoming everyone on the island, reminded them that it was a six-month-long settlement and nothing beyond that. Everyone had to be prepared to leave the island after the full moon on Holi. The Chaitra full moon was in the month of Baishakh and so that would have been too late this time. The mood of the water would change then and it would become turbulent. After the full moon on Holi which is the full moon of Falgun, it would not be safe to stay here. The old tortoise would then move in his sleep. The spirits of the pirates would then return to take rest on the island.

The six-month inhabitants would listen and move from belief to disbelief and back. They knew that the old man was largely correct. The tortoise held the island on his back. There was no dispute about that. The fishermen would go into the sea and stay there night after night. The spirits of the pirates were there. So many strange things happened at sea. How did that ship sink? Who did it? There are different interpretations but all agreed that the pirates might have been behind it.

'I am happy that everyone has reached the island. The old master hardly speaks to me,' Kunti said. 'I am as lonely as the old tortoise.

No markets, no videos, no young and strong men around. The labourers were sent off to Ghoradal by old Dhanapati after their work was over. This island is so large, but you look around and see no one. This place is the opposite of other places. There are hundreds jostling for space there like insects.'

'Would you be able to come here with young and strong men?' someone asked Kunti.

'How can I? I was already taken by the old master. I thought the firangs were young and strong, but master is so old and frail! I was so scared at first. I am alone here without any family or relatives. I feel scared going near the water. What if pirates lurk behind the tall grass?'

'What if they were there?'

'I would have gone with them. I like young men. They are strong, they laugh more, get angry easily, eat more and bring in more.'

'I am fed up with this young, mad woman I have brought with me. She keeps talking about markets and young men shamelessly.'

'We know she's deranged, don't worry.'

'She sat and wept all afternoon the other day for her parents. When I asked her, she said, what else could she do, if she felt like weeping?'

'This place brings out my old pains. I am able to cry in peace. I neither found the time nor the space to cry elsewhere,' Kunti said.

'You are supposed to come in with a clean slate like the clear blue Ashwin sky, forgetting your past. That's the rule here. On the island, I am your master and nothing else should matter to you.'

Once again, shanties come up one by one, a little away from each other. The space in between is used by the women to dry fish and grow vegetables like cauliflowers, tomatoes and chillies. The sandy soil is good for these vegetables. The women tend to their vegetables, as they add flavour to their temporary family life. The women follow on the heels of the fishermen. Sometimes, they latch on to their men right from banks of Ghoradal itself, where they gather on the night of the immersion of the Durga idols. Many pairs get easily forged before the journey starts, a day or two after the immersion. Fishermen try to pick up their partners for the next six months even before the journey starts. Those who don't find partners easily, come to the island in search of one. All the women finally find partners.

Batashi found Ganesh last time and decided to continue with him this time too. It was the same with Jamuna. Sabitri did not find her man from last year. He did not come. She cried for the first few days after she heard that the man had died of fever after suffering for three days. She then found another partner for her new home. This was common. It was not necessary that everyone who came one year automatically came back the next year too. Some died, some got ill and some got into crime and were sent behind bars. It was the same for the men too. Many didn't get their women from the previous year. Some women managed to settle down with someone permanently, some found jobs and some others just drifted away. Mumbai, Delhi, Watgunj in Kidderpore . . . brothels became their permanent homes from where they couldn't find release. The island of Dhanapati remained etched deep inside their hearts. Sometimes, they came to the island to find that the Kans grass hadn't dried up and still formed white undulating waves on the island. The southerly breeze would brush against the waves and come and caress the new inhabitants of the island, spreading a welcome cheer. Women who had once had a home on the island didn't forget it even within the dark confines of their brothels. They daydream about the island, their families of six months, the white waves of the Kans grass, the blue boundless sky and the seagulls that soared above. It seemed that the birds too were happy at the arrival of humans on the island. When fishing starts, the seagulls come down to the sea.

The shanties were readied in the first two days. Those women who did not find partners took up odd jobs after which traders came to the island and took them. When fishing started in full swing, no one remained unemployed. Daytime was so busy that they hardly got time to speak to each other. It was only in the evening that Jamuna and Batashi found time to be together.

'If something doesn't belong to you, can you sell it?' Batashi asked.

'I found something similar when I met my brother at the fair of Bhangar Pir. It's possible,' Jamuna said.

'What about the law of the land?' Batashi asked.

'They are the law, the government.'

'Who is the government?'

'I don't know, but the policeman is government man, even the Block Development Officer (BDO) is one, the accountant is one too!'

'Can they sell what doesn't belong to them?'

'Yes, they can. They are acquiring village after village. The land that belongs to you and me, can be sold off by them. No one will listen to us. My brother used to live in a hut off the highway. The government just asked him to leave. He had built that house on a land that belonged to him. Did anyone listen to that?'

Nine

There was a woman who smelled like fish,
Here's how she was sold against her wish.

Jamuna's words struck terror in Batashi's heart. The darkness all around made it worse. She held Jamuna's wrist tightly and shivered in fear. 'How is that possible, Didi? Did they evacuate the village?'

'Yes, the village was sold off.'

'If I don't sell my land, how will anyone else sell it?'

'Government can do anything.'

'Hai Allah! How can that be?'

'It happened! Villages are being acquired and then sold off in pieces to rich buyers.'

'Oh God! I am terrified now, Jamuna Di.'

'Why are you scared? Has your village been acquired?'

'I don't have a village, Didi.'

'You had one!'

'Just like your brother, my mother too had built her rooms in a village. I don't want to be reminded of the past. Let me go near the waters instead.' She released Jamuna's hand.

'Don't forget that you are a youthful woman. Why should you go there in the dark?'

'I don't want to go back to the empty shanty. It scares me to stay alone there. It seems to me that the pirates might break in any moment. It is safer near the water.'

'Come to my rooms. What has happened to you, Batashi?'

Batashi followed Jamuna quietly. Jamuna opened the lock to her shanty. They went in and locked the room from inside. Suddenly, it was very cold. The two women sat quietly in the dark. They did not light the lamp; no point in wasting fuel.

Batashi sat close to Jamuna. The older woman sighed while Batashi took in a deep breath.

'What has happened to you, Batashi?' Jamuna softly asked.

Batashi stayed quiet for some time. Then, dropping her wrapper on her lap, she prepared to lie down.

'Let me go off to sleep, Jamuna Di.'

'What will happen to your room? It's unguarded.'

'Who will steal anything there?'

'Who knows? You shouldn't leave your room open like this!'

'What do I have there that is worth stealing?'

'Hidden money?'

'Let that be. I won't go there now.'

'Why are you so scared? Are you feeling feverish?' Jamuna touched Batashi's forehead to be sure that she was not running a temperature.

'I am just scared, but otherwise I am well.'

Batashi was not sure if she should tell Jamuna. Not being able to share her fears was stifling her. She knew she couldn't share it with her husband, Ganesh. She thought of sharing it with the old man but couldn't do that either. But she had to spill. She felt scared sharing her secret in this room. She yearned to take Jamuna to the waterfront and would have comfortably told her there. Inside the room, her fear took a firm grip of her.

'Let me sleep then,' Jamuna said.

'It's not very late, Didi.'

'What else do we do? The batteries have run out and the radio will also get turned off soon. In seven days, the new batteries have gone dry. They sell false stuff on the island.'

'Why do traders come here, Didi?'

'Without them, who will we buy essential items from?'

'The trader is a devil.'

'Why do you talk about him?'

'I am scared of him, Didi. He has asked me to stay quiet, else he will make my life hell.'

'Jamuna could not see Batashi's face in the dark. She kept her hand on Batashi's thigh. The darkness inside the room seemed thicker. The stars lit up the darkness outside. The faint glow left by the daylight made it lighter there.'

'Which trader, Dasharath?' Jamuna nudged Batashi.

'Yes, Jamuna Di.'

'Why didn't you tell me earlier? I would have squared him up!'

'How will you? Government knows him and has given him all the power.'

'How?'

'Batashi broke down. She pressed a fold of her saree onto her eyes. Didi, the government has sold me off.'

'What?! Sold you?!'

'If government can sell villages, why can't Batashi be sold? Hai Allah! I got sold for two thousand rupees, Didi.'

'Which government?'

'I have been told not to take his name, Didi. If I tell you, I will conceive puppies, I have been told. But can government sell me without telling me?'

Jamuna screamed at Batashi. 'Is that trader Dasharath your government? If he has said all this to you, don't pay any attention.'

'No Didi, he has bought me.'

'Oh my God! What are you saying?!'

'I cannot tell you more, I am sworn to secrecy. I have sworn by Allah and the old tortoise chief. Please don't tell the trader that I have told you everything.'

'Don't be scared at all, Batashi. I will pack him off this island. Just wait for the fishermen to return.'

'If the government can sell villages, I am just a small blade of grass, Didi. Don't tell anyone that I have been sold. It's so cold, Didi.'

Jamuna wrapped Batashi in her arms. 'Shall I give you a thick wrapper?'

'No, please keep me in your arms like this, Didi.'

'How can anyone sell you? How can another buy you?'

'Does Ganesh own you to sell you?'

'Government has sold me, government can.'

'Who is this government?'

'I will be killed if I tell you.'

'You will die anyway! What have you got yourself into? It's like Punnime.'

Batashi started shivering in the dark. Her breath was quick and her bosom heaved with it. Jamuna was bewildered. She touched Batashi's head and loosened her hair bun. Batashi could feel the older woman's love. Jamuna touched her bosom and felt Batashi shiver. Batashi had filled out in this one month on the island. Jamuna appreciated her beautiful build.

'You are so beautiful, Batashi. Make use of your youth. There is nothing to fear.'

Batashi shook her head and murmured. 'I have been sold for two thousand rupees, Didi. I am helpless. I will have to go.'

'Where will you go?'

'Wherever I am taken.'

'Which government sold you? Tell me that. How much have you got?'

'That sweet smelling oil, soap, blouse, bra, snow cream . . . everything that will take the fishy smell away.'

'Are you a fool? By giving these things, can you be sold?'

'No, Didi. That trader has bought me and I feel he will buy some more. I am his now.'

'Who else will he buy?' Jamuna said in a low voice.

'I don't know exactly, but I think he will.'

'Why do you feel this way?'

'I might be mistaken. He is not taking me away because I still smell like a fish.'

'Fishy smell!'

'The trader hates that . . .'

'He comes to your room?'

'He wants to, but he hates that smell.'

'Has he touched you?'

'Not yet . . . because of the smell.'

'I don't get any smell. Does your husband smell that?'

'He loves the smell,' Batashi smiled in the dark. 'He tells me a fisherwoman should smell like fish. He tells me that my fishy smell attracts him.'

'The trader doesn't want it.'

'So, I scrub myself with soap and apply oil . . . to smell good.'

'Stop using those, you fool,' hissed Jamuna in anger. 'You are rushing towards your end!'

Batashi was shocked. She hadn't thought of it that way! Jamuna told her to stop bathing. 'You don't need to bathe every day in winter.'

Batashi saw a ray of hope. She had to nurture that fishy smell. If she stopped looking good, she would lose her worth.

Batashi kept quiet. Jamuna sat by her for some time, then opened the door and went out alone. The moon shone bright, washed by the sea water. She could hear the swiftly rising water of the high tide.

Jamuna thought to herself. What if the man who bought Batashi picked up the trail of her fishy smell and hid himself amid the bushes here? Had he already taken a round of the shanty? It was true that the fishy smell would give her away, but it would also protect Batashi, Jamuna mused.

Batashi came out and called Jamuna.

'Keep a cool head. Never lose your cool in the face of danger.'

'He told me to use soap twice a day for fifteen days.'

'Are you doing that?'

'I do. He told me I am coal but he will polish me to turn me into a diamond.'

'Don't you dare use soap!'

'He told me that after fifteen days of using soap, the smell will start fading. When the full moon comes, I will start smelling like the moonlight . . .'

'Tell him that on the island, even moonlight smells like fish. Darkness smells no different either,' Jamuna hissed. 'Tell me who your government is.'

'I don't know, Didi.'

'You know, tell me.'

'I feel scared, Didi. He is powerful.'

'I don't know him.'

Jamuna lost her cool suddenly and pounced on Batashi. Kicks and punches rained on her as Jamuna abused the invisible government. 'Tell me, you slut, who that government is, who has taken money by selling you. To hell with your government, the old impotent bastard. Let me set him ablaze. Go and sell your own woman!'

Jamuna lost control over her words. She started screaming at the top of her lungs. She seemed to be addressing an invisible enemy lurking in the bushes around her shanty. 'Lustful bastard, want to have fun with women and then sell them? Cannot stand fishy smell! She will not use your flavoured oil and soap. The smell of fish will remain on her. Let me see how you can rid her of that. I warn you, Batashi, I will take your happiness if you use any of those.'

'Didi, please calm down. Who are you saying all this to?'

'It's falling on the right ears. Who's your government? That Mangal police? No other government has come to the island. I wish death on him. Tell me what he has done to you.'

'I will tell you, please calm down now.'

'My brother is a victim of the government. He thinks he can sell women? Is she your property?' After screaming for some time, Jamuna stood there heaving, trying to catch her breath.

'He has sold me like one sells one's belongings. I will tell you all.'

Batashi started telling her story. Jamuna shivered. Mangal constable had left the island with the money. There was no way out now. The trader had paid for her. Why would he leave what was his?

Mangal constable had promised to put Batashi behind bars if she didn't go with the trader. She would be forced to use scented oil and soap. She would have to get rid of her fishy smell.

'You will not do it.'

'If I do not smell like a flower by full moon, the trader and the constable will not leave me. I will have to return to Ghoradal in the month of Chait, they will nab me there.'

'Your fate cannot be unwritten. Stay like a fisherwoman. They don't smell like soap and scented oil.'

'Only if this island was my home for twelve months, Didi . . .'

Jamuna knew that Batashi was right. In the month of Chaitra, they would have to leave the island again and return to Ghoradal. They couldn't undo this rule. If only they could stay on. But what would happen to Batashi when she left the island this time?

Ten

The dark night scary, when's the full moon?
Plans for that night, I will share with you soon . . .

A few days later, Batashi and Jamuna visited Dhanapati again. He had to be told about everything. He had set the rules of the island. There were traditions to be followed. Nothing could happen without his knowledge. Jamuna was seething with rage. She had seen the trader move from one end of the island to another, taking wide, confident strides, but couldn't confront him. She felt scared. She even walked up to his shop but returned, having done nothing. She knew the root of her fear. The trader had the government by his side. She knew she could do nothing against the police government. The name 'police' reminded her of her lame brother. She had heard from her brother about how the government came to the village and sold it. When villagers protested and said they would not give up their land, another, more fierce face of the government came forward to encounter them. There were hundreds of policemen with rifles and bayonets on them. Rushes of memories came back to Jamuna and she felt paralysed. She started avoiding the trader.

Batashi had said that the constable had sold her to the trader and left for Ghoradal to return only on the full moon night of Agrahayan. The constable came to the island only on full moon nights. He didn't like it when it was dark. He was used to electricity-lit Ghoradal and considered the island savage. The trader had asked him to come to the island in Pous. The constable would take some more money. The trader couldn't leave with Batashi unless he paid all his

66

dues to the constable. That would be criminal. If the police targeted him, he would be thrown two hundred miles away, shrivel up and die. Blood would spew from his mouth.

They went to Dhanapati but did not find him alone. Kunti woke up and came out on to the verandah. She rubbed her eyes and asked, 'Why have you come so late?'

'Why do you think it's late? We wanted to meet the master.'

'The master will not talk now.'

'Why? What has happened to him?'

'Nothing. He has met so many people since early morning that I have asked him to take some rest and pray to God.'

'Why should he pray?'

'We should all pray, Jamuna Di.'

'I fall asleep when I pray.'

'I just love thinking about God. I love Lord Krishna. I yearn to get married to him. That mesmerizing flute!'

'You are a crazy girl,' Batashi smiled.

'My heart goes out to Jesu Thakur. How they nailed him to death. If only I could serve him . . . bring some relief to his pain.'

'Will Khisto puja and Burradin happen this time?'

'Certainly, Didi, why not?'

> As the new star went up at Bethlehem,
> The stable saw the divine baby smiling at them.
> Hail mother Mary, Mother of the world,
> The baby in your golden lap, happily twirled.

Batashi and Jamuna were surprised at this beautiful rendition by Kunti. She would not go back to sleep again and stayed with Batashi and Jamuna. How could they broach the topic of the constable and the trader with the old chief in her presence? Finally, the old chief moved. He broke his silence. 'I was forced to be quiet all this while, Jamuna. This girl is so talkative. Give her a chance and she goes on talking non-stop.'

'Why do you blame me, master? You are the one who goes on talking. There have been so many you have spoken to since morning—the trader, Rama Mashi, Sabi Didi . . . there were many who I don't even know.'

'Which trader?' Jamuna asked.

'The tall trader, the one that looks like a palm tree.'

'What did he come here for?'

'Nothing! He just spoke to the master about God.'

'Nothing else?' Jamuna took off her wrapper. They had walked up to the chief's house and it felt warm.

'The master knows what he said.'

'You don't have to know what I told him.'

'Master, we wanted to talk to you.'

'Someone wants to talk to him again! Why do humans talk so much? Look at the trees and the animals around you. Do they talk?'

'Kunti, can you please get us some tea?' Batashi asked.

'Tea kills sleep. So, with the master's permission, I have thrown the tea and biscuits away.'

'What I hapless life I lead, Jamuna. I cannot even have tea!'

'There's a constant supply from the tea stall, what about that? Has that stopped?' Kunti wouldn't give up. 'You should all give up tea,' she told the women.

'Okay, now you go.'

'Okay, okay. Here I am, sealing my mouth. I will not talk anymore, I promise. Just tell me when the net ship will sink. Will that happen before Chait?'

'You will not stay here for that long,' the old man muttered.

'Why? Is she going away?'

'The trader has said that he will take her away. His younger brother is in the panchayat; the older one works in the BDO office and another brother is in the police. He will take her away and keep her at his house, give her a salary and food and clothes.'

'Will you go?' Jamuna asked Kunti.

She was busy shooing away a fly. 'Fish brings in these flies. I hate them,' Kunti replied.

Jamuna didn't get her reply but that didn't matter to her. It seemed that Kunti too had been sold off to the trader. But who had done it? Was it the government police or was it old Dhanapati? Could women be sold off to change hands?

'He said that since he is tall, he can never drown even in the deep-sea water!'

'He told you?'

'He was telling the master. I heard him. His height surprises me, really. I am reminded of another man who was so short that he didn't cross my knee!'

'A small boy?' Batashi laughed.

'No, he sat underneath a mango tree, smoking a bidi.'

'It's possible,' Jamuna muttered.

Kunti kept quiet. She took a break, at times, from her non-stop chatter, to catch her breath. She used that time to think of what else to talk about next.

'This mad woman cannot stop talking, I will go mad now.'

Kunti remained quiet. She looked tired. Perhaps she had stocked herself out. Her stocks were limited to her experiences in life, not beyond that. She worked her mind to manufacture words.

'What have you come to tell me, Jamuna, Batashi?'

Kunti got herself into the conversation again. What would they say? How much fish had been hauled up, what the price was, who had incurred a loss, how much fish brings how many flies . . .?

'Tell me, master, how much fish brings how many flies?'

'Oh! She's started off again. Shut up!'

'I am quiet! Am I talking? Whatever I say is known to you, master! Why do you listen to me? Do we listen to everything that is said around us? When we go to Ghoradal, we see so many traders who come from Delhi and Mumbai to buy cauliflowers and return with truckloads.'

'So what?'

'Master, you must start a weekly haat on the island. So many people will come here to buy and sell! There'll be so many things to look at and buy. You should start another haat for cattle. The whole day, they'll moo and bleat and fill up the island with their sounds.'

'Come with me, Kunti,' Batashi said. 'Did the trader tell you anything?'

'What will he say, Didi? I won't go with him. He's too tall for my liking, perhaps taller than Bachchan too!'

Batashi didn't know what to say. She didn't know whether she should be angry or whether she should agree with the woman. 'Where are you from?' Batashi asked Kunti.

'I don't know.'

'Your parents?'

'I don't know where they are . . . they abandoned me.'

'Where will you go after Chait?'

'I will marry the master. If I marry him, he will give me a home, Batashi Di.'

'What if the trader takes you?'

'I will never go with him,' Kunti said, making a face.

Batashi didn't know what to say. She couldn't share anything with this girl. She felt scared about Dhanapati chief too. The trader had sworn her to silence. The police wouldn't leave her so easily. Police was the government, one that could sell villages together. She was nothing but a mere blade of grass. Batashi turned her head and saw that Jamuna had moved up towards the master. Had she got a chance to tell him? Batashi felt heavy in the chest. If the trader got to know that she had spilled, the police government would also know. What would happen when she left for Ghoradal after Chait?

'Batashi Didi, have you ever seen Anna Bibi?'

'I wasn't born then.'

'Me too. Was she more beautiful than I am?'

'I don't know, dear!'

'Was she more beautiful than you are?'

Batashi shook her head. Kunti loved to talk, she couldn't stay without talking.

Kunti bit her lip. 'You know what, Didi, Anna Bibi did not leave the island even after Chait . . .'

'I have heard that.'

'She was pregnant then.'

'I've heard that too.'

'Why don't you ask the master?'

'What do I ask?'

'I want to have children and stay forever on the island.'

'Why do you keep talking nonsense all the time?'

Kunti smiled and playfully threw the part of her saree that was hanging loose, in the air.

'I want to have many children like hens or bitches. Then I will stay back on the island, bringing them up.'

'Do you daydream like this all the time?'

'Whenever I lie down to sleep at night, I do. Daytime is full of chatter with my old master.'

'This will remain your dream.'

'There's no one to stop me from thinking. You need a lot of children to live on the island. When I landed on the island on the first day, I was greeted by the Kans grass that swayed in the breeze and wild weedy vegetation all around. I told the master about having many children around me.'

'What did he say?'

'Nothing . . . just that no one on the island has children.

'Why?'

'He didn't tell me why but said that Anna Bibi was pregnant and stayed back on the island, but no one found her after that.'

Batashi stayed quiet. She wondered how Kunti could say all this with a smile on her face. Anna Bibi had eloped with Dhanapati. Her husband always kept himself busy with legal disputes since he loved to sue people. He couldn't get her pregnant but she conceived on the island. So how could Dhanapati say that no one got pregnant on the island?

'I know this story.'

'It's an old story, Didi. But I am desperate to do something. I don't want to leave the island in Chait. Where will I go?'

'You will go where you came from.'

'I belong nowhere.'

Batashi left Kunti and started moving towards Jamuna. Had she told the chief everything? What if she had?

Jamuna was on her haunches and looking up at old Dhanapati as she spoke. Batashi touched the older woman's shoulder as she bent down. 'Didi, if you have finished talking, let's go.'

Jamuna sighed. 'Nothing much to say.'

'Did you tell him?'

'I feel scared, Batashi.'

'What do you two wish to tell me?' Dhanapati asked.

'Nothing, master.'

'What about all that you told me?'

'That is all about fishing, master, and why Chait is the end of the fishing season.'

'The north wind starts blowing thereafter, drying up the fish, Jamuna'.

Jamuna and Batashi stood there quietly. Kunti came up. 'Batashi Didi, ask Jamuna Di about whether it is possible to have a baby in less than ten months. Animals don't take that long!'

Eleven

The constable will be back for new give and take,
Buy to sell and sell to buy, it's all for lust's sake.

'Wasn't it scary?' Batashi asked while returning.

'The trader has proposed to buy Kunti. So there's no point telling anything to the old master.'

'Has the chief taken money?'

'Will he tell us that?'

'Didn't the government take money?'

'Who knows!'

Batashi knew that it was not safe to share anything with the old man. But who would she share her troubles with? The fishermen? What if they asked her to go away? There was no dearth of women on the island. Would Ganesh also say the same thing? People who came here to earn a living would not like to go against the police. They hand over a fat sum to the constable every full moon night. He came to the island on that day to collect that bribe. They knew that the police could stop them from going to sea. Old Dhanapati might be the owner of the island but the rules were framed by the government. They are the real owners who have the power to sell off village after village. The government owned all land, water and air. They even owned the people and so, they could sell off Batashi and Kunti. Old Dhanapati knew everything. So, he allowed Kunti to be sold and was quiet about it. Dhanapati reported to government. He hosted the government every time he came to the

island. He offered cooked chicken to the government. Fear mixed
with sadness gripped Batashi. Jamuna, Batashi, Kunti, Sabitri,
Dhanapati, Pitambar, Ganesh—all belonged to the government.
Others knew it. Batashi had been stupid not to guess.

'What did that mad girl Kunti tell you?'

'She said she wanted to breed like a bitch or a tabby and fill the
island with her kids. She said that would make her stay on the island
permanently.'

'It's against the rule of the island. You're here to work. If you
conceive, it won't help the partner you're staying with.'

'That girl doesn't know that even her children would be
government property.'

'Who told you that?'

'If the woman belongs to the government, why won't her
children? The government will sell the kids.'

'I have seen at the fair at Bhangar how small babies are raised
inside vessels so that their limbs and torso get distorted. Such people
fetch better alms,' Jamuna said.

'That is definitely government handiwork,' Batashi said.

'Must be. All kinds of police move about in the fair and collect
money from beggars. The fair is a place for all kinds of exchanges.
You must see it for yourself, Batashi. I'll take you there.'

'That would be in Chait, Didi. Before that, the trader will
take me away.'

'Tell the trader that you are bound by oath to God for a year.'

'The worst misfortune will befall me then. I have already taken
time till Agrahayan and he doubts me for that. He keeps a tab on the
deadline. I don't think I will make it to the fair.'

'What a stroke of bad luck, Batashi.'

It was dusk and a dusty light enveloped the surroundings. Winter
was arriving and dust had settled on the leaves and everything else.
The sky looked dull and hazy. The water on the western side looked
like a feeble, immobile old woman.

'I am being spared because of my age.'

'But you were young once!'

'Once, two men raped me. The police quizzed me on it. In between, the constable took advantage of me, but no one did anything to those men. Now I know that they were government men.'

'I had a similar experience at Sonarpur.'

'They must have been government men too.'

Batashi looked at the melancholia in nature all around her physical space and said, 'So everything belongs to the government.'

'Yes . . . true.'

'Even the water there, the trees here, the sky above . . . everything?'

'Yes, even the chief's house and the land on which it is built or the patch of green around his house.'

'Nothing belongs to us?'

'No.'

Batashi sat down on the grass. 'What about our hair?'

'Every inch of you belongs to the government.'

'So nothing is mine?'

'Mine? Are you stupid? You are no one. You belong to the government and it can sell you to anyone it pleases, like you have been sold to the trader now. Later, you can be sold to someone else.'

'Even after selling someone, the government doesn't lose control over them?'

'No. Even the trader belongs to the government.'

Batashi knew that Jamuna was right. She was ignorant all this while. Jamuna had opened her eyes. Jamuna had told her that even her family of six months belonged to the government. If the government wanted, they could break such families. The straw and twig huts that they built for their life of six months also belonged to the government. Batashi started crying helplessly.

'So . . . we have nothing, Jamuna Di?'

'No, nothing. Earlier, the zamindars owned everything and now, it is the government.'

'Isn't there an iota of kindness in the government's heart?'

'How can you be kind when you have to live by buying and selling!'

'How did the government start?'

'I don't know . . . it is just there.'

'Why is it there, Jamuna Di?'

'For our greater good.'

'Is this good?'

'You should go to the city and see how happy people are!'

Batashi didn't fully understand. She was resigned to her fate now. Even Dhanapati belonged to the government, where would she go for help? Everyone knew the truth about the constable government. Ganesh, Pitambar and the other fishermen knew everything, it seemed. It was possible that not only Batashi and Kunti, even Rama and Sabitri had been bought by the trader. He chose the girls, agreed on a rate with the government and bought them. Sabitri had perhaps gone to Dhanapati to talk about the constable. Perhaps, she was just as scared and left things unsaid. Who would they complain to? Didn't Dhanapati know that he belonged to the government and that he was not the real owner of the island?

'Let's go back to our shanties, Batashi.'

'That tall man will come again. He is so tall that he can stand on the ground and pluck coconuts from the trees.'

'Then let's go to the waterside.'

They started walking. The winter breeze played with Batashi's hair. The dry breeze came from Ghoradal and chilled them to the bone. She pulled the wrapper tightly around her, covering her head. It was chillier by the water and their bones almost clanged. The tall man wore a woollen cap, a heavy woollen wrapper, socks and shoes, and sat by the water. Batashi put her hands around Jamuna and drew her attention towards him.

'He's sitting here!' Jamuna muttered.

'Perhaps he knew that we would come here.'

'How could he predict that? We took a sudden decision!'

'Never mind. Let's go back, Jamuna Di.'

They couldn't return. The man had seen them and called to them. The two had no choice but to go near him. He started inspecting Jamuna. What eyes he had! Jamuna felt as if he was running his fingers on every inch of her. She had heard about this somewhere—the customer would check every inch, even underneath the clothes, before choosing a woman. 'Do you need scented oil?' the trader asked.

Jamuna was astonished. Had he read her mind? The man reminded him of Batashi's scented oil every time she saw him or thought about him. Once, she had taken a few drops from Batashi and the scent had stayed with her for seven days.

'Yes, if you give me!'

'You don't need it much. Your youth is fading.'

Jamuna reached out to Batashi and held her tight.

'I didn't tell you earlier, but I have paid a price for you to the constable. Of course, you are not as expensive as Batashi because of your fading youth. Let the constable come back. We will finalize this. I will keep you to look after Batashi and Kunti.'

'Who else have you bought?'

'You will get to know everything. Just let the constable come back and give me a final price.'

Jamuna's face became dark and she hung her head. In this buyers' market, her price had fallen because her youth had waned. She hadn't realized that. Her husband, Pitambar, was a cool-headed man who didn't choose anyone else for the six months on the island, year after year. Pitambar loved her and never made her feel that she was losing her worth. This man was saying that from fourteen onwards, a woman's worth increased but started decreasing from twenty-five. They didn't know this. They moved like vagabonds on the streets to come back to the island after six months. For the rest of the time, Ghoradal, Sonarpur, Baruipur, Charan, Sasan, Canning Docks, Basanti, Sonakhali, Bhangar and Kolkata became their home.

'You sit apart now, you smell fishy. Let me talk to Batashi for some time.'

Now that Jamuna knew that she wasn't worth much, she felt relieved, in a way. She would request the constable to let her be. She would ask Pitambar to pay up for her in instalments. The constable would then sell her to Pitambar. That didn't mean she became Pitambar's property. She was now in the know of things. She knew that there was much more to the island than what met the eye. Jamuna felt emboldened by the fact that she would no longer fetch a good price.

'We too wish to talk to you, trader.'

'You will have to talk to the constable and not to me.'

'That bastard has already sold us. Why should we talk to him?!'

'Don't call him names. He is a good sort, remembers to return favours. Once, I had saved him. He still remembers that and tries to help me as best as he can. He represents the police, the government.'

'Who gave him the order to sell Batashi?'

'Orders come from above. Above the constable is the head constable, above him are the third, second and first officers, then the SDPO, the SP and then . . . above the police is the military. There are three wings to them . . . water, land and air. They are all part of the government.'

Jamuna choked inside. Her life breath seemed to ebb. She seemed like a dwarf in front of this definition of the government. Even the trader seemed insignificant.

'If we don't buy from the government, where will it get the money to buy aeroplanes, ships and arms?'

'Where does it buy from?'

'From us! We buy and sell and buy . . .'

'How is that possible?'

'We buy arms and aeroplanes and sell to the government and then buy women from the government to sell elsewhere . . . this is a cycle . . . the cycle of existence.'

Jamuna felt dizzy. She realized that the trader would sell Batashi to someone else. That man would again sell Batashi. This would continue till she lost her youth. The government also bought and sold aeroplanes, women . . . there was no end to this.

'The constable will be here soon. He has bought a bigha of disputed land with the money I gave to buy you. The person who sold this encroached land, naturally, doesn't have the valid papers to prove ownership. The actual owner of the land doesn't have control over it. The constable, in the meantime, has paid off for this disputed land and evicted farmers who were farming on it. It's a mess and it's taking time to resolve. He will have to take the help of his senior officer by greasing his palms. So, he will come to the island to extort more money.'

'Just let him come here. How dare he sell me? Does this country have rules in place?'

'The trader looked evil now. 'Don't you dare talk about the government like this. The laws are to aid the government in its give and take. If the constable hears you, he will simply throw you into the water and let the crocodiles feed on you. Don't you know how cruel he is?'

Twelve

She's a mermaid, she smells of fish,
She's gold and the object of a man's wish.

A few days later, the trader came to Batashi's hut. She had spent
the day drying fish of all kinds. She put the dried fish in baskets,
covered them with plastic sheets and then brought them inside her
hut. The dogs had to be shooed away all the time. In the evening,
she felt hungry and had just started chewing on puffed rice and a
half-burnt pomfret fish when the smell of cigarette sneaked upon
her from the rear of the shanty. She took her enamel bowl of puffed
rice and half-eaten fish and came out of the hut into the opening in
front. She looked a picture of misery in her dirty clothes, unwashed
hair and skin. There was no trace of soap or shampoo. When the
honey collectors or woodcutters left home to go deep into the forest,
their women looked like that till the time they returned. During that
period, the women didn't use alta on their feet or vermilion on their
forehead. They didn't wash their clothes with soap and didn't chew
betel leaves. Batashi looked like those women. She had deliberately
cultivated the fishy smell as advised by Jamuna. She chewed on her
half-burnt fish and waited for the 'tiger'.

'He is trying to get rid of the fishy smell for his selfish interests,'
Jamuna had told her.

'Tell me what to do.'

'Do something to make him loathe you. Fill yourself with fishy
smell or some such stench. This is the only way to keep men off. Even
sages and yogis cannot stand a foul-smelling woman.'

'What will happen to me, Jamuna Di?'

'He is asking you to get rid of that smell so that he can come near you. Women are left alone only when they age.'

'How will I become an old hag till God makes me one? Old Dhanapati had eloped with a Muslim woman, the wife of that man who lived off legal cases. Her name was Anna Bibi. "No one was as beautiful as her," he often said. He still talks of her perfect bosom and buttocks. She had fiery desire in her eyes. But despite all, she was left fasting by her husband whose only love were the cases he fought and won. He ignored her beauty that was enhanced by the snow and powder she used. He would ask her come closer only to say, "Anna, this time, I will manage that decree." Anna Bibi started hating him and gave up on her scented oil and soap. At this juncture, she came across fisherman Dhanapati and lost her sleep.'

Dhanapati, Dhanapati handsome and fair,
His full moon beauty was her heart's desire.

Dhanapati borrowed money from her husband, Hatem Molla, to buy fishing net and a boat. After a few days, he eloped with Molla's wife.

The trader came and stood in front of Batashi. 'You are such a horrible sight, Batashi. Is it the same woman that I had seen on the day of the Kartik full moon? Look at who stands in front of me in the darkness of the new moon—a raw and unclean woman of the honey collectors of the Sunderbans. But you are worse because they don't eat raw fish like this!'

Batashi knew she had been successful in her ploy. She had turned into the perfect fisherwoman. All day she handled fish and the smell had not just rubbed off on her but also seemed to have percolated into her skin.

Even Ganesh didn't miss it when he looked at her and said, 'You look like a woman who has just been orphaned or widowed.'

'Where have you kept your scented oil and soap? You are stinking. No one will dream of coming anywhere near you, Batashi,' the trader said. He was dressed in jeans, wore a gold chain, smoked a cigarette and had moccasins on his feet, Batashi noticed.

'Who cares for men? I have thrown your oil and soap away.'

'Why?!'

'They make me want to use them but it's so cold that I don't want to bathe.'

'But you have to do what I ask you to do because I have bought you. A woman's beauty lies in them. I will give you colour for your nails and lips too.'

'Not in this cold of the winter months.'

'You smell of fish all over. Pour scent on yourself so that I can touch you.'

'I am a fisherwoman and this is the only smell that suits me.'

'Do you know that I have to swallow medicines to keep me from vomiting when I come here?!'

'Have some puffed rice . . .'

'You have your puffed rice with that half-burnt fish.'

'I have fried the fish in its own oil. These sea fish are very oily.'

'Just get rid of your smell, Batashi. Did you watch *Mahabharata*?'

'No, I watched *Ramayana*.'

'You'll find this only in the *Mahabharata*.'

'No, it's there in the *Ramayana*. Sita was kidnapped by Ravana.'

'He was a demon! I am talking of the yogic powers through which mist covered the mythical Matsyagandha and took her fishy smell away.'

'Go to her!'

'She's an old hag now.'

Batashi kept quiet. The trader was becoming bolder by the day. He knew that Ganesh was on the island but would not return in the next three hours. The moon was overhead and would wane in sometime. The trader knew that Ganesh was having liquor somewhere on the island. Ganesh would raise an alarm if he found the trader there.

'You clean yourself with soap. Pour scent on yourself to chase the fishy smell away. This burnt and half-raw fish is giving your breath a foul odour. I will give you mouthwash. By the full moon, you should smell like a flower.'

'This smell won't leave me in this lifetime.'

'You're a fool to think that. There are so many like you whom I have bought and sold. One smelled like clay because her father was a potter who made idols of Lakshmi, Saraswati, Sitala and Kartik along with clay pots. The girl cleaned up the clay for him.'

'So, you failed to take off that smell, right?'

'It went away. I didn't hear anything to the contrary. If it hadn't, the customer would have told me.'

'What is a "customer"?'

'A customer is Lord Kartik, rich with cash.'

Batashi finished her puffed rice and fish. She kept her enamel bowl on the ground and picked up an enamel jug to drink water from it. 'They are all sitting there and having country liquor. So, I came here to have some foreign liquor with you in peace. But look at what you have done to yourself!'

'Give me the empty bottle after you have finished your drink. I will store mustard oil in it and use it to fry my lote fish.'

'Please take a proper bath tomorrow, Batashi.'

'Not at all! It's so cold these days.'

'Don't people bathe in winter? What nonsense is this?! Women are dirty for five days in a month and on top of that you don't bathe!'

'I will get a fever if I bathe and it will stay with me for a fortnight!'

The trader lit a cigarette with a wry face. Batashi thought Jamuna's advice had worked. Anna Bibi, the woman with whom Dhanapati had eloped, did this to save herself from the husband she hated. Perhaps old Dhanapati had told her to do that. Jamuna had stayed with Dhanapati for three seasons and it was she who had spread the stories of Anna Bibi on the island.

Anna Bibi's husband only loved to surround himself with litigations. His wife lay high and dry and could not conceive even after four years of marriage. Perhaps he couldn't sire a baby. But he wouldn't leave Anna, filling her up with stories of the cases he won.

She loathed him. Anna then realized that she had to turn herself into a honey collector's wife to keep the man away. She became dirty as she gave up soap; her clothes were equally dirty as she did not wash or boil them. She took off her bangles and stopped using oil, betel leaves and kajal. Because of that, she automatically lost half her beauty. Hatem Molla stopped calling her.

'That woman you brought the other day is irritating. How much have you told her?'

'You found that out for yourself, isn't it?'

'Why did you tell her? You knew that it was to be kept a secret. The constable won't leave you.'

'You were the one who told me. Why should the constable scold me alone?'

'Even after selling, the government remains the owner.'

'What about this island?'

'It belongs to the government.'

'No, it belongs to old Dhanapati.'

'Not at all! It's the government.'

'The original owner is the old tortoise chief.'

The trader laughed out aloud. 'Tortoise meat tastes good in winter. After that, if I sleep with you, I will have tasted the spring of my life. Tell your Ganesh to bring a tortoise. I will give you the oil and the spices with which to cook it.'

Batashi shut her ears with her hands. 'It's sacrilege to say this here.'

'Why?' Dasharath paced up and down. He lit a cigarette and after two drags, threw it down and crushed it with his shoes. Then, he surrounded the shanty. 'That constable is corrupt. He didn't stay on to hand you over to me. Instead, he said he would come back soon. He said that he would ensure that you come to me.'

'Go to Ghoradal and bring him here.'

'Not needed. He will come here on full moon. The trail of money will bring him here.'

'But my fishy smell won't leave me.'

'It has to go. I will take you to the city.'

'Kolkata?'

'No, Mumbai. Shahrukh's land. I will get you to act in films. You just get rid of that smell.'

'I don't care.'

'Shut up! Don't you value the money with which I bought your snow, powder, oil and soap?'

'Batashi realized that the trader was losing his cool. He was roaring like a tiger from Jharkhali that had crossed the water of the Hogol and Kartal rivers and was now looking for prey among the cattle.

Batashi sat down. 'You go now. My husband will be back any moment.'

'I will kick him hard and throw him in the water. This saline breeze, this island with water all around . . . it makes me lusty.'

'I know that.'

'Then get rid of that smell.'

'A fisherwoman is known by her smell, trader.'

'Let that bastard of a constable come and size you up. After all, it's his responsibility.'

'He will come to the island to collect tax.'

'That son of a bitch did not come on new-moon day. Now, he will have to ensure that my belongings reach Ghoradal and are put on a vehicle from there.'

'Will you really take me to Mumbai?'

'Get rid of that smell, Batashi. Even ghosts will get scared of you. I will get you a foreign soap, use it. Get yourself the Bangladeshi pink soap. It smells so good that I will make out from a distance. It can make a whole bus full of people smell good.'

'I don't want to bathe in this cold. What if I don't go?'

'You will have to pay back with interest.'

'I haven't borrowed, why will I repay?'

'There is a value against you in the government books. It was decided even before you were born.'

Batashi thought she could ignore the amount that was due against her name. She knew so many people who lived their life borrowing money and then kept escaping their moneylenders. One such man was her father, who didn't ever buy rice without borrowing money. Wasn't it natural that his daughter would continue that tradition?

The trader took out a bottle of scent from his pocket. 'Come, let me sprinkle this scent on you. This is a foreign perfume. Let me see if it kills that fishy smell.'

'It will make me vomit.'

'Come near. I can't look at you properly because of that stench. How beautiful you were that full moon night when I first saw you.'

'Ganesh is coming back. Leave now.'

'Really?'

'Yes, I can hear him sing his favourite song—I'll be reborn as a thread.'

'Keep this foreign liquor. He'll love it so much that he will leave you.'

'No, it won't suit him. Go now or he will beat me up. You don't know his temper.'

The trader walked into the moonlight. Batashi stood there alone. What if her fishy smell kept the trader away permanently? That would be a blessing.

'Hai Allah, Banbibi, Ma Sitala, make this smell sit on me permanently so that the government can neither sell nor buy me. Let it keep the trader off me forever.'

Ganesh came and said, 'May you be blessed. But so much of fishy smell can really put men off. Even your breasts taste of fish. Bathe with soap and become fair. A good sleep is the key to a good family.'

Thirteen

The Agrahayan full moon came with government,
Tax and money and all for gain.

Constable Mangal Midde was on his way to the island. He had
targeted to reach the island on full moon day but it could take a day
here and there to get to it. He had made it a point to spend all full
moon nights on the island. The moonlight made it easy to count
money, he would say.

Batashi and Jamuna knew about the visit just as the fishermen
did. The traders on the island knew about it too. Dhanapati knew, as
did the seventeen-year-old Kunti. He came to collect tax, money that
everyone kept aside to be given to him. One couldn't ask for relief or
for more time to pay up. The government had to be given his share,
every time. But he was never happy. He kept saying that more money
was needed since the number of people in the *thana* had increased.
He emphasized that to Dhanapati.

'I will meet your demands in full. I will make up for the gaps on
the full moon night in Chait.'

'You people are lucky to live on such paltry tax. Go to Kolkata
and see the myriad taxes that people pay. Here, you just have to
face me. I shield you from everything else,' the constable laughed
meaningfully.

Dhanapati nodded in consent. What the constable said was
true. In Kolkata, people roamed about like swarms of flies or crawly
insects. It was natural that to survive in that restless din, one had to
pay taxes for everything. Those who couldn't, had to physically work

to make up. On the island, the government himself came to collect tax, while in Kolkata, along with the government, many others came. It was difficult to categorize them.

The constable came a day before the full moon. He announced that the accountant would come again on a new moon night. His daughter was to wed on the full moon of Holi and so, he would come to collect tax again. Normally, he never came twice.

Batashi went running to Jamuna's hut. The full moon smiled in all its glory overhead. Its silvery sheen washed over the island end to end. 'He has come,' Batashi said.

'I know.'

'What should I do now?'

'Have you bathed, Batashi?'

'Yes, Didi. Who wants to remain unclean on a beautiful night as this? I started smelling so horrible that even I couldn't stand it any longer. Ganesh would chide me all the time for not bathing. He wanted me to clean up on the full moon night.'

'Did you use soap?'

'Barely smelled it.'

'I don't believe that.'

'Only on my hands and breasts.'

'The smell has left you. Did you wash your saree in detergent? Where's the fishy smell?'

'I just washed it in water.'

'No, I can smell detergent. Have you shampooed your hair?'

'No, I used mud from the sea.'

'Clay can never make hair this beautiful. Do you think I am stupid? Have you done all this for the government?'

'No, Didi, trust me. That stench was killing me. I stood out because of it.'

Your fishy smell has gone and now you will go too. The government is doing the final calculations at Dhanapati's house.'

'I won't go.'

'You will have to go, Batashi. Whether it's Agrahayan or Chait, it doesn't make any difference.

'I will not go in Chait.'

'If you stay back in Chait, your story will be the same as Anna Bibi. No one knows what happened to her. Whether the waters swept her away to the seven seas, whether she was eaten by the crocodiles, or whether she hanged herself and then vultures preyed upon her pregnant body. No one knows for sure.

'Never mind, Didi. I will stay back and so will Kunti. Join us. Let all the women stay on the island after Chait and not return to Ghoradal.'

Jamuna's man Pitambar came by just then. He had heard the conversation.

'How will you stay back? What will you eat?'

'I am too scared of going to Ghoradal,' Batashi replied and left in haste. Jamuna told Pitambar what had happened between the government and the trader. Pitambar said he knew everything. Every year, women were taken away from Sonakhali, Basanti, Jharkhali, Kakdwip, Namkhana and other places and sent to Delhi, Mumbai and all over the country.

'Some are even sent to foreign countries by flight. It is possible that they are taking Batashi too! She is young and definitely a prize catch! The constable is the main link in this and since he has sold Batashi, there is no point challenging that decision. Constable was the government. The constable has the junior, second and first officers behind him.' Pitambar lit a bidi. 'Let her go and work elsewhere as long as she has her youth.'

'The girl doesn't want that,' Jamuna said.

'Then let her stay back! But you said they sold her.'

'The trader said so.'

'How can that be? Why did she keep quiet when she was being sold?'

'She didn't know that she was being sold.'

'Possible. These days, it is difficult to say what is happening. Last Friday, when we were at sea, the breeze from Ghoradal . . . the southerly breeze I mean . . . kept pushing us towards Ghoradal. In the afternoon, it felt like spring, suddenly . . . as if Chait was about to arrive.'

'What! No one told us!'

'There was southerly breeze at sea and northerly breeze on the island. I have still not been able to fathom this.'

Jamuna thought about whether there a connection between the vagaries of these two winds that Pitambar spoke about and the buying and selling of women on the island. Finally, after not being able to establish the link she said, 'It's possible. That year, there was a storm at sea, but the island was safe!'

Pitambar also tried to find a connection. 'They were warning the fishermen on radio.' Even the poorest fisherman had a transistor. They were warned against going to sea and about staying put on the island as the storm raged on Henry's Island and Frederick's Island. The high waves lashed against the islands but the cyclone that swirled around from the east and west left the island alone. Except for a few drops of rain, the island remained high and dry. How was that possible? Old Dhanapati said that the tortoise chief swam away to safety with the island on his back in the darkness of the night.

'Our island was not here then,' Pitambar said aloud.

'I heard that too. But where did we go?'

'It's such a big sea . . . there's water all around and the skies had broken above it. In the midst of that, the tortoise chief had kept us safe somewhere.'

'We didn't get to know.'

'Imagine the storm raging at a speed of hundred kilometres in all directions, towards Ghoradal, towards Kakdwip, towards Namkhana and the tortoise taking us to a safe spot so that not a single tree gets uprooted and not a single hut gets smashed. Yet, in Ghoradal so many people were killed!'

Jamuna joined her hands and raised it to her forehead, paying respects to the tortoise chief. 'He took us elsewhere and we didn't feel it! Nothing on the island moved an inch!'

Pitambar gave a last drag at his bidi. 'No, nothing moved. People say that the earth goes round and round. Do we feel it?'

The moonlight washed everything outside Jamuna's hut till the end of the island. The soft brush of the waves against the banks could be heard from a distance. Jamuna sat on the small verandah and looked out at the expanse in front of her. Pitambar had dozed off after talking at a stretch. Jamuna touched him lightly to wake him up. 'Can we not help Batashi? She is a good girl.'

Pitambar rubbed his eyes. 'What does Ganesh say?'

'Nothing.'

'Why? Have they paid Ganesh?'

'I don't think so.'

'Then it cannot happen!'

'You menfolk should get together and find a way out. Say that there are rules that are followed on the island.'

'Since the constable is there, Ganesh isn't saying anything, perhaps. It could be a trick that the trader is playing.'

'Why don't you tell the trader?'

'Today, the constable has come to the island. We should keep quiet. He will stay at the old man's hut tomorrow and collect taxes. I will have to pay him there.'

'Then, what will the women do?'

'Nothing! Keep doing what you are doing!'

'This island will gradually go to the looters!'

Pitambar didn't answer and fell asleep again. Jamuna too dozed off. In her subconscious mind, she could hear the soft sound of the flowing water against the banks. Then she fell into a deep, peaceful slumber. There was deep quiet all around her and she felt like sinking into the water. She felt that there was blue water all around her and fish swam about her.

Jamuna called out faintly to the tortoise chief.

'Who is this?' a reply seemed to come, as if from within the depths.

'Are you asleep, tortoise chief?'

'Yes. I sleep my beautiful sleep . . . What else will I do?'

'Take this island somewhere else, old chief.'

'I cannot do it anymore.'

'Take it away like you did on that stormy night.'

'I have forgotten how I did that. I feel so sleepy these days.'

'Take the island away while you are asleep. Go deep into the sea and swim away, Dhanapati tortoise . . .'

No reply came thereafter. The blue water was still. Jamuna's breath was light and it made small waves in the water that broke easily. The winter water lay quiet and still under the moonlit cover. Jamuna slept a deep sleep.

In another shanty, Batashi slept under covers. It was dark underneath. It smelled of fish. Ganesh slept by her. He had had a lot to drink that evening and was sleeping a heavy sleep. Batashi remained alert. The constable had come and the trader was with him. What if they came at night? Did she hear a soft noise? Was someone there? Did the moon move towards the western side of the island? Was someone moving around the hut? One kick could unlock the makeshift door. The trader had threatened to forcefully lift her from her hut.

'What will you do then, Batashi?' he had asked her. 'I will stuff your mouth with cloth and tie your hands. Who will you call then?'

'I didn't say I won't go with you, did I?'

'Clean yourself with soap and wash your clothes with detergent. Use cream on your face and breasts and pour scent on yourself. If you don't stop looking like a vagabond widow, I shall kill you.'

'It's so cold, master.'

'I will make you warm. The constable is coming to the island. Is it good to stay so unclean? Do you think I am a fool that I don't know how long it takes to get rid of that smell?'

Batashi started using the soap again. She liked it. She rubbed away the dirt from her body and felt good. Her hair had become matted, so she shampooed to get rid of the knots. She had such beautiful hair! She followed up the shampoo with fragrant oil. Even the air around her smelled good. She washed her saree in detergent and it felt so good wearing it thereafter! Batashi realized that just as it felt good living in a clean space, it felt good cleaning up the body too! That fishy smell marred her happiness.

'Master, why do you sleep?' Batashi called out to Ganesh.

'What else will I do?'

'Batashi removed her cover and went closer to Ganesh. You move about in the waters all the time and have started smelling like the seawater.'

'Water . . . so much water everywhere . . .' Ganesh muttered in his sleep.

'Will you take me with you to the sea next time?'

'There's just water there . . . no huts, no shops, no video, no people, nothing . . .'

Batashi held him and cried desperately, 'Why do you sleep so much, master? The moon wanes, the night drifts away and the island sinks . . . taking Batashi with it. Wake up, husband, or you will lose Batashi forever.'

Ganesh woke up. The sea seemed to have woken up from a deep slumber. Its waves lashed against the seabed. Ganesh pinned Batashi to the ground and jumped atop her. 'You are smelling like a woman since evening. I will take you to the water, just loosen up and become easygoing. Sometimes, I feel so horny while sailing on the water that I feel like jumping in just to cool myself. Where does all this desire go when I come to the island? It's all because of that fishy smell. Thank God it's gone now!'

Fourteen

The island sinks in the Agrahayan moonlight,
Lord tortoise underneath 'lone sleeps tight.

The island of Dhanapati was a world in itself. A world within a world, in fact. Six months passed by at their own slow but steady pace. No one hurried. The fisherwomen were a picture of stability. It was as if they had been there for the last six years, and had spent innumerable days and countless nights there already. They behaved as if they were permanent residents of Dhanapati's Island. In reality, however, they hadn't seen many changes of season here—the long rainy season and the accompanying dark thunderous clouds, the beating heat of the sun in the summer months and the surge of the water all around.

To the fisherwomen, nature on the island resembled peace and tranquillity. Their seasons on the island—a slice of autumn, pre-winter rolling into winter and a sliver of spring—are quiet ones. They come in the autumn and leave at the height of spring every year to return in autumn once again. When they return to Ghoradal, hunger and starvation await them. On the island, they flesh out. Their hips and breasts fill out and make them comely, only to lose all of it gradually over the next six months.

The night before the Agrahayan full moon, while Jamuna and Batashi slept in their huts, Kunti was awake. She was massaging Dhanapati's foot. 'Why has the police come?'

'That's a routine. He comes every full moon night.'

'Lord, am I prettier now?'

'Who told you that?'

'The police and the trader.'

'Then they are right.'

'Why do they say all this?'

'That doesn't matter. Go to sleep now.'

'Will they take me away?'

'You will eat well and lead a better life. This is just a six-monthly world, out of which two months have already gone.'

'Winter won't go away from the island; there will be big waves in the sea. The sun will be so hot at Ghoradal that all ponds will dry up and all handpumps will be broken by people desperate for water. Only your island will remain safe.'

'Did you have a dream?'

'Sort of. If winter doesn't leave, you won't leave. The fishermen won't leave and their women too.'

'Good dream. Do you dream all day?'

'I love to sleep because of these dreams. I dream of that Friday market of Bakshigunj by the Padma River, exactly as I read in my schoolbook. The school is no more, just like my parents.'

'I will listen to the rest of the story tomorrow. Now go inside and sleep.'

Kunti nodded. She covered Dhanapati with the blanket and then arranged another cover around herself. Then she started moving her hands over Dhanapati's blanket. 'Bless the island so that winter never leaves it and the fishing season becomes permanent.'

The old man closed his eyes and sat still, listening to Kunti. How well she had phrased her dream, just like Anna Bibi. Her voice is beautiful, he thought and hummed,

> You are the creator that makes us, O Lord,
> For you, the moon shines and the sea we ford.
> Allah, you are the sunshine,
> The moon and the star of mine.

Your earth springs crops so good,
My hunger it fills with food.

'Kunti, can you sing?'

'Will that be good enough for your ears? Let me switch on the radio for you instead.'

'No.' The old man stretched out underneath the blanket. He lay motionless. Kunti nearly hummed. 'I dream that your island is full of permanent homes with roofs; crops are ripe and ready to be harvested; there are children playing noisily all over, restless like the ever-flowing water.'

The old man opened his eyes wide. The oil lamp had flickered out. Moonlight had brightened the entire island. It seemed to reflect on Kunti's face, making it visible even in the dark. The windows were shut to keep winter out. 'Open the windows, child,' he said.

Moonlight jumped into the dark room, flooding it and brightening up the old man and Kunti. A moonbeam curled up on Dhanapati's chest like Anna Bibi used to, once upon a time. The old man tried to clasp her with both hands. Kunti kept whispering. 'I see cattle all around on the island, mooing away in peace. I see children, all running to the village school clasping their books. I hear the gong of the school bell ring aloud. I can see the Vaishnav beggar singing, the flowering of the mango trees, the carpet of jasmine flowers, the cuckoo on the water apple tree and the blind beggar singing alone while trying to find his way.'

'What happens next?' Dhanapati wanted Kunti to go on.

'Then the dark, rainy clouds come, the frogs croak, the trees stand there and get drenched, taking me within their folds. Master, have you seen the rains on this island?'

'No, not the monsoon rains.'

Kunti laughed. 'Then why do you call the island yours? You should know everything that you call your own, just like husband and wife.'

Dhanapati opened his eyes and looked at Kunti. 'How do you know about husband and wife?'

Kunti looked out of the window at the moonlight drenched island. She sat quietly for a few moments, thinking, and then touched the old man's forehead, lulling him to sleep. 'Sleep, master. I will sleep too, so that I can dream. Let me put you to sleep.'

Dhanapati kept looking at Kunti. It seemed to him that Anna Bibi had come back to him, rising from the wild Kans grass overgrowth. He saw the same eyes and mouth, the same hair that reminded him of the north-western cloud. He imagined the raw mango-like scent of her breasts. The old man kept staring at Kunti.

'Master, I dreamt of the Poush Sankranti fair on the island last afternoon. The place was teeming with customers and traders, sadhus and those who were sad and lonely.'

'How strange is this!'

'What, master?'

'You talk like Anna Bibi . . .'

'Sleep, master, while I sing my lullaby to you. This is such a good island but there are no markets, schools or noisy children. So what can people do to spend time—nothing else but sleep.'

Kunti hummed,

> The island is soaked in Agrahayan moonlight,
> Underneath it, the master sleeps tight.
> The Agrahayan moonlit night moves to the west,
> The sea dips the moon without breaking its rest.

The old man reached out for Kunti in his sleep. 'Come sleep by me,' he whispered.

'You are my lord and master.'

'Come underneath my blanket, you are shivering in the cold.'

'I don't shiver, master. I just dream that the moonlit night remains forever, autumn doesn't leave the island, we wake up to dewy mornings always, and no one has to leave the island ever.'

'Come girl, sleep close to my bosom.'

Kunti moved. She pulled a part of Dhanapati's blanket over her and lay down on her side beside him, face to face. She laid her hand on his chest. Dhanapati took her hand under his, like he held on to the moonbeam. 'Talk to me.'

'I will never leave you and go anywhere, master.'

Dhanapati remained quiet. There were tears at the corners of his ancient eyes. It was not easy to hold on to his island. He had to offer returns to the constable. Obeying the constable was mandatory because it meant obeying the police station. The land revenue officers and accountants were just as important because it meant you were obeying the land office. One was expected to pay up the amount that was agreed upon after some amount of haggling. The constable said that the trader would take Kunti home. It didn't matter to him. After all, who was she? Just a girl loitering about at the banks of the river in Ghoradal. He picked her up from there, just like he had done earlier. She didn't mean much to Dhanapati, so it didn't matter who took her away, especially because it meant obeying the constable. The constable said that he would take the trader back with him this time and Kunti would accompany the trader. There was no question of disobeying the constable, else he would stop them from fishing in the sea or even prevent women from coming to the island. He would look for excuses to create trouble. A few years ago, he had done exactly that. There was an assistant sub-inspector who used to come to the island to collect money then. He started coming to the island twice a month and so, the fishermen had to pay double the amount. When the fishermen protested, he went back only to reappear with armed police who said that they had come to search for a murderer supposedly hiding among the fishermen. Finally, the police relented after Dhanapati agreed on a higher monthly fee.

'Shall I sleep now, master?'

'Come, let me put you to sleep.'

'You sleep too, master!'

'After what seems like ages—thousands and thousands of years—a woman sleeps by me. I am an old man now and have nowhere to go. Sleep overtakes me all the time, though I don't feel sleepy because at this age, sleep is denied to me. I have nothing else to do but stay afloat with the island on my back.'

'Who are you talking about, master?' Kunti laughed.

'Who else? Who will keep the island alive? Who will save it from the storms that surge? If the water turns turbulent, who will carry it to safety?'

Kunti was surprised. 'But that's another Dhanapati!'

'We are the same. When sleep evades me at night but my senses are dulled by it, I can make out that I am underneath the sea and there's blue water around me. Fish come and poke me everywhere but I cannot move because I have to hold the island safely on my back.'

'Is it true?!'

'Come touch me . . . lift up the blanket and feel me. You will see for yourself how I have held up the island for thousands of years. So many Dhanapatis have come and gone. There's no respite from the cycle. You say that villages and markets will come up here . . . fairs will be set up and children will play around . . .?'

'Yes, master! I will become pregnant and keep bringing more and more children to this island. I will give birth to them on full moon nights. They will come out of my womb and cry, "Ma, Ma . . ." I will fill up the island.'

Dhanapati touched Kunti's waist and moved his hands over her belly. 'It's so slim. Do you think you will be able to carry so many?'

'Certainly, master! No mother can fall short of her duty of birthing babies.'

'I am not your master. I am the original Dhanapati.'

'Which one, master? Kunti put her head on his chest and heard an ancient heart throb within. The old man's skin had thickened with age. He felt like a mammoth fish that weighed thirty kilos, covered with scales. The scaly exterior had somewhat softened from staying underneath the water all this while. Ultimately, it would soften so much that it would come off the flesh. But that would take many more years. Kunti tried to feel the old man and realized that he was not any different from the old tortoise.

'Are you asleep, girl?'

'No, how will I sleep when lying next to a man?'

'Have you slept with men earlier?'

'No! And when I did, it had to be an old tortoise . . . old Dhanapati!'

Dhanapati moved his hands slowly on Kunti's breasts. The soft, fluffed-up bosom heated him up somewhat. 'Will your babies come out of eggs?'

'I don't know that. If that's the norm, so be it!'

'These six months, there is nothing to fear. The next six months there is no one on the island. I just keep floating with the island on my back. Then, columns of water rise and ominous clouds cover the island. I just float away with the island on my back. My urge to save the island takes away my sleep.'

'I know.' She started moving her hand on his chest and then on his stomach and then below . . . first on the tortoise shell and then the soft parts of the tortoise's body. Old Dhanapati shivered.

'I was dead like a log all this while, girl, underneath the water for so many years.'

'Now give it to me . . .'

Dhanapati looked at Kunti, surprised at her transformation. Her nostrils were dilated, she heaved and her bosom moved like waves. Her eyes were like a tornado, ready to rip apart everything along its way. She climbed on old Dhanapati.

'I will become pregnant and stay back on the island, master. You will make me a mother. My mother said you need a man to get pregnant. She said a tortoise was the best sire. So, you should be good at your job, master.'

His eyes dilated wide and his heart was beating fast. Dhanapati found her lying in the moonlight—a female tortoise—waiting to take in his seed and then re-enter the water. The old man heaved and laboriously moved towards the female tortoise lying on the shore. The two bodies met, one above the other. They both lived underneath the water but mated only on land. While making love deeply, old Dhanapati savoured the sights of the island to his heart's fill.

Fifteen

The prowler at the door, he chills with fear,
The prey lays her trap, that the killer cannot tear.

On the north-western side of the island, near the riverbank, there was a Meena Bazaar where traders came from different places. In six months, the bazaar saw a lot of buying and selling. The six-monthly Meena Bazaar was where the hullabaloo was.

Traders came and settled between the Kojagori full moon after the pujas and the Kartik full moon. They brought with them rice, dal, salt, cooking oil, kerosene and also dry sweets, snacks, potato wafers, peanuts and condiments. Winter fruits like sour oranges, small apples, sweets made with jaggery and sesame seeds were also available. One vendor sold deep-fried snacks with tea. A little distance away, they brewed country liquor. These sold better than hot cakes. A happy cacophony filled the air. The island looked like a suburban town with the bazaar and its surroundings being the focal point. Transistors played round the clock. Old Hindi songs of Rafi, Kishore, Hemant Kumar, Lata and Geeta Dutt wafted in the winter air. The shops that sold paan, bidi and cigarettes were unique. If you didn't get a brand here, you didn't get them anywhere else, not even at Ghoradal! Four Square, Caesar, Passing Show, Number 10, such myriad brands! Where did they come from? Some said that these were made in factories near Ghoradal and must be fake. The island was the best place to sell fake stuff. Even if the original brands were not made any longer, the fakes had survived and had taken their place.

A fortnight after the Kojagori Lakshmi puja, when the new moon gave way to another phase leading up to the full moon, a new batch of traders would land on the island. They brought with them winter wear, sarees, petticoats and blouses, Bermuda pants, T-shirts with messages like 'Love Me, Kiss Me', dead sahibs' coats, pants and sweaters. There were some who came with scented oil, soap, snow cream, bangles, vermilion, bindi and whatnot. For this period, traders made a fortune by selling glass bangles and the *shankha pola* which was the sign of a married woman. The fisherwomen bought themselves their wifedom. The vermilion and the shankha made their marriage strong, they believed. When the hawkers carrying their ware of bangles and vermilion called out to the women, they responded like waves gushing towards the seller. It seemed that they had been waiting for him. When they filled their hair parting with vermilion and wore the new bangles, their happy responses sounded like ululations. It matched the sound of the breeze blowing in from the sea.

The fisherwomen dried fish in the afternoons. Winter was due to set in. It was a long stretch after which they would have to return from the island. Why wasn't winter permanent here, like foreign countries? These thoughts would crowd their minds, making them unmindful. Some would even doze off, only to be woken by the tuneful hawkers, 'G-l-a-s-s b-a-n-g-l-e-s anyone, shamfu, soaf, s-i-n-d-o-o-r . . .'

No one was sure of the trader who had been at the island for a month or so and lived with the owner of the shanty of a hotel that sold rice. He didn't have anything to sell particularly, but people knew that he was an ally of the constable. They didn't pay much attention to such things. It didn't matter to them. People came and went, some stayed back, some stayed for shorter stretches—these were irrelevant to their existence and didn't evoke any curiosity. Six months passed in a jiffy and then everyone had to leave the island. It was inevitable. The island would then fade from everyone's mind. Life in Ghoradal and beyond would then take over and no one would have the time to think of which stranger came to the island and stayed from one full moon to the next.

It was natural for one or two people to just be on the island without any fixed purpose. This trader was not one of those. Once, a madman had landed up on the island without any purpose. He would just not return to Ghoradal and would keep saying, 'I am fine and happy, give me some rice . . .'

This trader was not one of those happy-go-lucky kinds. He seemed to be a moneyed and whimsical man. The constable was his buddy. He had five such cops in his family too. He roamed the island with the constable the entire day of the Agrahayan full moon. They had tea together and marched across the island. People had become familiar with him around. The constable went around collecting money and people showed him the customary respect. Towards the afternoon, the trader found Batashi. She had locked up her room and was roaming about to avoid the duo, keeping a tab on their movements. If they moved in the east, she was sure to be in the west. She was desperate for cover.

'Be ready early tomorrow morning, Batashi. We will have to leave the island,' the trader told Batashi.

Batashi came face to face with the constable and gathered her wits about her, though she was scared. This man had sold her. 'Sir, what if I don't want to leave the island?'

The constable did not reply, the trader did. 'Here is Mangal Babu. He has taken approval from the first officer. He got the green signal from the police station, so no one can stop you. Just get ready to leave.'

'Who else?'

'You don't need to know that. You are sold and that is enough. You leave with him, even the first officer wants that,' said the constable.

'Did the government ask me while selling me off?'

'Why should he tell you before selling you off?' The constable laughed scornfully. 'The government is telling you now and that should be enough, Batashi.'

'What if I am unable to go?'

'That cannot be. The government decides everything, keeping the benefit of all in mind.'

'What if I don't want to go?'

'That doesn't matter, girl. You were sold at five thousand seven hundred rupees. If you don't go, who will pay the trader back? It would be a loss!'

Batashi was not sure if she understood. She had a vague idea of what the constable said. The constable said that the trader had spent the entire time between two full moons for girls like them. If one of them did not go, it would be a loss for the trader, indeed. He might sue her! The trader's entire month's income would have to be paid, the constable explained further. 'He has a book of accounts for noting his monthly income. He will simply produce it in court,' the constable said. 'Can you guess the amount? Twenty, thirty, fifty or, perhaps, one lakh. Who will pay that?'

'Government,' Batashi said.

'Even then, the government will come for you and hand you over to the trader for five thousand seven hundred again. The rest will be paid in instalments. The case would go on and on till you lose your youth. That will make the compensation amount dearer. The government will be in trouble and you too.'

Batashi's face grew dark. The use of soap and fragrant oil had made her beautiful. Ganesh had told her that. He had gone to sea to return the next day. How could she leave without telling him? Ganesh wouldn't let her go. She had a six-monthly contract with him. How could she break that?

'You will be happy if you go with him,' the constable said. 'Did you use such scented oil earlier?'

'I won't go, government. It was not right to sell me off without asking me.'

The constable lost his cool. 'You beggar of a woman! Do you know that there is a debt of lakhs on you? I am just trying to sell you and repay that. There is no question of keeping you.'

'I starve most of the time, government. Why should I be in debt?'

'I am not going to explain all that to you. You will have to go.'

'No, I won't.'

'Then you are doomed. I will stop you from entering this island. I fix the rules here and the senior officer is aware of it. He encourages all buying and selling. Yes, you starve most of the time, so I am giving you the opportunity to have a good life. When your youth leaves you and you turn into an old hag, come back here to collect fish on this island.'

Batashi did not wait to hear what the constable was saying. She marched away towards the eastern side of the island. Her hair and her saree flew in the air and the scent of her hair wafted towards the trader. 'Her fish smell has gone but now, she doesn't agree to go, constable sir. I thought it would be magical like I saw in the Mahabharata, where the fishy smell of the fisherwoman vanished as the sage read his mantras.'

'Don't worry. This is India of the Mahabharata. Everything will happen on time.'

The trader was sullen. 'Alone for a month on this saline island, saline breeze, saline winter, saline sun . . . I am yearning for women.'

'Only money can give me that yearning. Have you seen foreign currency? They are very expensive. From now on, I will take only foreign currency from you in return for women.'

That evening, when the moon rose from the east and the moonlight was not that clear, the trader and the constable reached Batashi's shanty. She had just finished eating puffed rice and burnt fish and was rinsing her mouth, when she heard the footsteps. She couldn't make up her mind and just entered her room and locked the door. She knew that the lock was made of bamboo and was unstable, but it still offered some protection, just like the plastic sheet that hung like a curtain to keep the cold breeze out, helped to hide her modesty. Once inside, she knew she had made a mistake. She could have fled in the opposite direction. These two stood outside the thin wall of her room. She could smell the cigarettes; the smoke came inside the room through the perforated bamboo and jute sheets that made up the walls. She was trapped. They could break open the door. She decided to break through the walls and run. Her home for six months was not too strong. Batashi shivered with fright.

'Batashi, do you think you will escape me like this?'

'Come out, girl. There is nothing to fear. I am the government police. The government pays my salary and the senior cops approve of my work.'

Batashi stayed quiet.

'Isn't she there?' The constable was not sure.

'The door is locked from inside,' the trader said. 'Batashi, I can smell that fragrant oil and soap. The government is calling you. Come out fast.'

'Come out, if you are there, Batashi.'

Batashi wrapped the quilt around her. It was full of fishy smell mixed with the musty smell of dust since it hadn't been washed in days. Why did she have to use oil, soap and perfume? It was becoming impossible to hide the floral scent. She couldn't smell it, but the trader could. The trader kept on calling her from outside. He was mad with lust. The scent had aroused him. In that fit of lust, he kept asking Batashi to open the door and come out.

'That woman won't come out. If she doesn't, then let's torch the rooms or throw water. The police know how to deal with such tricksters. Have you seen how they pour water in a rathole? Pour water from one end and the rat comes out from the other. You need to strike it with a stick then. Have you seen how they smoke a beehive?'

'Let's pour a bucket of water,' the trader said.

'Let's send smoke in through the holes in the walls and pour water too. The deadliest snake coils out behind rats and this is just a girl . . .!'

Batashi came out. The constable and the trader caught her. The trader caught hold of her.

'Constable sir, you stand guard. I shall pay you.'

'That's small money. Girl, tell me where your Ganesh keeps his money. There is no bank on the island. You must be keeping his money. Bring it out.'

Batashi stayed quiet. The trader tried to pull her inside the room. He was fully aroused like the sage in the Mahabharata, like the gods and kings of the Puranas. 'That floral smell, girl, will increase your price.'

'Let me take the money first. Where is the money, Batashi?'

'In the room.'

'Where in the room?'

'Inside a vessel, buried underneath.'

'Where exactly?'

'I will have to enter the room and show you.'

'Leave her. Let me take the money first.'

'No, let me finish my job first. Let me enter the room.'

'No!' The constable screamed. 'I will enter first.'

'You will run with the money, constable sir!'

'I need that money. The new officer is pressing me for money. He has threatened to replace me with another constable for this island. Tell me, Batashi, where is the money?'

'Leave me, trader. Let me first help the government.'

'Let me enter first.' The trader pushed Batashi aside and took up his position while the constable caught Batashi by the arm and pulled her. 'Tell me where the money is.'

'Wait, let me wear my clothes properly.'

'Do it inside. No one is looking at you here.' The constable tried to pull her inside the room. He went in first and Batashi followed behind him. The moment the constable was in, Batashi gave a sudden jerk to free herself and banged the door close, pulling the lock from outside.

'O Jamuna Di, Sabitti, Kunti . . . come and see who has done what. Come here, all of you . . . I have trapped a tiger.'

People came out from all sides like ants on hearing that a tiger had been trapped. The fisherwomen surrounded Batashi's room. 'Smoke the room, Batashi. Set it alight . . . let it get burnt alive. Let it suffocate. Beat it with sticks. From where has a tiger come? This is the first time on the island. Must have come for fish, but why did it enter a room? There are no cows here! Why did the tiger choose a full moon night?'

Everything was quiet inside. Dhanapati came. Some fishermen who had returned from the waters came too. 'Who's inside, does anyone know? They knew everything. Leave the government unscratched and put the two on the night boat. The government is not known to do such a thing.'

Sixteen

On the seas, an island floats,
Pirate Dhanapati, its owner gloats.

Deep in the night, the trader and the constable were packed off on a boat. The fishermen and women seethed in anger. The constable represented the government and so, he was spared. The trader was spared because he was with the constable. Otherwise, they would have been thrown into the waters of the Kalnagini for the crocodiles to feed on.

The constable was just as angry and threatened to come back for Dhanapati. All of them had to return to Ghoradal a few months later. He would then square up with Batashi, and Jamuna too. How could anyone keep a tiger away from flesh and blood? He had smelt blood. The constable growled in anger. How dare they touch a cop? He would stop women from going to the island. They were prostitutes and he knew how to treat such women, the constable thought.

These last words had driven fear into old Dhanapati. Mangal Midde had threatened to arrest everyone on the island. He said he would come back soon with the senior officer and a team of policemen. They would hold guns to the islanders' heads and throw them into the sea. The constable ground his teeth.

The fisherfolk counter attacked him. 'Go back right now. We will break your limbs if you dare to come back. You have committed a heinous crime.'

It was indeed heinous. In the six-monthly family life of the island, no second man could enter the lives of the women by force. That was against the rule of the island, otherwise its society would collapse.

After the motorboat left, the crowd thinned. Three fisherwomen went back together, but instead of going home, they reached their favourite spot under the velvet apple tree where the tortoise chief slept. Dhanapati, the tortoise chief.

'Why did we come here?' Batashi asked.

'The tortoise chief called us, so we have come.'

'I am so scared, Jamuna Di. What would have happened if I was not able to fight those two? The government would have taken all the money and the trader would have taken me.'

'Me too,' Kunti said.

'I won't return to Ghoradal, Jamuna Di.'

'We'll talk about that later,' Jamuna said.

'The constable has promised to come back with the senior officer and policemen with guns. What will happen to me, Jamuna Di?'

'What will happen to me, Jamuna Di? I won't return to Ghoradal. I will wake Dhanapati up.'

Jamuna was shocked. 'What are you saying?'

'I will disturb Dhanapati's sleep.'

'The old man sleeps less and remains awake most of the time, these days.'

'No, no,' Kunti shook her head from side to side. 'He sleeps when you think he is awake.'

'But we have tried talking to him and seen him deep in slumber,' Batashi said.

'The old man talks in his sleep.'

'What does he say?'

'He talks of Anna Bibi and says I am his Anna Bibi!'

'How is that possible?'

'He says Anna Bibi has been reborn as Kunti.'

'Do you think so?'

'Not at all!'

'So, what do you feel?'

'I feel like staying back on the island with a lot of kids.'

'You are so young . . . how will you have kids?'

'I will have them, Jamuna Di, Batashi Didi.'

'Are you sure?'

'Yes, I will give birth to Dhanapati's kids, many children in one go . . . they will laugh and cry. I will call out to them all day.'

'Mad girl!'

'Dhanapati has told me.'

'What has he said?'

'He talks of his sleep.'

'Who sleeps, he or you?'

'Sometimes he does, sometimes I do. In his sleep, he calls out to me. "Come to my lap, my beautiful."'

'Old Dhanapati?'

'There is still youth left in him.'

Both Batashi and Jamuna were surprised. What was Kunti saying? She was a tiny girl, with her breasts just forming and a yet-to-flesh-out body. How could she desire Dhanapati's kids?

'How much do you know of children?'

'They will toss and turn like fish in water.'

'What else do you know?'

'They will grow eyes and teeth and then stand up. They will suckle at my breasts.'

'You mad girl!'

Kunti seemed to be half-asleep while standing. In her delirium she said, 'I will wake Dhanapati up.'

'Which Dhanapati?'

'My master.'

'Which master?'

'The tortoise master.'

'The old tortoise has been asleep for thousands of years. Many winters, springs and summers pass him by. The rains and the storms too. He sleeps in the sun and the shade, by day and by night. Who can wake him up?'

'The way I try to wake my old master, I will awaken the tortoise too. My youth will help him.'

'Me too. Even I am youthful.'

The moon was ready to set in the west. The water which flowed into the sea reflected it. The moon too flowed along with it. The tortoise image that they worshipped during the last full moon had become ancient—drenched by dew, baked by the sun, anointed by moonlight and sunk by darkness. The three fisherwomen sat on three sides and touched the image.

'We'll wake up the tortoise and ask him to take us,' Kunti said.

'Take us . . . take us,' Batashi followed.

Kunti hummed,

> Dhanapati is awake on the Agrahayan full moon,
> He will swim away with us, all very soon.

'Wake up Dhanapati, old tortoise, wake up. I have come to the island to wake you up, my old master. Swim away to the sea with the island on your back.'

Batashi hummed on,

> Our nights of misery go with the Agrahayan night,
> Old Dhanapati, bring the sea to sight.
> Take the island away from here,
> So that the government doesn't find us here.
> Take us deep into the big sea.

Jamuna's eyes filled with tears. She had a sea of saline tears waiting to flow out.

'Hear us, O Dhanapati, we are in pain. Our homes will break up if the government and trader come back.'

Jamuna hummed and shook her head to keep up with the beat,

> After the Agrahayan full moon comes the dark new moon,

With you, let's meet the sea soon.

Look at the moon sink into the water,

Her pain is the only offering of your youthful daughter.

'Wake up, Dhanapati, wake up.'

The three women went on and on, imploring Dhanapati to wake up and take them away, carrying the island on his back. The government should never be able to trace them.

The three women hummed. Old man Dhanapati hummed too. He talks of the tortoise.

The old man awoke. He sat up on his bed and heard the humming sound. It flew in with the breeze. He brought out his fin and washed in the water. No, not water, but moonlight. Then, he rolled back to sleep on his bed.

Jamuna mumbled,

'He woke up just now, when did he sleep again?

He sleeps his sleep, his slumber deep.'

Batashi went on calling, 'Wake up, Dhanapati.'

'He will wake up on his own, old tortoise. He sleeps a lot,' Kunti said.

'Why can't he wake up?' Jamuna asked.

'Just now, he woke up and soon fell asleep again,' Kunti sounded tired.

'He sleeps all day and night,' she muttered. 'He sleeps from morning till evening.'

Jamuna whispered in her ears, 'You should know how to wake him up.'

'How do I do that!?'

Batashi knows. 'Ask her.'

'You will know it yourself . . . wake up, O Dhanapati, tortoise chief . . . wake up, please. Kunti implores you, the young maiden who hasn't yet tasted men, her breasts young like a flower bud, soft as a ripe mango, wake up to her,' Batashi said.

Far away, the old Dhanapati turned on his side on the bed.

Part II

One

Who was within the girl and who was out?
Where was the tiger and who gave a shout?

Three days after the constable and the trader were deported, an eerie silence hung around the island. The moon had waned in those three days. The night that day was a full moon night. The moon began coming up late. Its beauty too had waned with its size. Batashi and Kunti are tired of their beauty too. Jamuna has turned old. While bathing, she found that her breasts had sagged, just like the setting moon in the west. She felt sad. If her moon waned further, would she be accepted on the island the next year? Even if she was accepted the next year, what would happen the year after? Would any man accept her? Would she then have to live by collecting fish on the riverbank of Ghoradal or wash plates at a cheap hotel? Finally, one day, she would die by the wayside like a dog or cat.

For three days, people had kept their lips sealed. No one spoke about the incident that had happened on the full moon night. The next day, there was some murmur. But the day after that, it died down too. What happened on the full moon night was not something to forget so soon! Would the episode be completely erased from people's memory? The people of the island forgot it after reaching Ghoradal. They didn't even recognize each other, once they were back. Dhanapati, Batashi, fisherman Ganesh and Dhanapati the tortoise, who was floating with the island on his back for ages . . . everything was forgotten. Jamuna too wondered if she would forget what had happened on that Agrahayan full moon night.

> Agrahayan full moon night, the waters so deep,
> Humans awake with the high tide that leaps.

The people of the island—the fishermen who had returned from the sea, their women, the traders of the Meena bazaar, the fish traders and stockists—had all gathered on the riverfront. They had shouted at the constable and trader to go away. Such things were unheard of on the island. This was sacrilege that the seas did not forgive.

Thereafter, everyone fell silent as if nothing had happened on the full moon night. As if the beautiful and appealing moon had seen nothing. The island was asleep. Old Dhanapati slept with his youthful companion, Kunti. Batashi was asleep too, with her six-monthly husband by her side. Jamuna dreamt of her youth.

Batashi hummed deep inside,

> The boat of youth gently rocks,
> Do you hear its silent knocks?

Jamuna returned home to see that Batashi was waiting for her. Her face was dark in the light of the morning. The sky was covered with thin clouds and the sun was not that bright. There was a thick curtain of smoke in the morning. Fog made everyone tense. Would the fishermen find their way back to the island safely? What if they lost track? The big sea was vast; what if the fishing vessels and trawlers lost their way? It had happened once. Batashi didn't know of this but Jamuna did. Where had those people come from?! Dhanapati had called them savages. He wasn't as old at that time and Jamuna was his companion during that year.

They had a strange reddish complexion and their eyes seemed to be etched on their faces. They had lost their way and were caught in all together in a trawler. Most of them looked militant, but two of them were slightly different. Dhanapati understood their language. He too had lost his way once.

He had landed up in Chittagong. The old tortoise chief had shifted in his sleep, floating away from where he was supposed to be. So, while returning, fisherman Dhanapati could not locate the island. The fog took him far.

'Don't go away, Dhanapati stay here,
On this savage land, in our care.'

They set out on the third night after full moon and sailed through the new moon. The moon rose in the fog and dipped again. Finally, when land came into sight, they found that they were surrounded by mountains.

'What are you thinking of, Jamuna Di?'

Jamuna sighed. 'Nothing, I think of nothing.'

'Did the old Dhanapati share any news?'

'Why, what happened?'

'I don't know,' Batashi murmured.

Kunti came and said, 'Someone has come and we are to see him.' Jamuna changed her wet clothes and wrung the water out of them. It wasn't cold but foggy. 'They are all out in the big sea . . . it worries me.'

'Nothing will happen during daytime.'

'What if the sun gets covered and they lose direction?'

'I just cannot think anymore . . . I feel so scared when I think.'

'You haven't bathed yet?'

Batashi was quiet. She kept folding and unfolding the end of her saree border around her finger. She dug her toe in the ground and scratched it. 'Have you eaten?' Batashi asked.

'I had puffed rice.'

'You didn't make some rice?'

'Maybe I will . . . when he returns from the sea.' She moved about on the verandah unmindfully.

She had filled the parting in her hair with vermilion and wore new shankha-pola. Her man was out on the sea and so, she hadn't bathed because the clothes she wore had his smell. Her body still bore the scent of her man's sweat. Jamuna started sweating. Perhaps his body juice was still there on her thighs.

Batashi was trying to hold her home together by desperately keeping its signatures intact. That was her only escape route. The trader and the police government would not let her go so easily. God only knew who had come to old Dhana's hut. Was it a new customer? This had never happened on the island. Why were they being called? Men tried hard to dominate will all the time. On finding a woman alone, some even behaved like horny animals, but no one had heard of women being sold off to customers from the island.

Jamuna and Batashi walked towards Dhanapati's house. The sun's rays filtered through the fog. They walked quietly. In their silence, a wave of conversation of the same frequency moved from one to the other. The horizon loomed at a distance, empty as far as the sight went. Jamuna looked out.

'You are scared about your man, isn't it?'

'Yes,' Batashi said.

'You feel happy when he returns, isn't it?'

'Takes my worries away.'

'And what about the body? Do you feel the call?'

'Sometimes yes, sometimes no,' Batashi said, looking at her shankha-pola.

'I get nightmares about the boat sinking. How would he survive in the deep? I pray to Allah and bang my forehead facing the west.'

'Why do you wear the shankha? Muslims wear bangles.'

'The shankha-pola is a sign of a married woman. I want to display my marital status. Does religion matter to women?'

They walked for a few steps quietly. Then Jamuna spoke again. 'The storm in the seas can sweep the boat in another direction.'

'I leave it to Allah and Dhanapati.'

'Once, Dhanapati had lost his way and reached the land of the savages.'

'Which side is that, Jamuna Di?'

'Old Dhanapati says that to reach that land you have to lose your way in the sea. He says he has forgotten the way.'

'My master might know.'

'He might not. You have to lose your way to know that. You will then know where the harmads or the Portuguese pirates came from . . . they were old Dhanapati's forefathers. Many generations ago, there was a Portuguese Dhanapati. He was fair-skinned and blue-eyed.'

Listen to her, Batashi chided herself mentally. She kept quiet. Jamuna kept repeating her stories. She had very limited stories to share. If she stopped telling them, she would go dumb.

'Dhanapati reached the land of savages. It is surrounded by mountains and the sea.'

'Perhaps.'

'You pray to Allah . . . are you a real Muslim?'

'I don't know, really. For the six months I spend on land, I live with an umbrella seller. He belongs to a place beyond Bagerhat. It was with him that I developed these habits.'

'Where is he now?'

'He returns home in the month of Bhadra.'

Jamuna kept quiet. After a while she said, 'The mountain in Kolkata stinks.'

'Who told you?'

'It's a mountain of garbage with vultures hovering over it.'

'You call that a mountain?'

'I saw it when I was looking for my brother. There were vultures and dogs fighting over a dead cow. I covered my nose with the end of my saree.'

Batashi kept quiet. Dasharath, the trader, had spoken about mountains. They were made of stones. Who had built them—Allah or God. But that description did not match Jamuna's.

The discussion ended. They had reached Dhanapati's house. Batashi trembled inwardly. Had she not trapped those two? By now, she would have been in some far-off land. She would have lost her

way and travelled into Jamuna's savage land. Dhanapati managed
to return, the others wouldn't. Others would rot behind bars in a
foreign land. These days, you are not permitted to cross seas.

Jamuna recognized Nabadwip Malakar—the man who sat on
the red chair and puffed at his cigarette—sitting in front of old
Dhanapati. 'Come in,' Kunti came out and said. 'My old master has
been waiting for you two.'

The official from the BDO office of Ghoradal, Nabadwip
Malakar, turned his head to look at the two women. 'Okay! I know
now. I did not understand who this Batashi was. She was here last
year and the year before too!'

'Yes, she was. So, what brings you here, Malakar Da?' Jamuna asked.

Malakar was a tall and dark man. He had dyed his hair black and
wore a white dhoti and kurta. He had a diary in his pocket, some
papers and a ballpoint pen.

'How would I know that you have come?'

'Do you want to have paan?' Kunti asked the visitor. 'I have all the
arrangements for paan . . . betel nuts, flavoured masala, everything.'

'Zarda?'

'No, not that, because it is harmful for my old master.' Kunti
spoke like a mature woman.

Nabadwip was amused. 'Quite a good housekeeper, Dhana, my
old man! Where did you find her? In the Sunderbans?'

'No, no . . . in some other forest,' Dhanapati laughed.

'I envy you, old man. You have created a Vrindavan around you.
Tell me, Batashi, what have you done? There's so much commotion
at Ghoradal about a policeman having been roughed up! What did
the constable and the trader do?'

'I told you everything,' Dhanapati said.

'I need it from the horse's mouth. So, were you inside your room
when they came in together?'

'What will you do with the details, Malakar?'

'I will have to report to the BDO. He has sent me, Dhanapati
chief. This is called an inquiry.'

'Inquiry!?' Kunti laughed. 'There are no *kumaris* or maidens here.'

'You shut up or I will lock you inside,' Dhanapati snapped at her.

Kunti kept quiet but her expression communicated what she was thinking—she could lock him inside the room herself. She had come as a thin and frail girl, but now she had fleshed out into a young and youthful woman with a lot of vigour. She didn't care what the old man said. She was the one who lulled him to sleep, wrapped him in when it was cold and massaged him with oil under the sun.

Seeing her turning serious, even Nabadwip tried to pacify Kunti.

'Don't get angry with him, girl. After all, he belongs to the bloodline of pirates. Hence the temper. Actually, the incident has created a furore in Ghoradal. Newspapers have reported about it too. A cop being beaten up is unheard of. They have showcased it on TV as well. From the level of the DM and the SP, it has now gone to the governor! I have just come here to investigate. The police coming under threat is totally unheard of. They are the ones who run the country!'

'Then what about the government?' Kunti asked.

'Government!' Nabadwip scratched his head. The government is run by the police . . . I mean it is the police that helps the government rule over the land.'

Kunti kept shaking her head. It was not clear if she had followed. Batashi felt suffocated. She could now understand why there was an eerie silence on the island. The winds that blew in from Ghoradal had brought with them this message in advance. Mangal Midde was not beaten up but the trader was. But they had abused Midde. They called him and his entire family names. This little Kunti too was furious and had cursed him saying that he would die from his own gunshot for trying to force himself on a woman who belonged to someone else.

'You tell me the truth,' Nabadwip told Batashi. 'I will take notes and, from there, a report will be typed on the computer in English. Were you alone in the room or was there someone else?'

'My master was in the waters.'

'To hell with your master. Tell me who else was there in the room?'

'I was alone.'

'And where were they? Outside the room?'

'How many times will you ask the same question, Malakar Babu?' Kunti sounded irritated now. 'You just go on and on and on with the same question!'

Two

The man from Ghoradal, what did he say,
Which woman will come to make the night gay?

How old was Nabadwip Malakar? Fifty or sixty. Perhaps even more than that, some people said. The women of the island too said that. Women can guess the age of men. At least Jamuna could. If she had moved westward with the setting moon, it was true for men too.

For Nabadwip and Dhanapati too. She had seen Dhanapati grow old, year on year. He was so old that Kunti had remained a virgin. Dhanapati lay by her like an old tortoise, keeping her virginity intact.

'How old are you, Malakar Da?' Jamuna asked all of a sudden.

'Why?' Malakar was surprised.

'I am asking without reason.'

'How old are you?'

'No one keeps count of that but we have to be aware of how old people like you are growing.'

Nabadwip was the suspicious kind. He knew that there were deeper meanings behind what sounded apparently innocent. He wouldn't let anything pass off so easily, especially what women said. They always spoke cryptically.

'Let me first get over with the work at hand,' Nabadwip said.

Batashi, Dhanapati and Kunti stood on the verandah and discussed among themselves. Nabadwip lit a big cigarette of some foreign brand and stood beside Jamuna outside the verandah. The sky was a faded blue. On the north-eastern side, birds of the sea circled above. That was the direction from where the fish-laden boats would come in. Looking at the birds overhead, Jamuna asked, 'Why did you call me, Malakar Da?'

'Tell me what had happened.'

Jamuna stiffened. 'Ask Batashi . . .'she murmured.

'I am conducting an inquiry. I need to ask everyone.'

'Everyone will tell you the same thing.'

'No, that cannot be. Look at the fingers on your hand. Are they all the same? Similarly, people too aren't similar and what they say will also be different.' Nabadwip took a long drag from his cigarette and released the smoke on Jamuna's face. Jamuna moved away. 'You smoke expensive brands. It smells good.'

'What will I do with all the money?' Nabadwip asked.

'Get married again?' Jamuna said laughing away and then, she suddenly stopped. Hadn't Nabadwip bedded her too, on this very island? That was many years ago. He happily gave her money after that. But the matter ended there. He had promised to help her if she got into any trouble. She was young then. Jamuna was sad. She stood there, digging the ground with her toe. She kept quiet, not finding the right words to strike up a conversation.

It was Nabadwip who had called her aside. Shouldn't he be the one starting the conversation? Did he feel a tug at his heart? She stared at the empty horizon. The undulating sandy stretch combined with the water. Finally, sky, water and earth merged into one. Jamuna noticed that although he had dyed his hair black, Nabadwip had grown old. His face gave him away. Malakar would come to the island every now and then, but he never appeared to age. For them, he was just Malakar—a permanent factor in their lives—who didn't age with time just like Mangal police, the senior officer of the police station, the party musclemen and some others. One Mangal makes way for another. Jamuna felt that all men in uniform were the same. One couldn't tell them apart. Malakar was not a cop. Old Dhanapati would say that he was a key man of the government. The policeman too was a key man of the government. Malakar didn't look scary. He was a nice sort. He was a womanizer. But still, he was good.

'Why have you called me out, Malakar Babu?'

'To romance you. Why are you looking so pale? Didn't you get proper sleep last night?'

'When do I sleep?'

'Why do you say so?'

'When he is at sea, I lose sleep because I am tense and when he is here, he doesn't let me sleep.'

'My God! Even now?!' Malakar pursed his lips and made a crude sound. 'Tell me what happened to Batashi?'

'Let old Dhanapati tell you.'

'That he will, but you will tell me too.'

'Why me? I cannot talk that well.'

'You can . . . I know every bit of you, Jamuna.'

'Those days are gone, Malakar Da.'

'Why gone? You should know how to keep things that way.'

'My time is over. I don't fetch a good price in the market any more. After this, it will be difficult for me to find space on the island.'

'You will always find space in my home at Ghoradal.'

'Why will you take me and give me space in your house?'

'I will explain that later. You have a good body, Jamuna. I feel like eloping with you.'

That didn't mean much. Malakar was praising her for no reason. It was part of his sweet nature. He had a cordial relationship with everyone. Jamuna was aware of the reality but still hoped against hope that what Malakar said was true.

'Do you remember, Malakar Da?'

'What?'

'That Falgun night just after the full moon of Dol?'

'What happened then?'

'I didn't know you well enough.'

Nabadwip Malakar looked surprised. 'What happened at that time?'

'You don't remember?'

'What should I remember?'

'It was just after the Falgun full moon. You had come from Ghoradal and so had I. It was almost time for the fishermen to leave the island.'

'What happened thereafter?'

'I am surprised that you don't remember. I was new to the island and you took me in. Were you any less than a demon at that time?'

'Yes, age has broken me.'

'Even now you are good enough, but you were a different man at that time.' Jamuna was so overwhelmed that she was ready to cry.

'The month of Falgun? You mean not this year?' Malakar came back to his senses.

'No, no. Why should it be this year? Falgun is not here yet.'

'Which year are you talking about?'

'I really don't remember.'

'Junk it. It's not a valid case any more!'

'Why should it be a case? Have I ever spoken about it to anyone? It's just between the two of us. Towards the eastern side of the island, one fisherman left his shanty and went back to Ghoradal. Do you remember?'

'Why?'

'His house was on fire at Ghoradal. He had a partner here for six months but his wife at Ghoradal ran away with the youngest child, leaving the other two at home.'

'So how many children did he have?'

'Why, three children.'

'None on the island?'

'No. If we get pregnant on the island, we have to give birth at Ghoradal and leave the island.'

Malakar shook his head. Jamuna stopped. She too had conceived once. She had aborted the foetus and lived with her mother for a few days. That was many years ago. After that, she had remained empty. Ganesh often told them about an incident when he had lost his way in the high waters with no sign of land anywhere. He was scared that he wouldn't be able to return. She often thought her condition was just like that . . . alone . . . surrounded by water on all sides. Who knew how she spent her six months on the land after the time on the island got over?

'Tell me what happened that night, Jamuna. Tell me the truth,' Malakar insisted.

'That fisherman returned to Ghoradal in Falgun. The woman with whom he lived here also went away. I guess she followed the fisherman, not knowing that once they left the island, they forget everything about it.'

'What happened then?'

'I don't know. They went away!'

'I am saying what happened in the empty hut? Did the Mangal police and Dasharath bring Batashi into it?'

Jamuna looked surprised. Why was Malakar adding up two totally unrelated stories together? He was the boss . . . bosses always did such things. She was reminded of that beautiful Falgun night from many years ago. Malakar had followed her like a shadow. She was a woman labourer who had come to clean fish and took up any job that came her way—even washing plates in a hotel near the riverbank. Malakar took her to the empty shanty. She had no choice, after having starved for two days. Work was not available easily and the fishermen were at sea. Their women were trying to shoo her away. Even the hotel did not keep her. It was at this stage that Malakar caught hold of her and fed her rice and mutton, and bought her a striped saree from the market. After that, he literally pushed her into the empty shanty. It was a clean one and Malakar told her that this would be her new home for six months. She would be his keep.

'Do you remember, Malakar Babu?'

'Why did Batashi go there?'

'She was in her own shanty.'

'Why did she go to that empty one?'

'I went to the empty shanty, Malakar Da.'

'You are a witness in this case. Whether you went there or not, doesn't matter.'

Jamuna looked out to the big sea. The water had receded quite a bit because of the low tide, leaving a thick layer of smelly mud. The cranes had landed on them to peck out fish. The dogs followed them. There was a fishy stench all over. Even when the dogs barked, one would get that smell. They came all the way from Ghoradal in search of fish. How did they come? Not on boats, surely. Perhaps they swam, resting on the landmasses here and there. They ate fish and fattened up on the island.

'Did Batashi lure them into that room?'

'She was in her room.'

'So, who was there in that empty shanty?'

'You and I.'

Malakar thought that the woman was trying to dig an old wound. She was probably trying to confuse him. Who had the time to spare a thought about something that happened in passing, so many years ago? Such women went from one man to another and were taken every time a man came across them. They didn't have just one master. They were like vacant, state-owned land by the roadside— waiting and available to be encroached upon by anyone. But even in encroachments, some kind of ownership would develop since the encroachers wouldn't leave very easily. Such women, though, were to be grabbed, enjoyed and then let off. Something on those lines had happened between him and Jamuna too, but she was trying to bring it back to get him into trouble. He chuckled deep inside.

'I haven't forgotten anything, Malakar Da.'

'You don't have to, but that won't benefit you in any way, now.'

'I am not talking about privileges. I am just reminding you of a moonlit night from the past.'

'Keep it alive in your mind, then.'

'Why have you come here, Malakar Babu?' There was a change in Jamuna's tone. She realized that these men from Ghoradal had no emotions for the island or the women they took here. Jamuna still remembered how Malakar had pushed her into the empty hut. That was just two days after the full moon on Dol. The silver moon had come up from the edge of the sea on to the sky.

Malakar pushed her inside. He stood there smoking a cigarette and told her in a low voice not to make any noise. He was going to give her a home, family, clothes and ornaments, he said.

The walls of the hut were made of jute sticks, leaving innumerable gaps in between through which moonlight filtered in. It left shadowed stripes on the floor. She hid herself in one dark corner of the room. Malakar stood outside, smoking and readying himself.

'You are a woman so you will have to do what a woman does. But remember to stay quiet about it. I am a government worker and have immense power.' He flicked the cigarette and crawled inside. He was a tall man and couldn't stand erect in the small hut. The striped shadows were on him and Jamuna saw a tiger coming towards her.

'You thought I had come here for you?'

'No, why should that be? But why have you come?'

'The whole world knows it is for Batashi.'

'But why have you—another one of the government—come for her? Please save her, Malakar Babu.'

'You have roughed up a policeman! Are the people of the island starting a civil war? All of you are doomed.'

'What is civil war?'

'I don't know but the police fear it could be that.'

Nabadwip gave a long drag on his cigarette and observed Jamuna.

Looking at how frequently he dragged at the cigarette, Jamuna could make out that he was aroused. She had excited him, like she had on that night. The tall tiger sat opposite her and smoked. It was as if the shadowy stripes had come alive. His eyes burnt with lust. He puffed out the smoke on her mouth.

'Even if you don't open your mouth, Jamuna, you will not be able to save Batashi.'

'What has happened, Malakar Da?'

'You seem to have lost it all. You don't excite me anymore, Jamuna.'

'There are many women in Ghoradal.'

'There are women everywhere, but the ones on the island are special. Did they manage to take Batashi?'

'Perhaps not.'

'Who went inside first?'

'Both.'

'There was no woman inside, so why would they go in?'

Jamuna found her pulse racing with anger. Nabadwip noticed it.

'Batashi and that slip of a girl, Kunti, both of them are all at fault. Did they force themselves on the woman or force themselves in?'

'They have sold Batashi.'

'To whom have they sold her? Where is the receipt? Is she a piece of land that can be sold so easily?'

'The constable has sold her, the government has.'

'Don't talk nonsense. Where is the deed of sale? Show me the number! You'll not be able to do that. They went inside an empty shanty but Batashi wasn't there, is that possible?'

'Not possible?'

'No, it's not possible,' Malakar stressed.

'But it did happen.'

'No, nothing happened,' Malakar shouted to muffle Jamuna's voice.

'Then what happened?'

'That, I will have to ask around. I will spend the night here. You are an old hag; I cannot sleep with you. Send me a woman, will you be able to manage that?'

Three

Betel leaf and lime, your sweet hand gives,
Your dark night hair, in my mind lives.

Jamuna felt heavy in the head. She looked at Nabadwip Malakar, walking leisurely towards Dhanapati's house, swaying his satisfied body. She realized that Nabadwip had called her aside for that last bit he wanted her to do. He satisfied his urge by ordering her to do his bidding. Had Jamuna left early, he would not have been able to tell her what he wanted. So, he had pulled her away from the others. Nabadwip didn't have too many people on the island to talk about such things.

Such was the tradition on the island. From Ghoradal, government babus came there for such things. They would come with official work of inquiries. It was winter break and the scent of flesh had brought Malakar here. He was becoming old, at least on the outside, but he still had the teeth to chew meat off the bones. If needed, he could take his prey five miles away into the deep forest. He still appeared to have the strength.

Jamuna thought that Malakar didn't consider her to be a woman anymore. But her fisherman partner, with whom she would spend six months, loved her. He loved to put his head onto her sagging bosom and sleep. Jamuna was angry. Malakar was using her as an agent to get himself women. A woman who had lost her prime had to get into woman-hunting to survive. Jamuna would stay away from this, she decided.

She couldn't tell Batashi because she was already scared of the goings-on. Her husband, Ganesh Sardar, was an angry man. He would kill Batashi if he heard of such things. He was seething with rage ever since he heard of the incident where two men were caught locked up in his room. He cooled a bit when he heard that the people of the island had trapped them and it was Batashi who had raised the alarm. It was only natural. Ganesh was, after all, a man! Any man could get another woman if he wanted, leaving the one he had at home. When he had started a family, he had to respect its sanctity. Jamuna thought she would go to her shanty and wait but she was worried about Batashi. This man was even eyeing Kunti. Jamuna started moving slowly towards Dhanapati's house. Nabadwip and Dhanapati were talking. Kunti stood behind Dhanapati and behind her, stood Batashi.

'I was trying to ask around as is the rule in an inquiry,' Malakar said.

'I know. I have given many such statements myself,' Dhanapati said.

'When did you give statements?'

'I have. I don't remember where and when. It's been so many years that I have been looking after the island.'

'How old are you?'

'I don't know.'

Kunti suddenly whistled, '. . . six twenty, seven twenty . . .'

Nabadwip smiled. His eyes shone as he looked at Kunti. 'Tell me what happened on the island that night.'

'Is it more? Two hundred, three hundred, a thousand?'

Dhanapati was irritated. 'Ask her to be quiet, Batashi.'

Kunti was upset. 'You said it was thousands of years, one night. The very next day, you changed what you said.'

'That is the age of the tortoise, the one who holds the island on his back.'

'You say you and him are one.'

'Ufff! Will you shut up? Malakar, this girl will talk me to my death. Batashi, take her away.'

Batashi, Kunti and Jamuna left the verandah. They went and sat at a distance on the grass. The soil was sandy; they would have to dust the sand away.

'Now tell me,' Nabadwip Malakar said.

'What will I say?'

'They came during winter. Naturally, the babus needed women to spend the night with.'

'I am not saying no to that.'

'Then where is the trouble?'

'Nothing!' Dhanapati shook his head from side to side. He suddenly looked like a feeble ball of flesh. The corners of his eyes watered. He didn't pull off his monkey cap, though it was quite late in the day. There was a thick wrapper around him.

'I have known this island for so many years. No one has ever come to buy women here.'

'That was not serious. It's over now.'

'Then why the inquiry?'

'Because they touched the police.'

'That is not true. He wasn't roughed up.'

'They said so. They also said that the island was full of unlicensed prostitutes.'

'What license are you talking about? They have given us a receipt. Want to see?'

'Rubbish . . . that's tax for the land. Do these women have any license?'

Dhanapati was startled. Nabadwip had been coming to the island to drink and have fun with the women, for years. He would accept a *nazrana* from Dhanapati year after year, but he still hadn't developed a soft spot for the island. He had been fed so well by the island, but he didn't have any gratitude. The moment he got scent of the news, Malakar, who was known to be the BDO's man, rushed to the island. He insisted that women needed license to use their bodies on the island.

'Government gives such permissions?'

'That's the rule. No woman on the island has a license. This is illegal. And now, they have even touched the police!'

The old man was silent. He wanted to understand what was being said. It was not right to touch the government, Malakar Babu, but the trader is not the government!'

'I know everything. These women are not married to the men they live with,' Malakar said. 'You shouldn't be bothered with who is government and who is not.'

'So, what should we do?'

'If there was no woman inside the shanty, what harm did the two men do by entering an empty shanty?'

Dhanapati realized that Nabadwip Malakar had come to play a game and would use them as pawns in it. Two games were on—his own and that of the island. Nabadwip was the government man; Dhanapati would not be able to pack him off on a boat so easily. No one could touch him. A repetition of what happened that night would not be excused by the government from Ghoradal. The man had come for an inquiry which was a very expensive thing. A report could shake up the whole country.

'What do you want?' Dhanapati asked.

'I am doing my inquiry.'

'Yes, but what do you want?'

'Want?! Don't you know me?'

'That is exactly why I want to ask you whether you will take our side while writing the report.' Dhanapati's voice was deep with emotion, and it hit Malakar like a heavy stone.

'The government will take a decision based on my report.'

'Tell me what you want.'

Malakar lit a cigarette and gave a big drag. He then blew rings of smoke in the air and said, 'You are an old man, Dhanapati. You were the one who would talk about the storm of the fifties. You came to the island and saw bodies washed ashore.'

'Yes, we spent some days cremating those and finally, the vultures left the island.

'It has been sixty years since?'

'Yes, must be.'

'And you—an old man—are back on the island, this time with such a young lass! Is she fifteen years old?'

'Might be.'

'Give her to me, Dhanapati.' He gave a long drag at the cigarette and threw away the stub.

Dhanapati grew sullen. He raised his eyes to the sky and sat thinking, silently. Malakar took a diary out of his bag and started writing something with a ballpoint pen. A little later, Dhanapati lowered his head and said, 'Young women help to extend one's lifespan. I need her to stay alive. I have to stay alive for many years. That is why I have brought her . . . she will keep me alive. She is my wife. As government, why do you talk like this?'

Old Dhanapati's face grew pale. 'She's very young . . . I haven't harmed her. She just looks after me.'

'Six months later, she will not be with you. After the Chait month, she will go away and live on the streets like a dog. So many will maul her. Tonight, let her massage my hands and legs.'

Dhanapati shook his head. The pirate blood that ran in his veins was on the boil. The island was discovered somewhere in the Bay of Bengal by his forefather Pedru. The tortoise chief carried it on his back and came here, near Ghoradal. Otherwise the island would be hidden somewhere in the middle of the seven seas. No one would have known about it. That would have been better, Dhanapati thought. His forefathers were Portuguese pirates who looted the seas and finally came to this land. On the mainland, people attacked them. After their bullets ran out, they were killed.

To save them, the tortoise chief Pedru brought the island on his back. He knew the story of Pedru-Pedro. Their village was near Ghoradal. There were 182 *nakshas* at Ghoradal, which meant that there were 182 villages. Dhanapati's village, Firingitala, was located in the 169th naksha. The *mouza* was the same. Dhanapati sat in front of Nabadwip Malakar, thinking about all that. It gave him some inspiration.

'Have you been to my village in Firingitala, Malakar Babu?'

'The one that has the graves of seven foreigners?'

'Yes. One of them was my forefather, Pedru.'

'You told me so.'

'He brought the island here.'

Malakar laughed aloud. 'Who would believe such a story? Kunti! Come here and make a paan for me. Let me see how sweet your hand is.'

Kunti got up and dusted her saree before coming towards the hut. There was a rhythm in her step, Malakar thought. He started lusting for the girl and measured every inch of her, peering at her bosom from above her saree. She wore a red blouse. Malakar was aroused.

'Girl, go and make me a paan.'

Malakar kept looking at her back as she walked into the house. Her hips would flesh out further, he thought. But even now, she was a pleasure to watch. She had such thick and long hair; she must have shampooed yesterday, Malakar thought. Her long hair reached her hips and below, looking like a mass of dark clouds. He gaped at the receding figure as long as he could, lusting after every inch of that body.

'Limit yourself to that paan,' Dhanapati said.

'She is neither related to you nor me. If you can sleep with this girl, young enough to be your grandchild, why can't I sleep with her too?'

'Don't repeat this again. I am a descendant of the pirate Pedru.'

'I am no less. I am Nabadwip Malakar.'

'We know you are Nabadwip Malakar. What is new about it?'

'My forefathers came to Ghoradal from Nabadwip.'

Dhanapati scoffed at that. 'Nabadwip is not far . . . just by the Ganges. My forefathers came from Lisboan by the Atlantic Ocean. He was a huge man, had five wives, six boats with sails and a house with a garden.'

'This is a cooked-up story.'

'If it's a story, then did I fall from the sky?'

Nabadwip laughed. 'Look, old man, I don't want to debate this with you. I have come here for an inquiry. If I get this maiden for a night, I will go back and make a good report. The government is peeved with the women of your island. They don't have a license. Imagine how much the government would have earned if they had a license.'

'They don't do such work.'

'They do. How else can you sleep with Kunti?'

'I feel scared of sleeping alone, Malakar.'

'Why should you feel scared? After all, you are a descendant of the pirate Pedru!'

Old Dhanapati fell silent for a while. He didn't know how to ward off Nabadwip Malakar. Government was all powerful and could do anything. It could destroy village after village, killing many. Government brought on such misery for greater good. If Malakar said he would sleep with Kunti, no one could stop that.

Kunti came slowly. She brought just one paan, so she could come quickly. Malakar extended his hand and caught hold of Kunti's. She pulled it away and went to where Batashi and Jamuna were sitting. Dhanapati wondered at the grit of the girl. She had become so poised. He could not see the turbulent waves in her now.

Nabadwip chewed at the paan and jumped up. He tried to spit it out.

'My mouth is burning . . . so much lime and black catechu! You devil of a girl . . . you slut . . . come here.'

Four

Crossing the seas, swims one Dhanapati,
Floating on seawater, comes another Dhanapati

Kunti was beside herself with laughter. 'What happened after that, Jamuna Mashi?'

'What kind of an aunt am I? Your mother's sister or your father's?'

Ok, Didi . . . what then? Did that man turn into a lamb!?'

'Yes!'

'How did that happen, Jamuna Di?'

'That witch knew black magic.'

There was a roar from behind. Malakar spat the betel leaf out on the verandah and called for Kunti. She turned around and bent towards Jamuna to say, 'His tongue is burnt. That man's a bastard. I have stuffed the paan with lime, catechu and a lot of chilli powder.'

'What! He is the government!'

'I don't care. I loathe that word, government. God knows who he has come to sell this time, that bastard. They get a salary every month . . . master said this the other day.'

Batashi turned her head and saw Malakar pacing up and down in anger. She felt uneasy. She was the reason behind him coming to the island. Kunti had made the situation complicated. Now, if he got mad with rage and returned to Ghoradal, what would happen to her? He would be back with at least ten cops.'

'You tell me that story about the witch,' Kunti said.

'I told you what I knew.'

'I have heard that witches can turn men into stone.'

'Perhaps so. They can fly in the sky, riding on trees,' Batashi said unmindfully. She did not take her eyes off Malakar. The man picked up the water jug, rinsed his mouth and spat out on the verandah.

'Leave all that for now. Go and make another paan for him.'

'I cannot do that. My hands won't let me. Tell me all about witches and who turns into one.'

'Witches are initiated at Kamrup-Kamakhya. They are given secret mantras.'

'Where is that?'

'Very far. You have to cross seven mountains, seven rivers and seven forests.'

'I want to become a witch.'

'Shut up! You are still a girl. Don't be mad. If they hear you, they'll beat you to death,' Batashi scolded Kunti.

'Only witches can do something now. That man has dirty looks. He was literally eating me up with those eyes.'

'Men are like that,' Batashi muttered under her breath.

If I were a witch, I would have blinded those eyes from a distance,' Kunti hissed in anger. 'That man is my enemy.'

'Keep your mouth shut, girl. If men look at you like that, it means they are lusting after your youth. You have flowered from a bud, Kunti. That is natural, and it means you are a winner!'

'No, I like my tortoise master.'

'Dhanapati! Foggy old man, he is. God knows for how long he will be alive,' Jamuna muttered.

'My master won't die. He is a descendant of Pedru, the tortoise chief.'

Jamuna looked at Kunti in wonder. She then looked at Dhanapati from a distance. Malakar was bent down from the waist, trying to explain something to the chief. The old, heavy body filled the chair and looked like a motionless heap wrapped up in a shawl.

'Those are tales. Not true . . .' Batashi said.

'No, they are true. I can vouch for that.'

'What do you know?' Batashi suddenly got angry with Kunti. She had made Malakar angry and Batashi would have to bear the brunt of it now. She might be dragged out of the island by the government. She faintly believed that she had been sold off already. Her heart sank in terror. Fear simmered inside her.

'If there was no woman, why would the two—the constable and the trader—enter the hut? It wasn't a rape.' The last words were Jamuna's.

'I know a lot,' Kunti said, coiling her long hair into a bun.

'What is it?' Batashi asked, raising her finger. She sat down on her haunches and rested her chin on her knee, lost in thought. Kunti looked at the blue of the sky and the birds flying high, from the corner of her eye. The effort of tying up the hair knot pulled at her spine and strained her neck. Her bosom looked comely even to Jamuna. Her saree fell off her shoulders, exposing her blouse and the pulsating bosom underneath.

Men should savour this treat, thought Jamuna. Old Dhanapati was almost blind and turning deaf too. How would he taste such beauty now?

'I cannot tell you what I know,' Kunti said.

'What is it?'

'I cannot tell you what I have seen in the night. The old master has asked me not to reveal it. He is not human, you see.'

'Then what is he?'

'I cannot tell you. He has asked me not to.'

'You are a mad girl,' Jamuna laughed. 'Go, Malakar Da is calling you.'

'If he asks me to make tea, I will put salt instead of sugar.' Kunti got up and stretched. 'The old master gives me a lot of bodily pain at night, Jamuna Mashi,' Kunti said, like a grown-up woman. 'I will have to learn witchcraft, so that I can follow my master to the depths of the water.'

'Okay, now go.'

Kunti stretched once more before moving towards Malakar. He was mesmerized. His head reeled. He felt hot. It felt so delicious. 'Are you trying to weave a mystery around yourself, girl?'

Kunti didn't answer. She yawned and looked at old Dhanapati. 'Come here, little girl. You are immature. So, you must have done such an impudent thing. I am the right-hand man of the BDO. He is a young man and fully depends on me.'

'Nothing,' Kunti said and stood there unfazed. Her nose pin shone like a dew drop in the sun. Nabadwip Malakar couldn't take his eyes off her. 'Come here, girl,' Nabadwip called again.

'What do you want now?'

'Nothing. Tell me why you gave me such a paan?'

'I don't know.'

Dhanapati tried to scold Kunti. 'It's shameful, Kunti. Why did you have to do such a thing with a guest? We treat guests like Narayan (God), don't we? Go, get him another good one.'

'I am not liking it here, master. I will go away.'

'Where will you go?'

'To Kamrup-Kamakhya.'

'Who has stuffed your brain with such rubbish?'

'I will cross seven mountains, seven rivers and seven forests to go there.'

'It's very far,' the old man said.

'Never mind that,' Kunti muttered.

'I know of a man who went there. Listen to me, Malakar . . . this is from a hundred years ago.'

'Another cooked-up tale.'

'I have seen it myself.'

'How old are you?'

'Five hundred or perhaps a thousand years . . .' Kunti said.

'I just have to look out to the water and the darkness beyond it and, all the old stories from five hundred years ago get up and walk towards me. My pirate ancestors lay there in the water.'

Whenever Nabadwip came in the past, he only spoke about money and Dhanapati paid him his share. Nabadwip had given his word that he would get the additional district magistrate to give the island on lease hold to Dhanapati. The block land and land

reforms officer (BLLRO) didn't want that, but the additional district
magistrate (ADM) could be coaxed into it. Malakar had promised
to talk to the BLLRO too. He was given money every time he made
such promises. Such name dropping had got him a lot of awe from
the people of the island. They thought Malakar was close to such
powerful people. These people seemed distant, like the stars in the
sky and Malakar was their go-between. Old Dhanapati had seen
those men and even pleaded with them, but nothing had happened.
He left it at that. Every time Malakar came, he ignited that old desire.
The island belonged to no one; it remained submerged for a large
part of the year. Dhanapati wanted to enter into some kind of an
agreement with the government, else he would lose control, if the
government willed it.

'We are the government, Dhanapati . . . no one keeps track of
this island since it doesn't offer a permanent settlement.'

'It is a wasteland, Dhanapati.'

None of that familiar talk was happening this time. This time,
Malakar was on another mission, though. After seeing Kunti, he
wanted to return all the money he collected from the island, in return
for Kunti. He had never felt this way. These days, he was careful.
There were so many diseases that could be contracted.

'I won't listen to you, master. I am determined to go.'

'By the time you come back, you will be an old hag.'

'Why, can only the old turn into witches?'

Dhanapati gaped at her with wide eyes. Who had given her this
idea? The whole day, she stayed near him and breathed all over him.
Through the night, she gave him company in sleep, mumbling all the
time. But she had never spoken about Kamrup-Kamakhya!

'I know of someone who went in her youth and came back in
her youth too.'

'There you go! Why were you scaring me?'

'Don't forget that she died and was born twice in between! It's
like going to Lisboan across the seas. The boat keeps moving on and
on and on . . .'

Kunti's face was a play of light and darkness. 'Are you telling me the truth, master?'

'Why should I lie?'

'Dhanapati, you are such a storyteller. I don't know about the olden times, but now, you just have to take a bus to Howrah from Ghoradal and take a train to Kamakhya.'

'No, that is not it.'

'Why do you say so?'

'That is not the real Kamrup-Kamakhya.'

'Then where is it?'

'Only Ma Kamakhya can tell you that. Pedru, my pirate ancestor—there were seven of them actually—set sail for Kamakhya from their own land. Understood?'

'Yes, I did,' Malakar said.

'After crossing the Atlantic and many other seas, they came here to this bay. This island—the one you call a wasteland—wasn't there at that time.'

'So what was?' Kunti was surprised.

'The water and the waves played with each other as the dolphins played with the ship.'

'I can do that. Staying underneath water for a long time and swimming far, far away,' Kunti said excitedly.

Nabadwip stared at the two in wonder. The heat that Kunti had aroused in him had cooled a bit. That paan made him angry and then, excited. It was like setting a haystack alight.

'Have you travelled in such a ship, Dhanapati?'

'How am I telling you all this, then?'

'How, when and where did you go on a ship? You people are dependent on your fishing boats!'

'When I crossed the Atlantic, I was floating for days. Kunti, Dhanapati Pedru liked what he saw for the first few days. There were moonlit nights and then, the moon disappeared. There was a dark mass but the light of the stars lit up everything. The water was pale yellow.'

'Have you come from across the seas?' Kunti asked.

'Where else did you think I came from?'

'Not from your mother's womb?'

'My mother gave birth to me on that distant land beyond the seas. It had severe winters and summers. The ground was stony; no crops grew there. There was a forest all around.'

'You have seen all this?'

'What else?'

'You talk about Bankura and Purulia all the time,' Malakar said.

'Is Purulia by the sea?' Dhanapati asked.

'Not at all!'

'Then why do you mention that place?'

'Tell me what happened thereafter?'

'My master is one thousand years old. You men of Ghoradal won't understand all this. My master is Pedru pirate from across the seas. There are many more things I know but I am sworn to secrecy,' Kunti said.

Nabadwip thought that staying so close to Dhanapati day and night and having his breath all over her had affected Kunti's mental stability. Could any young girl stay happy with that old man unless she was mad? 'Who has sworn you to secrecy?' he asked aloud.

'Pedru,' Kunti said.

'Which Pedru?'

'One of the seven pirates. He is right in front of you. If you saw what I saw in the dead of the night, you would have fainted by now, Malakar Babu. I have mastery in witchcraft.'

Five

How little we know of the world so vast,
Pirates raid the seas lightning fast.

This girl knew witchcraft? Malakar had never heard something as strange as that. How could a witch declare herself to the world in broad daylight? Witches were known to hide their identity. You needed quacks and witch hunters to identify them.

'Do you want another paan?' Kunti asked.

Malakar shook his head. 'No.'

'Then why did you call me?'

'I want to chat with you.'

'It won't augur well for you. My eyes might harm you, Malakar master.'

Malakar looked at her in surprise. Kunti looked away. 'Don't look at a woman like that. Don't I know what that means?'

She's indeed a woman, Malakar thought. She was much more woman-like than he had initially thought. That big bun on her head, one could also make out her waist from behind. How could such a beauty be a witch? Only the middle-aged women and old hags became witches, he thought. At such a young age and with such a body, how could she be an old witch? 'You are wrong, girl.'

Kunti shook her head and went ahead. Then she beckoned at him. 'Come here, Malakar Babu.'

He lit a cigarette in excitement. 'Is she a witch, Dhanapati?'

Dhanapati did not hear him well at first. He had dozed off. Sleep got the better of him these days. He felt like going underneath the water and staying there with the island on his back. He, however, realized that it was more exciting to stay up. Looking up at the sky, looking out into the sea and the birds on water; looking at the women around him, all of this was far more exciting. So, he would wake up with a start every now and then. His wife of this year—Kunti—tried everything to keep him awake. Her soft tread and the smell of her body kept him alert. When Malakar asked the same question twice, Dhanapati was shaken up.

'Women are like the Atlantic Ocean. Have you seen the Atlantic Ocean, Malakar?'

Malakar looked irritated. He was a shrewd man and, in all these years, he had cheated people enough to become rich. He thought he could read people well.

'You keep your Atlantic to yourself, old man. Don't talk rubbish.'

'Since you don't follow what I am saying, you are calling it rubbish.'

'Do you know that the Atlantic is one of the seven seas?'

'I know. Even Kunti knows this.'

'It's called so because it's difficult to gauge its depth. Do you know that?'

'Why do you think I won't know?'

'Do you know how big it is?'

'Of course, I do. I crossed it to reach the island.'

'Are you acting mad or something? Only your Kunti can believe your tale. Listen, Dhanapati, the government are bothered about what is happening on the island. So, I have been sent for the inquiry. But I am not able to make any progress.'

'Do you need more money this time?' Dhanapati asked.

'You guessed it right. But tell me if you have kept witches on your island?'

'You ask her.'

'Do you get any hint of that when you sleep with her?'

Dhanapati called out to Kunti. 'Bibi, come here!'

'Tell me, master.'

'Get me my cigarette.'

'Take this.' Malakar held out his big pack for the old man.

'No. I smoke my scissor cigarette . . . *kanchi.*'

'That fake scissor brand from the island?'

'Why are you calling it fake? Everything here is real. There's nothing fake on this island.'

'You will not get any cigarettes now . . .' Kunti ordered from a distance. 'I will give you one after you have had your rice in the afternoon.'

'Malakar is making me yearn for tobacco,' Dhanapati said in a hoarse voice.

'Let me move away,' Malakar said.

'No, no, sit. This girl is sharp like freshly cut onions and chilli grown on saline soil.'

Malakar turned his head to look at Kunti once again. Her bun had uncoiled and her long, thick mane looked like the deep sea itself. He felt aroused again. He yearned to have the girl and break her pride. He had tackled so many women in the past, but none of them were like this one.

'Do you know that trader?'

Malakar turned his head back towards Dhanapati. His blood was still on the boil. 'Will you not answer my question?'

'Which one?'

'Is she really a witch?'

'How can I answer that?'

'Where did you find her?'

'She went to Kamrup-Kamakhya and returned after two lifetimes. I found her sitting on the banks of the river at Ghoradal. I hadn't found anyone this year. So I had chosen an old woman to cook rice for me and massage my sore back and feet. I asked her to go away and brought this one instead.'

Nabadwip Malakar felt that he was going mad. Could he believe all this? But it was true that he knew very little of the strange ways of the world. Much remained unknown even at the end of one's life. No one could vouch for the truth behind the mysteries of the world.

'Kamrup is in Assam, Dhanapati.'

'That is not the real Kamrup.'

Nabadwip stayed quiet. He turned his head to look at Kunti. She was standing alone and beckoned at him again. Nabadwip got up. It was broad daylight. What harm could a witch do to him at this hour?! He moved forward.

'Why were you sitting there, Malakar Babu?' Kunti barked.

'Tell me what you want to say.'

'You wanted to chat me up! Why should I have anything to tell you?'

'That cannot happen here.'

'Then where can that happen?'

'A little away from such a crowd!'

'Can anyone hear what we're saying?'

'One needs to be away from the public eye to talk to women . . . to talk to them clearly.'

'Don't you have any fear?'

'Fear?'

'You haven't understood yet?'

'What should I understand?'

'What will happen if my eyes fall on you?'

'What will happen then?'

'Don't you know that I will go back to Kamrup-Kamakhya? I have been a witch for three lifetimes. Look at my eyes.'

Malakar thought that there might be some truth to what she was saying. He couldn't look at her eyes. He tried to think quickly, looking away from her. The island was different from Ghoradal. These women on the island came from nowhere. They were vagabonds without any addresses to trace them back to. They had no village, city or perhaps even a country attached to their names. They had no family, no husbands, children, parents or siblings. They never mentioned their whereabouts here. It was against the tradition of the island. Dhanapati said that as long as they were there, they belonged to the island. The fishermen were their husbands. If women conceived here, they had to abort in Ghoradal. Most women did not conceive during this six-monthly life. The next six months were another world altogether. Malakar was aware of this rule and likened the six-monthly world of the island to the order of days and nights at the poles. Six months made a year here. No one could track the next six months in the life of these people. One couldn't clock the other six months of the island in the sands of time, even if one used the sun dial or measured the shadows of the trees.

Nabadwip realized that Dhanapati had cast a spell on him with his words. He had immobilized him somewhat. He belonged to Ghoradal and lived there for twelve months. He was a permanent clerk of the BDO office. He had been promoted to group C from the lowest rung, group D. In between, he had been suspended. After that, he had been transferred to another block. He had been in Ghoradal for eight years now. He would retire in six years and, till then, he had planned to stay on in the same place. With such a background, how could he get swayed by what Dhanapati had told him? How could he get distracted from his goal of getting that woman? He shook himself up like a predatory cat. He was on the scent of flesh. 'Tell me what happened exactly.'

'What do you mean?' Kunti was startled.

'I am on an inquiry. Don't you know?'

'Are you deaf, Malakar Babu? Why are you asking me to repeat the same old thing?'

'Batashi was inside the room, right?' Malakar smiled.

'Yes, where else would she go?'

'She was inside and those two came in together and pulled the door shut. Am I right?'

'No, no. She was not inside the room at that time.'

'Just now you said that she was there.'

'She was there before that.'

'That means Batashi called them in, isn't it?'

'No, no. Batashi Di came out of the room . . . I think. No, no. She was sitting outside and having puffed rice with burnt fish. That is what it was.'

'I cannot make out clearly. If they went in and Batashi went along with them, that would mean that Batashi called them in.'

'She is there. Call her and find out.'

'She would talk in her own favour.'

'She will tell you what is true.'

'Do you want us to stop women from coming to the island?'

'Why should I want that? All work on the island would stop then.'

'Let the men work.'

'Where will the men go?'

'Go? To the sea!'

'Are you stupid? Will they find women on the sea?'

'Those two are men, so they went to that woman. How will you know what happens to men when they go to women?'

Kunti was getting muddled up. He went on bringing in the same story in different ways to confuse her. He was trying to say that Batashi had laid a trap for the two men and that they were innocent.

'You will harm Batashi Di, Malakar Babu. You are not saying, even once, how that government and trader had sold her. Why did they go to her room?'

'The government will not allow women to come to the island now.'

'Go ahead and do that. We know other ways.'

'You will come through the sea route, straight to the island. We will stop that too. Women are the root of all trouble!'

'No, we will come riding trees and brooms.'

Malakar was shocked. 'How will you come, you said?

'I told you about witchcraft. Some of us can sit at a distance and sip the blood of the trader and the government.'

'What are you saying?' Malakar jumped away from her.

'That is the truth, Malakar Babu. How will the men on the island stay without women? I know it from my old Dhanapati master. Can you stay alone?'

'Nah! Will you stay the night with me?' Malakar muttered as best as he could. 'It would be me instead of Dhanapati. You will not be able to make out whether it's him or me in the dark.'

Kunti laughed aloud. 'What if I take out the insides from your body? Won't that damage you forever? Will another one be sent here for the inquiry then?'

Six

A husband of six months is not legal at all!
If the government takes you, why should you fall?

Kunti and old Dhanapati sat in the courtyard and drew patterns on the sand. They were playing an old game—trapping the tiger. Some of Kunti's thick hair was on her face. She tried to shove the rest of the mass of her hair backwards. Nabadwip Malakar looked at the girl from a distance and decided to leave her alone. She was not a good girl, although she was young, he thought. She suited that old Dhanapati. He called Jamuna.

'I will listen to what you say.'

'I have already told you what I had to say.'

'Do you think that girl is a witch?'

'I don't know.'

'If she is a witch, we need to throw her out of the island.'

'I have not seen anything of the kind. She is too talkative and goes on talking all the time. She doesn't have any parentage or anyone to go back to.'

Nabadwip took out a cigarette and then transferred it back to his pocket. He looked at Jamuna carefully. How she has changed . . . like a river that is dying due to too much silt.

'Don't you have any responsibility towards me?' Nabadwip asked.

'What responsibility?'

'You need to take care of my well-being. Don't you know that?'

'I am a temporary resident here—a fisherman's wife. How will I take up that responsibility?'

'Fisherman's wife, my foot,' Nabadwip cursed. 'Everyone indulges in prostitution here. Why blame the trader? I have been on the side of the women here for years. My office at Ghoradal says that I have been supporting prostitution on the island.'

Jamuna stayed quiet. His words had surprised her. Malakar would come to the island to have fun. The women here were at everyone's mercy. They were free to be enjoyed by anyone who came here and hoped that people like Nabadwip wouldn't give them away. Too much noise about these men from outside taking women here would get their own fishermen to disown them. Women had no value.

If there was no noise about it, the fishermen chose to ignore everything, even if they knew what was going on. If their prestige remained intact, they kept quiet. Batashi and Ganesh were still together because the trader and the government could not sleep with her. She turned around and trapped them. This had added to Ganesh fisherman's status. The people of the island showered praises on Batashi. She could put an end to her sale. No one else could have done that earlier.

'Why are you quiet?' Malakar asked.

'What will I say?'

'If this goes on, on the island, the government will not leave you.'

'Does this mean it will sell us?'

'Why has Dhanapati brought in a witch?'

'Does the old man know this?'

'I have understood the whole game now. Only a witch can trap a policeman and his accomplice. In this case, it was the trader. The police are so powerful and the trader has so much money. There must be some witchcraft involved.'

Nabadwip Malakar was not a simple man. He was a crooked kind. He could twist anything and make it complicated; make a light thing heavy.

'Unless it was black magic, why should the trader and the police enter Batashi's room? She wasn't there, so why should those two enter an empty shanty? I am sure Batashi was not alone, Kunti too was in on the ploy. She was the one who cast the spell.'

Otherwise, why was his body heating up with one look at her? He was so used to women otherwise. Why did this one feel different?

'Tell me what had happened,' Nabadwip said in a low voice.

'You've heard everything!'

'I've heard nothing. Tell me about Kunti's involvement in the whole affair.'

'You have created your own story. Why are you asking me?' Jamuna said.

'Did Kunti use black magic?'

'I don't know. You were asking about Batashi for so long. Why are you dragging Kunti into this now?'

Nabadwip looked at Batashi. She was sitting quietly, alone. The island felt lonely, like it usually is for the six months from Baishakh. Any woman would do for him. Batashi was good enough. The police and the trader were lured by her. The trader was a rich man. He had many income avenues. He was a womanizer and could not control himself. Mangal Midde told him that the island was a market from where women could be picked up. The policeman hadn't lied. If he could lay his hands on a good catch, he would first enjoy her and then sell her for good money. Everything could be bought and sold in the markets in this country. From a pin to the sea, rivers and mountains, everything. But it is the women who are always in demand. Nabadwip Malakar asked Jamuna to call Batashi. 'Let me ask her. The government needs the inquiry report so that action can be taken.'

'Malakar Da, you need to protect us. This island gives you so much,' Jamuna said.

She was right. Malakar just made money from each visit. He was a government employee and, by using his position, he tried to extract money every time he came to the island. He didn't have to share this money with anyone. Mangal Midde had to distribute what he collected. Malakar agreed. 'Yes, the island gives, but don't you get much more from me in return?'

'What do we get from you?' Jamuna asked suddenly.

Malakar controlled his temper. 'It is because of me that you are carrying on with your businesses. Do you think the government allows this? It's illegal to live with someone for six months and call him husband. Who owns you for the other six? These days, AIDS is raging everywhere; it's a killer. It is me who is keeping the BDO sir in check.'

Jamuna just stared at the man. She knew about the disease. If you had it in your fate, you couldn't escape it. But how was Malakar involved in that? Was he protecting them from the disease? How was Malakar useful to them? Dhanapati coughed up money every time to keep him in check. The islanders paid their share to the old man.

Malakar could gauge Jamuna's mind. He laughed. 'I am sure you didn't understand. Does this island belong to Dhanapati's father?'

'Yes, that's true!'

'That's a joke. If you said that at Ghoradal, even the animals will laugh at you. The land belongs to the government.'

'It's true. Dhanapati's father was Dhanapati and his father too was Dhanapati . . . don't you know all this?'

'Trash that story. Did Dhanapati buy this island?'

'No, they captured the island.'

'Don't talk rubbish. For six months, people catch fish and dry them on the island. It is I who keeps the government in check. Otherwise, you people would have vanished from the face of the island.'

'Tell Dhanapati.'

'He knows everything. But this time, they have attacked the police. It's not an easy thing to do. The government is so unhappy. They will not take it lightly.'

Jamuna couldn't remain silent now. She retorted. 'Why are you going on and on with the same thing? Let them take Batashi away and sell her off. Come away, Batashi.'

Malakar, smiled. He caught hold of Jamuna's hand. 'Do you think that by going away, you will get rid of the problem? Call Batashi.

Let her tell me if there was black magic involved in the whole episode. Otherwise, how can a woman overpower two strong men?'

Jamuna called her. Batashi came closer. Jamuna stood slightly apart from the two and then, as an afterthought, went away to stand with Kunti. 'Let's push that tall Malakar into the water, Jamuna Mashi. Bastard.'

'Shut up. He is the government's man.'

'There is no government here.'

'The government is everywhere. Without it, the world cannot run.'

'Forget that. Do I need to go to Kamakhya to become a witch?'

'My girl, don't talk about all that. Witches go through a lot of pain.'

Batashi finished describing everything to Malakar. 'I have told you everything now.' Malakar made a sound with his tongue, as if sympathizing with Batashi. 'You missed an opportunity of a lifetime. What do you get by living with the fisherman in his hut for six months?'

'I get a family, babu.'

'Does this kind of a temporary family matter?'

'For six months, I am happy, babu.'

'The trader would have given you happiness for twelve months. With your body, you could have gone far, earned a lot. Why did you miss such a chance?'

Batashi stayed quiet. Malakar lit a cigarette. He kept moving his eyes all over Batashi, shamelessly. He took a long drag at the cigarette. You were lucky that the trader chose you. They are experienced people and have seen women of all kinds, all their lives. Is there any dearth of women for them?'

Batashi dug the earth with her toenail. Her eyes were downcast. Malakar softened his voice. 'Did Kunti help you?'

'What?' Batashi looked up.

'I think she did. How else would you shove the two into your house?'

'They came on their own.'

'On their own? Is that possible?'

'That's what had happened.'

'Were you inside?'

'I repeatedly said no.'

'Then why did they enter?'

'Had I failed to trap them in the shanty, the trader would have taken me away.'

'Where was Kunti then?'

Malakar paced up and down. 'Is Kunti a witch trained at Kamakhya?'

'I don't know.'

'She said so.'

'She is like that. A talkative, mad girl. There is no sense in what she says.'

'So, what should I write in my report?'

Batashi stayed quiet. Malakar went very close to her. She could feel his hot breath all over herself. 'Do you wish to stay on here or go away?'

'Where will I go?'

'With the trader. That will solve everything.'

'Have you come only for this?'

'Not really. I have come for the inquiry. I have to know how those two entered the hut. I also need to know if there's any witchcraft behind this.'

'You are the government man, isn't it?'

'What else?'

'You will only speak on behalf of the government then, isn't it?'

'That's right.'

'Then stop questioning me and write what you want to. I am prepared for the consequences.'

Malakar shook his head. 'That cannot be. I have to get to the bottom of this and know the truth. Such a thing should not be repeated in the future.'

'I will not tell you anything more,' Batashi said.

'Then be prepared for the worst.'

'I don't mind that. I have nothing else to say.'

'I will not have that for an answer.'

Batashi swelled with anger. 'I don't want to answer.'

'I will not hear that. You will have to tell me.'

'What if I don't?' Batashi turned around to face Malakar, squaring him up.

'Then you are doomed.'

'Are you trying to scare me?'

'No. Why should I?' Malakar observed her. He could see her nerves throbbing. Her breath was fast and her bosom heaved. Malakar was aroused. This woman was not bad at all! Kunti had clouded his vision and he hadn't noticed her carefully before.

'I am there with you,' he said out aloud.

'I will go now.'

'Where is your master now?'

'In the waters.'

'When will he return?'

'Tomorrow, at the crack of dawn.'

'Then it should not be a problem.'

'I don't understand.'

Malakar lit another cigarette. His hands trembled in excitement. 'I will make you happy and I will protect you too,' he said in a low voice. 'With Malakar around, no one will touch you again.'

'Okay. I am leaving now.'

'See, let's make this very clear. You take care of me and I take care of you in return. Instead of you, I will hand over Kunti to the trader. Will that make you happy?'

'Are you sure?' Batashi was surprised.

'Why should I lie?'

'Will the trader agree to take her instead of me?'

'Yes, he will.'

'Let my master come back.'

'No, not when he is around.' Malakar grabbed Batashi's hand. 'When I come to the island, you are my wife.'

Batashi extracted her hand from Malakar's, forcefully. 'I am someone else's bibi. He hasn't left me!'

Malakar laughed a short dirty laugh, spewing a cloud of smoke on Batashi's face and cursed.

'Keep your wifedom aside. Wash it off and come to me at night. Yours is not a marriage where vows were taken. In an arrangement like yours, even God doesn't mind who you sleep with at night.'

Seven

Why wait for the government when I am here?
You get dearer in government care.

Malakar had spoken clearly enough. He had asked Batashi to become his wife on the island.

'Is this man good?' Batashi asked Jamuna in a low voice.

'You cannot judge people of Ghoradal easily. Malakar is good. He is the government man.'

Batashi and Jamuna walked back. Malakar stayed back at Dhanapati's house. He said he wanted to take rest. He had finished his initial inquiry. He said he would stay back for the day to rack his brains and come up with some more questions.

Batashi looked thoughtful. She walked fast. From the east of the island, the two walked to the north. The air was filled with the smell of fish and it felt heavy. Batashi prayed for her body to start smelling of fish once again. Jamuna saw that Batashi was restless. She was panting for breath and found it difficult to cope with Batashi's pace.

'What did Malakar say?'

'What did he tell you, Jamuna Di?'

'Let that be.'

'Once the government is gone, can some other government come in?'

'Yes, that's the norm!'

'We sent the government packing on a boat and some other government has come to take their place. The government has changed but their ways remain the same!'

'That is not possible. Listen, I have told Malakar already. He is a powerful man.'

Batashi caught hold of Jamuna's hand. 'He wants to sleep with me, Jamuna Di. What will I do? My entry to the island is at stake.'

'Why? Who will stop you?'

'If my master gets to know, he will not keep me.'

'How will he know?'

'When they come back from the water, the smell of their women tells them everything.'

'Rubbish! That doesn't happen.'

'No, Didi, they do.'

'If it stays hidden, will you relent?'

Batashi started digging into the grass and the sandy ground underneath with her toe.

'How many months are left? We have to return to Ghoradal and then, from there go by bus or train . . .'

Batashi was reminded of the end of Ashwin . . . not the last one, but the one prior to that.

> I am headed to the island, anyone for me?
> The men of Ghoradal, I am free.
> Doesn't your master look for other women?
> No, I would have known then.
> You will have to survive, won't you?
> My master will save me.

'For that, you will have to go to the waters. It is not possible on land. We are women. Our lives are like this.' Jamuna put an arm around Batashi's shoulders.

'What if I say no?'

'Malakar has asked me to convince you and get you to understand.'

'My master is at sea. When he is away, I cannot sleep, Didi,' Batashi's eyes welled up.

'Same with me.'

'If I sleep with an outsider, it might affect the well-being of my master.' Batashi wiped her tears.

'You will have to survive, Batashi, and that is of utmost importance now.'

'My family will break up.'

'No one will know.'

'You know.'

'Not a soul more.'

'That Malakar will know.'

'He has chosen you.'

'That's not my fault.'

'Your body has attracted him.'

'I cannot help that.'

'Just give him two hours. It won't harm you and it will keep him happy too.' Jamuna tried to counsel Batashi.

'Yours is the family of a poor man. A lot depends on the contribution of the woman of the household too. A fisherman's family is a small family.'

Jamuna was older than Batashi and more experienced too. 'To help the family, women have to come out of their homes and into the streets. This is not new! If children are hungry and cry for food, can a mother still afford to stay at home? She has to come out and find a way to get rice. Doesn't she?'

Batashi was listening to Jamuna intently. 'But I don't have children, Jamuna Di.'

'You have a husband! If he falls sick and lies in bed, the wife has to go out to get money. She can do anything to save him. There's no harm in that.'

Batashi shook her head slowly. She was not living in want. Her husband of six months was a strong man. He went to the bay and came back on time. By what logic then, should she sleep with Malakar? And if she agreed to sleep with Malakar, why did she decline Dasharath trader?

'The trader had bought you; he wouldn't have allowed you to stay on the island, Batashi.'

'I could have gone.'

'He would have bought another one again. This island would have become a market for buying and selling women.'

'I really don't care about that.'

'Do as you please. But remember that if you please Malakar, no one will touch you.'

'Mangal Midde . . . Dasharath trader . . . when you return to Ghoradal, do you think they will let you go?'

Batashi remained quiet. She walked slowly towards her shanty. Jamuna followed her. Batashi was reminded of that dawn at Ghoradal. No one had taken her. Her skeleton of a body had not attracted anyone. She was sick with hunger and malnutrition. For three days, she saw the man coming to the riverbank. He was searching for someone. He had forgotten all about her from Baishakh to Ashwin. But when monsoon was over and the nights started getting chilly and starry, when two stars among the seven brothers were lost in the northern sky, he heard the call from the island. The rains of Shravan and the high tides of Bhadra had sunk the island. But then, the waters receded. The kans grass flew about like white feathers. That picture had stirred him up. It reminded him of the woman with whom he had lived for those six months on the island. How was she? He hadn't seen her for so many days! It was time to once again to set up home on the island. He had to share this home with her for six months once more.

'Master, which is your real home?' Batashi asked Ganesh while going to the island with him.

'What do you mean?'

'Do you belong to the island or to Ghoradal?'

'I don't know that myself.'

'What do you feel?'

'When I come to the island, I feel that I belong to it while at Ghoradal, it feels like I belong there. It feels like I have returned home from another land when I reach the island.'

Batashi stretched her arm over Ganesh's back. 'I feel the same too. I was elsewhere and now I am returning home to the island,' she said.

'You don't have a village of your own. So, it is easier for you, perhaps . . .'

'There was one, but now I don't remember anything about it.'

'Perhaps because you don't want to remember it.'

Batashi had become quiet after listening to that. Just like she had quietened down after hearing Jamuna just now.

'Why are you quiet?' Jamuna asked.

'What should I say?'

'Shall I inform Malakar?'

'No.'

'Women should not say no.'

'What has happened to you, Jamuna Di?'

'Why?'

'You helped me escape the trader and now, you are pushing me to Malakar!'

'What do you do from Baishakh to Ashwin? How do you get your food then?'

'I had my umbrella seller from across the border.'

'Bangladeshi! Why didn't he take you with him?'

'So what? Does that stop him from being my husband?'

'Leave it. Make Malakar happy and save yourself.'

Why are you taking the government side?

He is different from the other governments. I know him. He is kind.'

'If he is, the ask him to leave me alone.'

'The government has to complete the job at hand. He has come for the inquiry. That has to be completed. Otherwise how will he pinpoint whose fault it was?'

'Is this also part of the inquiry?'

'Malakar will write the report in your favour. If the government is happy, he will speak on your behalf. Just take care of him.'

Batashi tried to comprehend. She realized that this government was good as long as one listened to him. If she disobeyed him, he would take revenge. So how was this government different from Midde and the trader?

'Did he sleep with you too, Jamuna Di?'

Jamuna was sad. She looked up at the sky, her eyes reflecting the emptiness above. 'Women of the island have to give in to them. This is part of one's family life. Our fishermen know everything, but they ignore it.'

'Your husband knew?'

'He didn't tell me.'

'Wasn't he sad?'

'He was. But you have to do as the government pleases. Else we will be stopped from coming to the island. What will happen then, Batashi?'

Batashi did not speak. She stood in one place and muttered, 'If I have to sleep with another man, then how does it matter if it is one government or the other? It's the same thing!'

'But you will be saved from the trader at least . . .'

'How does that help?'

'Malakar and the trader are two different things altogether. Malakar is doing an inquiry and that is definitely not an easy thing to do.'

'At least the trader was young. This one is old, Jamuna Di. Perhaps he has slept with you, your mother, my mother and now, he wants to sleep with me. He wants to sleep with that little Kunti, who is probably his daughter's age. How big is his appetite?'

'There are men who never have enough.'

'He has lost his youth.'

'Till they reach their pyre, their hunger is insatiable.'

'I can't do it, Jamuna Di. I might hide it from my master but I cannot bring myself to do this.'

Jamuna touched Batashi's shoulders and pressed on her upper arm, as if to reassure her. 'Let the inquiry be over. Let him go and say that Batashi was not at fault, but the trader was. Don't delay this.'

Batashi shook her head. 'My master is in the deep sea. If I sleep with Malakar, it will bring a curse on him. When the fisherman was at sea, if his woman slept with another man, he would not be able to net fish. That's just one problem. If he falls asleep when his woman is sleeping with another man, because of the curse that will befall him, the boat will be led astray. What will happen then, Jamuna Di?'

'That's just a belief.'

'No, it's true.'

'I have never heard or seen anything like that.'

'Dhanapati, the old master, said this.'

'That old man! He just says anything that comes to his mind.'

'My master says the same thing.'

'This is a matter of government inquiry. You won't sin.'

'Let me think again.'

'You will be doomed if you don't listen to the government, Batashi. Jamuna was plain irritated now. 'You will then have to lie with countless men. If the inquiry goes against you, neither will you be able to come to the island nor will you be able to think about the welfare of your master.'

Eight

Her frail frame and tired face, her beauty they hide,
The island will bring it back, along with the tide.

The bay was yet to fill up. But it would. Enough blood and flesh would also cover her skeletal body. Keeping that in mind, Ganesh, the man from Ghoradal, held her hand. Batashi was not the woman with whom he had set up home last year or the two years before that. He had waited for that woman at the bank of the river for long. Then, finally, he chose Batashi.

> The man from Ghoradal looks for his lady gem,
> He gently takes the hand of one of them.

Batashi told Ganesh that she had heard of the island from Nibharani. She had met Nibha at Baruipur station first and then again at Ebadat Miyan's guava garden.

Nibharani! Was that her shadow in the dark water of Kalnagini? The fisherman who was rowing the boat looked back at her. Which Nibha? When did she come to the island? Who did she live with? 'She was as dark as the endless night,' muttered Ganesh.

> How dark was she, can you tell?
> Dark as the night, you knew her well.

'Okay, let me try, though there's not much to say. She spoke about the island that gave a husband to those who didn't have a mate, a family to those who never had a home. The island gave everything to those who had nothing.'

'But why didn't she come?' Ganesh asked.

'Baruipur station was full of fruits then—mangoes, litchis and guavas. So many months have passed thereafter, from Ashar to Ashwin. She probably stayed back at Baruipur station. But master, why are you asking about her? Aren't you happy with me?'

Ganesh tried to avoid the answer. 'She was like the water of the Kalnagini.'

'That's full of poison like this bay.'

'Yes, she stung. But I knew how to handle her fangs. She was so supple and attractive, so full of youth and vigour. She was so beautiful.'

'Was she your wife?'

'I think so.'

'You haven't forgotten her. Throw me into the waters, let the crocodiles feed on me.'

That was so long ago. Two years, three years or perhaps even more since they spoke like that while returning to the island. Today, the island seemed like her own land, where she was born, raised, entered puberty and got the first taste of a man in her life. She imagined that she was a permanent resident of the island as she was someone's wife. She had to leave every Baishakh because of poverty. There was no other choice. The waves grew higher and the water became restless. The turbulent sea woke Dhanapati tortoise up. The men of the island left for Ghoradal. The southern winds pushed her towards Ghoradal. She had to return alone. She was compelled to. The tortoise chief would carry the island and move away. The old Dhanapati said that he had once taken such a ride on the back of the tortoise and reached his country. He was young then. The island floated away and then floated back in Ashwin.

> Ashwin is over, Kartik follows soon,
> Dhanapati's Island floats moon after moon.

It had to come back. A certain draught woke Dhanapati up, another one at Ashwin lulled the tortoise to sleep. Ganesh fisherman knew this story. Batashi listened to him intently while on the boat. Ganesh told her the story slowly. Batashi realized that the old master and the tortoise were both Dhanapati. Old Dhanapati was the tortoise himself, while the tortoise was actually a human.

In the midst of the story, Ganesh went back to Nibharani.

'No one had seen anyone darker than her. She was like a dark flame. At other times, she was like the dark cloud. As dark as the new moon night. Like the dark sea water at night. What does the sea look like? The darkness of the sea is broken by the light of the stars, a pale shimmer on the water. You just had to wipe it off. You could even scoop it out. Her touch made me so happy.'

'Do you like dark women, master?'

'I am a fisherman who is out in the dark sea. After the sun sets, there is a cloak of darkness all around. That is the only colour I can relate to. The darkness is broken by the fireflies. And then, that too goes out. Then there is nothing to break the dark. I love that colour.'

'Like the big, dark sea?'

'You had heard of the island from her. So, you should know how dark she is.'

'You tell me, I would like to hear from you.'

'I had spent so many days and nights with her. I had seen so many shades of dark.'

'She still rules your heart. Throw me in the water and go to the island.'

Ganesh laughed.

'If you didn't like me, why did you bring me here, master?'

'Help me row the boat, come here.'

'Please give me an answer.'

'I am not attracted by the island so much. It is that dark girl and her youth that has cast a spell on me. The day Ma Durga left us, the island seemed to be calling out to me.'

'Did you like me, master?'

'Nibharani clouds my mind now. Why did you remind me of her?'

'She sent me here.'

'Why didn't she come?'

'Ebadat Miyan of Baruipur is a huge, tall man. She went to work in his garden and that saved her. Miyan liked her and kept her back.

He has given her silver ornaments, silk sarees, bras and blouses, a case
for her betel leaves and what not!'

'I would have given all that to her.'

'There's more. He has given her salwar kameez, snow powder,
scent that gives off such fragrance, colour for her lips and cheeks,
kohl for her eyes, net for her bun . . .'

'What else has he given her?'

'Soap, scented oil, and then . . . I cannot tell a man this . . .
packets of what she needs monthly.'

'I would have given her everything,' Ganesh sighed.

'What would you have given her, master? What is available on
the island?'

'You get everything on the island, or I would have bought them
from Ghoradal.'

'You can give them to me.' Batashi laughed.

'Yes, I will. Then she will be jealous of you.'

'How will she know?'

'Women get to know everything.' Ganesh looked up at the sky a
little unmindfully. Nagini had flown into another river, they were one
now. There was an island at a distance. You could see the forest and
some huts. Soon, the island disappeared. Batashi observed Ganesh.
He had removed his wrapper because the rowing made him hot.
He glistened with sweat. The north breeze blew in, bringing the chill
with it. But that didn't cool him. 'You forget her, master.'

'What if she doesn't let me?'

'Just think of me.'

'Will you think of me when I go into the sea?'

'Yes, I will.'

'It's so lonely in the sea with no one to talk to. What if she talks
to me then?'

'Think only of me, master.'

'It's dangerous to think of women when you are at sea. You
would want to return then. Even if there are no fish in your net, you
will still come back. The sea is so big, the horizon is ever elusive and
you could even lose direction, if women cloud your mind. But that

dark Nibharani . . . so what if she hasn't come, she pulls me back
from the water.'

'I will, too.'

'You won't be able to.'

'Just wait and watch.'

'Your youth is not like hers.'

'How was she?'

'Like a slithering snake.'

'She is fat and round now.'

'Who told you?'

'Didn't I meet her?'

'No, she is in the prime of her youth now. Just like the big sea.
You cannot make out when the Kalnagini enters the big sea and
becomes one with it.'

'She is round, fat and dark. God knows why Ebadat Miyan
chose her.'

They went on and on with it, even after reaching the island. They
bought jute sticks, bamboo sheets and split bamboo poles for their new
home, but they continued to talk about the dark Nibharani. In the
afternoon, as they sat eating flattened rice and jaggery, they continued
to talk about her. Just before dark, when they finished building the
hut and had dug up the earth to make the earthen stove and filled it
with firewood, they kept talking about her. He left Batashi at home
and went to meet Dhanapati master. The old man came back with
Ganesh. Even he hadn't forgotten the dark woman. Then, the moon
came up from the sea. It was four days after full moon. It had flattened
a bit but hadn't taken the shape of a boat yet. Dhanapati saw Batashi
in the moonlight and then the two went back, chatting about the dark
woman again. After finishing his rice and dal with a big bite of onion,
the satisfied Ganesh said, 'She was a sorceress. Do you understand?'

'Leave me then, master.'

'She's a sorceress who is casting a spell on me from that garden.
But you stay with me, since you have come with me this time.
It's another matter that she won't leave me.'

'I'll make you forget her.'

'Will you?'

'I'll die if I can't, my master. Let the crocodiles feed on me.' Batashi started taking off her clothes. 'That woman has cast a spell on Miyan, who had an eye for me.'

'He has managed to keep her back in his garden, but you have come here.'

'Miyan will understand who he has landed up with.' Batashi touched the knot at her waist. She called out to Ganesh in a low tone. 'You will know me when you see me, master.'

She slowly took off her clothes in front of Ganesh. The island was quiet, save for the sound of the flowing water. Batashi realized that the tide was rising. Ganesh looked at Batashi with surprise and then jumped on her, almost like a butterfly rushing for the flame.

'Yes, you will do it.'

'I will, master?'

'Yes, my wife of the island.'

'What if she comes?'

'You are far more beautiful.'

'Is that so, master?'

'Yes.' He seized her waist and entered her. 'Where were you all these years, Batashi?'

'I was near you. You hadn't seen me.'

'Why weren't you there?'

'I was at sea.'

'Yes, you are right. You were my starlit water.' He saw that pale shimmer on Batashi's body. Her face, breasts, stomach and navel, thighs, lay bare under the moonlit sky. 'You have hidden the dark woman with your light, Batashi. I cannot see her anymore. You are my starlight.'

'Master, please don't fall asleep, else the government will catch me,' Batashi said in her mind. She got up and started pacing under the sun. She spat on the ground.

You are showing off that cursed inquiry!' She seethed in anger. 'Go to that dark Nibharani, she will cut your member off. To hell with Malakar and that government. Let them die the worst kind of death. I don't want that inquiry.'

The sun was about to set. Not knowing what to do, Batashi entered her hut and lay on her mat. If Ganesh master got to know, both would be doomed.

She had fallen asleep and woke up when Jamuna came to call her. The sun had set and it was about to become dark. 'Come with me, Dhanapati master is calling you.'

'Why?'

'Only he knows that.'

'I don't want that inquiry, Jamuna Di.'

'Don't think so much.'

'I won't go there. My master is at sea.'

'We are just their mistresses for six months.'

'No! Who told you that?'

'Malakar did.'

'He's a bastard. May he be cursed with death,' Batashi cursed.

'Quiet! He's the government's man!'

'To hell with your government.' Batashi spat on the ground.

'Listen Batashi, Malakar is old. He will not be able to manage. Old Dhanapati has said the same.'

'Let that old, cursed man die too.'

'What are you saying, Batashi! He keeps the island afloat on his back.'

'I don't know anything. I am yearning for my master. Oh my God! If he falls asleep on his boat in the water, I will be finished. I won't go, Jamuna Di.'

Nine

Look at the mermaid, what a beautiful sight,
Entering the water, setting the world alight.

The sun was about to set. A shadow cloaked the island. The sandy earth cooled fast. Nabadwip Malakar was telling Dhanapati how powerful he was. There was nothing to worry as long as he was there. He would settle things in such a way that even if the government went up to the high courts and the Supreme Court, it would not be able to do anything. Malakar said he knew all the tricks of the law and even after retirement, he would continue to do this work. He would earn his livelihood by giving legal advice to people. Nabadwip said that as long as he was in service, he would speak the language of the government. But after retirement, he would go against it. These days, things were easy with the computer and Xerox machine. He would keep all the documents of the government so that he could start helping Dhanapati.

'Are you against us now?' Dhanapati asked.

'Not exactly against the island, but I am the government man after all. I have come for the inquiry and a lot will depend upon my report, isn't it?'

'Please ensure that it is good.'

'What is my interest in this? The island should ensure that my interest is protected too, isn't it?'

'We have taken good care of you Malakar, since the time you started coming to the island. Do you think I sleep underneath the water?'

'No, no . . . you are very much on the surface and awake too,'
Malakar laughed.

'I can see everything.' Dhanapati looked out into the dark water.
'I get to know everything.' His voice sounded as dense as the darkness
outside. 'Whether I am inside the water or above, whether I am
asleep or awake, nothing escapes me. I get to know what happens on
every inch of the island or in the water, even when a fisherman loses
direction. My ancestors were pirates. Seven or fourteen generations
ago, they crossed the dark waters to land here. Their spirits still rule
the seas and the island.'

Malakar felt eerie. Kunti came and stood behind Dhanapati.
She kissed Dhanapati's cheek, not caring about Malakar's presence.
'My master, please get up. It's getting chilly, you should not stay
under the open sky like this.'

Nabadwip Malakar looked down. The excitement he felt at
the sight of Kunti in the morning had ebbed now. His attention
had shifted from Kunti and was glued to Batashi now. Malakar
was suspicious of Kunti. It was possible, perhaps. Who knew if she
had magical powers? He was scared of Kunti now. If she was really
trained at Kamrup-Kamakhya, she had to be avoided. You couldn't
be successful with everyone. These kinds needed to be respected from
a distance. A few years ago, a BDO madam had come to Ghoradal.
She was beautiful and attractive, as hot as fire. Malakar didn't have
the courage to look up at her. He would look down at her toes while
talking. He would recite the Devi mantras in his mind when in front
of her. She was a powerful woman; one had to lie low.

The two sat under the shade on a mat. It was chilly here too.
'How old are you, Dhanapati Sardar?'

'I have lost count. When I shut my eyes, I can see Lisboan
across the sea.'

'The land of the seven foreigners? No one believes that story, actually.'

'I don't care. I can see how the dark water of the sea swells.'

'I had asked the BDO sahib about the dark sea. He said there
was no such thing.'

'Everyone doesn't know everything, isn't it?'

'I agree, but BDO sahib reads a lot of books.'

'You think everything is there in the books?'

'That's what people say.'

Dhanapati changed the topic. 'Are you still capable, Malakar?'

'What?!'

'I mean, are you still able to handle women?'

'At your age, if you can, why can't I?'

'Don't forget that I am a descendant of the pirates of a foreign land. They are able to hold their virility even after they are a hundred years old. They can even sire babies at that age. I have that strength.'

Nabadwip kept quiet. The change of topic had unnerved him. He looked out in the dark. Jamuna had gone to fetch Batashi. There was foreign liquor in his bag. Malakar knew that he was not as strong as he was earlier. But he had become more lustful. Young women attracted him more these days. He felt sad. If you lose your strength, what do you live for?

'Get some tiger ribs and have them with powdered milk and honey. You will get back your strength, Malakar.'

Malakar was startled. He stared at Dhanapati's face. Wasn't it looking unusually dark? Dhanapati stared back, not batting an eyelid. He looked lifeless yet alive. It seemed that he was asleep with his eyes wide open. He seemed to be afloat in the dark water. 'Who will give me tiger ribs?'

'You have to look for them properly. I am sure you'll get them.'

'Who told you about this cure?'

'This is an ageless cure that has come down to me from my pirate ancestors. When they were crossing the big sea, they came across an island floating on the China Sea.'

'That is so far away.'

'Yes, that island was floating away.'

'You are mad! Keep your stories to yourself, Dhanapati.' Malakar had lit a cigarette and puffed in the air. 'Tell me about tiger ribs.'

'You get that in the China waters. The Chinese people are able to hold their youth for a hundred years. In my country, they used the juice of a leaf. If you are not able to pleasure women, they turn into wild tigresses and bay for your blood.'

Malakar was not prepared to give women any pride of place. 'Oh! What rubbish. I have seen many like that. You need to know how to control them.'

'You are lucky that you have been able to take your eyes off Kunti. You need to know all about her. You will come to the island often and look for women. Just ensure that you don't catch Kunti's eye.'

'Is it true that she is a witch?'

'I am not sure.'

'This is not good. The government doesn't support such things.'

'What does she understand of the government?!'

'My BDO sahib tells me that many of the tales of the island are false.'

'May be, maybe not.'

'I don't believe in all this.'

'That's your call but keep your eyes off the girl.'

'No, you have tamed her. Why should I have eyes for her?'

'You did it in the morning.'

'I have come for the inquiry. Don't I deserve something in return? You are an old man. What are you able to give her? I thought about this and so my eyes fell on her. Nothing more than that. I think that Batashi would be better. She has some spirit in her, otherwise she would not have been able to trap those two.'

Dhanapati was muttering something. After Malakar stopped, he spoke up. 'Do you know what a mermaid is, Malakar?'

'A fish-woman? Mermaid?'

'Kunti may be that!'

'What rubbish!' Malakar gave a long drag at his cigarette. The fire at the end of the stick was bright.

'You are full of tales these days.'

Malakar bent towards Dhanapati.

'It is true, Malakar.'

'How will you prove it?'

'I know.'

'How do you know?'

'I have seen her enter the water,' Dhanapati lowered his voice.

'When?'

'Well past midnight, when everyone is asleep.'

'Why were you awake?'

'I woke up and did not find her beside me. The window was open. Malakar, everything that I am telling you is true.'

'You didn't ask her?'

'She said that I was dreaming.'

'That is possible.'

'I clearly saw her . . . it was her face but her body was full of scales and there was no mistaking her fins and tail. She took off her clothes and got down into the water.'

'You saw that after she disrobed?'

'There was no mistake. I saw it all by the moonlight. The moon was right overhead and the sky was not foggy. I could look out at the sea.'

'Can you see the sea from your room?'

'Yes, a sliver of it. The rest is covered by the casuarina trees.'

'You saw through the casuarina trees?'

'I saw it clearly. She took off her clothes and went into the water.'

Nabadwip thought for a while. Something bothered him. He was a bit embarrassed to ask directly. 'So, doesn't she feel like a woman underneath her clothes?' Malakar asked in a faint voice.

'Mermaid.'

'You didn't know about this?'

'How could I?'

'You sleep with her, so you should have found out!'

'Yes, I did. The saline smell of the sea, the smell of green moss . . . I am familiar with these smells.'

'Did you ask her then?'

'I thought the smell was coming from my body. I live underneath the water for long, so the same smell comes from me too.'

Nabadwip looked out into the dark. There was no one in sight. Not even Kunti. Was she hiding somewhere, listening to their conversation? Was she looking at him from her hideout? She was a clever girl. Malakar did not believe what she had told him. But he couldn't bring himself up to disbelieving Dhanapati either! It was not easy to rubbish her. He had heard many kinds of stories about the island and Dhanapati too. These could be half-truths, who knew?

'Do you sleep with her like one sleeps with a woman?'

'Yes. One look at her arouses me.'

'Did she look and feel like a fish then?'

'I think, no.'

'Then why did you see her like that?'

'Dream.'

'You said, it wasn't a dream!'

'Never mind what I said. She said it was a dream.'

There were women's voices in the dark. He could recognize Kunti's voice.

Nabadwip got excited and stood up. Dhanapati asked him to calm down.

'They are still quite a distance away. It's like this in the dark of the night on the island. Voices from afar reach you as if they are near. Voices are reflected back by the sky above. Do you know who will be the next Dhanapati?'

'Next Dhanapati? You don't have a son!' Malakar was surprised.

He heard those voices again. They were nearby. Jamuna was bringing Batashi. Kunti was there too. When did Kunti go out? Malakar's skin broke out into goosebumps. He was excited.

'They are still quite a distance away.'

'They seem so near.'

'If they come here, you will see them.'

'I think they are standing nearby. I cannot make out in the dark. Let me bring out my torch.'

'No, don't use the torch. Let me call out to them. If they are nearby, they will come here.'

'Jamuna!' Malakar called out.

No one answered. He called again. Malakar was surprised. He sat down. The voices had quietened. There was silence all around. He believed that they were standing somewhere in the dark, behind the house. They were lurking among the casuarina trees, perhaps. He lit a cigarette and puffed out slowly. No one could trick him so easily. He had to show them his power. He had found an excuse to come here from Ghoradal and couldn't let it come to naught. He wanted to find out how spirited Batashi was. It was not easy to trap two men, one of them being a government employee! It seemed that the women of the island—those prostitutes—were becoming more fearless than ever! He had to break their fangs.

'Tell me, who will be the next Dhanapati?' the old man asked again.

'You were the one who had shown these fishermen the way. If you don't come, do you think the fishermen won't come to this island of six months for their livelihood?'

'But I do need someone to take my place when I go down into the water, isn't it?'

Malakar strained his ears. Did he hear a whisper? Had they come? Why did Dhanapati say that they hadn't come yet? Malakar grew restless. He thought he had heard Batashi's voice. He got an erection.

'Let me go out into the dark and see for myself,' he said.

'They are still far from here.'

Malakar did not trust that, but he could not get up either. Dhanapati held his hand tight.

'I am the seventh or the eighth Dhanapati. I am looking for my successor. Someone who has the pirate's blood in him. Once I get him, I will give him my place and go down into the water. I will sleep with the island on my back. I will relieve the one who is holding the island on his back now.'

Ten

Government was there and government is here,
Government is the only reality to fear.

The three women sat at the back of the house and spoke in low voices. 'Those two old men will talk themselves to sleep,' Kunti said.

'Malakar is not the kind to sleep,' Jamuna said.

'He's sitting there,' Batashi said.

'They are waiting for us,' Jamuna muttered.

'Every time, he gets up to go out with his torch, Dhanapati stops him,' Kunti said.

Jamuna sighed. 'I know Malakar. He is the government's man. The government doesn't forget anything. Even after three or seven generations, it seeks compensation.'

Batashi touched her forehead. 'I know, Jamuna Di. Now let me go.'

'Let them finish talking.'

'My man will fall asleep on the water. I am scared for him.'

Kunti shook her head. 'Don't worry, I will keep him awake.'

'Don't joke about such things.'

'Don't worry. If that Malakar touches you, I will kill him. I will . . .' Kunti said.

'Stop, stop. He will hear.'

'Don't you worry, Jamuna Di. I will suck his blood. I have been to Kamrup-Kamakhya. Don't forget that.'

'You are mad!' Jamuna gave an endearing pat on Kunti's shoulder.

'We will have to stop him,' Kunti muttered.

'That will affect the inquiry. He will give a bad report.'

'Let that be. We don't want an inquiry on the island.'

The torchlight touched each of them. It shone like a tiger's eyes. You three are sitting here!'

'Yes, you too join us,' Kunti said.

'On the ground? It's chilly and the dew will drench me.'

'There are three women here and you are still scared of the dew? Come here, let me test your manhood. We are waiting for you,' Kunti laughed.

Malakar did not feel comfortable. 'Bring Batashi in,' he told Jamuna, clearly avoiding Kunti.

'Why should she go in? We have been waiting for you for so long! Why were you talking so much?'

'Dhanapati is calling you,' Malakar said.

'If he calls me, I will hear his voice, won't I? He is like a small child these days. He sleeps in the evening. I wake him up to feed him . . . my little baby.'

'I am carrying foreign liquor, Jamuna.'

'Bring it here. Let's all have it together.' Kunti laughed. 'I've had a lot of that at the house of that ship owner. His ship sails on water and his house is also like a big ship.'

'Where is that?'

'I don't know. I ran away from there.'

'Okay, okay . . . let that be. Jamuna bring her in. Let me go inside.'

'The room is locked,' Kunti stood up and said.

'Which room will I stay the night in?'

'I will open the lock when you wish to sleep. Do you want that to be as early as this? Let me bring out the bedding then.'

Malakar stiffened. He had come to the island so many times in the past. He had almost gone there every year. But this had never happened before. He had not met a woman like this. The others had been so obedient. They never said no to him. The government had to be kept in good humour if they wanted food and shelter for six months. Some money, snow powder, soap, etc., were add-ons.

They knew that even Dhanapati had to obey the government. No one could bypass the government. Sea, water, sky, fishermen, boats, fish, tortoise, the island and its trees, everything belonged to the government. The government collected tax for everything. If you didn't pay tax, your land would be lost forever. Malakar was aware of this law. The government even owned a part of the sea. If a fisherman from another foreign land entered Indian waters, he would be taken to prison. Once, so many fishermen from Siam were caught like that. There was no way out. This young girl did not understand that.

Jamuna understood what was going on in Malakar's mind. She admonished Kunti, in an effort to please Malakar. 'Don't you know who you are talking to? We are safe on this island because of Malakar Da.'

'Don't I know that, Jamuna Mashi? The old saying . . . make hay while . . .' Kunti laughed.

'Please keep quiet.'

'I will catch a cold standing here. Jamuna, take the keys from her.' Malakar did not want his position compromised any further.

'The three of us will keep you warm, Malakar Babu. Take the wrapper and cover your head. Come here,' Kunti laughed again.

Malakar was deflated. The heat of arousal that was throbbing through his veins at the thought of entering the room with Batashi was ebbing now.

'Let me go and sit in the covered sit-out.'

'No, no, why so? Batashi, go with him, he had been waiting the whole evening for you . . .' Kunti didn't let Jamuna complete the sentence. She went up and held Malakar's hand.

'Come, come, let's get you warm. The three of us—Jamuna Mashi, Batashi Didi and me too! Why are you trembling?!'

Batashi was quiet all this while. She was looking at the faint stars in the sky. There was no moonlight now. Under the light of the stars, her husband was rowing his boat. There was another one who balanced it. The tide pulled the boat along. The helper was the illiterate Fatik Midde. He had to throw the water out of the boat and help to row it at times. Ganesh would then net the fish. Earlier, three men would go together. Now, only two of them did. Cutting down on the numbers helped increase their income. What if Ganesh dozed off and a shark entered his net? It would cut through the net and escape with the fish. Batashi was lost in her thoughts when she suddenly realized that Jamuna was pulling her up.

'This man is not like the trader, Batashi. He has not come here to buy and sell. If we keep Malakar Da happy, he will help us have a permanent home for twelve months on the island. We will all have our permanent homes here, Batashi.'

'I have given *patta* to so many people in the past.' Malakar suddenly felt alive again.

'What is patta?' Kunti asked.

'You stay quiet, girl. You don't have to know everything.' Malakar showed his temper now. 'I will talk about such things with Dhanapati.'

But there was no stopping Kunti. 'So go to Dhanapati and wake him up from his slumber. You don't know how deep the tortoise sleeps. Deep inside the water, bubbles rise and there are ripples.'

'Never mind, Kunti. Our work needs to be done.'

'That will happen in any case. We will not leave the island.'

'How can you say that? We will all have to leave after Chait.'

'There's still time for that and there are ways of doing it. I know it. What will Malakar Babu do now? Inquiry? You ask me, Malakar Babu. Batashi Didi is a bit sad. Her man is at sea. The inquiry will make the sea god angry.'

'Aah!' Malakar stepped aside. He could sense anger rising inside him. Batashi stood up. He knew that he was not as strong as before. He had to have that bone dust and young women. He lit a cigarette, trying to measure Batashi from the light of the matchstick. He could feel that he was getting aroused again. Kunti had to be removed from there. The clearing behind the house was good enough. Malakar pulled out monkey cap from his pocket and wore it. He had forgotten about it. 'Kunti, you go from here.'

'Where will I go?'

'Go to your Dhanapati.'

'He is asleep.'

'Wake him up.'

'It's not time yet.'

'Go and sit by him.'

'No, no. I will stay here with them.'

Jamuna took Kunti's hand and tried to lead her away.

'Why should I leave?'

'Come, let's wake up the old master.'

'Then take Batashi Didi too.'

'No, let Batashi stay here with Malakar Da and complete the inquiry.'

Kunti looked at Batashi strangely. Batashi was looking crestfallen. 'Come with us, Batashi Didi.'

Batashi shook her head.

Kunti looked defeated. 'Will you stay here alone?'

Jamuna tried to pull her away. 'Malakar Da will stay.'

Kunti started moving in the dark as Jamuna pulled her. A few steps later, she pulled herself away from Jamuna. 'He will choke to death.'

'What are you saying?!'

'That Malakar government will choke to death.'

'Shut up or you are doomed.' Jamuna tried her best to quieten Kunti.

'What will happen to me?' Kunti dropped her saree and bared her heaving bosom. 'Come, see me under your torchlight now. I will take off all my clothes. Come, do your inquiry on me. Else you will die.'

Malakar had inched towards Batashi. He cringed when he heard Kunti. Was she cursing him or was she foretelling his future?

'You don't have the strength anymore. You will choke to death,' Kunti said aloud. 'You will land up at the burning ghat, I tell you.'

Malakar moved towards the covered sit-out. He was caught between anxiety and fear. There was a turmoil within him. On one hand, his ego was crumpled and on the other, the fire of anger seethed inside. After Malakar left, Jamuna and Batashi ran away together in the dark. Kunti stepped onto the verandah. Malakar was sitting there cursing himself. He was such a powerful man. He had been telling Dhanapati that he would get him the lease of the island. He could do that. He was an employee of the BDO office and had access to all offices of the block. What has happened to this island of prostitutes? Malakar spat on the ground. Why did Dhanapati bring a witch with him? Would the night pass safely? He would leave for Ghoradal first thing in the morning. He had never failed like this before. It was then that he heard Kunti's voice from the dark.

'Malakar Dada, Government Dada . . .'

Her voice had changed completely. Malakar was so scared that he didn't dare to look in that direction. Kunti touched his shoulder and spoke in a low voice. 'Come, Malakar Da.'

'Go away. I will return tomorrow morning.'

'No, you come with me. I have unlocked the door and have a bed ready for you. The old master will not wake up till I call him. Come, Malakar Da.'

Malakar thought that he was being tricked. She had tricked him to save Batashi already. He didn't want to walk into her trap. He would return to Ghoradal and ensure that the island was rid of women.

Kunti kept talking in a low voice. 'Come. Batashi would have cried the whole night, tomorrow morning and night too. Her Ganesh master would not have come back.'

Malakar turned his head now. He could sense her bosom on his arm. Kunti pulled him. 'I won't cry. I cannot make out whether my master, Dhanapati, is in the room or on the island outside. Come . . .'

Malakar got up. He followed Kunti in the dark as she led him to another room at the other end of the verandah. An earthen lamp was lit. Malakar saw that a neat bed had been made. Kunti smiled at him.

'I was the one you wanted first, isn't it?'

Malakar lit a cigarette in excitement. Then, he puffed out and asked, 'I hope I will be fine after this?'

'Batashi would only have wept. She doesn't think beyond her husband.'

'If I get you, I don't care for Batashi.'

'You can consider me to be her for now.'

'No, no. You are Kunti.'

'No, you can take me to be Batashi for now. I am playing Batashi in your inquiry. Come to me now.' Kunti got up on the bed propped up by bamboo sticks. She grabbed Malakar and ran her nails deep on his skin. She tried to feel the part below his abdomen. 'Now, come quick. Just ensure that we get to stay here for twelve months. I dream of mothering a hundred children from Dhanapati.'

Malakar got ready. Within a split second, he lay Kunti under him, parted her legs and asked, 'Is your Dhanapati capable of giving you a hundred children?'

'He can go on all night. I have learnt it all from him. But now, I am not me. I am Batashi. I have come to sleep with you. I am not sinning, I am not sad. Now, let me see how you do it!'

Nabadwip pounced on her with the ferocity of a tiger. He removed her clothes and got ready to enter, when he heard a nagging wail.

'My husband has fallen asleep on the water . . . he has fallen asleep in the dark. His boat floats away and no one knows where it goes. With your husband in the water, you need to be a good woman. O my man . . . where are you?'

Malakar could see Kunti's hidden treasure in the light of the lamp, but could not enter it. His manhood sagged and he fell on her like a heap. Kunti patted his back. 'Sleep, sleep . . . you government. It is only when you sleep that we are safe.'

Sleep government babu, it's best that way,
Awake in your sleep, night and day.

Eleven

Tell me who's the government master,
Obey you him or call for disaster!

The inquiry was over and Nabadwip Malakar returned to Ghoradal early in the morning. Kunti walked him till the bank of the river. She had made *bori* with urad dal paste. She filled a packet with it and gave it to him.

'The inquiry was good, Jamuna Mashi. The government is a good man. I patted him twice and he fell asleep. He didn't speak of Batashi Didi even once.'

Dhanapati looked thoughtful. 'He would always tell me before leaving the island. God knows what he will write in his inquiry report. You should have woken me up, Kunti.'

'You are my master. You were deep in your slumber like the tortoise chief who holds the island on his back.'

Dhanapati cursed aloud. But one couldn't make out whether he was happy or sad. Kunti moved about happily, swaying her plait from side to side. Jamuna looked tense about what that raucous Malakar must have done. Kunti hadn't let him touch his prey. He was not going to forget that in a while. The government never backtracked. The government never lets his target escape and sticks to his decision. Otherwise Malakar wouldn't have come. One government left and another came. The government never ended. The government would exist as long as the world would.

Kunti relayed the entire episode to Jamuna . . . how she had managed to tame the tiger and put him to sleep, finally. She said that she had sung a lullaby to put him to sleep. He couldn't harm her and couldn't sink his teeth into her but the inquiry had got over. He had promised to write in their favour.

'Okay then . . .' Jamuna was relieved a bit but a nagging thought didn't leave her. 'Will he help us stay on the island for the entire year?'

Kunti stuck her tongue out. 'Oh! I forgot to ask him!'

'That was the real deal, wasn't it?'

'Let him come back.'

'Will he come again?'

'Yes, he will come back with a bigger sahib. Jamuna Pishi, inquiry doesn't get over. It continues for life.'

'Then why did you say it's over?'

'This one got over. Another one will start. I will put him to sleep again. Next time, I will say that Batashi Didi has gone away.'

They sat discussing. It was best to say that Batashi had gone away. But was it safe to lie? The government would get to know anyway. You couldn't hide anything from the government. It didn't help.

Dhanapati strained his ears trying to catch their conversation. He shook his head in assent. 'The government knows all. Three Bangladeshi families had come to the island once. They were from Khulna. There was no way of distinguishing them from us. But the police knew. They came and arrested them.'

'How did they find out?'

'The water around us mirrors everything to the police.'

'What?'

'A bowl of water and some alta in it does the trick.' Jamuna explained how the police saw faces in that water.

'Have you seen that happen, Jamuna Mashi?'

'No, I've heard.'

'How do you identify foreigners?'

'Foreigners like us are easy to identify. The pirates are tall, fair and have the strength of demons. They have red hair, blue eyes and very wide shoulders. They are strong like the mango tree but have dry skin.'

Kunti looked at Dhanapati in surprise. She tried looking for such features in the old man. 'Were you like that when you were a youth?'

'My youth hasn't left me.'

Kunti tried to hide a smile, and shared a glance with Jamuna. She helped Dhanapati put on his monkey cap and said, 'No, no . . . you are still young, master.'

Dhanapati looked happy. He smiled at the sun. His expression showed that he was thinking of the old times when he had come here, crossing the seas. The eastern sea. 'My youth will never leave me, Jamuna . . . it cannot. I am a descendant of the pirates and I can still do wonders. If I wake up fully, this girl will not remain alive.'

Jamuna agreed. She remembered how strong and manly Dhanapati was in the past. She had been with him. Even when his youth had waned, he was unstoppable. When he beat the water with his fins, he created such ripples.

'Tell me clearly what Malakar said when he left.'

'Nothing much, my master.'

'That's what I fear. When the government says something, there's much to fear and when he doesn't, that too is worrisome. Why did I not wake up on time!'

'He asked me not to wake him up,' Kunti said softly.

'You should have done the opposite. That is the government's way. You will learn all about it.'

He asked me to walk him to the riverbank. 'Does that mean he didn't want me to go with him? Was he unhappy that I went? It's so difficult to read the government.'

'You have to know what keeps the government happy. You cannot go against the government. Remember, Jamuna, how the criminal who had committed a double murder was nabbed from the island?'

Jamuna nodded. Kunti asked, 'What is double murder?'

'When someone murders two people together.'

'Why did he murder?'

'He had no choice. His wife slept with another man daily.'

'So, he killed them?!'

'Yes, he killed his wife and her lover together . . . battered them to death. Then, he came to the island.'

'The government catches people if they kill humans?'

'Yes, the police do,' Jamuna explained.

'If a man kills his wife and her lover, how does that affect the government?'

'That's the law,' Jamuna explained.

'What is law?'

'Don't you know anything? Are you fresh from underneath the water?' Dhanapati was irritated.

'Why is the government so powerful, master? The very name gives me gooseflesh.'

Eventually, they came to the end of the topic. Kunti had no more questions to ask. In the end, all of them agreed that Malakar returned happy from the island. They agreed that since he had asked Kunti to accompany him till the riverbank, he must have been happy. 'He has promised to be back,' Kunti said in a low voice.

'Then there's nothing to worry. He's taken a fancy for you,' Jamuna whispered.

'I don't know why and how, because all I did was patted him to sleep. But he has said he would be back.'

'Did you scare him?'

'No, but I will learn witchcraft, Jamuna Pishi. It will help me survive these men.'

Jamuna left. 'You saved Batashi. Else, she would have set herself on fire,' she said before going.

'I know,' Kunti said.

'Did she tell you?'

'No, she didn't. But I thought so.'

'I have seen such things happen. After three men took her one after the other, a woman set herself on fire.'

'But why did you think that Batashi would do it?'

'I feared that she would set herself alight. Women live in so much pain.'

'I would have been a sinner and I would have consumed poison too.' Jamuna stopped.

Jamuna went back. She was not worried anymore. Kunti came back to the verandah. Dhanapati's eyes followed her.

'Come here.'

Kunti shook her plaits and almost danced her way to Dhanapati. 'Tell me, my master,' she laughed. Dhanapati kept looking at Kunti. He didn't know what had happened at night. He had dozed off. He faintly remembered that Kunti had woken him up and literally carried him to his room. He had finished his dinner early in the evening. So, he had plunged on his bed and coiled underneath his blanket to sleep heavily. He couldn't remember if Kunti was beside him at night. She was his new bride; she should sleep beside him at night. What did Malakar do with her behind his back?

'Shall I make payesh today, chief?'

'Don't call me your chief. I am your lord, your master and husband. Don't call me by two names.'

'Chief also means lord and master, doesn't it?' Kunti laughed aloud. 'Don't you lord over me?'

'Did you sleep with Malakar?'

'No and yes.'

'What do you mean?' Dhanapati boomed in anger. 'What did you do with him?'

'Both yes and no are true.'

'Tell me the truth.'

'I don't know it myself, my lord.'

'If I had been awake, there would have been twin murders. Don't forget that I belong to the bloodline of pirates. The sea is under my control. I used to go to Ghoradal and bring nine to ten women on my boat. I would tie their hands and put them in the hold of my boat and feed them there, only to bring up one at a time.'

'I know that, my lord.'

'How do you know?'

'I thought this was normal for a foreigner like you.'

'Who told you?'

'No one. I thought it up in my mind.'

'Can you think so much?' Dhanapati was surprised.

'Not always . . . sometimes.'

'Tell me, what could be my next question to you.'

'Why did I have to sleep with Malakar, right?'

'Why did you? You are my wife, my property.'

'You wanted to give me up to him.'

'When did I say that?'

'When he asked for me, did you deny him?'

'What is mine, I can give or keep, isn't it? And then, he is the government.'

'That's true.'

'But if he touches you without telling me, that is sacrilege.'

'Master, is Malakar capable?'

Dhanapati didn't hide his anger. 'Do you know I am capable of twin murders? If I was awake, I would have chopped your heads off your bodies.'

Kunti shivered. She cringed. She seemed to imagine the scene. Dhanapati got up slowly. He tried to unlock his waist that had stiffened. He dragged his slow and tired feet and walked about in the sun on the verandah. 'Pirates cannot control their anger. Once, one of us took three women and threw them in the water for sharks to feed on.'

'Poor women!' Kunti said with tears in her eyes.

'You may end up with that fate.'

Dhanapati came and stood in front of her. 'I don't care if Malakar is government or not. Remember, I am the descendant of Pedru, the dangerous pirate.'

'I know,' Kunti said.

'I am Dhanapati Pedru, whom you call Sardar.'

'I know that too.'

Dhanapati touched her shoulder. 'I am the king of the island, the badshah.'

'Yes . . . badshah . . . badshah-begum . . .'

'Yes, you are my begum.'

'Badshah-begum . . . *chhum chhuma chhum* . . .' Kunti rhymed. 'Am I begum?'

'Yes, queen . . . king-queen . . .'

'Queenie . . .' Kunti laughed.

'Not queenie, rani.'

'Rani? Am I a rani?'

'Yes! Don't equate yourself with that Jamuna or Batashi. You are my bibi, this island is mine, the water is mine and so are the fish in it.'

'Mine too.'

'Then why will you let Malakar take advantage of you?'

'I will not.'

'You will order him like a begum.'

'Then, let me order you . . . Can I?'

'Try.'

Kunti stretched her arms and wound them around Dhanapati. 'You are my lord, my master, my chief. You are my life.'

Dhanapati licked her eyes with his tongue popping out of his toothless mouth. He placed his hands on her breasts and squeezed them. 'This massive island is ours. All the fishermen and women on it . . . they are all our subjects. We are their overlords. I am Pedru Dhanapati. You belong to me. If you go to anyone without telling me, I will chop your head off.' He squeezed her breasts as he spoke.

Twelve

The water takes the woman's form,
Sailing alone, his body longs for the storm.

The boats came ashore in the morning. The fishermen had spent the night longing to be back home as the waves bobbed them up and down. They scooped out the water from the boat relentlessly, keeping their eyes on the north star. It seemed to shine above Dhanapati's Island. Once back on the island, the star seemed to have moved towards Ghoradal. The way back from the water to the island, guided by the star, was Dhanapati's way. It was also the route Dhanapati Pedru took to come and land on the island. He had shown the way.

The fishermen never lost their way, no matter how deep they went out. Mistakes happened only when there was a curtain of fog and the north star was out of sight. The north and south seemed to merge then. If they sailed south, thinking they were heading north, they would lose their way for life. The south would lead them to their doom. The water changed its colour in the south and you saw black, maroon and purple water all around you. Once Dhanapati too had lost his way but managed to come back. He came back and told the fishermen how the black water was home to the dark woman seated on a lotus. To meet this woman in the water was a signal of death. You couldn't think of women in the water. If such thoughts came, you had to return to the island. The journey would go waste. If thoughts of women clouded your mind while at sea, you were bound to lose direction. All stars would look like the north star then. Dhanapati had

related a story once. It was the month of Falgun. This could have been
the third, fourth or fifth Dhanapati. He was aroused suddenly.

His entire body was aroused thinking of women. The pirate
blood ran fresh in his veins and he couldn't ignore the thoughts
of a woman's body underneath him. He felt like jumping into the
water since it looked like a woman who had laid out herself for him.
She was inviting him with all her curves. She had bared all for him.
It was the month of Falgun. Dhanapati had forgotten that in Falgun,
the Agastya star rose from the northern horizon of the water.

The spring breeze blew suddenly, pulling the boat. Dhanapati
mistook the Agastya for the pole star and lost himself forever. There
was another reason for losing the way. If the tortoise chief decided to
move away with the island on his back, it would be difficult to locate
the island then.

'Where did Dhanapati float away?
When did he come back, what was the day?'

The tortoise chief did not have to move too far. He just had to shake
his huge yellow legs underneath the water. The island would change
place naturally. The fishermen would not find their island in the
old place.

'Is this possible, master?' Batashi asked.

'Yes, it is possible,' Ganesh replied.

'Have you faced such a thing when you were in the water?'

'Yes, I have.'

'How did you return then?'

'I know the degree,' Ganesh said, sinking his teeth into Batashi's
soft bosom.

'What is degree, master?' Batashi asked.

'You won't understand till you go into the water.'

Poush was coming to an end. The moon was a sliver in the sky,
just a ribbon width more than the previous night. For fifteen days,
the ribbon increased in width. Ganesh knew how the ribbon grew in

width day by day. Sitting in the deep with nothing else in sight, he trained his eyes on the moon.

The end of the month was near. The day after was the full moon day of Magh. A ripe moon washed everything on the island. Moonlight melted through the cracks into Batashi's hut. It looked like pure coconut oil. It was somewhat fragrant, Batashi thought. Her hair was spread out on the pillow and on the mattress beyond. Ganesh inhaled the scent of her hair and said, 'This time, I was aroused while I was at sea.'

'That's not good!' Batashi shivered.

'As the boat swayed, I became more and more aroused. The fire of desire burnt me.'

'What did you do?'

'I prayed hard to the sea god, our Dariya Pir. There's no other way, when you are in the water.'

'You are not in the water now. You are on the island, atop the tortoise master's back. I am your boat. Come . . .'

It was such a beautiful night that followed a wonderful day on the island. Ganesh was back from the water. Malakar had returned to Ghoradal. Ganesh did not know what Malakar had asked for. He came back and slept all day, only to wake up in the evening, looking fresh and big like the tortoise himself.

'Tell me, what is degree?'

'Have you ever been to the sea?'

'You have never taken me.'

'I cannot take a woman there. The boat will rock and all will sink.'

'Will I never get to know what degree means then?'

'Why do you want to know that?'

'To save myself if I am in trouble.'

Ganesh started removing Batashi's clothes with his hands and said, 'Degree will not help you on the island. It comes into use only in the water.'

'I stay alone here when you are gone. What if I get into trouble? Who will save me then?'

'Whether you know the degree or pray to the pir of the water, ultimately, you have to save yourself, just like you saved yourself from the trader.'

'You have your pir. Who do I have?'

'You have me.'

'You are in the water most of the time.'

'What happened again?'

Batashi kept quiet. Ganesh climbed on top of her. His desire was like a sea in high tide. 'I will not pack them off on the boat this time. I will cut them to pieces and throw them to the crocodiles.'

'You cannot.'

Ganesh seethed. 'I swear by the pir of the sea. Let that bastard come here again, I will not leave him.'

'It's better that you teach me that degree.'

'There's not much to understand. It is useful when there is a storm at sea and you have to return to the island.'

'How will I save myself, master?'

'Later . . . now, come.'

The night progressed silently. With all the strength that he had gathered from the sea, Ganesh entered Batashi . . . again and again. She felt like the familiar wave that rocked his boat at sea. He bypassed his hand below her waist and pulled her close. Then, he swore again. 'Anyone who comes near you will be castrated.'

'Uufff . . .' Batashi grunted. 'You cannot castrate the government. Its bloodline continues. One government dies, only to give birth to another. Let them come, no bastard can lay his hands on me. Hai Allah! You have looked after Batashi, Allah.'

Ganesh literally drowned Batashi with his strong caresses now. 'Yes, the pir has kept us well. We are happy, I swear in his name. If anyone eyes you, Batashi, his boat will sink and he will get eaten by the crocodiles. He will have no one to carry on his bloodline. Even if he is a government.'

Batashi groaned in pleasure. 'Yes, we will castrate them and turn them into eunuchs . . . hee, hee, hee . . .'

Ganesh started relating his previous night's experience. He had drifted off course. The moonlight had spread out on the water and there was a veil of fog that messed with it. One moment he could see the stars but in the very next moment, they vanished. There was a sudden waft of breeze. Ganesh was scared. It was an ill wind. There was no sign of it just a little while ago. The breeze reminded him of a bare woman.

'Oh my God! Who was she?'

'I don't know . . . you or perhaps someone else.'

'Who was it?'

'I cannot recall.'

'Someone from the island? That Kunti or that nag Sabitri?'

'I don't know, really.'

'Are you hiding something from me, master?'

'Why should I?'

'Who would bare herself for you in the water?' Batashi sounded angry.

'What if I say it was you?'

'I was here all the while. Why should I go into the water and bare myself underneath the sky?'

'Then, perhaps, it was someone else.'

Batashi's waist shook in the rhythm of their union. 'Who is more beautiful or youthful than your Batashi? Why should she go to your boat and bare herself? Be careful, master. That slut will sink your boat.'

'I know. There are such women at sea. I only remember her ripe wood apple breasts and her waist that was like a boat, ready to sail away with me. She had full buttocks, like the bottom of the boat. Her thighs were like two stems of banana plants and I felt like a king between them. It was a maddening experience.'

'Hai Allah! She was a witch, trying to bewitch you in the middle of the sea.'

'Possible. She had such thick hair. She had uncoiled it and then she lay on the water, her thighs apart, inviting me there.'

'Hai Allah! She will kill you, master. She is not Batashi who prays for your well-being.'

'I know that.'

'She would have led you through her thighs into darkness.'

'I know.'

'That's a land of darkness. You would have floated in darkness forever.'

'I am aware.'

'It's like floating in the water inside your mother's womb.'

'Now stop all this and relax. It seems like I haven't had you for the past seven lives!'

'You can take me as much as you want, you are my master. I just have one desire.'

'What do you want? A silver anklet?'

'No.'

'A gold chain?'

'No.'

'I will give you all you want.'

'That woman was evil and couldn't do it, but I am pure . . . I want you inside me, master. Give me a son.'

'How is that possible?'

'You don't have to be careful, I won't be either. Leave all those restrictions aside and come straight inside me. She rolled over to the ground and spread out her legs. Come in, master, give me a son. I will stay back on the island with your son through the year and wait for you for six months when you go back to Ghoradal. I will think that my man has gone for work for six months to come back to me thereafter.'

Ganesh stared at her in surprise. She looked exactly like the woman at sea. He couldn't take his eyes off her. She kept calling him. 'Come, my master, give me a baby. I will have you inside me for ten months and ten days and then I will stay back on the island.' Ganesh felt that his relaxed body was rising again. He dived into the water, leaving his boat empty.

'Look at that beauty, who is she?'

'My tired body floats in glee!'

Thirteen

The island will be yours, the water and the sky,
No child you'll bear, don't ask why!

Dhanapati, the old master, had sent word through Kunti that there would be a public meeting at his house. 'Jamuna Mashi, please send your husband to the meeting. You are not invited. Ask him to reach early.'

'What if I go?'

'This meeting is reserved only for men.'

'Jamuna looked serious. She knit her brows. 'Why is the master meeting only men?'

'Only he knows that.'

'You don't know?'

'No.' Kunti nodded her head. 'The men are the masters. They will talk.'

'What will the men talk about?'

'Why? Even when we meet, we talk, don't we?'

'No, I don't think it's that simple. Kunti, sit here.'

'Where's your master?'

'He's asleep.'

'Why is he sleeping till this late?'

'He doesn't sleep well at night, Kunti.'

'That's not normal.'

'He remains awake at night when he is in the water. When on the island, that habit continues. He sees just water bubbles at night.'

'Does he let you sleep well?'

'I just give in to sleep and cannot stay awake.'

'Give him the message.'

'I will. Let's all of us have a meeting too.'

'What meeting?'

'A meeting of the wives as the husbands hold theirs. Tell your master that you will be attending a meeting here at that time, at my place.'

Kunti stayed quiet. She was not sure if she would make it. The men would come home for the meeting and she would have to give them paan-supari, serve them water and batashas. She would be the only woman among fifty men. The thought got her excited and made her happy since she was mentally preparing herself for it. She loved to live large and wanted to have a hundred children, giving birth to four or five at a time. She would often tell Dhanapati of her plans. Even Draupadi, who had five husbands, would be jealous of her. She would have fifty! They would all assemble at home and she would be the lone woman they would look at. She was very happy.

'I don't think I will be able to come, Jamuna Mashi.'

'Why? What will you do?'

'I will have to stay home and take care of the guests.'

'Your master will take care of them.'

'Let me see if I can come. Let me leave now.'

She went to Batashi's hut next. Kunti met Ganesh on the way. From Batashi's house she went to Sabitri's, then to Ghennabala's, Kandni's and Namita's. She loved it . . . moving from one house to another with her message. She told everyone that only men were invited. She would be the only woman present in the meeting. Those were Dhanapati's orders. However, there was a meeting for women that Jamuna Mashi had called for, she told the women. 'You can go there in the evening; I shall find out from you what happened.'

Kunti returned home after finishing her round and sat down to cook. She then made old Dhanapati sit in the sun as she bathed him. The old man loved it. She put a cloth on the line to create a curtain. Dhanapati's body had to be bared for the bath. After the bath, she

wrapped him neatly in a lungi at the waist and a wrapper on top.
'Master, you are ready now. Go and walk in the sun for some time.'

'Go and bathe now, Kunti.'

'Not today.'

'So many men will come.'

'So what? You are my master,' Kunti said deliberately.

'Remember that. Don't look at them. Eyeing outsiders is a sin.'

'I know.'

'Don't look up at the men.'

'I won't.'

'Men will look at you as a matter of habit.'

'True.'

'You have to be careful, Kunti. Understood?'

'Yes, my lord.'

'Don't answer them if they call you.'

'I know, my master.'

'Don't let anyone touch you.' Dhanapati pinched her cheeks
playfully.

Kunti was quiet. Dhanapati paced up and down in the sun.
Kunti felt like giving him a hard push and throwing him on to the
ground. Why was he trying to dictate her? Had he bought her? From
whom and when? Kunti rubbed her feet on the ground in anger,
almost like an angry tabby cat. She tried to keep her temper down
and stared hard at the old man.

'Don't go out in front of anyone.'

'Who will give them paan-supari?'

'You don't have to serve them yourself. Just keep them on a plate
before the meeting starts.'

'Do you think no one looks at me, master?'

'That's a different thing. Fifty to hundred men staring at you
together has a different meaning altogether.'

Kunti shook her head. She couldn't agree with Dhanapati.
He was trying to establish his right on her. He suspected that Kunti
had slept with Malakar. 'I know what I should or should not do,'
she growled.

'You are my woman,' Dhanapati asserted.

'If you continue to behave like this, I will return to Ghoradal.'

'Yes, go if you can. Malakar will be waiting for you there.'

There had been a sudden change in Dhanapati since that night. Kunti had noticed that. Previously, he obeyed her like a child, but now it was the exact opposite. 'I will go to Jamuna Mashi's house then.'

'No, that cannot be.'

'Then what should I do?'

'You will stay inside. I will call for you if necessary.'

Kunti couldn't hold herself any more. 'I don't want a family. I will leave for Ghoradal. Leave me, master,' she screamed.

'Will you be able to leave me and go?'

'Why certainly! I can.'

'No, you cannot. You are my wife. No boat will take you without my permission.'

Kunti broke into tears. 'Why are you behaving like this with me, Dhanapati master?'

'Why did you sleep with Malakar?'

'That's a lie. I just put him off to sleep. Wasn't I there by your side that night? Didn't you find me?'

'I was dead in my sleep that night. I don't know . . .'

'Then how did you know that I slept with Malakar?'

'I was told.'

'Who told you?'

'Nabadwip Malakar has been coming to the island for so many years. He has always respected me as the master of the island. I have paid him enough and he has tried his best to get me the government papers that will make my ownership final. He will give me a receipt. It won't be a six-monthly arrangement any more.'

'This is good news, master.'

'Bring a mat and lay it out in the sun. You are not a prostitute. You are Dhanapati's wife. Remember that. Only I have the right to your beauty. Go get me the mat now.'

Kunti brought the mat and laid it out. Dhanapati sat on it. He asked Kunti to sit across him. Kunti seethed in anger but softened

at times. She couldn't understand Dhanapati fully. She looked down.
Kunti understood that Dhanapati was trying to establish a complete
hold on her. She could not even get up without his permission. She
yearned to sit on the shore and look out at the water. It would have
given her such relief.

'I've never had a young wife like you before.'

Kunti stared at him.

'You will be able to hold on to your youth for long.'

'With your blessings.'

You are not like the others. Jamuna was there for two seasons.
She would never remove her veil.'

'You want me to cover my head with a veil?'

'Yes, you should. But you are so young that I didn't want to order
you. I wanted to be rather playful with you.'

'What game?'

'You don't need to know that. It's my game and I play it my way.'

Kunti was quiet. She was scared. Where had she landed up?
It would have been better to look for a man in a shanty beside the
railway tracks. Even a rickshaw puller would have been better than
this. She would have expected food, sex and a normal family life with
eight to ten children around her. This man didn't have the strength
to give her children. Kunti cursed the old man in her mind. Bastard!
He had brought her here by telling her tales of the sea. Now, he
didn't allow her to sit by the seashore. That cursed pirate's descendant!
Had he bought her?

'Why are you quiet, Kunti?'

'What should I say?'

'Listen, you are different from the other women here. If you
listen to me, you will have them.'

'Have what?'

'This island is yours. You are the lady and I am the lord.'

'What about the other Dhanapati?'

'I will give everything to you. I will sign off on it and give
everything to you.'

'I am illiterate.'

'That doesn't matter. My word is enough.'

'What will you give me?'

'This island, the fishermen and their women, the shops, the riverbank, the big sea, the water in the sea, the fish therein, the nets . . . everything . . . they are mine and yours too.'

'How strange?! They will be mine?'

'Yes, I don't need another Dhanapati. These days, women rule the world. Look at Indira Gandhi.'

'Who is she?'

'You wouldn't know. She died before you were born.'

'Give all this to me now.'

'I will teach you how to manage the island first. You have to learn how to run everything, like I do. My forefather Pedru had seen such a woman owner at Satgaon port. She had a command on everyone and everything. I will make you like her.'

'What about my children?' Kunti asked in a low voice.

'That is not allowed on the island. Why do you need children?'

'What will I do with so much property if I don't have children to look after them? This island, water and the sea . . . they will have no meaning for me then.'

'Owners of such huge properties don't need children. They only help to destroy the property. Once you become the owner of everything that I have, you will no longer want children.'

Fourteen

Look at the government on the banks of Ghoradal,
The island afar, no give and take at all!

'Why didn't they call us to the meeting?' Jamuna asked.

'Let them not call us,' a woman said.

'Why? Don't we belong to the island?'

Everyone was quiet. The winter daylight paled off early. A shadow replaced the sun spot in the opening outside the shanty. Fifteen women sat there, some on straw mats, some directly on the ground. They were looking at Jamuna and their faces looked tense.

'If we don't come to the island, will it function normally?'

'We get food to eat for these six months. It is equally important for us to be able to come here,' someone said.

'Yes, we also get a family.'

'Clothes, shankha-pola and vermilion too.'

'We get a man to ourselves. The other six months at Baruipur, Ghoradal, Sonarpur, Joy Nagar and Kolkata . . . five men together . . . Oh God! Do we live like humans then?'

'It will all be over, it seems,' Jamuna said.

'Why? What happened?'

'We have been excluded from the meeting. This has never happened before.'

'Men go to the sea without us too! The meeting can be about that,' Sabitri said.

'Why should we not listen to that?' Jamuna argued.

'It doesn't concern us,' Sabitri reasoned.

'We sit here thinking about them when they are at sea. The dangers they face are ours too!' Jamuna looked around for support. She met Batashi's eyes who looked very tense and withdrawn. 'Tell me, Batashi, am I wrong?'

Batashi kept quiet. She thought Jamuna was right. Her man told her all about what happened at sea, including the thoughts about being with women in those lonely hours at sea. He spoke about the mystery woman of the sea who tried to lead men astray in the unbounded waters. What else could they talk about that the women couldn't listen to? Jamuna was tense about something deep inside and wanted to share her thoughts with the other women, Batashi realized. Was Jamuna aware of something that the others did not know? It had to be, Batashi thought. Was it about the outcome of the inquiry? Batashi lowered her head.

'I think women are in danger,' Jamuna said.

'We are wives—bibis—of the fishermen. They cannot live without us on the island.'

'There's no dearth of women,' Jamuna said.

'Why? What have we done?' Batashi asked.

'Perhaps nothing. But this is the first time that the government has turned its attention on the women of the island. It is not good.'

'Isn't that over now?' Sabitri asked.

'No, it will continue. Nothing about the government gets over. He will come back.'

'Why will he come? What is Batashi's fault?' Sabitri jumped up. She was an otherwise quiet woman, but when she started talking or trying to argue a point or complain about something, she lost her cool easily.

'Come, sit. There is no point arguing about the government. It is bound by its own rules. The law is by the side of the government.'

Sabitri sat down slowly and cursed.

'There is no challenging the power of the government,' Jamuna said. She took out a paan from a box and started chewing on it, making a lot of noise as she did. Sabitri tore open a sachet of paan masala and emptied it in her mouth. 'Batashi is unlucky,' she said.

'I really cannot judge that,' Jamuna said.

'You really don't know, Jamuna Di?' Batashi flared up for a second and then deflated again.

'The government doesn't do anything without a reason,' Jamuna said.

Sabitri pawed the ground fiercely. 'Do you want to say that buying and selling women is a good thing? Have you called us to listen to this?' Sabitri growled.

Jamuna kept quiet. Sabitri stopped. The others were quiet. One could even hear them breathing and see their heavy bosoms heaving, as if keeping pace with the waves of the Kalnagini. Jamuna looked at everyone. After some time, she spoke again.

'We have to come back to the island every year and start a family. We have no other choice. We have to think about what is good for us.'

'That is true,' Sabitri agreed.

'Let us accept that the government is powerful.'

'Don't we matter,' Sabitri asked.

'We?' Jamuna laughed. 'We are like the small insects that seek shelter among the grass blades. They die when they get trampled by the feet.'

'We don't care, let that happen,' Sabitri was agitated again.

'You cannot die that easily,' Jamuna muttered. 'I have been coming to the island for years, Batashi. Once upon a time, I was Dhanapati's wife . . . I am not that anymore . . . but have I stopped coming?'

'That doesn't stop anyone from coming to the island.'

'Yes, today Dhanapati doesn't matter to me. I have a husband. But that's another matter. I am saying that the government can do anything.'

'What can it do?' Batashi asked.

'The entire country is run by the government.'

'How does that concern us?' Batashi asked.

'The island is part of the country, isn't it?'

'This island belongs to Dhanapati,' Sabitri said.

'Yes, it does belong to him, but it first belongs to the government and then to him,' Jamuna explained.

'Let me go home, Jamuna Di. I cannot follow what you said.'

'Sit. I am saying that the government are all powerful and control all lives.'

'How powerful?'

'Very, very big.'

'Like the sea and sky?' Batashi asked in a faint voice.

'Like God?' Sabitri asked.

'I don't know. But I know for sure that they are discussing the government in the meeting there,' Jamuna said.

'We know that,' someone said.

'Will that harm us?'

'Has Dhanapati told you anything?' Batashi asked Jamuna.

'Nothing directly, but I can understand. Listen, Batashi, Malakar Babu was very angry when he left the island and that is not good.' She was nearing her fifties and thought that she could understand much more than what other women did. The meeting was to discuss men and that is why they were not being allowed. It was against them. No matter how much Dhanapati insisted that he was a descendant of foreign pirates and that the island belonged to him, he held the island because the government was allowing him to. Jamuna knew everything. That season she had been Dhanapati's wife. She was at the height of her youth then and Dhanapati was madly in love with her. Trouble arose and the government was about to evacuate the island. Dhanapati sent his young wife to appease the big sahib. He was a small man in his fifties but full of vigour. He had announced that they would have to vacate the island because it belonged to the government. Such encroachment was not allowed. Jamuna spent three nights with him and, after that, he left for Ghoradal from where he headed to Kolkata. Dhanapati then gave her *talak*.

'Go and look for another man now,' Dhanapati told Jamuna. 'I am the descendant of Pedru the pirate, I cannot have a disloyal woman in my house.'

'It is the government that does everything for us,' Jamuna said.

'What does it do?' Sabitri asked.

'Lots, actually.' Jamuna seemed to be at a loss for words. She thought hard. Roads, towns, bridges, jails, hospitals, ration shops . . . our food and clothes . . .'

'It doesn't give us clothes and food,' Batashi said.

'It does. We don't realize that. If we are forced out of the island forever, what will we eat for the six months that we used to spend here? Have you thought of that, Sabitri?'

Sabitri tried hard to follow, but she was not sure what brought the government to the island. Who the government was and what it did didn't really concern her, she thought. Jamuna seemed to have read her mind. 'You have to keep the government in good humour, Sabitri. We women have no say in anything.'

'I am totally confused.'

'You are not. You know what I am saying and why. You got away the first time. Next time, you could have pleased the government. I am sure the government has sent some news and that is being discussed in the meeting there. It's true that women spoil everything.'

'Let me leave.' Batashi stood up.

'Why will you leave? We haven't finished talking.'

'Yes, we have.'

'No, we have not. You have to understand that the government needs to be pleased all the time. Only then will it protect you. Women can easily please the government with their youth and beauty. There are some who like money and some who like women.' Jamuna looked at each face in front of her. Most faces had no expression. Only Batashi spoke up.

'They come here looking for women. Who is the government's father?'

'What!' Jamuna was surprised.

'Who is the government's master or lord? Who will sleep with the government's wife?'

'What are you saying, Batashi?!'

'I am only saying what is right. Government is our master—our master's master—and so we are forced to sleep with him. But who is the government's master? Who forces Malakar's and Mangal Midde's wives to sleep with him?'

'Shut up! Don't say a word.'

'I am Ganesh Sardar's wife. Don't I have a status?'

'We are poor and have to compromise in every way. The government is rich, prints notes, makes money and gives gold jewellery to his wife. Why should his wife sleep with someone else?'

'I have done the right thing by not sleeping with that old man Malakar. I have a husband and a family. My husband is a strong man. He can kill Malakar. Why should I be forced to sleep with another man?'

'Sit down. What is past is gone. Malakar has left the island. But you need to remember that once you have touched the government, your name has entered his books. He will look for you. The government does not forget anyone.'

'Let it do as it pleases,' Batashi growled in anger. 'I am leaving.'

'No, you won't. What if the government comes and tells us that women will not be allowed on the island?'

'What if we don't listen?' Sabitri asked.

'We will be forced to. They will post policemen on the riverbank at Ghoradal to stop us from getting on the boats. What will we do then?'

Sabitri looked surprised. She hadn't thought about that possibility. She bent towards Jamuna and asked, 'Is that possible?'

'Quite possible.' Sabitri's face turned purple in fear. She suddenly shivered in the cold and started rubbing her palms. 'What will we do then?'

'We will have to return.'

'Will such a misfortune really happen?'

'It might.'

'What will the men do then?'

'Let that be their problem.'

'How will they live then?'

'Let them think about that. But if we are unable to come to the island, we will be in great trouble.'

Batashi realized that Jamuna had her in mind while she said all this. Jamuna had wanted her to spend the night with Malakar. That had not happened and Malakar had returned to Ghoradal the next morning. Malakar was the government's man. Would he place policemen on the banks of the river at Ghoradal? Batashi was scared now.

'Are the men talking about this at the meeting?' Batashi asked Jamuna.

'Perhaps. When they are in trouble, men don't think of others. Dhanapati didn't think about me and left me instead, in a fit of rage.'

'But my master is a good man.'

'Let him get into trouble first and then we will see.'

'What do we do now?'

'We will not leave the island.'

'Why should we leave the island now? It's not time yet,' Batashi said.

'We will not leave when the time comes, in the month of Chait,' Jamuna stated.

'How is that possible?'

'The government has never returned empty-handed from here. This time, it had to return twice. If we return, the trader, Midde and Malakar will pounce on us at the riverbank itself. They will not leave Batashi. The government doesn't leave anyone.'

'Let Batashi do what suits her best. She is too stubborn and boastful of her beauty,' someone said.

'No, she's not alone in this now. I am an old hag now. I will not be left alone too. I know the government well.'

All fell quiet. The shadows of winter darkened and enveloped everyone. Some of them remembered Anna Bibi at that moment.

Fifteen

Move to the south with Pedru on your mind,
A little more to the south and you will have to leave your life behind!

'No one will be spared. Was Anna Bibi spared? Have you forgotten her?' Dhanapati said this and waited to catch his breath. 'If we were just men on the island, such a problem would not have arisen. The government would not have repeatedly come for us.'

The men looked at each other. Was this even possible? Dhanapati himself had brought such a young bud of a wife! He wouldn't be able to stay alone either! If the government came there repeatedly, let Dhanapati hand over his wife to them, they thought!

'We are breaking the rules of the government.'

'There is no government here on the island. Its rule doesn't matter to us. Such laws do not work in the water.'

'Don't talk like women. The government's rule is applicable everywhere. The land, sea and sky are under different governments. They don't meddle in each other's affairs.'

'Do you mean to say that even birds follow the government's rules? Don't you think what you are saying is weird, master?' Someone laughed.

'It might sound strange but it's true. This sky overhead is owned by India's government. Pakistan is on that side. If a flying machine comes into this sky from Bangladesh, there will be so many Indian planes gunning for it and chasing it like a preying kite.'

'Understood,' a man said, reaching for a bidi on the big plate kept in the middle. But we are poor people who neither wish to reach the sky nor play with guns or open fire on anyone. Why should all this bother us?'

'There's ample reason why. The government has given me just this island to rule. I am the descendant of Pedru the pirate. If you reach the big sea and move to the southwest, you will get the island of Khejuri. You will see the lighthouse of the pirates there. If you move further south, you will see the salt godown of the pirates. Keeping west, if you move further to the south, you will see huge houses, all built by the pirates—my forefathers. They are all broken now. But they belong to me. I have patta—ownership rights—over them. Pedru pirate got the rights from the Delhi badshah. Do you want to know more?'

Daylight had waned and sunlight had left Dhanapati's courtyard. The chill was less biting. There was a thin blanket of cloud in the sky. One fisherman yawned and looked here and there. Dhanapati's young wife was nowhere to be seen. Most of them thought that she would spice up the meeting. Many were disheartened. Dhanapati's story seemed to make up for her absence. If Kunti had been present and walked in and out of her rooms, they would have felt better. One of them closed his eyes and thought about Kunti. There was rhythm in her step and cheer in her voice. His wife had told him how Kunti wanted to give birth to hundred children. What if he helped sire them?

'Pedru pirate looted so many countries as he headed here. He sunk ships and boats on his way. The hold of his ship was full of gold, treasures and women. After Pedru enjoyed the women, he punched holes in their palms and tied them up. When his ship neared land, he sold them off. The younger ones fetched a good price,' Dhanapati continued his story.

Those listening to him could almost see scenes fleeting in front of them. 'Pedru's pirates caught many women from here too. After reaching Ghoradal, Pedru jumped on to the shore with a gun in hand and entered the village. He chose some women and put them on his ship. The villagers had no choice but to stand and watch. The pirate had a gun in his hand and was very strong. He could kill villagers by just slapping them. I am the descendant of that pirate.'

'We know that,' a fisherman said.

'Even the Badshah at Delhi was surprised at the amount of gold and gems that Pedru had brought along in his ship. 'Have they been gifted to you by some djinn?' the Badshah asked Pedru.

'Does Delhi have a sea like this?' a fisherman asked.

'It did, in those days. That was so many years ago. Pedru bought the island from the Badshah with his gold and treasures. The Badshah paid him a lot of respect because of the gold and gems he brought and gave him the title of Dhanapati. Since then, Dhanapati has become my family name.'

The fishermen were a bit confused. Why had Dhanapati called them to narrate an old tale? Even the women knew these stories. Then why were they kept out of the meeting?

'Pedru's ship was very majestic. It was blood red in colour and bore the sign of a skull. Pedru knew that women could be the cause of all undoing. So, he caught women and sold them off in different markets. Some were even packed off to Arab countries. He believed that women had secret powers. He had a harem of his own, I believe, where he kept the most beautiful women. But they were women after all . . .'

'But what is it that you wish to say? We set up home with the women on the island.'

'Wait, let me finish. Had Pedru not crossed the seven seas to come here, I would not have been here. I would have been born across the seas.'

Some fishermen laughed silently. All this made no sense to them. There would have been no Ramayana without Ram; no fruit without seed and no seed without a flower . . . Dhanapati noticed the smiles and looked sullen. 'I was born on this island,' he said with a heavy voice.

'We didn't know that!' Pitambar Das, a fisherman, spoke up.

'That's because I never told you. All Dhanapatis were born here. Badshah gave the patta to Pedru pirate saying that the island

would belong to the Dhanapatis from one generation to the next.'
The master stopped to catch his breath again. He got breathless easily
these days. Even the sea breeze did not seem enough. 'My mother
gave birth to me and went down into the water. She came from a
far-off sea. My mother and father became one in the month of
Ashwin, on the island. Did I ever tell you that?'

All the fishermen looked surprised. They had never heard all this
before. This was very different from what they had believed all these
years. Not that they believed everything. But what Dhanapati was
saying now seemed to be limitless and had no fixed direction. They
were confused. There was something eerie about the falling light
all around. Dhanapati seemed to be talking from a great distance,
perhaps from the middle of the sea. This was not Ghoradal. This was
the magical island where everything seemed possible. Dhanapati's
strange birth story seemed true. It was the story of a mother tortoise
who travelled across the seas to give birth on the island.

Dhanapati's voice was low. 'Don't compare yourselves with me.
The more you hear, the more confused you will be.'

'No, no, please go on. We have come to hear you . . .'

'The shell of the mother tortoise was olive green. If you look at
me in the dark, you will find the same colour on me.'

The fishermen remained quiet. Everything seemed to look
and sound so real to them. They had seen him sitting in the dark
so many times. Around the month of Falgun, when the south wind
was about to start blowing, a green glow seemed to emanate out
of Dhanapati's body. They could see him in their mind's eye. They
would ask him why he sat there by the sea and looked out. He had
lived his annual six months on the island for ages. Didn't that quench
his thirst for the sea? He would tell them that he wanted to see
the Agastya star come out into the night sky. That would give him
the sign of the end of the time on the island for the year. Far away,
in the southern sky, towards the middle of Falgun, the Agastya star
came out in the sky, as if from the depths of the sea on the horizon.
The Agastya star would also come out in the night sky in the pirate's

own land across the sea. His father and mother had left home to meet and become one in the month of Ashwin. They swam up to a lonely island and enjoyed their union, away from the eyes of everyone.

'My father swam away back home thereafter. But my mother tortoise crossed the water and came to this island finally. She crossed so many seas and new depths to come to this island to give birth.'

'Is this true, master?' Ganesh could not hide his surprise.

'Why should I lie?'

They agreed. There was no reason for him to lie. He had special powers. Otherwise how could he rule over such a big island for years? They looked out at the shadow that the night had started casting on the island. Everything seemed true.

'My story is never-ending like the bountiful sea.'

'What happened next?'

'My mother came on to the island and placed me safely underneath the sand, before getting down into the water. I broke open the shell of the egg to come out.'

Pitambar Das agreed. Tortoises were indeed born that way.

'Even humans are born like this.'

Pitambar Das said he wasn't sure about that but he knew that tortoises were born like this. He had once been employed to collect tortoise eggs. He could take one look at the sandy island to guess if a mother tortoise had come up to lay her eggs. They left their mark on the sand. He was a fisherman now, but he had worked for several years as a tortoise-egg hunter. He had myriad experiences but did not feel the relevance of sharing all that here.

'Now, if you have finished, I can start again,' Dhanapati said.

'I have finished.' Pitambar could only talk about mother tortoises and how they laid their eggs. Nothing more. He had seen olive green tortoises laying eggs and hiding them under the sand and then going down into the water, weeping all the while. They had to save themselves or the people of the island would catch and kill them.

'You can still hear them weep,' Dhanapati said.

'Really? Have you heard them weep?'

'Yes. I have never seen my mother. My father had left her long ago. I came into the world and opened my eyes alone. Two kites or, perhaps, eagles, protected me with their wings, shading me from the sun. Then, the god of the Firingitala came and took me under his wings. He was a kind god.'

Pitambar Das said he did not know any of this.

'I never spoke about all this.'

'Why did you call us?'

'We have to save the island.'

'Why, what has happened?'

'Don't you see how the government folks keep coming back, again and again? Can we afford for our women to be like that? It is because of them that the war happened in the Ramayana due to which Ravana was killed in Lanka. Now, even the island will be gone forever.'

Ganesh reacted now. 'Who are you talking about?' His voice sounded gruff.

'I meant all women, why are you getting excited?'

'I was feeling cold. So, my voice was hoarse. What have the women done?'

'These women of the island do not follow the law. Since when have the women of the island started behaving like virgins?'

'Please don't talk in riddles. Batashi is my wife.'

'Wife!? She's pretending to be one.'

Pitambar tried to cool both men down. 'Please stop. Dhanapati, you have created the rules of the island. You have said that this is a world of six months. Don't go back on your words!'

Dhanapati realized his mistake. It would be difficult to control the island if he broke the rules that he himself had set. Swallowing his words, Dhanapati spoke again. 'See . . . the island belongs to the men who go out to the sea and bring in fish. The women stay home. They are here because the men need them. They take up the status of their wives. But they are wives for just six months. There's no dearth of women in this world. How can we go against the government for them?'

'Why didn't the government think of women earlier?'

'Times have changed, Pitambar. We pirates look at women as commodities that we buy and sell in the market. You shouldn't give them too much importance or they will try to rule your life. You should keep them underneath your thumb or else they will create trouble. Mangal Midde, the trader, and Malakar have all returned empty-handed and are very upset. What if the government asks us to leave the island after the inquiry is over?'

'But the island is yours!'

'That is true. Right from the time of the Mughal Badshah and the Badshah of Gour, the island is mine from Ashwin to Falgun. Pedru's ship was anchored here, full of women and treasures. His soldiers would go to Ghoradal and other places on boats to loot them. They returned with their spoils that filled the hold of the ship. I can see everything clearly.'

'Why are you saying all this?'

'Tell your women that they will have to please whichever government they come across: Mangal Midde or even the other big and small officers.'

'How can that be possible?' Ganesh stood up.

'Quite possible. When you return to Ghoradal, what happens to your woman of the island? Take another woman as your wife. There are so many women available. Let the government take Batashi away.'

Ganesh seethed in anger. 'You have called us to say this?!'

'I am scared. If the government takes over the island, where will we go? Let us please the government by giving it the women we have. If you don't agree to this, then I will not push you, but remember that you have to keep women in control. They should not start dictating terms. This is what Pedru Dhanapati would say.'

Sixteen

Ashwin to Chait the black water rules,
Six months later, the south wind pulls.

The men looked grim and unhappy. Dhanapati had finished saying what he had to. Earlier, there was another rule; men used to enjoy women and throw them in the water, Dhanapati had said. No value was attached to them. That was the time of Pedru, Vasco and Gonzales. Much later, the island started this rule of a six-monthly family. That was started by the current Dhanapati. Chief Dhanapati. The men used to go to the water and come back lusting for women. They used to grab the women who used to come to work on the island. To stop this, Dhanapati started the family rule. This brought some order on to the island. He had to look after so many things. Now, if the government desired someone, it was his duty to send her. The government was supposedly above all else. A fisherman could have another wife. That would help to keep order on the island and keep the government happy at the same time.

'Will you do that yourself?' Ganesh asked Dhanapati.

'They don't even look at Dhanapati's wife. They dare not. That will spell doom on them. They will not be able to leave the island.'

Most fishermen were unhappy. Some traders seemed to agree. They started talking in low voices among themselves. 'We have to somehow keep our lives on the island intact; we depend on the income from these six months on the island.'

'We have to earn from the island. Otherwise why should we come here?'

'This is not a real family.'

'No, not at all!'

'If these women bring trouble to the island repeatedly, it won't be good for us!'

'I agree.'

'These women are nothing more than prostitutes.'

'Quiet! Don't talk loudly. We will have to take steps if our business gets ruined.'

The first trader spoke up. 'At Ghoradal itself, there are cinema halls that screen half-naked women. These halls are crowded all the time.'

'TV, newspapers . . . everyone is selling women's bodies!'

'Who doesn't know that?'

'Films are full of sex.'

One trader laughed. 'Pleasure for our senses,' he said.

'Isn't it natural for the government to seek such women who go as fishermen's wives on the island? Is the government a fool to not know that women can be judged by their faces and bosoms?'

As the traders continued their banter, the fishermen started murmuring among themselves. Clearly, Dhanapati's role had changed from the time when Mangal Midde and the trader were pushed out of the island. He was trying to change the rules that he himself had established. Dhanapati was, however, trying to say that there was no change. Didn't the fishermen change wives? Didn't women change husbands? Did Dhanapati have the same wife all the time? Ages ago, he had eloped with Anna Bibi. After that, so many six-monthly periods had passed on the island and so many wives had come and gone. So many Ashwins and Chaits had melted into the sea. The north wind had blown towards the south, and the south wind brought with it the starry sky of Ashwin. Pitambar's wife Jamuna was Dhanapati's mate once upon a time, in her youth. The fishermen looked confused and didn't know what to say. Pitambar Das cleared his throat and tried to mouth out a few words.

'This will only help to increase the demands of the likes of Mangal Midde and Malakar Babu.'

'What do you mean?' Dhanapati asked.

'If they are able to paw women so easily, they will come again and again, like the man-eaters from the jungles.'

'Yes, that's possible.'

'They used to come for money all this while. Now, they have started smelling the womenfolk too!'

'That was always there, you didn't know.'

'It's one thing to look and smell and quite another thing to snatch them away.'

'That was there too, you didn't know.'

'That's not possible. We would have known.' Ganesh sounded angry.

'How do you know what these women do when you are at sea?' Dhanapati said this and looked out at the dark sea. He helped to bring in that darkness on everyone around him. A chill descended on them from above. Dhanapati pulled his monkey cap onto his ears and wrapped himself tighter. The verandah suddenly lit up as his wife placed the lantern and went inside again, like a shadow. Everyone was surprised. They didn't know that Kunti was present inside the house. Why was she kept out of the meeting too? Perhaps because Dhanapati didn't want her to know that he had changed. Next, he might try to keep her underneath a burkha. Her presence would have made the evening beautiful. She would have spoken and made everyone laugh, driving new energy into them.

'I don't have anything more to say. I just needed to tell you that we should unite together to protect the island. The government might stop us from coming here. If that happens, I shall not stay here alone. I will simply get down into the water.' Dhanapati said that and looked at everyone in front of him.

'You said that when we go out to fish at sea, our women do things they aren't supposed to do. Is that true?' Ganesh asked.

'I am a descendant of Pedru Dhanapati. Why should I lie?'

'Is there any proof?'

'Why do you think the trader and Malakar want to sleep with her? They are used to it.'

The darkness around seemed to concentrate on Ganesh's face. He loved Batashi and considered her to be his wife. He wanted to take her to the village, get her a place to stay in and look after her. In the month of Ashwin, when he would return to the island, he would bring her with him. Dhanapati Sardar had hit where it hurt most. It was as if a cannon had landed from the pirate's ship into his fishing boat. He tried to protest, though the effort seemed to lack teeth.

'You are making this up. When we are at sea, our women don't even touch hair oil or soap.'

Dhanapati smiled a meaningful smile. He didn't laugh aloud but there were layers of meaning in his expression. He seemed to have said a thousand words without opening his mouth. Ganesh seemed totally deflated. Others seemed just as depressed. In all these years on the island, they had never faced such a crisis. Who knew so much was happening behind their backs! Ganesh held his head in despair.

From Ashwin to Chait, these six months took Ghoradal away from their minds. They forgot about their wives and families they had left behind at Ghoradal. That life seemed like a stagnant water body. No ripples could happen there anymore. There was no honey left in those hives. It was the turbulence of island life that gave them the will to spend those six months at Ghoradal. They spent the six months there counting down the seconds to escape to the island six months later, again. From Chait to Ashwin, the fishermen waited desperately for the endless sea, the horizon that beckoned, the limitless sky and the abyss of darkness. They could almost hear the schools of fish sending out bubbles and strained their eyes to see the pale yellow light of the stars. They yearned for the Ashwin full moon when the island and the sea got together to call them.

'You need to keep an eye on them,' Dhanapati said in a low voice.

'That's not possible when we are at sea.'

'That is why, in some countries, they make women wear burkha. So that other men do not lust after them,' Dhanapati advised.

'What are you saying, Dhanapati?' someone asked from the dark. 'First you said that we need to hide our wives. In another moment, you are saying we need to give them up to the government. This cannot happen!'

'I am only telling you the truth. If these women can have secret affairs here, why will they not go if the government calls them?'

The fishermen got up. The traders followed them. They had been silently supporting Dhanapati. They were not happy with what happened to trader Dasharath. These days, everything was openly done and that included the buying and selling of women. In some countries, they heard that men managed to earn for their families just by buying and selling women. Dasharath traded in women and there was no harm in accepting that. It was a trade like other trades. Why did the fishermen have to harass him? Who knew how much the government and police harassed him after that! Naturally, the fishermen and women would have to suffer for what they had done. What if they were driven out of the island? All trade on the island would come to an end. Sudhanya was a trader who held such views. He dealt in clothes—vests, sarees, salwar kameez, cheap woollens— and had brought in fresh stocks only a few days ago. He had heard it all at Ghoradal, but here, the story seemed different. The story of the traders differed from that of the fishermen. He had heard colourful stories about the island and that had brought him here. He knew that sleeping with the fish picking women here was easy. He travelled with his wares from one market to another, from one fair to another and knew that only capital-poor women sold their bodies.

Sudhanya quietly supported what Dhanapati had said. If someone came with money, he should be allowed to lay his hands on the woman of his choice. These women were not the wedded wives of the fishermen. They had been projected as wives, just to give a name to this temporary arrangement. Leaving such wives should not be difficult. It was in their own interest that the fishermen should give them up when needed so that the government was pleased and their claim on the island remained unchallenged. That was good for everyone.

'I find a lot of sense in what Dhanapati said so far,' Sudhanya said.

'Let us ask the women. They should be allowed to give their opinion. Why are we speaking on their behalf?' someone said from the dark.

'We are their owners, we can decide for them,' Sudhanya said.

Finding one supporter put Dhanapati at ease. 'This is exactly what I was saying. These women are my servitors. I am a descendant of Pedru. I can keep two hundred women as my slaves. But I don't do that nowadays. I expect them to follow my orders.'

'Then how will they be our wives?' Ganesh asked.

'They are mine first and then, yours. They are not your wives by law or religion, so they cannot be so choosy.'

'You didn't talk like this earlier!'

'I have no choice now. The government has gone back twice and is very angry. It is not good for us.'

'Didn't the government return like this earlier?' Sudhanya asked Dhanapati.

'Everything would happen peacefully and there would be no protest from anywhere. Even the fishermen know what I am saying.'

Some fishermen said they didn't know anything.

'You are trying to turn the island into a prostitute quarter.'

Dhanapati fell silent. 'Isn't the whole world like that?'

'What do you mean?'

'There are no rules anywhere. Anyone can do anything,' Dhanapati said.

'Make yourself clear.'

'Men and women, who's doing what, no one knows. There's no guarantee that your wife will stay only with you and cannot go with anyone else.'

'What if a woman doesn't agree?'

'They cannot disagree. They don't have a choice.'

'What if I say no?'

'You are no one to say no. You have to follow government's orders.'

'What if I decide not to follow?'

'It won't be good for you.'

In the midst of all this, Kunti came into the courtyard with a lantern in her hand, a veil covering her face. Ganesh stopped midway. Dhanapati could smell her presence. 'Why did you come here?' Dhanapati asked Kunti in a serious tone.

'You will catch a cold, master.'

'I will take care of that. Dhanapati's wife will not come out in the midst of men,' he ordered, without turning back to look at her.

'Can she go to the government?'

'No, she doesn't have to.'

'Then even our wives won't go to the government.'

'Dhanapati owns the island, the sky and the sea.'

'You are not saying the right thing, Dhanapati,' Ganesh stated, not hiding his anger and frustration.

'What do you mean?'

'Not you, it is the government who owns these.'

'The government knows that I own the island. There is no other government but me here. You have to obey me as the government. Dhanapati is the only master for this island.'

'Then the government should have no say on the matters of the island.'

'That is true. But at a little distance, Ghoradal onward, the government's rule starts. They come here as my guests and should not go away unhappy. If the government desires a woman, we have to give her to them.'

'Yes, the government has to be given what he wants. Master, come inside. If someone doesn't go to the government, someone else will go. If the government is left alone in the market, he will find someone of his choice.'

Dhanapati looked out into the dark and said, 'How do you know that?'

'I know. Government doesn't depend on anyone. He can only seek the help of the bigger government, no one else. Otherwise he can arrange for everything—money, women and anything that he needs.

Dhanapati sighed. 'You are right.'

'So, let me drop my veil, master? I am not quite used to it. I am feeling suffocated. I am Dhanapati's wife. Dhanapati is the master of the island and so am I, as his wife. Can I not be the government? Does a government need a veil?'

Seventeen

The Ghoradal breeze blows, Chait takes the man,
Love peters away, 'twas a six-month span.

The men carried Dhanapati's words to the women, almost like male birds carrying seeds to women who waited like the earth to receive them. Ganesh took Pitamber along with him.

Jamuna had finished her meeting and her hut was empty. She had lit up an oil lamp and sat there with Batashi. They had pulled rag-like wrappers around themselves to ward off the chill and looked like ghosts in the dark. The men sat down with their legs stretched out. 'Dhanapati's wife said government did not need veils,' Pitamber said.

'That is why she kept her veil on her face for some time and then threw it down. She was laughing then,' Ganesh added.

'Is Kunti a government that she threw her veil down?' Jamuna asked.

'Seems so.'

Jamuna laughed. 'She's a mad girl. Does she ever use the veil? None of us do in the daytime, for that matter. At night, the cold forces us to pull our veil over our heads.'

'Not just the head, the face too,' Ganesh said.

'What does that mean?'

'I am repeating what Dhanapati said.'

'What was the meeting all about?'

'Dhanapati wanted to tell us that he is also a government,' Ganesh said.

'Dhanapati is a government!' Jamuna laughed aloud, nudging Batashi. 'Say something, why are you quiet?'

Batashi looked out into the dark. She knew that the meeting that happened here and the one that her husband attended were all focused on her. She had nothing to say. But she also realized that she had to take a call, once and for all. There was no other way out.

'If the government had given orders that women would have to cover their faces with a burkha, it would have been another matter.'

'Why?!' Jamuna was surprised.

'Then they would not have identified the women here.'

'Not right,' Jamuna said. 'If the government wants, can a woman stay underneath her veil or burkha?'

'No, not possible. If the government wants, you have to give her up. He is the guest.'

'But the trader is not government,' Jamuna reasoned.

'But if the government asks on the trader's behalf, he has to be given the woman,' Pitamber said.

'Then the trader will bring the government with him now.'

'So Mangal Midde will get his commission and the trader will lift the veil to choose his woman, is that what was decided?' Jamuna's voice was sharp and shrill.

'You are quite right,' Pitamber said.

'What about the woman's opinion? Doesn't she have a say?'

'No, she doesn't.'

Jamuna looked sullen. She had feared this. It was a meeting to take a decision against women and hence they had been excluded. Why did their men accept such a decision? Weren't they their husbands? How could they accept such a proposal without protest? How could they come back with smiles on their lips? Wasn't there any value attached to this family that they set up together for six months? Did they have any status at all or were they still beggars?

'Will no one ask us for our opinion?' Batashi asked.

'It is finally the opinion of the government that matters,' Pitamber said.

'Will the government spell our doom? Don't we have the right to know what its plans are?' Batashi asked.

'The government is all powerful. We have no control over it,' Pitamber shook his head.

Jamuna was listening to them. She stared at the flame of the oil lamp intently, as if searching for answers there. 'Do these things happen at Ghoradal too?'

'Yes, possibly.'

'Does the government visit your wives there?'

'You cannot compare life on land with that on the island. Ghoradal, Firigitala, Firingnagar, Harinbari, Kakdwip, Nangkhana, Baruipur, Kolkata . . . there are hundreds of beauties in those places. How fair they are, what smooth skin. The government looks at them and forgets our wives.'

There was logic in what he said. 'The land area is endless. There are never-ending rail lines, leading to Delhi, Mumbai, Agra, etc. The government will get as many as it wants. But here, on this island, they have just Batashi, Kunti, Sabitri, Kandani . . .' Jamuna and Batashi felt very sad.

'Our families have no value, isn't it?' Batashi asked Jamuna sadly.

'Why should that be?' Ganesh asked.

'Our husbands are not real husbands,' Batashi continued in a low voice.

'Why are you saying all this?' Ganesh asked.

'A husband who gives up his wife to the government is no husband at all, that family is doomed!'

Ganesh had no answer. He couldn't deny what Batashi had said. It suddenly seemed that they were living with prostitutes, not wives. He could see Batashi's face in the light of the oil lamp. The yellow light lit up her face and reminded him of the starlit water of the sea. Tears drenched her face.

'We haven't said yes to the suggestion. Why should we obey such a proposal? We are seamen, why should we listen to the government?'

'Have you said no?' Jamuna asked.

'We have neither said yes nor no,' Pitamber replied.

'Staying silent means saying yes,' Jamuna asserted. 'I don't know whether they are government or not, but Mangal Midde and Malakar are devils. So, I asked Batashi to serve Malakar. We are women of the island; we have to compromise a bit. There is no alternative.'

'Then let that be!' Ganesh sounded angry.

'No, it's not that easy. My youth is almost over now. I was Dhanapati's wife once upon a time. He then chose someone else. This husband of mine accepted me and made me happy. Dhanapati does not treat his wives well. After he is satisfied, he asks women to get down from the bed. He was foul-mouthed. I was scared of him.'

'Let's not discuss all that,' Pitamber said, speaking from the dark corner where he sat.

'Why did you push my wife towards Malakar?' Ganesh asked.

'I tried to save her from the inquiry. Malakar came to complete the inquiry.'

'She tried to escape from the two and locked them in and you were pushing her to another government. Batashi would have lost her chastity.'

'Don't talk about that now. Can one woman save another's chastity? The six months that we live on land outside the island is literally hell. So many take us randomly, without reason. Even the old women are not spared.'

'At that time, you are nobody's wife,' Ganesh reasoned.

'Can we forget that wretched life? The government is even more powerful on land,' Batashi said in a low voice. 'Every second man is a government. Even the one who steals from the wagons is a government. He has been asked by the government to do so.' Batashi was choked with tears. She remembered how four government men took her one after the other one night when she was on land away from the island. She had bled profusely. The thought of that night gave her gooseflesh. Jamuna cleared her throat, as if asking Batashi to carry on. When Batashi did not speak up, she said, 'Batashi rejected

the man and spat on him. Malakar had to return empty-handed.
I couldn't reason with her into going with Malakar.'

'So, what will happen now?' Ganesh asked.

'When the government comes for inquiry, Batashi will not
go there. She will stay indoors in her house.' Jamuna breathed in
slowly. She felt happy after saying that. Batashi had done a daring
act. There was no denying that. Ganesh was her food provider but
did that make him her husband? Theirs was not a marriage around
the fire with mantras recited by the priest. But still, Batashi thought
that this one was real. Jamuna did not realize that in the beginning.
She thought that even if she had a family, she should make herself
available for the government, if she was wanted. Jamuna thought that
although Batashi sought her advice and tried to ward off the trader
with her fishy smell, she would have to give in finally. She had seen
Batashi fight the trader and Malakar. Now no government would be
able to take her easily.

'I will not go to anyone else. My husband is at sea. If I sin, he will
not be spared,' Batashi said.

'I have never had your kind of belief, Batashi.'

'I have started hating men, Jamuna Di. Except for my husband,
everyone else is evil.'

'How can you say that?'

'Let's not listen to what Dhanapati said,' Ganesh said.

'No, you shouldn't. Look at how he has changed his colours!
Dhanapati's veil has fallen off,' Jamuna was angry.

Pitambar Das lit his bidi. He released smoke gradually. 'He was
an all-new Dhanapati today.'

'True,' Ganesh said.

'Only a few days ago, it was this very Dhanapati who had packed
off Mangal Midde and the trader,' Pitamber said.

'He's a changed man today,' Ganesh insisted.

'The old tortoise,' Jamuna cursed.

'Dhanapati treated us as his subjects all these years. He thought
about the welfare of the island. But today, the way he spoke made
him look like a changed man.'

'He had set the rules. Today, he is talking about breaking those rules. He is talking about veiling women and that no one can refuse the government. We will oppose Dhanapati this time. Why should we allow our women to go and serve other men? Our women will stay at home,' Ganesh declared.

Ganesh and Batashi stood up, preparing to leave. They walked back home in the dark. Batashi took his hand.

'Batashi, Dhanapati will never realize why you love your family,' Jamuna said, addressing the dark.

'Even our men don't understand. One man is always better than seven. They will never know our pain,' Batashi replied from the dark.

'If I decide to breach my own chastity and sleep with many men, it is something I should be doing by choice. No one can force me to sleep with an outsider,' Jamuna said. 'Dhanapati was wrong.'

They walked silently in the dark. No one spoke. They had spoken enough on the matter. Ganesh reached their house and lit the torch. 'Hope no tiger lurks here.'

Batashi was quiet.

'What will you do for the next six months, Batashi? I have to make some arrangements for you, near Ghoradal.'

'You will forget me.'

'I won't.'

Batashi tried to sit down on the mattress made with leaves on her verandah but found that they were drenched with dew. She had forgotten to keep it inside the room before she left. She started folding up the mattress.

'Let Chait come. I will see if you remember then, master.'

'I will remember.'

'It's always forgotten.'

'Why so?'

'It's all in the air. The north wind blows and pushes men to the island and the south wind pushes them back to Ghoradal. You will forget when the south wind blows.'

Ganesh remained quiet. She was right. He has forgotten his family that he has left at Ghoradal. Once Chait comes, that family beckons, that home pulls. Batashi and their island home seem suffocating.

'Jamuna Di and I will stay back on the island.'

'What! What will you eat?'

'If all of us stay back, we will be able to survive.'

'The sea will be rough then and you will find it difficult to move out of here.'

'I know. But still, we will have to do something.'

'Let Dhanapati decide. After all, this island is his.'

'I will not go back to Ghoradal. The trader, the constable and government will kill me. They will skin me alive. I had another master, the umbrella seller from Bagerhat. I don't know what has happened to him. I cannot leave the island. This is the safest place for me. Let us stay back. In those six months, just come back twice to see me. Don't forget me, master. I too am your wife. When you are at sea, I don't touch soap or oil. I don't wear washed clothes.' She wept helplessly in the dark.

Eighteen

Like your prawn and myriad fish,
I've known you, like every dish.

'I've known you, master, for seven lives. How will you pull a veil over my face?'

In the evenings, Dhanapati felt drowsy. He sat on the mat with his legs stretched out. Kunti had wrapped him to the toe and covered his head with a monkey cap. She sat by him and stroked his chest, reaching him from underneath the blanket. She could almost hear his old heart throb non-stop.

'You confused everyone, Kunti. You have to remember that you are my wife and have to protect my interests above everything else. Why did you drop your veil?'

'I just felt like it.'

'You could have done that later. While we were talking you should have kept your face covered, as I had already instructed. You must listen to what the government tells you.'

'Why should the government want to keep me underneath a veil?'

'To take control of women.'

'How can women be controlled by just veiling them?'

Dhanapati reached out and caught hold of Kunti's hand underneath the blanket. He dragged it to the cusp of his thighs. 'Keep it here. This is part of your duty as a wife.'

Kunti started laughing suddenly. 'It's as still as a dead fish now, your youth is gone.'

'It will return.'

'That's not possible, master,' Kunti murmured. 'The cuckoo cannot speak.'

'It does. You just have to teach him. Nothing is permanently lost. The sun sets to rise again and so does the moon that dips in the horizon across the water of Kalnagini. The moon keeps losing its vigour after the full moon disappears on the new moon, only to come slowly back again.'

'Can you compare them with humans?'

'I am not a human,' Dhanapati said.

'Then what are you?' Kunti whispered.

'I am the descendant of Pedru pirate. He wasn't human.'

'Then what was he?'

'He was a devil.'

'That I agree with. Else he wouldn't have filled up the hold of his ship with women and slaves. I have heard that story from you, master.'

'He was a devil and not a human. A devil who challenged Christ and everything holy. Even the gods above feared him.'

Kunti listened and tried to understand.

'Even the devil cannot escape the rule of God and Allah and is punished by him.'

'You won't understand this so easily, Kunti. Pedru would have thrown you into the deep water by now. He had no emotion for anyone.'

'You can take me to the deep and throw me in too. Who's stopping you?' Kunti sulked.

'No. I am the seventh in line from that first pirate, Pedru. In all these years, that devilry has been wiped out of me.'

'Master, I cannot understand most of what you say. You must make things easy for me, since I am your wife.'

'What is it that you understand?'

'You should know that you are my master!' Kunti laughed again.

Dhanapati took his hand out of the blanket to reach Kunti's face and said, 'I too don't understand you completely, Kunti.'

'What is so difficult?'

'I am your master. You have to say things that I understand, my darling.'

Kunti stared in the dark, not batting an eyelid. She seemed still like the dark water. The pale light from the lantern made the stone from her nose pin shine. Her cheeks seemed fuller. This old man was ancient! He was a thousand-year-old sea tortoise whose body touched hers. He touched her breasts but didn't hurt her. Was he wading through the water?

'Kunti, I cannot throw you into the water like pirate Pedru. I have started loving you. Your eyes, the way they stare helplessly, make me tender.'

'It is the same with me. You are one and so many!' Kunti said this while still staring out and not turning to look at Dhanapati. 'I feel tender towards you. You are a descendant of devil Pedru; you are the tortoise chief and you are the government and talk like one. You want to be the government but you have become old, master.'

'No!' Dhanapati shouted. Underneath the blanket, his member throbbed like the mouth of the tortoise. Kunti removed her hand. Her glass bangles jingled as she brought it out of the blanket and laid it across Dhanapati's chest. He moved a bit.

'Instead of allowing the government to take the island away, isn't it better to become one, Kunti? Mangal will not leave us so easily. He is arranging his army at Ghoṛadal so that they can come here and train their cannons on the island from the water.'

'Start preparing to counter that.'

'You cannot fight the government with an army of illiterate people.'

'Then what will happen?'

'You have to do what the government wants you to do. If he wants women, you have to give him that. If the government comes here and doesn't get the women he wants, is that good?'

'Why should women suffer?'

'Nothing, really! They have to do what the men want them to do.'

'Why did you ask me to veil my face?'

'Not just the veil. You have to use a burkha too.'

'Impossible! That will cover up everything!'

'That's what is needed. That way, women will understand that they cannot have any opinion. If men ask them to drop the burkha, they will. If men ask them to keep it on, they will have to do that. If men ask them to go to people like Malakar, they will have to obey that order too!'

'Master, even I am a woman!'

Dhanapati laughed. 'You are the government's wife, you are Pedru devil's descendant's wife. You are a devil's wife. Anyone who looks at you will be blinded instantly.'

Kunti breathed out slowly. Then she turned her face to look at the dark again. Dhanapati was moving underneath his blanket. The tortoise was waking up from his slumber. 'Take me inside the room, Kunti.'

'Why can't you go alone?'

'Stay by me.'

The blanket fell off and so did the lungi as the knot loosened. Dhanapati stood there naked. Kunti quickly pulled it above his waist and tightened the knot. 'Master! How can you be so careless!? What if there were people around at this time?'

'Who cares about that?'

'They would have seen your dead fish and known how old you have become.'

'You are a prawn seedling, too juicy.' Dhanapati laughed aloud and walked towards the room. He sat down on his chair. Kunti would feed him now. He was used to his wives serving him since the time he was a youth. His wives had always bathed and fed him. After all, he was the descendant of Pedru pirate. Towards the west, near Khejuri (or was it Talshari?) the ruins of Pedru's palace still existed. Dhanapati reminded everyone about it. In present day, the palace is a snake pit, only visited by men who loot women, enjoy them and kill them before leaving. Once upon a time, the palace had a harem where Pedru kept hundreds of women.

> Hundreds of women he had, hundreds of slave wives,
> Lived in that harem, sun-moon staring on their lives.

His slaves served him night and day. Dhanapati had just borrowed this bit of Pedru. All these years of living on the island, at Ghoradal and at Firingitala, had ripped Dhanapati of the devil's skin. He just kept one wife now. Couldn't he afford many slaves and wives? He was the government after all!

'Is the government like Pedru?'

'Pedru was a giant, he had hundreds of wives. The men were all eunuchs. Pedru had all of them castrated. Pedru ensured that they didn't have the strength to be with his wives. A ship, filled with spices, was travelling from Arabia to Moor . . .'

Kunti knew the story. She had no interest in Pedru. She just wanted to measure how big or cruel the government was. She was happy to know that Pedru the devil was stronger and more powerful than the government. She was not sure if she was scared. She couldn't sum up Pedru and hence her summation of the government remained incomplete. She was not sure if Pedru was a real pirate or just a story. The first Dhanapati came seven generations ago. He was so cruel that the water around the island remained blood red all the time. He had once killed a ship full of women just on a whim. He enjoyed killing them.

'Please stop your story. You don't resemble Pedru at all. You cannot be that cruel.'

Dhanapati slurped at his big bowl of milk and puffed rice, flavoured with jaggery made out of date juice. 'I will start a new rule. All women will have to wear burkha on the island.'

'I will not.'

'I will not allow any woman to disobey me.'

'We will not follow your orders.'

'You will be forced to. The government and the traders come to the island and the women are making them go hot. They are not at fault.'

'Master, this is just not right.'

'Women cannot go into hiding.'

'Master, the women are here to struggle and earn some money. They start families for six months with the fishermen and help them in their work. Women work hard otherwise men will kick them out.'

'They can work wearing burkhas.'

'It is not possible. They have to tuck the loose end of their saree at their waists to carry the wicker basket on their head. To separate good fish from dead, they have to sit on their haunches with the saree picked up to the knee.'

'They will have to get used to it. I am the lord government of the island. My rule has to be obeyed if they want to avoid the jail or the noose.'

Kunti stayed quiet for a while. Dhanapati finished his bowl, drank some water and wiped his mouth with the loose end of Kunti's saree. 'Then no one will come to the island anymore, master.'

'Hunger will force them to don the burkha. They will even wear sacks then.' Dhanapati stood up with effort and walked up to the bed. He lifted his legs up. Kunti wrapped him with a blanket. The window was slightly open through which darkness from outside flowed in.

'Don't worry. I will not keep you underneath a burkha. How will I see your body otherwise?' Dhanapati laughed aloud now. 'Come now, sing a song.'

'Which song?'

'A lullaby.'

'Master, don't frame any rules. People are scared of such rules. They go on ordering you all the time about the dos and don'ts.'

'Don't worry. I know what is best for me. I am the owner of the island since the time of Pedru pirate. I cannot let the island go. This is where Pedru would kill and throw women into the blood red water . . .'

'Please stop, master. I feel giddy while listening to this tale.'

'I cannot let the island go. I will have to keep it. I will have to keep the government happy and give it all it wants. The government is to be worshipped by all. It cannot be questioned. Now, sing.'

Kunti was not sure if she wanted to sing. She was angry. She didn't want Dhanapati to start any new rule that would suffocate the women underneath burkhas. They would be able to take the burkha off only after dark, because darkness would then envelop them naturally. It would be such a suffering. 'I won't sing,' Kunti said.

'Why?'

'You will first have to forget this order.'

'No problem. I will listen to the radio but I will make sure that I implement this rule. Next, I will stop women from singing on the island.'

'You have lost your head, master.'

'You have to keep women under your thumb to make them serve you.' Dhanapati lay on his back on the bed and closed his eyes. He fell asleep instantly. His head tilted on one side. Kunti looked at the old man as went into a deep sleep. The she started humming, almost by habit.

> Dhanapati, Dhanapati master of the world,
> In his sleep he lies there curled.
> Six months of days leave six months of night,
> Dhanapati doesn't have a partner, quite.
> Dhanapati, Dhanapati, let's go to the sea,
> No one else, just you and me.

Kunti hummed and the sleeping Dhanapati's breath kept the beat.

Nineteen

She's a happy fish, lively and gay,
Why should I cover myself, you hear her say.

'You will cover yourself in a burkha. It is a woman's duty; she has to do it.'

Kunti was awoken at the crack of dawn when she felt that Dhanapati was climbing on her almost like a tortoise, his face coming out of his shell. He enjoyed her warmth. 'Your wish and mine will both be fulfilled. The rule will be for all the other young women of the island. They will all have to cover themselves up in burkhas.'

Kunti tried to breathe under his weight. Would no one be able to see her youthful body?

'No, not at all.'

'Master, youth is to be displayed to all. Why should one cover it?'

'No, it's to be covered for all except for the husbands. Otherwise other men become hot and create trouble.'

Kunti extricated herself from underneath the huge tortoise and lay him on his back. He looked like a turned turtle and stared at her. 'It's too hot to bear,' she said, while taking off her clothes and climbing on to Dhanapati almost with the agility of a swimmer.

Jamuna Di has a song,

> The youth is like a flower, the bud in bloom,
> Just as the island rises from the ocean's womb.

'Sing again,' Dhanapati said.

'You said you will not let anyone sing.'

'Yes, I will definitely implement that rule. Songs, laughter and all those coy ways in which women attract men will all be stopped. I have to save the island.'

'What if you aren't able to save the island? Where will you go?'

'My rules will save it.'

'People won't follow them.'

'I will not allow those who won't.'

'They will stay on the island but will not follow your rules.'

'That will not be allowed.'

'You will see for yourself, not a single woman will wear burkha.'

'They will be doomed.'

Kunti laughed aloud. 'I will wear it on their behalf. You are my man and I will wear the burkha in front of you. That will keep you safe and well.'

Dhanapati stared at Kunti, his eyes wide open and mouth gaping. He grabbed Kunti's hips as best as he could, but he just couldn't manage anything, lying on his back with the woman on top. He was used to pinning them down. Pedru pirate had said that women were to be held below all the time. When he said it and whom he said it to, the seventh descendant, Dhanapati did not know. He did not know Pedru's language either. He just knew that Pedru came to this pagan land of no religion and was able to enslave everyone. He crushed the men. The women with babies in their wombs ran away to the villages or the jungles. Dhanapati knew that many of the fishermen who came to the island had Pedru's blood in them. Pedru resided in him and that is why he got those flashes of anger from time to time.

'Why are you quiet, master?'

'You don't have to wear a burkha.'

'No, I will wear one.'

'Why?'

'To hide my body.'

'Wear it when you are outside the house, when you have to go to the market.'

'No, master. They all know me in the market. They know I am your wife and they dare not look up at me. But at home, you get excited looking at me, time and again. That is not good for your health.'

'That's not your lookout.'

'It certainly is. Once you were gasping for breath and I was helplessly searching for your tablets. I was so scared. I know my breasts and hips make you hot. My gold and jewel of a master, my only hope, it is my duty to keep you fit. You have to keep calm.'

'Get off my chest now.'

'Yes, yes, I will get off. I will wear a black burkha and strut about in front of you. You will neither see my face not my breasts or hips. You will not make out whether I am Kunti or Sabitri or Jamuna.'

'No.'

'The rule will come into force.'

'It will, but Dhanapati, the government of the island, is not part of that.'

'But how will the government stop his wife from wearing a burkha? Batashi Didi and I will both wear it.'

'No.'

'Yes. I have been thinking of so many ways to keep you calm like a mammoth tortoise. There are some like that in Kolkata. They must be as old as your Pedru foreigner, one of them might be Pedru himself!'

'No. He is in Lisboan.'

'Why so?'

'Pedru returned to his land, sowing his seeds in so many women's wombs. That's a long story.'

Kunti got off Dhanapati's chest. 'Tell me . . .' she said, stroking Dhanapati's chest. The winter night was about to end; the chill had thickened like wet sand. The water glistened with the light from the stars. The waves landed on the sand softly. They matched the breath of old Dhanapati, who lay still, matching the stillness of the wintery sea. But life ebbed and flowed in him. Dhanapati's huge body lay on his back and Kunti felt that he looked like a huge wave that had frozen on the sand. Sometimes he looked like the big sea itself, the dark sea. He breathed in and out slowly. Kunti moved her hand at the cusp of his thighs.

'Tell me what happened at Lisboan,' she said.

'That's my ancestral place,' Dhanapati said.

'Let's go there together.'

'How will we go there?'

'Following the route that he took to come here!'

'That would mean crossing so many seas.'

'I don't mind at all!'

'We will have to build a ship.'

'Yes, let's build one.'

'A ship with many sails.'

'Yes, white sails . . .' Kunti murmured.

'Like pigeons?'

'No, like the seagulls.'

'We need people to row the ship.'

'We'll take them.'

'What about the cannons and guns?'

'Yes, those too! But let's go to Lisboan.'

'Yes! We'll loot the traders on our way as we go to Lisboan.'

'Gold, jewels, clothes, sweets . . .' Kunti said.

'You will wear a gown.'

'I will wear a burkha.'

Dhanapati touched Kunti's chin. You will not need a burkha on the ship because there will be water all around us.'

'The water will see me.'

'So what?'

'It will pull me in.'

'Water doesn't do that. Is it a man?'

'The sea man . . . like the one you are!'

Dhanapati soaked in the warmth of the blanket. His manhood was gradually coming alive and felt heavy like a live fish. He took it within his two thighs and started breathing in deeply. Kunti brought up her hands to his chest again.

'I have explored the waters like no one else, but I never realized it,' he said.

'Women understand better.'

'Am I a real sea man?'

'Yes, you are . . . you feel like the sea to me.'

Life seemed to ebb out again and Dhanapati seemed to lay still.

'I have gone from sea to sea, from Arakan to Dianga where the Festa ruled. There was so much song and dance, and liquor flowed throughout.'

'Where is Dianga, my master?'

'In the Arakan Sea. That seems to be so many years ago, I cannot remember everything clearly now. There was another island near Dianga called Patanga and then you had to sail on to Sandip. Do you know what Sandip is?'

'Must be an island?'

'Yes, from there one goes to Sabaspur, then to Sogol Island, which is filled with gold and jewels. The pirates kept their treasures hidden at Sogol Island. I can still smell the lemons of Sabaspur. I didn't realize in all these years that I am the real sea man, the one and only. While sailing on the water day and night, I would sometimes feel scared of the dark, with only the light of the stars on the water, when there would be no moon. The water would be a pale yellow and there was no horizon to look at. It felt as if I would row myself to death and never reach the shore or the islands. It felt as if I would never reach Lisboan, Ghoradal, this island, Sandip or Sabaspur.'

'Who taught you about Lisboan?'

'A pirate came sailing here.'

'When?'

'I cannot remember.'

'Who told you about the other islands?'

'Another pirate.'

'What was his name?'

Dhanapati pulled Kunti near his chest and said, 'Dhanapati, another Dhanapati.'

'Are you him?'

'Yes, I am. I am the one who went to Arakan and then came to Bengal. I had my wife from Lisboan with me at that time, Maria.'

'Was she a beauty?'

'She was like the sea at high tide, just like you.'

'Am I beautiful, master?'

'Dhanapati only chooses beautiful women. I had looted Maria from Lisboan; she was a foreigner.'

'Who told you all this?'

'A pirate.'

'Which pirate?'

Dhanapati smiled. Kunti saw that there was a tinge of sadness there. The flame of the lamp was about to die, it had to be refilled with kerosene. Dhanapati's shadow on the opposite wall looked like a huge wave. Kunti lifted her head from Dhanapati's chest. The pirate's eyes were blue and his hair was golden. He could make women pregnant by just looking at them.

'Where is the blue of your eyes, master?'

'At Lisboan.'

'Let us go to Lisboan and get back the blue of your eyes and the golden colour of your hair. You will get back your youth there. Whatever is lacking here, we will bring from there. Tell me what happened at Sabaspur. Where did you go next?'

'I just sailed on from one water to the next. There would be crocodiles on the banks and deep forests on both sides of the water, not a single hut anywhere.'

'What happened next?'

'The storm came.'

'What kind of a storm!?'

'How the wave surged . . . We were together on the island and hadn't noticed that the sea had vanished, taking the water with it. It was soon back like a violent column of water and carried Maria away.'

'The sea man! What happened next, master?'

'The pirate was swept away.'

'Then what happened?'

'The pirate was brought back to the island.'

'Thereafter?'

'This is that island.'

Kunti murmured, 'Dhanapati, Dhanapati, this island is his.'

'So many days and nights have crossed the island thereafter.'

'Is Maria your Anna Bibi?'

'Let's forget that.'

The first birds started chirping outside. It was dawn. 'Let's go to the big sea to reach Lisboan. You will see how endless the water is, from one sea to the next. After crossing so much water, I landed up at the island. I experienced a strange feeling. The island beckoned me to come and sleep there.'

'Let's go to the seaside, master.'

Kunti clothed him and stepped out into the early light of the day. Chill was stuck at every bough, every grain of sand and in the emptiness in between. 'It snows in Lisboan,' Dhanapati said.

'Who said?'

'I know. Snow covers the ground. Its colour is like the kans grass or like the flower of the almond tree.'

'Master, let's go there.'

'I want to, but who will I leave the island to? Who will take care of it as I go on this endless trip that takes a lifetime to complete? There will be so many days and nights and water columns and storms to cross before we reach Lisboan!' Dhanapati started walking ahead.

The island was silent. The blue of the early morning sky hung on the curtain of fog. 'Lisboan blue . . .' Kunti murmured.

'Yes, the blue of the big sea, the Atlantic.'

People were still asleep on the island. Dhanapati took Kunti's hand and started walking. 'If this is a journey of a lifetime, will we never come back to the island?'

'Exactly. One who goes from here to Lisboan never comes back just as one who comes from Lisboan cannot go back. Pedru and

Dhanapati can never go back. We can only sit by the sea and wait for the breeze that comes from Lisboan.'

'Can we search for breeze?'

'Yes! You can hear stifled cries in the breeze.'

'You mean sadness? There is sadness in the breeze?'

'Yes, the breeze from the west brings with it laments, cries and tears.'

'When does that breeze come in?'

'When the storm comes.'

They reached the shore. On the left, the fishing boats were lined up one after the other. Dhanapati could not make out whether they were ready to leave or whether they had just come in. Earlier, the fishermen would come to him, bringing news from the sea. This year they weren't doing that. Had the island changed after the incident with Mangal Midde and the trader?

'Master, if I journey a whole lifetime, will I really reach Lisboan?'

'The water in the sea is never-ending. One day, it will drown everything, Kunti.'

'What about your Lisboan?'

'Even the sky will drown one day, breaking the slumber of the great tortoise.'

'What will happen then?'

'Only Dhanapati will remain alive then. He will take a boat and sail towards Lisboan, with a crow, a pigeon, a tortoise, a snake, a sheep and a woman to keep him company.'

'Which woman?'

'One who knows no one else but her master.'

'What else will be there on the boat?'

'The boat will sail alone, with its sail reaching for the sky. The boat will move on and on, not stopping anywhere.'

'Let that be.'

The sun rose like a fiery red ball from the south-eastern side of the water. Dhanapati stared at it and remembered that this was the sun that his ancestors also saw at the beginning of each day. He was the seventh in that line. It was the same sun that the people at Lisboan

saw and so did the emperor of India. Tears flowed out of his old eyes.
He remembered his youthful days with Anna Bibi. How beautiful
she was. He kept staring at the red sun. The colour seemed to fade
but he kept his eyes on it. After a long while, he put his head down.
'It is dark, Kunti. Let's go home.'

'It is morning, master!'

'Take me home, it's dark.'

'Didn't you see the sun rise?'

'Yes, I have seen so many of them. They are still stuck to
my eyeball.'

'I think you need to splash some water in your eyes, master.'

'Have I lost my eyes? How will I see my Lisboan after waiting
for a lifetime?'

'Not at all, master.' Kunti led him away towards his house.
'My eyes have become weak and I cannot see well. No one knows
that. I thought the sun's rays will bring back my vision. My eyes were
born in Lisboan, the sun god is my Lisboan. I thought he would be
kind to me. But that is not to be, my girl!'

'I am your wife, master.'

'No one should know that I have lost the light of my eyes.'

'Rest assured, my master.'

Dhanapati grabbed Kunti after reaching his courtyard.
He touched her breasts, her hips and her waist and tried to measure
her with his hands.

'Will I never see Lisboan with my own eyes, Kunti?'

'You will, master, trust me. I will bring back your Lisboan to you.'

Dhanapati sat down on the verandah. The sun had climbed up
now. He liked the warmth.

Twenty

Bring back his youth, Lord Dhanapati arise,
The waters gush, as the waves reach the skies.

Days passed but the darkness of Dhanapati's eyes did not fade.
He hid himself indoors.

'Can you see, master?' Kunti asked.

'I see what others cannot.'

'What do you see with your eyes, master?'

'I see the fog; I see the world cloaked in a burkha.'

'I think you need to go to Ghoradal.'

'I will have to wait for Chait. I cannot go before that.'

'You need to see a doctor.'

'My eyes will get well on their own. They are Pedru's eyes,
Pirananda's eyes too.

'Who is Pirananda?'

'My father's father, another foreigner.'

'You have never spoken about him in the past.'

'All my forefathers' faces are brightly visible in my cloaked eyes.
Pirananda was Fernando, his father was Salvador, whose father was
Gama . . . they were all Dhanapatis ahead of me.'

It was afternoon now. The room was lit up by the afternoon
light. The window was shut and darkness hung around it. Dhanapati
was covered in a blanket and sat with his back to the wall.

'If the fishermen get to know about my eyes, I will lose control of
the island. This island is mine. It used to be known as Sogol Island.'

'I never heard that name, master.'

'You are a young girl, how will you know such old stories?'

'What do you mean?'

Dhanapati spoke in English now. 'What is your age?'

Kunti had never heard such language. She was dumbfounded.

'I cannot understand what you are saying.'

'You will. But tell me why this dark veil on my eyes is not lifting.'

'I will get you some herbs that will bring the light back to your eyes.'

'Who told you about those herbs?'

'No one.'

'Then how did you know?'

'I know rose water and kewra water are good for the eyes.'

'Who said that to you?'

'No one. I just know.'

'I knew that one day my eyes will become dark. It happens to all Dhanapatis. My grandfather Pirananda became blind. He forgot everything and walked out of home in search of Lisboan. He got lost and never came back.'

'What happened after that?'

'I don't know. Dhanapati turned his sightless eyes towards Kunti. She wanted to hear more and kept pestering him. She wanted to know about the pirates, the seven seas, Lisboan, Sabaspur and Sogol Island. Even after Dhanapati finished talking, she wanted more.

'Where did your Pedru Pirananda go?' Kunti asked.

'He got hold of a few sailors and set sail.'

'But he had lost his eyes and his head too!'

'Much remains in a Dhanapati, even when all is lost.'

'Like you?'

'I can see quite well.'

'Really?! Can you really see?!' Kunti bent over Dhanapati.

'No one should know that Dhanapati has no eyes. Get me dark glasses from the market.'

'Why one? I will get you two.'

'What will I do with two? One is enough for two eyes.'

'I will wear one.'

'Why should you?'

'Since you cannot see, I should not see too!'

'What nonsense! You are the owner of the island like me and you will collect taxes on my behalf. People will come to pay you. When I am gone, you will become Dhanapati.'

Kunti laughed. 'But that's impossible, master!'

'I will carry the island on my back and stay afloat at the bottom while you will rule on top. Keep track of the women on the island. If the government asks for a woman, give her up. Give them to the traders too. Tell the fishermen that this is the law of the island. Those who protest can leave the island for good.' Dhanapati started gasping for breath in excitement. 'We have owned the island for seven generations. My father, Pirananda's son, Salvador, gave me this island.'

Kunti thought she heard the name Salvador for the first time. She often got confused from one story to the next. 'Master, I will get you some holy clay from underneath the velvet apple tree where we worship the tortoise idol. That will cure your eyes.'

'If my eyes don't come back, I will have to depend on you. Get ready.'

'What will happen then?' Kunti asked almost by habit.

'You will have to consider yourself as Dhanapati then.'

'Can a woman be a Dhanapati?'

'Why not? Do you know Indira Gandhi?'

'Who is she?'

'She was the owner of India.'

'Where is India?'

'This is India. The sea, sky and land, everything. Just like the pirates have their Lisboan, we have our India.'

'Government?'

'That is also India. She was the government of all governments but would cover her head with her saree, always.'

Kunti was mesmerized. She wanted Dhanapati to go on. He was her husband. They behaved like man and wife. Whatever happened between man and wife happened between them too. Just a while ago, he had removed her saree and unbuttoned her blouse. It remained that way. He was her master. But sometimes, he seemed to her like an old grandfather, and entertained her with a sackful of stories. She loved those stories, those never-ending tales, like the waves of the sea.

'People would tremble at the name of Indira Gandhi.'

'Why? What would she do?'

'She owned the military, the government.'

'I don't have all that, why should they be scared of me?'

'You will be the owner of the island. You are a woman and have a lot of strength. You will do it. I will teach you everything. Your youth will be your weapon. The government will be scared of you. It will stand and talk to you from a distance. You are a witch, I know that. Otherwise how did you become the owner of the island in such a short time? My eyes are cloaked. How did that happen? Have you done something to my eyes, Kunti?'

'Oh my God! Why are you saying this, master?'

'You are the master now. You have done what no one else could do. You have taken away the island of the pirates for seven generations from me. My eyes are dark like a new moon night. I am floating in endless darkness. You have done this to me.'

'No, master, no.'

'It is true. You know witchcraft. You learnt it in Kamakhya. The great goddess, the source of all shakti, resides there. She has bestowed that power on you. Otherwise how can a slip of a girl mesmerize me and become the owner of my island? You will be able to control the government. Send out word that the woman whom the government wants has to leave with the government. Otherwise you will stop women from coming here. If you want to rule the island, you will have to do this.'

'You should give orders.'

'I will not give orders anymore. I will call people and say that my boat had capsized in the big sea, taking Maria Bibi along with it. That Maria Bibi has come back now as Kunti Bibi. It took her several lifetimes to cross the sea and come here via Kamakhya. She came walking for most of the distance and crossed Kalighat, the church at Baruipur, Ghutiari Sharief and so many other holy places en route. Maria Kunti has come back to me. I recognized her finally when she started talking about Lisboan to me. I have handed over the island to her and retired.'

Kunti stayed quiet. She listened intently to what Dhanapati had said and felt excited. What was he saying?! Was it true? This huge island with so many fishermen and their wives, so much money and accounting, so much trade and so many traders, from Agrahayan to Chait, would all be under her control? She would have to order Batashi, Sabitri and the other women to go with the government if he so desired! Dhanapati had said that Batashi did what she had to, but times had changed now. They will now have to obey not only the government but the traders brought by them too. She felt as powerful as the government. Batashi had trapped the government and sent him packing to Ghoradal but that couldn't be repeated. Dhanapati had realized his mistake.

In the present day, traders controlled the government. They were the ones who armed the police. They footed the cost of the guns and bombs. The fact that the government enjoyed itself and had a fat pay was courtesy the money that the traders gave to the government.

Kunti was surprised. She wouldn't have known the government had she not come to the island. She thought that the police had all the power. It could forcefully put anyone in prison or could beat anyone black and blue. She thought the country belonged to the police. Once, when she was residing beside the railway tracks at Taldih, people had stopped the train on its tracks. The police simply came and beat everyone up. So many people were injured. So many had their clothes torn to tatters. She was also caught but managed to pull herself free. Now, she realized that police was government. Malakar was also government. Government was everything. Those who didn't follow the government had to face inquiry.

'Master, I will not be able to handle so many things.'

'You will manage.'

'You be in front, I will help you from behind.'

'No, you take the lead. I have lost interest.'

'Why?'

'I have lost interest in the island.'

'What?! The island is yours!'

'I will give it to you and go to Lisboan.'

'No, no, master, don't say such a thing. Am I not youthful anymore?' Kunti embraced Dhanapati.

'You have the youth of the sea.'

'So why will you go to Lisboan?' Kunti removed her saree and brought out her supple breasts. She moved close to Dhanapati and pressed them on his eyes.

Dhanapati wrapped his arms around her. He felt that he was rising from the bottom of the ocean, like a huge tortoise or a whale or a submarine. 'I will be your slave, Kunti. Keep me alive. You are the new owner of the island.'

Kunti had bared herself in the light and dark of the room. Dhanapati stared her with his blank eyes. Kunti jumped on him, hissing in excitement.

'What use is my youth if I cannot arouse my master?!'

'Will you really arouse me?'

'I will. What am I a woman for?'

'I have never heard any woman talk like this,' Dhanapati murmured to himself. Then he pinned Kunti on her back on the bed. There were huge waves in the sea and a column of water rose up to the sky. The south wind raged and it sounded like the breath of a man and a woman becoming one.

Kunti writhed on the bed, beating it with both hands. 'You are aroused, master, your slumber is broken. You are my good master. You don't know how good you are! Why should you go to Lisboan? Who has told you about Lisboan? This island is your Lisboan. You and I will stay here and not return to Ghoradal even in Chait. This island is my country. We will rear a hundred babies together on this island.'

Dhanapati rubbed his mouth on Kunti's breasts. 'I have become blind, my wife. There cannot be a blind king or a blind pirate. The rule says that he will be thrown into the water. But am I blind? Can Dhanapati become blind?'

'You will see through my eyes.'

Dhanapati gradually became limp. Kunti too gave up. 'You couldn't do it, Kunti. But I will do it myself now.'

'When? How?' Tears rolled down Kunti's cheeks.

'The day you break my slumber . . .'

'Are you asleep, tortoise chief?'

'Yes, wake me up. You will do it, I know.'

Kunti laid out her bare body in the half-dark room. 'Open your eyes, master. You will wake up only if you look at me.'

'I will then prepare to set sail with your island on my back, my Maria Kunti. I will sail to Lisboan.'

Twenty-One

She's a witch who came here,
Turning the day dark with fear.

Old age turns one senile. One moment you say something and the next moment, you forget it. New things are said, old ones forgotten. It was difficult to make out which one was true and which was made up; which one might be true and which one a half-truth. All these years, one knew that Dhanapati was Pedru's descendant. Now Kunti got to know about Pirananda. She had never heard of him. No one on the island did. Kunti was filled with wonder. Dhanapati had seen so many foreigners, pirates, Burmese folks . . . he had crossed so many storms and seas to reach Ghoradal and then this island. He was a superhuman, Kunti thought.

He wasn't human, really. He was a giant tortoise who carried the island on his back. Kunti watched Dhanapati closely. He was in deep sleep, like the tortoise that slept for thousands and thousands of years underneath the water. It was not easy to break that slumber.

Kunti was now Dhanapati's permanent wife. Dhanapati had called the people of the island, wore dark glasses and announced this. He called Kunti his Maria Bibi who had been lost in the storm as the sea surged. She had come back as Kunti.

She was not just his wife of the island but that of Ghoradal too.

She was not his wife of six months but of twelve months too.

She was the next Dhanapati, he had announced. One Dhanapati lay at the bottom of the sea in deep sleep which was him. The next Dhanapati was Kunti. Someone asked if a woman could be Dhanapati. This had never happened in the past. Was Pedru or Pirananda a woman?

Kunti lifted a portion of the loose end of her saree to cover her head in such a way that her face remained uncovered but the veil was still in place. 'So, do you mean to say that a woman cannot be Dhanapati? she asked.

'Exactly. Why should we be ruled by a woman?' a fisherman asked.

One more spoke up. 'Why should we pay tax to a woman? How can the owner of the island be a woman?'

'Yes, why not?'

'This has never happened in the past.'

'You are wrong. Do you know about India's Dhanapati, Indira Gandhi?'

'We all know her.'

'She was murdered.'

'Bullets were sprayed on her.'

'Kunti will be like her. You must understand she is Maria Bibi reborn as Kunti. There is Pedru's blood in Kunti's veins. Who knows which blood flows in whose veins? Look at her face, you will be reminded of Pedru. Stop staring at her from now on. Keep your eyes to her feet. She is your mother. Respect her like Dhanapati.'

There was magic in Dhanapati's speech. They accepted what he had said and lay prostrate on the ground. In the end, Jamuna came to her and said, 'Do you really know magic?'

'Why?' Kunti was surprised.

'We too had been with Dhanapati. He would push us out of the bed after the job was done.'

'He cannot take it anymore. He wants to go back to Lisboan.'

'What is Lisboan?'

'That's the land of the foreign pirates. Have faith on me.'

Kunti lowered her head on Dhanapati's chest. The old man had fallen asleep. 'Get up master, it's getting late.'

Kunti's life has become restricted now. She could not move around with her head uncovered or could not sit anywhere she pleased like before. Dhanapati had barred her from doing that. She had to behave like the owner of the island now, like a proper Dhanapati Kunti.

Knowing well that it was not the right thing for her to do, she went to the seaside and sat there alone. It was quiet and the sea was placid. There were no waves. Soon, she grew tired of sitting there alone and came back home. Dhanapati was asleep. He had to be woken up. How would she arouse him? She had to get hold of powdered tiger ribs and honey, mix the two and give him the mixture. That would bring his youth back. Jamuna had said that. 'Get up, master. I shall bring you tiger ribs. That will arouse you.'

Dhanapati was lying on his back. He opened his eyes a little. 'Is it dark now, Kunti?'

'No. It's evening now.'

'My world is dark.'

'I will bring your youth back. Your eyes will also be back then.'

'That is not possible.'

'I have married you to bring it back.'

'Will you do magic?'

'I will, master.'

'Do you know how to cast a spell?'

'Haven't I cast a spell on you?' She lowered her mouth, rubbed it on his chest and murmured, 'I have brought the black magic of Kamrup-Kamakhya with me.'

'Is that true?' Dhanapati turned his blank eyes towards her.

'Yes, it is true, true, true. I swear by Pedru god.'

'He was a pirate, not God.'

'The god of the pirates built the island.'

'Who told you that?'

'You had said it.' She lifted Dhanapati up and made him sit. She helped him put on his dark glasses. After that, she helped him on his feet, tightened the lungi around his waist and wrapped him in a thick wrapper. Then, she kissed his cheeks.

'My master is so handsome. May God keep you safe from evil eyes.'

> The moonlit Kartik night comes to an end,
> Dhanapati master wakes on sleep's bend.

'Dhanapati protested. It's not Kartik now!'

'It's all in the mind.'

'How is that possible?'

'I can bring it back.'

Dhanapati touched her lightly. 'Then even my eyes will come back, Kunti.'

'But magic cannot make it permanent.'

Dhanapati sat on his chair. 'I will bring a doctor for you. How can I do that?'

'Send a message to Malakar.'

'Government Malakar?'

'Yes. He will call the doctor.'

'Let's go to Ghoradal instead.'

'No. I won't go to Ghoradal now, Kunti. It's of no use. I had seen a doctor in the months of Shravan Bhadra. They said it's no use. I have lost my eyes. There is no use bringing a doctor.'

Kunti smiled to herself. She knew her master could not see her. He could not make out that she was sad. 'The doctor doesn't know anything. I will get herbs from the forest. You stop worrying, master.'

'Just cast your spell on me and make me see everything now and then.'

'I will.'

'Show me now.'

'It's almost dark now.' She looked out at the distance across the sand. She had lied. It was still broad daylight; there was still time for the sun to set. The shadow of Dhanapati's house lay on the courtyard. The shadow of the mango and jackfruit trees merged with it.

'Is it dark now?'

'Yes.'

'Have the stars come into the sky?'

'They have.'

'Should I go inside?'

'You've just come out.'

'Cast your magic spell on me and make me see the sky.'

'It's so foggy now. You will see nothing.'

'Where's the chill of the night? It feels like day now.' Dhanapati took off his dark glasses and looked around suspiciously. Kunti's heart skipped a beat. She silently moved and came in front of Dhanapati. He moved his head from side to side. His eyes looked blank. All light had gone out of them, Kunti could make that out. Was it true or was Dhanapati deliberately trying to fool her? He was, after all, a descendant of the pirates and knew the art of trickery. She had heard so many stories in these two-and-a-half–three months. She thought she knew so much about him. She was no longer the Kunti who had come to the island for the first time. She was now the owner of the island. She was Dhanapati now. The old man put on his glasses. 'I think it's not dark yet,' he murmured to himself.

'That's my magic, master.'

'What kind of magic?'

'It's dark but you are seeing light. Do you hear the crickets chirp?'

'No, I don't feel that it is dark at all. What kind of a night is this?' Dhanapati brought his hand out of his wrapper and tried to touch and see whether it was really dark. 'I cannot feel the darkness, Kunti.'

'That's my magic. Otherwise why should it feel like day to you when it is actually dark.'

'Yes, it feels like daytime.' Dhanapati breathed deeply. He rolled his hands in the air, trying to create invisible waves. 'I didn't feel like this in the past.'

'What do you feel now?'

'I feel that it is not yet dark now.'

'How do you know that?'

'I can smell it, my goddess wife. You are a goddess, not just Dhanapati. You are Ma Kamala. You are Goddess Lakshmi who comes out of the depth of the ocean and sits on her lotus seat.'

'Tell me that story.'

'I will tell you, but tell me, is it dark now?'

'It is. Let's go in.'

'Why is it not cold then?'

'No, it is not cold.'

'Is it clouded, my goddess?'

'Who is the goddess?'

'You are. Goddess Lakshmi. I had seen you in the deep, Kunti! My boat was caught in the storm and the sail burst. The boat capsized.

'I am Maria,' Kunti said.

'You are Ma Kamala. Tell me if it is day or night?'

'I have kept the daylight on for you. When you woke up, it was dark and cold. I brought you out and magically converted the night into day. Can you not feel that?'

'Is that true?'

'Yes, it is true.' Kunti was surprised at her own story-building skills. She said whatever came to her mind. Everything seemed true. She had indeed cast her spell on Dhanapati. He accepted all that she said.

'Has the sun set, my goddess?'

'Yes.'

'Was it red just before it vanished?'

'Yes.'

'Three hours later, will the moon come out?'

'Yes. It's Krishna Panchami today.'

'No, it's Chaturthi now.'

'Could be. I lose track of time, easily.'

'You have to keep track of everything. Otherwise the tax that you collect will be looted, my Dhaneshwari, Dhanapati's wife! I will call everyone and say that you are goddess Lakshmi. I have brought you from the lotus forest.'

'I am not that, master.'

'Then where did I get you, Kunti?'

'I was sitting at the riverbank of Ghoradal. You were looking for a young maiden and finally selected me.

Dhanapati let out a sigh. 'You will do it. I had cast a magical spell and controlled the island all this while. You will continue to do that. I am Pedru's descendant and you are Goddess Lakshmi, Dhaneshwari Devi. Your words are magical. I know it is daytime now but you are trying to make me believe that it is dark. You are trying to say that the daylight is your doing.'

'Yes, master.'

'Tell me if you really know witchcraft.'

'Otherwise how could that beggar girl turn into Dhanapati?'

'Tell me more . . .'

'I have become the owner of the island by magic.'

'Pedru took control of the sea and the island. You have now taken control of the seas—big and small—and of the island,' Dhanapati said.

'So you agree that I know magic?'

'It's the magic of your youth.'

Kunti smiled and took Dhanapati's hand. 'Let's go in.'

'Why should I? It is not dark yet.'

'Let's go in, master. I am tired.'

'So am I, Kunti. I am aching to see your body but I am falling asleep.'

'You will see me. Just think of me.'

'You are Mother Lakshmi. I am imagining that.'

'Bless me with a hundred children. I need a roomful of babies.'

It was dark now and Kunti led Dhanapati inside. She put her arms around him as he told her the story of Goddess Lakshmi. He knew so much and could go on and on. One couldn't make out how much of it was true and how much he made up. Kunti had learnt to weave stories from him.

'She is Ma Kamala, the goddess of wealth. She sinks boats and then brings them out of the depths of the water. She sits on her lotus seat in the deep. It is her wealth that had attracted Pedru here. His was from a poor country.'

'Whose boat had sunk?'

'Pedru's.'

'What happened next?'

Pedru prostrated himself at the feet of the goddess. She took pity on him and brought out the boat from the floor of the sea, filled it with gold and jewels and gave it back to him. She also gave him the island.

'That is a new story.' Kunti realized that she too would have to tell such tales of the past. Otherwise the fishermen would never obey her and be at her feet.

Part III

One

Who became Dhaneshwari and why let me tell,
She listened to the story as the night fell.

It was dark. But that made no difference to Dhanapati's dark world. Kunti sat at the doorstep and looked up at the sky. It hung like a saucer on the world, rising from the sea. There was a screen of fog outside but that couldn't hide the stars above. Till the time the old man could see, he would identify the stars for her. He would show her the star in the north that used to guide him back from the sea. In the month of Agrahayan, the seven brother stars were not visible in the northern sky. In the month of Ashwin, the old master had shown her the seven stars and told her that they would go to sleep together to rise again from the west in the month of Falgun. Kunti hummed as she was reminded of the seven stars.

> Seven foreign brother stars, live in the sky,
> Dhanapati sits here looks up high.

'The seven brothers fall asleep, but the star above Ghoradal stays awake in the north, all the time without fail,' Dhanapati had said.

'Master, do you know all of them?' Kunti had asked.

'I know them by heart; which star lives in which part of the sky in which month and who sleeps when.'

'Look, master, I think I can spot one of the seven brothers in the sky.'

'They are so far away that sometimes you can see them and sometimes you cannot. I will teach you how to identify them and where to find them. Otherwise who will you live with on this island?'

'But you cannot see them anymore.'

'My mind's eye can see everything—the sky, the sea, the deep water and the soil of the island. Before I bequeath everything to you, Dhaneshwari, let me tell you the story of the Pedru pirate.'

'Does Pedru pirate live in the sky in Agrahayan?'

'Both in the sea and in the sky.'

'Is that possible? Can someone stay under water, holding the island on his back, and also live in the sky at the same time?'

'He said so, so there must be some truth in it.'

'What happened to Pedru pirate, master?' Kunti sat close to the old man. Sometimes, he felt like an old grandfather. While spinning his story, the old man would run his fingers over her, sometimes loosening her hair from a bun, sometimes feeling her cheeks and then taking his hands to her breasts. She couldn't make out whether it was the fond touch of a grandsire or that of a desirous husband. She felt lonely on the island. She was living with a pirate's descendant who had looted and brought her here.

'Listen, Dhaneshwari. I am a descendant of Pedru the pirate. He was one of the seven foreign pirates. He was the first Dhanapati and I am the last one. After this, the island will be ruled by a woman. This is what Pedru had foreseen too. You are that woman.'

Kunti lowered her forehead on Dhanapati's feet. 'This is a blessing, master. I will accept it gracefully. A beggar like me will be given a country to rule, this is unthinkable!'

'You will certainly get it all—the sky, the sea and the island.'

Kunti grasped his hand and pressed it on her chest. 'I have also given whatever is mine to serve you, master. Take me and continue your story about the pirates.'

Dhanapati closed his eyes. These days, whether he kept them open or shut, the world remained dark. Keeping his eyes closed while talking was an old habit. He had no idea that he would get someone like Kunti at the fag end of his life. He removed his hand from Kunti's bosom and tried to concentrate on what he was saying.

'He came from Lisboan, my girl, beyond the seven seas.'

'Still, tell me how far that is.'

'Very far. You have to cross seven big seas to get there. Pedru was a dangerous pirate. He was seven feet tall. Those who came from Lisboan or Ispahan were like that. The saline breeze of this country changed their looks and robbed them of their height.'

'What happened next, master?' Kunti bent down on Dhanapati.

'Upon reaching here, Pedru got lost in the lotus jungle and finally came face to face with a beautiful woman seated on a lotus.'

'The goddess on a lotus throne?'

'Yes! How did you know?'

'My grandmother told me, perhaps.'

'Good! So, you know now that I am always right. Pedru was an infamous pirate. I will leave this island, the sky with its stars and the deep sea to you. But you have to know these stories about Pedru and Mother Lakshmi, before you take over the reins as the ruler, as Dhaneshwari.'

'Please go on, master.'

'The pirate used to loot villagers. There were so many women in the hold of his ship. But the woman on the lotus was a beauty who could not be compared with anyone he had seen before. There was no one so beautiful at Lisboan.'

'Then?' Kunti held her breath.

'Looting was part of Pedru's daily activity. I too was like that in my youth. The island, sky and sea were all under my control. At least ten women took care of my needs. They massaged my body with oil and gave me drinks and food on time. I had the best meat that was available and they put me to sleep.'

'I can do all of this alone,' Kunti murmured.

'I know that and so I am giving it all to you. After Pedru saw the woman atop the lotus in the jungle, he was mesmerized. There were guns and bullets in the hold of the ship and cannons and ammunition. But his pirate's brain had been aroused at the sight of the woman. He had never seen a woman atop a lotus in all these years that he had been stomping the sea.'

'Please don't stop, carry on.'

'The ethereally beautiful woman carried a golden pot at her waist. She was beaming and her eyes shone with laughter. "Who are you, why do you look so startled?" the goddess asked. What else? Without realizing what he was doing, he attacked the lotus jungle with his cannons and ammunition. He wanted that woman at any cost. She would fetch him a good price in the market of Arakan. He wanted her golden pot too. That would give him enough money to buy a ship.'

'Goodness! How would he sell Goddess Lakshmi in the market?!'

'Yes, my Dhaneshwari! It was the full moon night of Ashwin, awash with moonlight. Everything was bright like daytime. The moon shone overhead. Pedru thought of selling the woman at Arakan and Rosangar. He also thought of gifting her to the Badshah of Arakan and seek his permission to be a pirate on his waters. Just then, a white owl circled overhead. Pedru didn't recognize the sign and shot at the night bird. The bullet misfired. An angry Pedru rushed into the jungle to catch the goddess. The sky was pitch dark and a storm surged. The Kojagori full moon, when the rest of the world welcomes Goddess Lakshmi home, suddenly disappeared. Pedru's ship capsized with all its women and riches. The big waves reached the sky. They lashed at Pedru in the lotus forest.'

'Thank God, master! I literally held my breath to get to hear the end of the story.'

'Since then, my Dhaneshwari, Pedru has been on this island like a beggar. The lotus jungle had disappeared to give way to wild grass. Snakes, tigers and crocodiles ruled the jungle. Pedru sat on his tree perch and wept for Lisboan, praying to Mother Mary.'

> His ship got lost, his treasures too,
> Goddess Kamala robbed all of pirate Pedru.

'His condition was worse than a beggar's. The pants that he wore became a rag and fell off.'

'Such a strong man became naked!'

'So what?' Dhanapati scolded her. He turned into a pauper and saw so many full moon and new moons pass. Several seasons passed by too. His tears brought Mother Mary down. She was herself a mother who lived in great pain. Her son had been nailed and crucified. She felt sad about Pedru's misery. But she knew that he had sinned and was thus suffering. She went to heaven and asked goddess Kamala what had happened.

> Tell me sister Kamala what has he done,
> He cries in misery, consoling him none.

After hearing the entire story from Kamala, Mother Mary came back to Pedru and scolded him severely for his heinous act. 'From now on, you will stay awake on Kojagori full moon night and worship her. Just as I am your Mother Mary, she is Mother Kamala. We are two sisters.'

> Mother Kamala, Mother Mary, sisters they are,
> One lives in plenty, the other weeps her scar.

Kunti was surprised. She had never heard of any lotus forest on the island.

'Mother Kamala was finally happy with Pedru and blessed him. She tilted her golden pot and out came the capsized ship and everything that he had looted, including the women. She gifted him this island and its sky, the water and its depths. Since then, Pedru was the owner of the island.'

The present Dhanapati was seventh from the first. The present Dhanapati would also be the last one.

> Come Kunti, in front of me,
> I am there but you don't see!

Show me your twin breasts, come close;
That won't help, your vision froze.

'I am confused, Dhaneshwari. I cannot make out when I could last see with my own eyes. Perhaps that was many years ago. Now, I don't see anything but endless dark. Several years ago, I saw you at the peak of your youth—your ripe, wood apple breasts, how appealing your face was, your cheeks and those full lips. Your thighs were like the insides of the peeled-off stem of a banana plant—pristine white. Your buttocks were like a perfectly shaped pot. When you would sit on the ground, I would see a boat on the water. When I was atop you, it felt like floating on a boat, Dhaneshwari. Where has my youth gone?'

Kunti cried. 'Your eyes were intact when you brought me to the island in Ashwin. You would identify the stars for me, the seven brother stars . . . Have you forgotten that?'

'I cannot believe it anymore, Dhaneshwari. It seems like a previous birth when I had light in my eyes. Let me feel you, come close.' Blind Dhanapati touched Kunti's breasts. He unbuttoned her blouse and examined them closely. 'They are still so beautiful. Your youth is intact, Kunti. The beauty that had mesmerized me many years ago and cast its spell on me.'

'It's all yours to take.'

'You youth is like the sky, the sea, the fish in it and the breeze . . . never ending. Your youth will be alive forever. I will leave everything I have to you. They all came out of the pot of Goddess Kamala. The gold pot of Goddess Lakshmi never empties out. Take as much as you can. Pedru had received his wealth from the goddess's pot. Today, I give it to you.'

'Master, I was a beggar.'

'You are Dhaneshwari now. Answer me.

Who does the island belong to now?
What was yours is now mine.

Who do the sky and the moon belong to?
All are mine that belonged to you.
Kalnagini, Kartal and Beula are whose?
All will be mine, if you choose.
Gomar, Bidya and Betana, don't forget those!
Those rivers are mine too, I'll keep them close.
What about the sea fish?
All are mine, if you wish.

Dhanapati stopped talking for some time. He breathed slowly.
He seemed relaxed now. 'You will get more, all that belonged to me,
movable and immovable—the winter chill, the north breeze, the date
juice and the jaggery made from it. All that is there on the island is
yours. You will receive all the tax. You are young. I know you will be
able to keep everything under control.'

Kunti felt like Dhaneshwari indeed. The master just had to call
the fishermen and tell them that she would rule the island from now
on. How wonderful would that be! Tears of joy welled up in her eyes.
She has come a long way.

The old order changed and Dhaneshwari came,
The sky, sea and land were hers to tame.
Goddess Kamala took over her land,
Pedru paid for his sins with his hand.
Hail Mother Kamala, sister to Mother Mary,
You've granted us all, like the boon giving fairy.

Two

The pirates and looters were of the same clan,
To catch women, they made their plan.

This was Ghoradal. The breeze from the island blew in here from Chaitra onwards. It was Ghoradal that sent chilly, wintry breeze to Pedru's Island the whole of winter. The island was known by many names—Pirates' Island and Pedru's Island were two such names of the island of Dhanapati. It was Ghoradal, atop which the pole star shone, that guided the fishermen of the island. The seven brother stars remained awake on top of the sky of Ghoradal all night long. It was Ghoradal that sent the government to the island. Government and traders. The police, the accountant and Dasharath, who bought and sold women, they all went from here.

There were no government officials on the island, they all came from Ghoradal. They went to the island countless times throughout winter. When the police returned, the tax collector, Malakar, went. After he came back, another went. Lathi in hand, the police went when no one else did. Sometimes traders, whom the government liked, went along with them. They looked at the moon and kept an account of time. In the size and shape of the moon, the traders saw women.

The women of the island were scared of the government from Ghoradal. They came to remind the people of the island that the sky, the moon, the planets, the seven brother stars, the pole star, the waters, the fish within and even the tortoise that carried the island on its back, everything belonged to the government. As soon as the government stepped out of his boat to come on the island, the

278

fisherwomen Batashi and Jamuna knew that they had gone under the control of the government, just like darkness takes control of the world after sunset.

There was no government on the island. Here, only Dhanapati ruled. He lived with his young wife, Dhaneshwari Kunti. All these years he collected tax and now, the island dwellers would have to pay the tax to Kunti.

> Hail, hail Kunti, Pedru's wife,
> She got the wealth that changed her life!

It was Ghoradal from where the fisherwomen went to the island. Ghoradal ruled the island from a distance. At least the accountant said so. Dhanapati listened to him quietly. After all, the tax collector was a government. When the government left, Dhanapati would say, 'We are under no one; we are free.'

The tax collector had said that the whole world was under the control of the government. Those whom the government did not recognize were considered foreigners.

> You come from another land, you are a foreigner,
> So says the government, do you follow, mariner?

The government could do anything. It could cage you like a bird. The tax collector had said that the government did not cage birds that belonged to the country, but they could always put foreign birds in cages. Birds in flight belonged to the government, just like the clouds, the floods, the storm and the rain. The sun and the stars were all under the government. Nothing could exist without it.

The tax collector of the BDO, Malakar, had said that the women of the island could all be jailed by the government. Everyone knew that.

'You have to understand how powerful the government is.' Constable Mangal Midde sat there. shaking his leg. He chuckled.

The government knew that the women here did not belong to Ghoradal. No one knew where they came from. It wasn't enough to just come to the island and set up home for six months without the permission of the police.

'You have to take permission from the District Magistrate (DM). Whether you will do business or whether you will set up home has to be decided by the DM. The DM has given the entire responsibility of the island to the BDO and the BDO has, in turn, given the responsibility to me.' Malakar tried to explain as best as he could.

'Will you get another promotion, Malakar Da?' the constable asked.

'I think so. I joined as a fan puller. When electricity came on, the fans rotated automatically. Today, I can even work on the computer. I am tax collector, *gumasta*, and assistant to the BDO.'

Mangal Midde let out a sigh. 'How the times have changed. Today, there's a market for women too. Trader Dasharath said so.'

'Where has the trader gone?'

'He's gone for some work. He told me that he would take Batashi to the market in Mumbai and sell her. She would fetch a high price. Apparently, each body part sells there for a price.'

Malakar shook his head. 'You two are good for nothing. How did you get trapped by the fisherwoman? You should have completed the job before coming out of the room! I would have done that.'

'No, no. It's a government service after all. I have to be careful.'

'Yes, no one should know and you should not leave any trace. But why do you fear? Are these women citizens of India?'

'What do you mean?' Mangal Midde was surprised.

'Who knows where they come from? Where do they stay the rest of the six months? Do they vote?'

'Where will they vote?'

'Do they have voters' cards?'

'I don't think they do.'

'Then why did you run out of her room? She is not a citizen at all!'

'Really!'

'I am raising this issue for the first time. I had completed my inquiry and written this clearly.'

'I have not written anything like that.'

'You have to write that they are Bangladeshis.'

'All of them!'

'Yes. They have no voters' cards. They speak in Bengali. I am Nabadwip Malakar, I will take my revenge. I will throw them out of the island.'

Midde kept quiet. He realized that, despite his intelligence, the women of the island had shown Malakar his place. He had returned hurt but had kept his anger alive. He had kept the matter secret, unlike their own incident which the whole island got to know.

'If they are Bangladeshis, they have to be pushed back. That's what the first officer said.'

'We will teach them a lesson before pushing them back.'

Mangal Midde kept quiet. He had been sitting with Malakar the whole evening. He just went on and on and on about teaching the people of the island a lesson. Do you think that Batashi is also a Bangladeshi?' he finally asked.

Malakar became alert. He wanted to sleep with Batashi but could not. That did not mean that he had lost his chance forever. Age was silently creeping up and took him in its grip. He told Midde that he would have done the job before coming out of the shanty, but would his manhood permit that? He was gradually losing his strength and had to come back with just an inquiry report. 'Where does Batashi come from?' Malakar asked, feigning ignorance.

'You don't know that yet?'

'I did not try to find out.'

'Not from Ghoradal, Namkhana, Kakdwip, Pathar, Sagar, nowhere . . .'

'Then what place does she belong to?'

'What if she is a Bangladeshi?' Midde asked.

'I don't think she could be traced to back there.'

'Then what will happen?'

'She is a floating woman. Such women do not have a village or a locality to call their own,' Malakar explained.

'I will send a report to the first officer and send her to the lockup.'

Malakar thought about this. If Batashi went to jail, would he benefit at all? There was no use trying to punish her like this. If she stayed on the island, there was some chance of getting her one day. There was always a possibility of a second chance. Sending her to jail meant giving her another chance to set up home, like she had done on the island. Malakar tried to mislead Midde.

There was no end to their conversation, though daylight had come to an end. Lights came on. There was no electricity on the island but generators were used. The light from the island lit up the route to Ghoradal till a little distance. The light was dim as if it was shy of the dark. Ghoradal was where Batashi and Jamuna's government belonged. The two governments sat at a tea stall, deep in conversation. The riverbank was a few steps away. The Kalnagini river moved like a serpent as she touched the island and moved towards the sea. The river was dark and the lamps on the boats shone like stars. The spots of light danced with the ripples on the water. They could hear the water softly splashing against the river bank and the boats. The tide was coming in, filling up the river again. This was the river bank from where Jamuna, Batashi and others sailed to Ghoradal. Dhanapati had found his Kunti here. Mangal Midde looked up at the sky. The island lay far to the south. It was impossible to find it in the dark of the night. The tortoise moved here and there with the island on its back during the night.

'Tell me, Nabadwip Da, how did that woman gather so much courage? She locked me up, a policeman!'

Dhanapati's wife Kunti had put him in place and sent him back red-faced. Nabadwip kept quiet. Thoughts of that day filled his mind. Mangal Midde too kept thinking of how to take revenge.

As the two governments sat together at Ghoradal to talk and plan, six leagues away, Jamuna and Batashi also got together to chat.

'Tell me about your parents, Batashi.'

'My mother did not know who my father was. She was called Panchi Bibi.'

Jamuna laughed. 'Does that mean government is your father?'

'I really don't know who my father is. The very word "government" scares me. Government will sell me.'

Jamuna did not reply. She knew what Batashi said was right. Earlier, Dhanapati was the owner of the island but now Kunti has taken over from him. She was a mad girl. Would she be able to save Batashi?

'What will happen to me, Jamuna Di?'

'The government is keeping an eye on you.'

'I am so scared.'

'Run away.'

'Where will I run to?' Batashi dug her nails in the ground and scooped sand out. The veil fell off her head. Dew drenched her rough and dry hair.

'Yes, I know . . . Where will you run? There's government everywhere.'

'Is there a place that has no government?'

'No, there is none.'

'What will happen then?'

'I think you should still try to run. People do.'

'Where do they go?'

'I don't know.'

'Perhaps they run away into the sea.'

'How long will you stay in the sea?'

'Isn't there any place for me, Jamuna Di? Will the government finally take me?'

Batashi cringed at the thought of captivity. At least for six months in a year, she was assured of food and a shelter above her head at the island. Just as people try to take control of an unclaimed island, the government was now trying to stake a claim on her. She was not being considered a fisherman's wife at all, but an unclaimed woman on whom anyone could stake a claim.

'If government is my father, why should the government want me?'

'That's the way men are,' Jamuna said.

'It is possible that a policeman or a tax collector may have slept with my mother when they were young.'

'Yes, possible. But snakes eat their own young, tigers too. That is why tigresses escape with their cubs.'

Batashi shivered in fear. Jamuna looked at the sky and the stars and thought that if the island, the water and the sky belonged to the government, the trader too belonged to the government. He was a favoured man. Even if the people of the island had sent the trader back, he was likely to return. He had invested money on her, so he would want his returns now.

'Look at Kunti, how lucky she is! She has become like the government now. The island, sea, fish and everything else is hers too,' Jamuna said.

'They belong to both government and to Kunti?'

'Yes, that's what it is. Actually, everything belongs to Ma Kamala. She gave it to Pedru pirate and from Pedru, the Dhanapatis got them generation after generation. Now, Kunti has got it from Dhanapati.'

'Then how can it belong to the government?' Batashi was intrigued.

'Government is the final owner. This is what Malakar the police and even my master say.'

'What I don't understand is that, on this island, there is no thana, no police, no BDO and no bolaro. Then how is the government there?'

'The government can be present even when it is absent,' Jamuna said. 'I am Pitambar Das's wife, but have I not slept with Malakar too? I did it because he is government and would stop me from coming to the island. I would be blocked at the ghat itself.'

Batashi sighed deeply. Her breath was hot. Some invisible power seemed to carry her hot breath to Malakar at the Ghoradal riverbank. 'The sky is clear but I feel a waft of hot breeze,' he told Midde.

'Perhaps it's because of the clouds,' Midde said.

'Then how can we see the stars?'

'The clouds are there, Malakar Da, whether we see them or not. Hot breeze is good, actually. Without it, the breeze from the island will not come to Ghoradal and they too will not leave the island and come back to Ghoradal,' Midde said.

'It's still some time before summer.'

'Once spring had ended in the month of Falgun itself and the fishermen had returned early without waiting for Chait. Do you remember that? That might happen this year too.'

'Why should that be?'

'If you pour water into a rat hole, they come out automatically. If the hot breeze comes early, they will leave the island faster than usual. We want it that way, don't we?'

'That's what we wish, but I doubt if that will happen in reality.'

'I will pray that it happens. The moment those women step on to Ghoradal, we will get hold of them. Then they will know what it is like to insult the police.'

Nabadwip thought about his limitations. Could he do what the police did? Perhaps it was his boss who could do what the police did. He tried to draw up a plan. He wanted revenge. He would impose a fine on them when they alighted at the ghat. He would snatch away all the money they would bring with them. He was sure that to save herself from the police, Batashi would seek his help. Standing at the ghat, Nabadwip waited for the strong winds of Chait to blow.

Three

Tell me government, how much you'll take,
Money comes later, there's a contract that we need to first make!

Two months later, the trader returned to Ghoradal. Mangal Midde thought that he had left for good. He could not repay the trader's two-and-a-half thousand rupees. Once you have taken money, it is very difficult to cough it up again. Later, he justified his act to himself. Never mind if she was a woman from the island, she was a woman after all and her youth was valuable. How can the price of her youth be just Rs 2500? He should have got much more than that! The trader should have at least offered ten thousand rupees.

So many well-built men came to Ghoradal from Bihar, Uttar Pradesh (UP) and Punjab to look for women to marry. Marriage brokers came from Kolkata too. They first paid twenty–twenty-five thousand rupees to poor farmers to buy their daughters before marrying and taking them away. No one got to know what happened to them after that. Did the girl ever come back to the island with a child in tow? It was true that Batashi had no parents and was literally a beggar, but that couldn't reduce her price to two-and-a-half thousand rupees! She had government Mangal Midde as her guardian! Whoever did not have a family had the government as their guardian. Government owned everything. Midde was, therefore, expecting to get at least Rs 7500 more. He had analysed the situation and come to this decision. The trader would take Batashi away from the island and Midde would have to provide security to him. Such a

big service couldn't be provided by just charging Rs 2500. He needed
at least five.

> You've given a pittance, give me the rest,
> Then take the girl, who you consider the best.

Mangal Midde spoke to the trader in a room at the Shanti Nivas
hotel. People came here as couples and rooms were available even at
hourly rates. Dasharath Singh was not one of them. He stayed here
every time he visited Ghoradal.

They sat facing each other. Mangal was not in his uniform and
looked quite shabby. But there was no mistaking those shrewd, sharp
eyes. A bottle of vodka, water, some peanuts, grams, onions and
chana chur sat on the table between them. Just a single sip brought
back memories of the island to Midde's mind. It had been the full
moon night of Kartik. Had this vodka been there, things would
have been so different! Mangal only wanted money. He was myopic
about money and did not see any further. Money begot money, and
money was Midde's only God. He would not have agreed below
ten thousand.

'Constable sahib, what happened?' The trader called out to
Midde, seeing him distracted.

'What will happen? You have offered a pittance.'

'What more should I offer for a woman of that category?'

'Is she any less than any other woman? She keeps the island alight!'

'No one knows where she is from. She has no parents nor any
family. There's hardly any price such women fetch,' the trader said,
filling up the glass.

'Why do you want her parents? Do you wish to take them along
with you?'

'No, but at least we would have known where she comes from,
what her background is.'

Midde understood what the trader was hinting at. Perhaps
the presence of parents made matters more complicated because

if their girl went missing, they could go to the police. Often, the police shooed them away and then they went to the TV channels which would broadcast the news everywhere. Then, they went to the Human Rights Commission. To avoid this, many sealed poor parents' mouths with money. Women who came to the island had no home or parents. Whether they were traded off to Mumbai or Bangkok or eaten by the crocodiles and tigers, no one would bother to find out.

'I will not accept such a small amount,' Midde said.

'Okay. I will make you happy.'

'How? I am only asking for a fair price! I am the government, how will you please me?' Midde sounded stern.

The trader was a shrewd man. He did not mistake that tone. Only once had he lost his balance at the island and cursed himself for it later. The saline breeze, the fishy smell of the island and the absence of fishermen had all combined together to make him horny beyond reason. Otherwise he would not have tried to take Batashi on the island itself. He would have arranged a passage for her from the island to one of the resorts at Diamond Harbour, Bishnupur, Amtala or some such place. After his work was done, he would have transported her to Kolkata and then to Howrah. From there, she would have been packed off to her destiny. 'You have got me wrong, Mr Constable. I run an international business but wanted to look for rustic women too. So, I went to the island. There's a global demand for women of that kind. Otherwise, there is no dearth of women anywhere.'

'What do you mean?'

'It means my business is big and is conducted from multiple centres.'

'What is your business?'

The trader took off his wrapper and threw it on the bed without folding it. He wore a yellow t-shirt that had two eyes printed on it. Mangal thought they looked like the eyes of a woman staring at him.

'I am into the biggest trade in this world. Have you ever been to Bangkok?'

'No, how will I?'

'Have you been to Singapore and Hong Kong?'

'No!' Mangal said and stretched out his hand with the glass for a refill. He hardly got a chance to taste foreign liquor and had to stay satisfied with local brew. The vodka seemed to have excited him. 'Why are you trying to impress me?' he asked.

'Have you seen fashion channels?'

'Where?'

'On TV!'

'I did, once. Half-naked women walked about. I am not interested in these things.'

'What are you interested in?'

'Money and only money.'

'To get money, you need to act! Just send women and see how much you can earn. This is the biggest business in the world.'

The constable's head started reeling with what the trader said. He dealt in women throughout the globe. How did the girls who walked half-naked on TV reach there? This man was saying that there was a growing demand for women from India, especially from Bengal, in these places! Could that be true? He said that these rustic women just needed to be polished up a bit and then their prices soared. The constable thought that he was just a middle-class man with no idea of such big things. He was to become an assistant sub-inspector next. He was interested only in small things like collecting bribes from marketplaces and sending them to his bosses while keeping a share for himself. Some of his bosses helped him in this. He waited for his bosses to tell him how much he could keep. He obeyed his seniors. The trader was showing him a world that was too big for a small fry like him to handle. Could he manage all of this?

'It is less risky to deal in women like those of the island and so I went there. I also wanted to entertain myself. Everything was moving according to my plan, but I did not succeed. I still want to put my plan into action,' the trader said in one breath.

'I think you should speak to the first officer,' Midde replied.

'I have spoken to everyone but the knot needs to be loosened at the ground level. The first officer won't go to the riverbank!'

'Do you think I will manage?'

'Certainly.' The trader tried to reassure the constable.

'Can you do this without Batashi?'

'But why?'

'I can speak to others and find out who is ready to leave.'

'No one will agree.'

'I will tell them that they will lead a comfortable life and will be seen on TV too.'

The trader laughed. 'Do you think being seen on TV matters to these starving women?'

'Get into a better contract with me first,' the constable said.

'We are big traders. I am the seventh generation.'

'Ok, what will happen next?' The constable spoke with a slur. The vodka was acting fast.

'Intoxicated so soon?'

'Give me the details of your trade. Never mind if I am drunk. It shouldn't matter.'

'This is original vodka from Russia. Do you know what kind of girls are in great demand in Russia?'

'How will I know?'

'They fetch the maximum price in dollars.'

'I am not aware.'

'If you start working with me, you too will earn in dollars.'

'American money?!' Mangal Midde's eyes bulged out in surprise.

'One dollar is equal to fifty rupees, do you know that?'

'Wonderful,' Midde said with a slur.

'It is safe to get paid in dollars. If you take rupees, you might get caught.

> Dollar you will earn as your payment,
> It's a lot of money, my dear government.

'Will I be able to use that money in the market?'

'Certainly! There's a lot of demand for dollars.'

'Will I be able to buy rice, oil and salt?'

'Dollar will soon become the only currency.'

'Hurrah! I am with you, trader!' Midde raised his hands above his head in excitement. 'I had always dreamt of American money.'

'I hope you will manage?'

'I must.'

'Hope you will not be scared of tigers.'

'Not at all.'

'You won't bat an eyelid?'

'Never.'

'Then, it's a contract.'

'Where is the contract? We haven't agreed upon any amount,' Midde said. He reached for the expensive cigarette packet and pulled out one. Even when he was drunk, there was no cheating him. 'First tell me how much of hard cash I will earn and then, I will think of entering into an agreement with you.'

'You will get paid for every woman.'

'How many do you need in a year or in six months?'

'As many as you can give.'

'You will take them all?'

'Yes. You will have to bring them out of the island. That's your responsibility.'

'You will not go to the island?'

'I don't need them. I have slept with half the tribe of Seychelles.'

'Who will choose?'

'Once you bring them here, I will choose.'

'No, that won't do. You will have to come to the island with me. I will take responsibility for you but you will have to exercise restraint.'

The trader smiled. Mangal Midde was completely drunk now. The trader looked like a huge figure who was sitting on a chair but his head has reached the ceiling, crossing the ceiling fan overhead. If he stood up, his head would break the ceiling, Midde thought.

'What will happen then?' he murmured.

'What has to happen will happen,' the trader said.

'What about those who don't get chosen?'

'Throw them in the water.'

'What about those who are past their prime?'

'Shoot them like they shoot old racehorses.'

'Is that possible?'

'There is no market for old hags. Don't you look for fresh vegetables and fruits? It is just like that.'

'Lots of fertilizers there.'

'That is possible here too. Small breasts can be pumped up with injections. Do you know that?'

'No, I don't.'

'We have been traders for seven generations now.'

'All this while, you dealt in women?'

'That was a side business then. If we had to plead with the Badshah, we had to offer women for his harem.'

'That must have been ages ago.'

'That is exactly what I was saying. You need women to please men everywhere. That's the universal rule, hence this business keeps flourishing. Their price never falls.'

'Then what will happen?'

'What has to happen will happen, constable!'

'What will you do?'

'I will only buy and sell.'

'But the island . . .'

'That comes much later. I have to talk to the higher authorities.'

'I will help you there. Enter into a contract with me.' Midde started laughing. He was pleased with his suggestion that the trader should buy the island and own all women there. He could choose at will.

'How much will you take?'

'How much will you give?'

'Do you want it in dollars?'

'Some in dollars and some in our local rupee notes.'

'Why do you need local money?'

'I will give it to Dhanapati. The old man has been looking after the island for years.'

The trader was swaying like the waves. 'He also has a wife.'

'Yes, he does.'

'There is a demand for very young girls in the eight-, ten- and twelve-year range.'

'Go to the island and take your pick.'

'Yes, I will. We have been in this business for generations. My forefathers used to pick and choose and sell.'

'Sell what?'

'Many things . . . clothes, sugar, rice and whatnot.'

'Women?'

'Why are you making me repeat what I have already told you? You are growing old and it is time to retire. Join me in my business and I will give you an agency. Without an agency, how will you do business with me?'

Four

The evil pirates go hand in hand,
Taking the government along, they head to the island.

Aniket Sen had first heard of Dhanapati's Island from a staff member called Nabadwip Malakar. It was in the middle of Shravan, when monsoon was at its peak. He had just joined the office. One evening, in the dim light of the kerosene lantern, the tall Malakar sat by him in the verandah of his quarters and explained the Ghoradal block to him. He was taking him through Firingitala, the tomb of the seven pirates, the ruins of the indigo planters' bungalow and the one that belonged to Tom Sahib, the banks of river Kalnagini and then came to a stop. He then took him on a boat to Dhanapati's Island. It was a stormy night and it rained torrentially with the angry sea occupying most of the island. There was no one in sight for as far as the eyes could see. Malakar brought in a lot of drama into his storytelling, making the description as graphic as possible. Aniket felt that he had reached the island. The darkness of the verandah, because of a power cut, coupled with the rain outside, made Aniket feel that he had actually stepped on to the island. He felt it shake underneath his feet. Malakar was telling him about the giant tortoise below the island. It had crossed the Atlantic and had now fallen asleep with the island on its back. It was still asleep. Nabadwip Malakar hummed, punctuating the story now and then.

Shravan-Bhadra go, here comes Ashwin,
Dhanapati's woman makes him grin.

'I have learnt these songs from a fisherwoman on the island, Jamuna Dasi,' Malakar smiled. Let me try one more.'

It's the Ashwin full moon, peace rules the night,
Dhanapati sleeps as the moon takes flight.

Aniket was filled with wonder. A giant tortoise slept with the island on its back! The tortoise was called Dhanapati. Malakar unpeeled the story gradually for Aniket. When it stormed and rained incessantly in monsoons and the sea raged, Dhanapati woke up from sleep. Aniket felt that he had entered an unreal world. Malakar had repeated the story exactly as he had heard from the fishermen.

Aniket wrote in his diary that night,

'I stepped onto the island. It was a monsoon night and rained heavily. It was pitch dark. It felt as if the island was sinking and I was being drifted away. The tortoise chief, Dhanapati, had woken up. Was this a floating island?'

Aniket had then fallen asleep. He dreamt of a huge boat. The sails were massive in size. It looked like a big sea bird. The sea seethed below while clouds took control of the sky. This dream stuck to his head as he went about his work at Ghoradal. He had to go to the island someday. Malakar went on tour to the island for three days and drew up a report for him.

'Sir, I have completed my inquiry.'

No one knew who had sent him to the island for what inquiry. BDO Aniket had got to know Malakar well over the past six months. He assumed responsibilities on his own without waiting for anyone to direct him. No one from the island had complained to the BDO about anything. Then why did Malakar go to the island?

'You are a young man. I should not be telling you this but the women there are young and have such amazing bodies!'

Aniket had found out a few things about Malakar and the constable on his own. Some news had come to him from the grapevine. The constable had also gone to the island on his own.

Malakar had told Aniket that there was a lot of money floating about on the island and the constable had gone there to collect *hafta* for his police station. The constable and a trader had got into trouble with a woman there.

Aniket was dribbling with the idea of going to the island. He was in a dilemma because he had heard that the constable had been roughed up on the island. His bosses had asked for a report. They inquired whether Aniket was aware about the fact that in winter, the island turned into a bazaar for the buying and selling of prostitutes. The impression they had was that the constable had been beaten up for trying to curb this trade. The police station would give its own report; the BDO had to give his. He had to also give a general status report of the island. How much of it was habitable, who the encroachers were, etc.

'Malakar Babu, I need to visit the island.'

'Why should you take that pain? I can go again and do an inquiry.'

'How many times will you go?'

'I love to go to the island.'

'What do you do there?'

'It's like an outing.'

'Is the allegation true? You have already told me that it is.'

'Much of it is true. These women live with the fishermen as their temporary wives. They keep changing their men every year. Rather, I should rather say that the men keep changing their women.'

'Should I return the same day?'

'Yes, you can. But why take the trouble of going at all! These days, even Dhanapati has grown old, though he has a very young wife.'

Aniket did not know why Malakar spoke the way he did. But who else would bring him information about the island? From being a man who would pull fans in the BDO office to a group C clerk, Malakar had come a long way. But no one had taught him how to talk properly. Everyone knew Malakar and he knew everyone too. He was perhaps the most resourceful person in the BDO office, even more than the BDO himself. He had risen from the level of a peon and so, he knew everything that lay documented in the files. He would locate the right file at the right time when others failed. He knew each *mouza* and all the residents of the block. He knew all the party leaders too.

'Old Dhanapati must be hundred to hundred and fifty years old. His wife is about sixteen or seventeen. Why should the sahibs from here go to the island? You should call them here.'

'You are mistaken, Malakar Babu.'

'I know, sir. There were so many big bosses for whom I brought supplies from the island. You are young and so you don't know all this. I have grown old here. Let the big bosses come; you will see how things work.'

'Let's stop this now. You talk too much, Malakar Babu.'

'Okay then, let me leave for now. But you should not go to the island, sir. The atmosphere is not good. The island teems with prostitutes, beggars and fishermen. I will get you an inquiry report and will write it the way you want. Earlier, they would pay to the BDO office too. Dhanapati is a good man. He knows that unless you pay to the government, it will not look after you.'

Aniket smiled. He knew that Malakar did not twist words. There were no hidden meanings. 'When did that hafta stop?'

'During the previous BDO, Manisha madam's time. She was so strict that you had to see her to believe that a woman could be that severe! It was tough to work under her.'

Manisha Chatterjee was the BDO before Aniket. She had recently quit and had joined a big newspaper as a journalist. She was a poet too. Aniket had met her the day she had gone to the district headquarters to collect her release letter. 'Go to Ghoradal and experience that strange world for yourself,' she had laughed.

Aniket decided to step into the strange world and meet Dhanapati. Otherwise he would have to wait till Chaitra. He said so to Malakar. He understood what his boss wanted to convey.

'Let us go in the morning and return in the evening. If you wish to stay back, you will have to spend the night at Dhanapati's house. It's not a good place at all. There are bad women all over.'

'First, let's go. We will think of how to return later.'

'Okay, sir. First, we can go so that you can see what the island is all about. I will go later and collect the tax. They call the money that they pay to the BDO office as tax. They know that they have to pay to the government. The old tortoise doesn't mind at all!'

'I am going there to investigate.'

'Both will happen together.'

'No, Malakar Babu. We will not collect tax. It will remain suspended now.'

Malakar reacted sharply. 'That cannot be, sir! That pirate cannot enjoy the island without paying tax. They used to pay to Emperor Akbar.'

'That was more than five hundred years ago.' Aniket could not help laughing.

'It's an old tradition, sir.'

'Who told you this?'

'Old Dhanapati, the tortoise. Akbar's minister had started the system of measuring land and imposing tax.'

Aniket was impressed. Malakar knew a few pertinent things. Though he did not know the name Todar Mal, what he knew was good enough! Malakar said that it was from Emperor Akbar that the pirates had got the right to stay on the island on lease against a tax.

'Who gave you such details?'

'Dhanapati did. He showed me the paper that had the signature of the Mughal emperor.'

'Really!?' Aniket was confused for a moment. Was Malakar making up a story yet again? Had Dhanapati really said all that? 'You said you had seen the paper, Malakar Babu?'

'Yes, brittle paper . . . it fell off if you touched it.'

'Is it still there?'

'I don't think so. It is five hundred years old!'

'But you said you saw it!'

'That was twenty-five to thirty years ago!'

'So, it is not there now.'

'No, it isn't. I think it was destroyed in the floods of 1978. During that time they were not on the island, but they still couldn't save it. So, sir, let me take you to the island and show you around.'

'But remember, no collection of any tax now.'

'That's up to you, sir! Am I dependent on the tax? There are so many avenues for such tax collection. I was just trying to say that the pirates have been paying tax since Badshah Akbar's time for using the land.'

'Let the land revenue department look into that and give them a receipt.'

'I don't know if the land revenue department collects tax, but I consider this a *nazrana* that they should be encouraged to pay. Dhanapati says that he had been instructed by his pirate ancestors to continue to pay tax. Earlier, the badshah would get the tax, now government gets it. We get it.'

'The Badshah in Delhi knew about this island?'

'He didn't have to know anything. He was happy receiving the tax from the pirates. How could they be allowed to rule the sea without paying for such a right? How could they be allowed to loot women without paying the badshah for use of such power? Sometimes even women were given as gifts to the badshah.'

Aniket was overcome by a strange feeling. Malakar now took him through the story of Pedru's shipwreck when he came face to face with Mother Kamala and how he spent his first days on the island before being rescued by a fisherman.'

'Who got the lease from the emperor?'

'Pedru got it. He got a lease for the river and the sea too. No other boat was allowed to float on these waters.'

Aniket mentally readied himself for a visit to the island as Malakar poured out the lore effortlessly. He had to prepare a report on whether the island was a free mixing zone and whether prostitution was a trade on the island. Malakar continued to tell him how Pedru and Dhanapati were related through generations. He also told him about how Dhanapati was one with the tortoise. He would die and become a tortoise. This was the natural progression of a cruel pirate who had tortured women. These women had cursed Pedru and turned him into a tortoise that floated with the island on its back.

'Were the pirates Portuguese?'

'Yes, sir. Dhanapati carries the same blood in his veins.'

'Who knows which blood runs in whose veins, Malakar Babu.'

'No, no, sir, we cannot compare ourselves with those pirates. You have to see it to believe Dhanapati's empire. He lives with a wife young enough to be his granddaughter. He has lost his eyes but not his desire. It is the pirate's blood that still gives him an erection.'

Aniket kept quiet. The more he spoke with Malakar, the more he got to see the man that lived inside him. He did not know about the Huns, Sakas, Pathans and Mughals, but that didn't affect his happiness. The pirates did not come empty-handed. They came with pineapples, custard apples, guavas, cashew nuts and so much more. They brought with them so many words that are now part of the Bengali dictionary. No other foreign race brought in so many new words to the language. Malakar would never know all this, Aniket thought.

'Let me leave now, sir. I will go to the island before our trip to inform them.'

'Why is that necessary?'

'The island lives in a time that existed five hundred years ago. There isn't a phone on the island even today. Even letters are not delivered. Perhaps we could use a dove or a pigeon to deliver the message, then?'

Aniket's mind was filled with images of a world that was still hidden from civilization.

Five

The horse trader came, he was the Ispahani,
The starving husband died, there was neither food nor money.

Nabadwip Malakar gave a patient ear to the constable and said, 'You won't be able to do it alone.'

'Why?'

'You are undisciplined and I cannot go against the law. You are not the only government here.'

'Did I ever say that?'

'My boss, the BDO sahib, will visit the island.'

'Why will he go there?'

'To complete the inquiry about why the police and the trader were trapped together. What had they done?'

Mangal Midde looked deflated. The BDO would visit the island. He had heard that the BDO was a bad man. The first officer of the police station said so. The BDO was the head government official of Ghoradal. He had to maintain his stature and so threw his weight around. Why should the head visit the island? Why should he investigate? What was there to investigate? That the constable had been roughed up with the trader should have been enough for the government to take a call. The BDO should have accepted what the police had said. Whenever there was trouble, only the police report was sought.

'Will he take a guard with him for the visit? I mean, do I have to go along with him?'

'No, he won't take a guard.'

'A visit without a guard?'

'You are the only guard here. If you go, you might land him in trouble.'

Midde looked sullen. That incident had descaled his rate in the market. But if that was the case, why did the trader who had his business in Hong Kong and Singapore try to rope him into his business? Why had he held a meeting over vodka?

'Today, he will make the final contract. After that, we will celebrate over a drink.' Midde got drunk the previous evening and slept on the trader's bed in the hotel room. 'Go with your boss, let me seal the deal with the trader,' Midde said.

'Don't get into the contract alone. After all, they are foreign traders!'

'No, no, he speaks in Bengali.'

'Naturally he will, because you do not understand English.'

'His name is Dasharath.'

'That is natural. Would you have spoken to him had his name been Clive or Pedru?'

'Then how can he be a foreigner?'

'He trades with foreign countries.'

'That's true.'

'These are Indian agents of foreigners.'

'That doesn't matter, really. He will pay me in dollars and that is all that matters. Whether he is Indian or not should not matter.'

'You are right. Colour doesn't matter. But will you manage?'

'You think I won't?'

'You might get trapped.'

'Rubbish.' Mangal was angry now.

'You did get into trouble.'

'That was the trader's fault, not mine.'

'He will get you into trouble again. Let me go to the island with my boss. Ask the trader to give me some money so that I can meet and talk to Batashi. I will help to bring her here, if he wants. We are already into Falgun and there's not much time left for them to pack up from the island. I will not do any inquiry during this visit.'

The two sat at a tea stall near the riverbank and chatted. Motor-fitted boats were coming in and leaving in quick succession. People landed and got busy to go about their work. Empty boats got filled up fast again. The motors spewed out dark fumes that spiraled upwards and spread out. Some crossed the riverbank to come inland while the rest headed towards Ghoradal. The huge banyan tree at the riverbank looked dusty and tired, but it did not fail to spread its shadow around, though there was no one to rest underneath at this hour. The riverbank was full of smells coming from spicy food being cooked at cheap hotels, some of which were sharp and tangy enough to make people cough. The smell of spices mixed with the smell of cheap cooking fat. Both took in that smell as they spoke.

'Even you won't manage,' Midde finally said.

'What will I not manage!' Malakar looked surprised. He was mentally devising a plan to take his boss to the island. He had been planning this but the visit hadn't happened yet. He was waiting for the winds of departure to set in. It brought the message to the fishermen and women to get prepared to pack up. That was the right time to go to the island. His boss would not find anything of interest on the island then. The people on the island would then prepare to torch their huts and leave. The BDO would not be able to investigate much. But that was still a month-and-half away. Towards the middle of Chaitra, the fishermen were reminded of their homes at Ghoradal. The BDO would not be able to reach any conclusion then since the year on the island would be over by then.

'Batashi is a tough nut,' Mangal said.

'It won't take time to soften her,' Malakar replied.

'If you are able to bring her, I will give you good money. Once here, I will take charge. It is much safer here.'

'Then arrange for that money,' Malakar said.

'Rupees or dollars?'

'You keep the dollars. Pay me in rupees because I will have to spend on the island. I will have to pay Dhanapati also.'

'Let me speak to the trader then.'

'Do that quickly. Now.'

'How can it be so fast? The trader will have to speak to you.'

'I am a government man and cannot deal with outsiders like this. If the BDO gets to know, he will take action against me.'

'But I keep talking to the trader.'

'You are the police and it is your job to deal with crooks.'

Midde seethed. 'He is part of a multinational company, not a miscreant.'

'I didn't say he is.' Malakar stretched out his hand. 'Give me a cigarette.'

'Wait, I will give you a foreign brand. The trader gave it to me. He is quite a generous man. Come with me to his hotel and I will introduce you to him. No one will know.'

'Why should I go? He needs me to get things done, not the other way round.'

'No. We need each other. Don't forget that he will pay in dollars—fifty times more valuable than our rupee. Can you imagine how much we will earn?'

'But he needs to come to me and request me.'

'Don't be so foolishly rigid. There is no dearth of women and he can pick up the likes of Batashi from anywhere. There are so many governments who are ready to enter into agreements with the trader.'

Nabadwip did not argue. He knew Midde was right. A man whose purse was fat with dollars did not have the compulsion to meet the likes of him. Let's go and see him then,' he said to Midde.

'Let him do the talking. You insist on an agreement.'

'Yes, that's right.'

'Ask for an advance.'

'Obviously! Otherwise why should I start work?' They started walking. This was common in Ghoradal. When officers came from the headquarters on tours and stayed at the bungalow, he supplied women to them. He was handsomely rewarded by the bosses. No one thought of transferring him out of Ghoradal. People knew his reach. He took women from Ghoradal to the resorts at Amtala for the bosses. Once, he had trapped a BDO by getting a maid to enter his rooms. Later, that BDO became his pet and did his bidding. Malakar was yet to fathom the current BDO. He had been here for the past six months but Malakar was unable to understand him. But now that he was eyeing the island, Malakar would keep an eye on him too.

When Midde and Malakar reached the hotel, Dasharath trader had just woken up. He was a late riser, Malakar understood that. This meant that he remained awake till very late.

'Namaskar, babu,' he told the trader.

'I know you,' Dasharath said in reply.

'How do you know me?'

'We have been trading for seven generations. My forefathers traded with Jagat Seth; before that my ancestors were into maritime trade and took ships to Arabian countries. Even before that, one of my ancestors who was into horse trading, moved across the length and breadth of the country with his horses. He had been extremely successful in his business and earned a lot.'

Malakar was fascinated. He had heard of this trader but had never seen him. 'I have never seen any horse trader, sir, but I have heard that horse trading happened at Ghoradal too.'

'Why only Ghoradal, it was popular at Mahishadal too. You must have heard about how my ancestors, the wealthy horse traders, captured one whole state!'

'No, I have forgotten,' Malakar replied.

'It's easy to forget. Not all can remember everything.'

'Yes, that must have been a long time ago,' Malakar smiled.

'It is easy to start varied businesses because it is easy to forget. One of my ancestors traded in jewels. There is no trade that we have not dabbled in. Kathmandu, Lhasa, Basra, we have been everywhere. The government has always been on our side. That makes it easy for both sides. We earn and give a share to the government. We have been in trades where there was no direct selling but we have earned well. Just by renting out boats and ships, we have earned so much! We took leases of the riverbank and earned from those. Just by arranging for boatmen or by bringing in grains from the villages and selling them in the market, we have earned a lot! These are old trades. Government too has sustained losses in these trades. Now, I am into a trade that only gives me very high returns. Tell me, what brings you here?'

'Sir, Malakar Babu is a man of the government and has immense contacts on the island. He will bring in supplies from the island,' Mangal said.

'Will he manage?'

'I think he will and that is why I have brought him to you,' Midde assured the trader.

'I want this to be done quickly. I cannot let go of my target. I have to get Batashi.'

'You will get her,' Malakar assured him.

'When?'

'Very soon. I speak better with a drink, sir. You will know my mind better then.'

Glasses were placed and a bottle of vodka sat beside them. 'You will get her. She is very clever; I will have to tackle that first.'

'That's the kind I want. She would walk the ramp, and give and take like an expert. When will you bring her?'

'Whenever you desire.'

'What if she doesn't come?'

'Sir, please don't forget that you have Malakar to do the job for you.'

'What if she lays a trap?'

'I will entrap her in return.'

'I get turned on the moment I think of her voluptuous body. Listen, I know her biodata. No one is sure whether she is a Hindu or a Muslim or whether she's an Indian or a Bangladeshi. She neither comes from a village nor a city and doesn't have a voters' card or a ration card. She herself doesn't know who she is. She just has that body that she calls hers. Such girls are ideal for my business. Tell me if you will really manage to bring her.'

'I will, sir,' Malakar said and emptied the glass to the dregs. I am a practised hand too. Though I work for the government,

I understand these extras well. I know that the government cannot run on its own till traders like you give. The government depends on traders for money. I had ancestors too. We amassed so much land just by collecting taxes. My great grandfather was a tax collector. People would run when they heard his name.'

'I know,' Dasharath Singh said.

'We used to lock up grains in the godown and starved people. Hope you remember that, sir.'

'The Ispahani Company was ours at one point in time. Hope you know that!'

'Why not?! We earned so much from it!'

'You got hundred rupees per head.'

'How many got killed?' Nabadwip Malakar asked.

'People roamed the streets looking for some starch from cooked rice. Dead bodies looking like skeletons lay strewn on the streets. Once in 1176 and then in 1350, I remember it all. People ate leaves but did not survive,' Dasharath said.

Mangal drank quietly all this while and had drunk up quite a bit. 'How true is all this?' he asked.

'Absolutely true! Don't you know that traders can do anything! They can create famines and throw grains at hungry mouths at the same time,' reminded the trader. 'The government will do what the trader wants.'

'Sir, my grandmother was saved, but her two daughters and husband died,' Mangal said.

'I would have sent rice had I known!' Malakar laughed.

'You are the government now, constable sahib. Grab and loot anything you can lay your hands on. Have fun. Want to go to Bangkok?'

'No, I need money.'

'You will get it. Just do my work. You have not done much all your life. Now that you have opened your door, leave it ajar. I will enter with my warriors on the chessboard and checkmate everyone.'

They kept talking. Mangal was drunk and went back to the episode of his grandmother and her daughters several times.

Nabadwip put his hands on Mangal's back and said, 'The Ispahani trader will be back with his horses again. You just have to be on his side.'

'Absolutely true. If you go against me, you will die. Bring me that woman. I cannot wait any longer. I will leave this evening and come back a fortnight later. I have already given you an advance. Do you need any more now?' the trader asked.

Nabadwip stretched out his hand. Mangal could not bring his hand out of his pocket. This happened to him at times. His hand swelled and fitted tightly between the gaps.

Six

Dhaneshwari Kunti asked, what's the message?
An inquiry again is the government's presage.

Nabadwip Malakar came to the island again. The north wind was almost dying, though the south wind was yet to start. The sun had moved slightly to the north which meant that when one followed the east-west route, the sun had inched towards Ghoradal. It was much hotter now. A few more days and, the fishermen would be reminded of their homes at Ghoradal. The women here were about to enter the dark half of the year again. At this juncture, Malakar came to Dhanapati's house and informed him that his boss would come for a visit to the island.

'You better tell Dhaneshwari Kunti about it,' Dhanapati said.

Malakar was surprised. Did she really know some magic? Did she really walk up from Kamrup-Kamakhya over three or perhaps seven life times? Was she really a witch? How did Dhanapati chief's island go to her? How could a woman rule the people here? What kind of a joke was this?

Kunti was decked up with vermilion that filled up the parting in her hair, shanka-pola on her two hands and a cross hanging around her neck. She came and sat by Dhanapati's chair. She didn't ask Malakar to sit. There was no chair in front of Dhanapati. The old man wore dark glasses. Malakar went inside the house and got himself a chair. Then, he lit a cigarette and tried to gain some confidence.

'So, what news have you brought?' Kunti asked.

'Quite a serious one. The BDO sahib is coming here.'

'Why is he coming?'

'For the inquiry.'

'But isn't that over?' Dhanapati asked.

'The matter is quite grave and cannot get over so soon. After all, government's men have been heckled! The government is looking at it very seriously.'

'Leave Batashi out of the inquiry,' Kunti said. Her voice was serious.

'What do you mean?'

'Batashi will not sleep with the government.'

'You leave that on me. She laid the trap for the tiger. Naturally, the tiger won't leave her so easily! Get me water and some sweets.'

'That will come,' Kunti said and then called out to someone. 'Buli's Ma, where are you? Give him some batasha and water. Make some tea too. He will have lunch and return in the evening.' Malakar realized that Kunti did not wish to let him stay at her house that evening. His days on the island would not be as beautiful as they used to be, Malakar rued. The island had changed now. But he was not to be defeated in this game. He had to look for Batashi and talk to her. Otherwise, there were many who could carry news of who was coming to the island from Ghoradal and at what time. The boatmen plying between the island and Ghoradal could do that easily. They carried goods for the traders and also messages about which sahib was due to arrive on which day. Malakar did not have to visit Ghoradal to carry news of the BDO's visit. That was just an excuse, actually. He had come with a different purpose altogether.

'I will not go back in the evening. I will stay till tomorrow afternoon.'

'What work do you have till then?' Kunti asked sharply.

Malakar felt uncomfortable. He wanted to sleep with this girl! She was not in the mood to spare him now. 'You took your share of money in your previous visit, isn't it?'

'Why should I visit the island only for money?!'

'Money and fisherwomen, these are the only two things that men from Ghoradal are interested in, isn't it?' Kunti asked.

Malakar laughed. 'I need to talk privately to Dhanapati. Unless you leave us alone, that won't be possible.'

'I am the chief now, so you will have to tell me.'

'Has he retired?'

'Yes, he has. Things are different now, Malakar Babu. You cannot be expecting money and women anytime you want, anymore.'

Dhanapati raised his hand to stop Kunti. 'He is a respected man, government. The head of the government will also come. You cannot talk to the government like that.'

Kunti dimmed. She adjusted her veil properly and sat down. Her face looked dark. Malakar had asked her to leave, but she decided not to. When two men spoke in private, it had to be about women. They would talk about Batashi and Sabitri. They would leave her out of this because she had become Dhaneshwari. Kunti sat there shaking her legs.

'We need to be alone.'

'No one is stopping you. But I am the master of the island now. So what if I am a woman? You cannot leave me out of any conversation.'

'No, it is just between him and me.' Malakar sounded irritated. He was used to striking deals with Dhanapati. How could he talk to this woman now? How could he tell her which woman the government was looking for? This seat was not meant for her. It seemed that Dhanapati's wife was behaving more powerfully than Dhanapati himself, like a dwarf reaching out for the moon.

'You leave for some time. Has Malakar Babu been served water and sweets?'

'Coming.'

'He is our government guest. We need to take care of him.'

'How many times can we serve him? If he has come for the inquiry, Batashi will not go.'

Malakar noticed that earlier, Kunti would call her Batashi Di. But now, it had come down to Batashi. He also realized that he would have to broach the topic in front of her. But why should he be bothered? The inquiry report that had gone to the superiors clearly indicated that it had become an island of prostitutes and they had to go to anyone who paid for them. They had no right to raise their voice at him! He was government. He could not be spoken to like that. This slip of a girl needed a tough man to control her and teach her a lesson. He softened his voice and said, 'So, chief, should I start?'

'Yes, please speak in front of her. She's the owner of the island now.'

'Why did you choose to leave? You are still strong!'

'Mother Mary instructed me.'

'What did Mother Mary say?'

'She asked me to give the charge of the island to her and wait.'

'Wait for what?'

'Ma Kamala and Ma Mary will come to take me.'

Malakar joined his palms in prayer to the two goddesses. 'But will this little girl be able to run the island? It's not easy!'

'I will be able to do it,' Kunti said.

'Will you not be scared to face the government?'

'No.'

'The big and the small governments will come.'

'I know.'

'Will the government get his due?'

'He will.'

'What will happen when the government comes for an inquiry?'

Kunti looked at Malakar squarely in the eye. 'There will be no inquiry.' She said this without batting an eyelid.

'Government will come for inquiry, whether you want it or not.'

'Money and inquiry will not happen together.'

'But that's the rule. Without money, inquiry will not be good.'

'Not a single woman will be part of your inquiry,' Kunti said, spacing out every word for effect.

'It is about women, how can we leave them out?'

'I have told you what I had to say.'

'Let me go back and report this. You will have to do what the government wants. Are you outside the purview of the government?'

Kunti's face turned even more sullen and dark. She got up and left. It was clear that she was angry. An old woman, who served them as a maid, came with water and country-made candies. 'She is Mother Mary and Ma Kamala's sister. Please talk to her with reverence.'

Malakar snubbed the woman. 'I know what to do. Please leave.'

'Please remember that the government is not the end of the world. God is there above all.'

When she left, Malakar turned towards Dhanapati. 'This island has become infested with prostitutes. The government will not like it. It will evacuate the island.'

'You know everything.'

'Do you trust me?'

'I do.'

'Will you do as I tell you?'

'I will.'

'Will your wife Kunti also do as I say?'

'She will, if I tell her.'

'Will she go against you?'

'No.'

'Look at me.'

Dhanapati turned his lightless eyes, shrouded behind the dark glasses, at Malakar. Everything appeared in different shades of dark to him.

'Can you see me?'

Dhanapati made a gesture with his head to mean assent.

'She has blinded you, Pedru's descendant.'

Dhanapati sat still and silent. For a second, he felt that Malakar was right. And then, he shrugged the thought off. Kunti loved him. She reminded him of Anna Bibi of his youth. So many women had come as his wives thereafter, but no one was like Anna Bibi or Kunti. Her kisses were hundred times more powerful. The thought of her body left him with goosebumps even at this age. When Kunti mounted him, it was a never-before experience. Kunti had promised to cure his blindness with a potion made of powdered tiger ribs. 'She loves me,' Dhanapati said aloud.

'Listen, Dhanapati, when the government comes to visit the island, it looks for women.'

'They get them.'

'Will the BDO also get when he comes?'

'You just name whom he wants and she will be his.'

'Batashi.'

'Why her? Aren't there any more women on the island?'

'Yes, there are many but the inquiry is about Batashi and the government will need her for it.'

'How long will this go on?'

'Till the file is settled.'

'You can arrange for that.'

'Yes, once the big sahib visits the island.'

'Let him come, the people of the island will give him the respect that is due to him.'

'There is one more thing that I wish to say. In Chait, when it is time to go and the huts are burnt, I will take Batashi with me.'

Dhanapati sighed. 'Yes, it's time to go.'

'Then, why should Batashi stay back? Ask her to come with me.'

'Now! It's not even the full moon of Dol!'

Malakar was excited. Dhanapati's tone indicated that when the time was up, he could take Batashi. 'But there's not much time left for people to vacate the island and it won't cause any harm if Batashi could look at the Dol full moon from Ghoradal! How long can the trader wait for one woman? After all, what is her worth? They live only to serve men! Let me take her. There isn't too much time left now. She can face the inquiry there,' Malakar said.

'Then why will the big sahib come here?'

'There will be inquiry both here and there. Even if Batashi is not here, sahib can question others on the island.'

'So Batashi won't be needed here?'

'Let me take Batashi for inquiry to Ghoradal. In her absence, there will be no inquiry on the island. That is the safest option for the island.'

Dhanapati weighed the options. Malakar was speaking the language of the law. He liked the idea. When the head government, the BDO sahib, would come for the inquiry, Batashi would not be there. Where had she gone? She had run away. If the criminal was not there, the inquiry wouldn't happen. At the most, the government could ban her from coming to the island the next year. She could change her name to Jyotsna, Purnima or anything else and re-enter the next time. Six months was a long time and made fishermen forget a lot. No one would contest Batashi if she changed her name.

'Let me take Batashi with me. Otherwise it will be very risky for the island. After all, she had roughed up the police.'

'Tell Kunti. We will do as she tells us.'

Kunti strode forward. 'No, she won't go.'

'Why?' Nabadwip faced her and asked.

'Why would she go?'

'She would face an inquiry on the other side.'

'No need for any inquiry. Women are not cheap.'

'She should have realized that before attacking the police and the trader. If she doesn't go now, she will be in greater trouble when she leaves the island in Chait.'

'We will take care of that,' Kunti said.

'Your opinion has no value outside the island,' Malakar laughed. 'The moment Batashi steps on to Ghoradal she will be caught.'

'I told you, I will take care of that.'

'You are making a mistake.'

'None of your business. Batashi will not go for the inquiry. No one can enjoy her for free.'

'She will get money and even walk about on TV.'

'I stick to what I say. I am Dhaneshwari, the master of the island and I have the last word here.'

Seven

The sky, earth and water belonged to God,
Now it's the government's, isn't that odd?

It was still some time before moonrise. It was pitch dark all around. Old Dhanapati spoke to Kunti. 'You shooed him away?'

'Where will he stay?'

'Why, they have always stayed here.'

'No, he won't stay here. Last time, he shuttled between Batashi and Kunti. All he wants is women to put him to sleep.'

'He is government, that's why.'

'Let the government bring his own women.'

'No, Kunti, don't speak like that. The government has a right over all women on the island.'

'I will not accept that.'

They sat on the covered verandah and spoke. Nabadwip Malakar went back to Ghoradal in the evening itself. He was unhappy and expressed his displeasure to Dhanapati. The old man said he was helpless since Kunti was the present ruler and he was living under her care.

'Kunti, we cannot go against the government. That will not be good for us.'

'No one's body is so easily available, master. For six months, these women are wives. Why should they sleep with outsiders? Why should someone's wife sleep with the trader?'

'To ensure that her home remains intact!'

'No, that will break her home.'

'Not at all! The fishermen are aware of these things. They just pretend not to know. Otherwise the government will stop them from coming to the island. What will happen then?'

'Is that possible?'

'Quite possible.'

'Why? The sea is owned by us . . .'

'That is what we think. Actually, it belongs to the government.'

'Is government God?'

'Yes, for the moment.'

Kunti shook her head. She could not agree. 'Government cannot be God,' she muttered. 'Can the tax collector, police and trader be government?'

'You have to understand that the water is owned by the government. That is why it catches all foreigners who stray into our waters. Remember that if the government gets angry, it will not be good for any of us.'

Kunti kept quiet for a long time. There was pin-drop silence in the verandah. The sky overhead was full of stars. It was not so cold any longer. The was no mist in the air. The scent of a wild flower wafted in. Dhaneshwari breathed in deep. It was a familiar smell. It came from the neem flowers from behind the house. There were countless stars in the clear sky. She looked at the pole star in the north that used to guide Dhanapati back to the island in his youth. Just after Falgun, a star came up from the sea onto the south sky. Dhanapati said that once this star was located, people on the island knew that the water would surge and the time to leave was near. That was many years ago, when the boats were not run by motor and the fishing nets too were not made of nylon. It was this star that signalled the time to depart.

'Does the Agastya star still make an appearance?'

'Yes, it does!' Dhanapati answered in the dark.

'Why don't the fishermen talk about the stars now?'

'Perhaps they tell their wives.'

'Have you given everything you had to me?'

'I have.'

'How did you get them?'

'From my pirate ancestor, Pedru.'

'How did pirate Pedru get it?'

'From Ma Kamala.'

'Ma Kamala poured it out of her golden pot?'

'Yes.'

'Have you given me the sky?'

'I have given you my sky.'

'The island, the water, all of that too?'

'Yes.'

'This dark night and the sun-filled day?'

'What is mine, why should I not give you?'

'This scent of the wild flower that comes through the dark?'

'Yes, yes, yes. Everything came out of the golden pot of Ma Kamala. The island, trees, fish, water, sky, flowers, sea, stars . . . everything. Ma Kamala and Ma Mary gave them to Pedru. He was the first Dhanapati. He sleeps underneath the water carrying the island on his back.'

'That is the tortoise chief.'

'They are the same.'

'So, if the sky, island, water and everything else is mine, given to me by my husband, why should I give it to the government?'

'You don't have to.'

'Then why should the government demand Batashi?'

'Batashi is also yours.'

'Why should she sleep with the government?'

'She will go because you will ask her to.'

'No! That cannot be. I will not give anything that is mine to the government,' Kunti seethed.

'Don't call anything yours, Kunti. That's not good. Everything belongs to God. To Ma Kamala, Ma Mary. They have given everything to us.'

'I know that, master.' Kunti joined her palms at her forehead to pay her respects to the two goddesses. I understand that, master. If everything belongs to God, why should it be the government's?'

'You must obey the government.'

'What if the government asks for the sky and the water?'

'We must give.'

'Why?'

'Government is everything, all powerful.'

'You are a man, master. You have only enjoyed women, but never understood how it pains them.'

Dhanapati became quiet. No one has said such a thing to him ever. He had lived with so many women. So many came and went but no one spoke like this. Not even Anna Bibi, though she too was hot-tempered. That is because she was the first real woman in Dhanapati's life.

'You talk like Anna Bibi,' he said.

'Anna Bibi?!'

'Yes, Hatem Molla's wife.'

'You had eloped with her and brought her here.'

'You know that!'

'Yes, I heard from Jamuna Mashi.'

'I told her the story.'

'You left her here and went away to Ghoradal.'

Dhanapati hung his head. He couldn't speak any more. His face was as dark as the darkness in his two eyes. A deep, dark silence fell between them. After a long pause, Dhanapati spoke.

'There was no way in which she could go to Ghoradal. Hatem Molla had sent lathi-wielding men to the riverbank.'

'But how could you leave her alone on the island?'

'She didn't want to leave the island. She wanted to make Dhanapati's six-monthly family a permanent one.'

'I know everything,' Dhaneshwari said.

'What do you know?'

'You were scared that Hatem Molla would kill you. He was a moneyed man and very powerful.'

'Yes, he was capable of that.'

'Anna Bibi was pregnant then and you were scared that both of you would be killed the moment they reached the riverbank of Ghoradal.'

'I am a descendant of pirate Pedru. Do you think I would be scared of such lathi-wielding men?'

'You had not become Pedru's descendant then.'

'What!?'

'Tell me if I am wrong.'

Dhanapati was quiet. Kunti roamed about in the dark verandah, as if wanting to encircle the darkness. Dhanapati sat with his head lowered on his hands. He seemed to have grown older in the dark. Who knew that this slip of a girl would come into his life and give him his youth back? How did Kunti know so much about Hatem Molla's wife? Jamuna did not know so much, and neither did Saraswati who was with him before Jamuna. So many women's lives were intertwined with his. None knew so much. Anna Bibi's face appeared in his mind's eyes suddenly. She had to use her veil at Hatem Molla's house.

'Let me see your face, bibi?'

The moon came up from the depths of the sea. Much of the moon was covered with a dark veil. The little that remained was so beautiful!

'You've seen my face. Now leave, quickly. Molla will return any moment.'

'He has gone to Baruipur.'

'He will come back by even after the registry of his land.'

'Show me your face just once.'

'I am his wife. Who are you? Go away. You give me a strange feeling.'

'He is not here now. Let Ashwin come, I will go away to the island.'

'Ashwin! Island! Where is it?'

Anna Bibi had called it Dhanapati's Island, for the first time. She couldn't stay with Hatem Molla after Ashwin. He had a lot of land and remained busy with them, registering them, visiting the sub-registrar's office, JLRO office and what not. He fought so many cases at the Baruipur Court and Alipore Court all year long. On some days, he came back with a lot of sweets.

'Bibi, I won the case. Let them go to the court as much as they want. They can do no harm to me! I will end up winning every time.'

He had no time for Anna. Fighting so many cases and looking after his land, left him exhausted. He suffered from acidity all the time too. Anna was left barren, childless. He had no time to take her to the doctor as well.

'When will these cases end, master?'

'Never! That will be the end of me!'

'What if you don't fight these cases?'

'How will I keep so much land then?' He would go on and on about how to get witnesses, how to grab more and more land, deeds and what not.

Anna Bibi made a resolution. Pulling her veil over her head, she visited the dargah and prayed for a son. She went to the river and prayed for a son. She went and tied a thread at the trunk of the banyan tree. She went to an old grave inside the jungle and wept alone.

'May my husband forget his cases. May I get what I deserve.'

The man shadowed her. He had come to the jungle after her. 'Why do you weep, Anna Bibi?'

'You!'

'I will go to the island in Ashwin.'

'Go away! Don't ever come back here.'

'I will take you with me.' He lifted her veil. The moon came out. He laid her on the bamboo leaves on the ground. The dry leaves crackled like they do when two snakes unite.

'If you brought her here, why did you leave her behind?'

'I did not.'

'Men forget women after their job is over. They are cruel.'

Dhanapati was quiet. During Ashwin, he went to Anna Bibi and said, 'I will go to the island now.'

'Where is the island, Dhanapati?'

'You have to cross sea after sea after sea to reach the island. I will go there to fish, dry them and send them to the market.'

'I will go with you.'

'What about your husband and his home?'

'Let them be.'

'What about the land you own?'

'Never mind that.'

'What about your clothes, jewellery, betel leaves and betel nut, and snow powder?'

'I don't want anything.'

'You will leave them all?'

'I have forsaken all that I had for the only man in my life. That is you, Dhanapati. Take me with you.'

She had a lot—land, jewellery, clothes, money . . . she left it all and became Dhanapati's mate. She loved the island and called it Dhanapati's Island.

'How do you know so much, Dhaneshwari?'

'You still talk to her in your sleep, master.'

'What do I say?'

'She hasn't left you. She comes to you in your sleep, master.'

'She wanted to stay back on the island. She did not want to go to Ghoradal. The foggy old Molla looked for her all over the place.'

Eight

Listen to the market, Dhaneshwari dear,
Power controls the market, and makes everyone fear.

'Why did you leave Anna Bibi on the island, master?'

'You don't know the whole story.'

'I know everything from what you blabber in your sleep.'

Dhanapati seemed to coil into his shell. Dhaneshwari had said this earlier. Did she cook this up because she was jealous of Anna Bibi? Anna Bibi was almost wiped out from his memory. That was so long ago that he could not even dream about it. He couldn't remember any such dream after he woke up.

Was Dhaneshwari trying to interrogate him? Dhanapati dragged his words now.

'Listen, Dhaneshwari, fishermen coming from the sea after a round of fishing cannot live without women.'

'What's new about that?'

'Go to Khidirpur dock and see the market for buying and selling women with your own eyes.'

'Where is the dock?'

'In Kolkata.'

'Does Kolkata have such a big sea?'

'No. Ships come in through smaller water channels.'

'What do you mean by a women's market?'

'Women are bought and sold there.'

'Is that a government's market?'

Dhanapati breathed out happily. He had been able to distract Kunti from the topic of Anna Bibi. Kunti went on asking about the market. Dhanapati kept on answering her. The biggest buyers were those who were returning from the sea—the sailors. They were not fishermen but those who sailed on ships from one country to another. They were traders, like pirate Pedru was. Tired of sailing on the saline water, they jumped like animals onto the land when the ship anchored at a harbour.

'So, what about the market?'

'The sailors choose.'

'Who takes the money? The government?'

'Government is there everywhere, Kunti. In these markets, the women put on make-up and wait to be taken. Suddenly, the government comes from nowhere. They have lights flickering about their cars. People simply run away.'

'What happens next?' Kunti bent down towards Dhanapati. It seemed to him that his wife was just a child, waiting to hear tales from her grandfather.' He touched her bosom. 'Are you feeling scared?'

'The police are the government, isn't it?'

'Yes, and the government owns the police too.'

'Then who is the government, really?'

'You can say it is the police.'

'The tax collector and Malakar, who are they?'

'Yes, they too.'

'It seems that you are confused too, master.'

'I know everything. Listen. One government can share his power with another person and make him government too.'

'I still don't understand who the real government is.'

Dhanapati lay his hands on Kunti's back. 'There is no big or small government, Kunti. Do you know why a Muslim man is different from a Hindu man?'

'Yes, they cut the foreskin off. That increases the power of a man. Were put through it too?'

'I don't know, my parents knew.'

'I don't think you are a Muslim.'

'That was so long ago. Perhaps in another birth. My parents were Kestans. Kestans don't do it.'

'Tell me about the government.' Kunti sat closer to Dhanapati.

'The government gives power to people to perform different tasks, collect tax, buy and sell, shoot and kill, destroy the women's market and loot whoever comes in the way, impose fines on others, jail them or hang them, etc.'

'How did the government get so much power that it gives it to its chosen few?'

'That's what being government is all about.'

'Why didn't the government give it to you?'

'The fact that I rule the island and these fishermen obey me is because the government has given this power to me.'

'Then you too . . . really are you one too?'

'Yes, I am government of the island.'

'But has the government given you any power?'

'Otherwise why would the fishermen listen to me?'

'I think they listen to you because they wish to.'

'Nothing happens without a reason, Dhaneshwari. You must understand what the government wants if you have to keep the island under your control.'

Both kept quiet for some time. Kunti ran her fingers over Dhanapati's cheek and then came down to his lips. 'Does the government get its power by circumcision?'

'I don't know.'

'I wonder where it gets its power from?'

'But that is the power to be with women. It's a different kind of power.'

'Ultimately, both are the same,' Kunti said.

'I haven't thought of it that way!'

Dhaneshwari stared in the dark. She was totally confused. She tried her best to find out where the government got its power from. What could be the root of this power? How could the

government transfer this power to someone else and how could that
person gradually turn into a government? Kunti nudged the old man
again. 'Tell me more.'

'What else do I say? They pick up all the women from the market.'

'What happens to them thereafter? Are they killed?'

'No, why should they be killed? The government takes its share
from the sale of the women.'

'What happens finally?'

'They are released in the maidan in the dark.'

'Is the government so much in need of funds that it has to earn
it in this way?'

'It's a common thing. It is called tax.'

'That the tax collector is supposed to collect?'

'The tax collector collects it on the island. The police collect
everywhere else.'

'The police collect money on the island too.'

'Yes, the police are government. On some days, they just come
wielding their lathi, collect the money and vanish.'

'The government sold Batashi here. Who does this elsewhere?'

'Look, the sailors pay to the government; the women who get
sold also pay to the government. This shows that everything belongs
to it and, it allows buying and selling at will.'

'Buying and selling of what?'

'Women.'

'This is impossible.'

'The government owns women's bodies, every part. It decides
their price after inspecting their bodies. Tax is collected per woman
when the sale happens.'

'O Ma Kamala, O Ma Mary, please help us. Is the master true?'

'Your master is saying what he has learnt over the years.'

'Tell me what happens in the end.'

'You must remember to please the government and meet its
demands if you wish to keep the island to yourself. You are the
youngest ruler that the island has ever got. Neither Pedru nor me got

to rule the island at such a young age. For many years now, you will have to rule the island and look after the fishermen and collect tax from them. Days will roll on and, before you know it, you will turn into an old woman, but the island will remain yours.'

'Will I turn into an old woman, master?'

'Yes, that is natural!'

'The sky, the earth and the sea . . .'

'They too grow old. You and I don't realize that. You don't realize at all, while I, because of my age, can imagine a lot more. No one can go against this rule of the universe.'

'Will I finally lose my youth?'

'No. But that's a long way off. You will not realize how time flies.'

'You too did not realize?'

'No. Days just rolled by.'

'I will bring back your youth.'

Dhanapati smiled. 'Had I not got you, I would have become older much faster. You have helped stall my age.'

'I know I will never lose my youth. I believe it. Now, tell me the rest of the story.'

'Which story?'

'The one about Anna Bibi.'

'That's the story of my youth. Why do you need to hear that?'

'Tell me what happened to her.'

'She came to the island and became pregnant.' Dhanapati's face became as dark as the sea in the night. He hung his head and sat without speaking for a long time.

'It's not allowed to get pregnant on the island, isn't it?'

'After Anna Bibi's episode, I, government, made that rule.'

'Did Anna have a boy or a girl?'

'Anna told me she was pregnant and refused to leave the island. I told her that the baby was due to arrive two months after we left the island.'

'Did she say that she would give birth on the island?'

'Yes.'

'Was she carrying a hundred babies?'

'Only she knew that.'

'Human babies crowded the island like red crabs on the seashore.'

'You are talking about yourself.'

'I heard you talk to her in your sleep.'

'You will get them.'

'What will I get? I have already got everything!'

'You will get your hundred children.'

Dhaneshwari shivered in joy. A strange feeling stirred up from the depths of her stomach and reached her throat as she let out a cry. 'I will give birth in winter. The fisherwomen will help me deliver my babies.'

'Yes.'

'Will you manage, master?'

'I will. But if you give birth, other fisherwomen will also want the same freedom. What will happen then?'

'That will be very good, actually.'

'They will then refuse to leave the island after six months.'

'Why should they leave this island, the sky, the water, this breeze or these birds?'

'That would mean the island will get occupied.'

'Who will occupy it?'

'The fishermen, women and children.'

'Instead of six months, it would be for twelve months.'

'That would mean that no one leaves the island the whole year. The year starts with Agrahayan and ends with Kartik.'

> With Agrahayan, the year started once upon a time,
> Pirate Pedru changed that chime.

'Let the world of six months turn into one of twelve months,' Dhaneshwari said.

'You will not get tax then.'

'Why?'

'If you allow them to stay for twelve months, they will become owners of the island too. They will never leave the island and go. If they don't leave, they will not pay tax!'

'Then what will happen, master?'

'You will give birth at Ghoradal, not here. The same rule will apply to other women also. No one will come to the island with a child. Fishermen will not accept women with children. Only women without children can set up home on the island. Let the island stay alive for six months. That will ensure its continuity. The government and the traders will also have to continue to come here. You have to think of them too!'

'Anna Bibi stayed back with the baby in her womb, isn't it?'

'Yes.'

'How could you leave without her?'

'She refused to leave. I could not stay back beyond the scheduled time. That was the month of Chait when Ghoradal beckons all fishermen. Anna Bibi was beautiful, no doubt, but how could I sacrifice my life for her? She was, after all, nothing more than a woman! I would have also died had I stayed back.'

Nine

Fermented rice, a dash of lime leaf and hilsa fish,
The trader will eat as per his wish.

Malakar returned and gave a detailed report to the trader, Dasharath Singh. It was for him that Malakar had gone on the official tour. He would claim his travel allowance (TA), daily allowance and night halt allowance, which was double the daily allowance. Then, he would draw up a report and start planning for the next part of his project.

'Malakar, one day, this report will become the official one. It will be a government-to-government report.'

'Are you government?'

'You can call me one.'

'How is that possible?'

'Times have changed, Malakar. If I come here officially, your government will roll out a red carpet for me.'

Malakar did not understand what the trader meant but he did not say so.

'Did you mention my name there?'

'No, I kept your name under wraps.'

'You were wrong.'

'I went and told them that an official inquiry would happen on the island. I told them that it was the order of the government.'

'What did they say?'

'They said no.'

'Why didn't you mention me, Malakar?'

'They had attacked you, so I didn't think it would be advisable.'

'That was because of that coward Midde.'

'He gets into trouble repeatedly. Once, they took off his clothes in the Firingitala market and left him in his underpants.'

'What had he done?'

'I cannot mention that to you.'

'After that, a lot of raids happened at Firingitala and many were nabbed. In a few days, everything was forgotten.'

'Will you drink vodka?'

'Why not?'

'Do you know where Bonbibitala is?'

'Yes, that's where the fishermen live.'

'They go to the island in Ashwin and leave it in Chaitra.'

'Yes, sir, you seem to know it all.'

'Their wives have them for six months, from Baishakh to Ashwin.'

'Yes, sir. For the rest of the six months, their men don't stay with them.'

'Do they stay alone then?'

'They take care of the household.'

'Can we not wrap up some women from Bonbibitala?'

Malakar cringed. He realized that Batashi was just the icing on the cake. This man was about to cast a wide net on the island. Malakar had never thought on these dangerous lines. From Baishakh to Ashwin, the wives have the husbands with them. From Ashwin to Chait, women would be picked up both from the island and Ghoradal. Unless one worked doubly hard, dollars wouldn't come that easily.'

'Sir, they have families. It won't be possible.'

'You just have to give them the taste of dollars.'

'Sir, but they hold their families close to their hearts.'

'Lust for money is a dangerous thing. Don't forget that my forefathers amassed a lot of money during the war by creating an artificial crisis by hoarding food grains. They fed the black market.'

'But that's an old story, sir.'

'Now that there is such a viable market for women, shall I not make money out of it?'

'Yes, sir.'

'The trader took out his money bag and pulled out a note from it. Can you see this?'

'Money?'

'Dollar.'

Whose picture did Malakar see on the note? The trader told him that it was the picture of Abraham Lincoln.

'This is a hundred-dollar note, worth five thousand Indian rupees. One such note is good enough to break families. No one can say no to dollars. Gradually, this is the only currency that will work here. Without dollars, one will not be able to buy and sell anything in the market.'

Malakar was confused. How could everything be bought and sold in dollars? The trader started laughing. 'Nothing will move an inch without dollars. You will first have to buy dollars and then go to the market.'

Malakar sipped his vodka. I don't trust you, trader, he said in his mind.

'Don't think that I am as gullible as that lathi-wielding Midde. So what if you are an Ispahani, Malakar has been with transformed pirates and foreigners too. For two hundred years, seven generations of his forefathers had served them and earned titles of Rai Bahadur and Babu. They also kept at least five women in their harems. You cannot weigh Malakar with your dollars.'

'Malakar, try and understand what I am saying. Indian money will soon have no value and you will not be able to buy anything. You will have to earn dollars to survive. So, start as early as you can.'

'Show me the way.'

'I will show you the way but you give me news of the island now.'

'They are about to wind up for the year. They will light up the shanties and leave the island to come to Ghoradal.'

'When is that?'

'Not too far from now.'

'If they don't come back on time, I will send someone to set everything on fire.'

'You will not need to do all that. Batashi will come here on time. It is with her arrival that the southern wind will start blowing at Ghoradal.'

'Are you sure?'

'I am certain, sir. Until these women set foot in Ghoradal, the south wind stops at the island and doesn't reach Ghoradal.'

'Do people know this?'

'Yes, they do. I know it.'

'No, tell me if others know it. Not just you and me.'

Sir, I don't know about everyone else. Things are changing these days but this fact hasn't changed. I have been going to the island for thirty-five years now. But things have changed. The scene on the island is not as happy as it used to be. Earlier, I have myself slept with four women at a time. I had that strength.'

'And now?'

'Earlier, you could order not only the women but the men too. These days, they have learnt to speak up for themselves. That is why they harassed you so much last time.'

'I can get the military to whip them back to shape. They will all fall in line then.'

'That is the government's job, isn't it?'

'I have my own military. I will tell you that story later. But now, tell me the story of the island.'

'They are about to return.'

'What about Batashi?'

'She will go with you.'

'How do you know that?'

'She said she will not come for the inquiry to Ghoradal now, but will go with you when she leaves the island and comes to Ghoradal in Chait. She yearns for you, sir.'

'I don't want to know all that. I just need the woman. Tell me clearly what she said.'

> A foreign trader he is, almost a pirate,
> Malakar tell me, when I need to be at the gate.

'You are giving me goosebumps, Malakar.'
     'There's more, sir!'

> Where will he take me, to which land?
> Will there be water or will there be sand?

The trader said, 'I leave it to God.'
     'Yes, he will take care of you. Batashi said she will cook lotke fish with green chillies and turmeric.'
     'Won't she apply a paste of turmeric on her face and body?'
     'Yes, that too. She is ready to apply turmeric and salt and get packed off.'
     'Batashi yearns to go with you.'
     'Why didn't you bring her?'
     'I had to spend time to understand her.'
     'Tell me more . . . I am eager to know what she said.'
     'Trust me, sir, I have your best interests in mind.'

> You will find Ghoradal of great interest,
> Women are cheap and you can rest assured, they are among the best.

'I am so happy, Malakar.'
     'She is using powder, shampoo, cream and scent. She is using alta on her feet and her back and there are red marks on her sarees now.'
     'What did you say?'
     'Sir, I will give you all those details later. But for now, can you tell me about my money?'

'I will give you dollars. Give me more news about Batashi.'

'She wears see-through sarees now and spends time rubbing salt on the fish.'

> Lotke fish she will cook with turmeric,
> Chillies with it will cause you hysterics.

Dasharath was not being able to fathom Malakar. He was not an easy man. He had come for business but could not stop lusting for Batashi.

> Hilsa fish in small pieces and bits,
> Being dried in the sun, in preparation for the feast.

'You are great, Malakar.'

'She yearns for you. But she cannot come before the south winds start blowing.'

'You are making my heart go pit-a-pat.'

'Really, sir!

'I yearn for Batashi.'

> Ask your south wind to start blowing fast,
> I will do all that, but give me my money first.

'Take dollars.'

'But is that pure?'

'You can take dollars or Indian rupees, as you please.'

'Thank you, sir. I will be at the Ghoradal ghat so that no one lays his hands on Batashi.'

'Okay. Please tell me again what she asked about me.'

'I am only scared of Dhanapati's wife, Kunti. She is a witch and might use a tree to send Batashi away to the Himalayas.'

'Malakar, we are in the twenty-first century!'

'That doesn't change the fact that Kunti is a witch and knows witchcraft.'

'That's your problem, Malakar.'

'I know that her witchcraft can work only on the island. Once at Ghoradal, she will be powerless and I will take over.'

Malakar went out in the dark and started laughing. For generations, his family had cheated many an Ispahani or pirate. Dasharath was no different. Malakar decided to take leave and go to the island. He didn't know that Midde had come from nowhere and stood behind him. The trader had asked him to keep vigil on Malakar.

Ten

The big government walks ahead; look at his style,
Small government follows him, wearing a smile.

The sahib, who got down from the motor launch and crossed the
wooden jetty on unsteady steps to finally get on to the island, was
the big one. Dhanapati had said that there was no government as
big as the BDO at Ghoradal. He had sent his wife to welcome the
big government and bring him over to his house. Chait was about to
come and people knew that they were soon to leave the island. The
sun was hot. The big sahib had come with Malakar.

'This is Dhaneshwari Kunti, the present owner of the island.
She is the second-in-command after Dhanapati,' Malakar explained.

Dhaneshwari wore a big veil and welcomed the big sahib.
Behind her were many other fisherwomen. Malakar was surprised.
He hadn't seen anything like this before. Why had these women veiled
themselves? Perhaps because Dhanapati's wife was using the veil.

Malakar whispered to his boss. Dhanapati must be over a hundred
years old, but his wife is not more than seventeen. Dhanapati had
brought the woman from somewhere but it was not certain whether
he would keep her after Chait, when people left the island.

'This girl is from Kamrup and claims to be a witch.'

BDO Aniket was irritated with Malakar and stopped him.
There were many veiled fisherwomen in front of him. Their leader
addressed him.

'This is our world of six months, sahib. The women come
here for six months and set up home with the fishermen. For the

337

remaining six months, they roam about like vagabonds. Once back at Ghoradal, they lose the security that the island gives them. Why has the sahib come? Has he come again for inquiry? Sahib, how many times will the inquiry happen? We plead to you to stop this inquiry on the island.'

Malakar scolded them. 'Will you stop? I don't know which of you is talking because all of you have veiled your faces.'

'I am Dhaneshwari Kunti.' She dropped her veil for a moment to put it back again.

'You are a wife of six months. It is soon going to get over.'

'If you go on like this, we will send you back by boat. Sahib is here and we will tell him everything.'

'Sir, this is not a good place. I told you that. These women are all prostitutes. Next time, you should stop them from coming back to the island. Let the fishermen come alone to catch fish.'

'Please stop this, Malakar.' Aniket Sen was clearly upset with him.

'Okay, sir, I will tell you everything after we return. This woman is a sorceress. She will trap you. I know her well. Do not listen to her. Let Dhanapati do the talking.'

Dhaneshwari guessed what Malakar was whispering to the BDO.

'I am the chief of the island now. The chief has passed on the rulership of the island to me. I am the government of the island.'

'Ridiculous! How can you talk like this in front of the government himself?'

'He is one government and I am another. The island has survived so long because of chief Dhanapati.'

A woman spoke up from the crowd. 'Pedru Dhanapati got the island from Ma Kamala. Are you aware of this, government?'

'Stop cooking up stories,' Malakar laughed. 'Pull back your veil, let me see your face.'

'No, we will not lift up the veil when the government is here,' another woman said.

'Whose order is that?' Malakar asked.

'Dhaneshwari Kunti's,' the woman replied.

Kunti continued the conversation. 'Government comes here to buy and sell women. They look at their faces and bodies before choosing. So, I am keeping all women veiled when the government is around so that he cannot choose easily.'

Aniket was surprised. He hadn't heard such conversation ever. These veiled women did not wish to hide themselves. They were doing this for a reason. Was Malakar true or were these women speaking the truth, Aniket thought to himself.

'Has Dhanapati registered the island and given it to you?' Malakar asked.

'What do you mean?'

'How has he transferred the right of the island to you?'

'It is easy! He decided first and then called everyone and declared it to them.'

'You are an idiot to talk like this in front of the government. The laws of the land have to be followed.'

'Dhanapati chief is a descendant of Pedru the pirate. Pedru got it from Ma Kamala. Dhanapati called everyone and said that, from now, I am the ruler of the island. No one questions Dhanapati's decision here. He has not only given me the island but the sky, the water, day and night, high and low tides and the six months from Ashwin to Chait. So, as the present ruler of the island, I have asked the women to keep themselves veiled when the government is around.'

'Did everything belong to Dhanapati?' Aniket threw the question at Kunti.

'Yes, government sir! Dhanapati's land is Lisboan, beyond the seven seas. You will get to know the entire story. He is blessed by Ma Kamala. I will tell you how he became the government of the island.'

'Listen, stop your stupid stories. Don't forget that you are talking to the government. He is not an illiterate person like you people on the island,' Malakar snubbed them sharply.

'We know that he is the big government. We will appeal to him. Who will listen to us if he doesn't?'

Aniket sat listening. Beside him sat Dhanapati chief, wearing dark glasses. Aniket wasn't sure if he was really blind or was acting like one. Aniket was of a small build, just the opposite of Dhanapati. He was a huge man and looked appropriate as the ruler of the island. Perhaps his massiveness had helped to keep discipline on the island, Aniket thought. The fishermen had put up a shamiana in Dhanapati's courtyard, when they got to know that the big government was coming.

Malakar was not there. Aniket did not want him to interfere and create trouble. He tried to poke his nose in everything, Aniket thought and was happy that he was not present. 'Who is Pedru?'

'He was the king of Lisboan or perhaps his messenger.'

'Wasn't he a pirate?'

'That cannot be, sahib,' Dhanapati said. He was a godly man. I can vouch for that. He was caught in a severe storm but prayed to the heavens to save himself.

'But people talk about Pedru the pirate in this place, isn't it?'

'No, sahib. I am talking about the saint Pedru, who left his kingdom, the hundred wives in his harem, and his treasures and riches, to set sail on the water one moonlit night.

'No one knows this story.'

'That's because I have not told them.'

'Why didn't you tell me before?' Aniket felt that he had been talking to Dhanapati for many years now and was continuing that conversation. It was as if he had been transported to another world. Scenes from his childhood flashed before his mind's eye. One part of him said that there was no link between where he was and reality. He was sitting in an unreal world with unreal people and losing himself gradually in it.

Kunti sat in the verandah, resting her chin on her palms. Dhanapati had bequeathed this unreal world to her and she seemed to be at sea. Did she veil her face because she wanted to hide the fact that she was nervous of her inheritance? The old woman who served them, Buli Ma, went about her work. She made tea and took instructions from Kunti for cooking.

'Make a spicy lotke fish curry. Put enough turmeric, salt and green chillies. Make spicy hilsa too. Make it so hot that their mouths burn with the heat. Let the Ghoradal government realize that the government on the island is no less when it comes to attitude.'

'The big sahib is a guest, he has come for the first time,' Buli Ma said.

'Make it less spicy for him then. But make sure you put at least a bowl full of extra chillies in the portion that you keep aside for that bastard Malakar. If you cannot do it, I will do it myself. Just remind me.'

'He, too, is a guest.'

'If a thief comes here as our guest, should I treat him like a relative?'

'I understand.'

'I will make him realize that times have changed. Dhanapati is no longer the head of the island and they can no longer take our women for granted. They cannot extort money anymore. They have used the island for entertainment for years. I will not allow that anymore.'

'Should I keep myself veiled? I am neither young nor beautiful. They will never eye me.'

'Yes, you will veil yourself. If the old women drop their veils, the government will know that those who are veiled are young and can be used.'

'I am not used to this.'

'Change your habit then. When on the island, all women will remain veiled. Let me see how they choose their women or buy them.'

Dhanapati continued his conversation with Aniket Sen. 'Sahib, when I look up at the sky full of stars at night, it looks nothing less than a divine tapestry. I have never seen anything as beautiful as that. Had I not come to the island, much of the world would have remained unknown to me.'

'I can understand that.'

'I will help you understand everything. I am a descendant of Dhanapati the saint. When I am awake at night, I hear the sounds of an oar on the water. I know that the saint is coming to the island from the distant Lisboan.'

'We had never heard of any saint in the past but only about pirates.'

Dhanapati shook his head. 'They mix up the two Pedrus. But that is not right.'

'We hadn't heard of the existence of two Pedrus earlier.'

'How will you know, sahib? You have heard the story only from Malakar, who is a looter himself and thinks others are criminals too.'

Aniket saw that Kunti had inched towards them to listen to their conversation. She sat on the ground and looked up at them. 'Sahib, when will this inquiry by Malakar, Midde and the trader end? When will the buying and selling of women on the island end?'

Aniket Sen did not know the whole story well, but he could guess what was going on. 'Let me see what I can do. Tell me what happened next.'

Dhanapati seemed tired and hung his head.

'Dhaneshwari, would you like to continue?'

'What will I say?'

'Whatever the sahib asks you.'

'Inquiry? Why me? I am Dhaneshwari.'

'No, no. I mean the story of Pedru.'

'He is my forefather-in-law. I cannot take his name.'

'That doesn't matter, really. Okay, tell him the story without taking his name directly.'

'Okay, let me try. But I might get mixed up between the two Pedrus. You will have to excuse me for that, but I will try my best.' Kunti came and sat closer to Aniket.

Dhanapati butted in. 'I have given all that I had to my wife, Dhaneshwari. She is the present owner of the island and will take all decisions.'

'Yes, I have heard that,' Aniket said.

Kunti started humming,

There were two Pedrus; pirate and saint,
One was a king and other without a taint.

There was something mesmerizing about her rendering. It seemed to cast a spell on Aniket. Dhanapati corrected her once in a while as she explained how a pirate could also turn into a saint like Valmiki and it was also possible that this pirate-turned-saint might have gone back and written an epic in his country.

'Let me go back and check on the internet,' Aniket said.

'What is that sahib?'

'It gives news of the world.'

'You must find out about the two Pedrus there. Who is the saint and which one was the pirate? Were the two same or different people? Once, a man had come to meet my master from Magrahat. He called himself Pedru Laskar. Who was he?'

Kunti started humming again,

> There was a Pedru pirate from Magrahat,
> Owner of a fishing pond, he came for a chat.

Eleven

Who was that, sailing all alone?
No other than Pedru, now here, now gone.

Dhaneshwari Kunti couldn't go on relating Pedru's story with the ease with which Dhanapati could. She stopped in between and Dhanapati picked up from there effortlessly. There was much for Kunti to learn. Weaving lore and imagination together was one of them.

'Pedru was not a pirate, he was a saint,' Dhanapati said. 'He belonged to Lisboan across the seas. What a house he owned! It had seven majestic buildings and courtyards between them. He was a prince. He had a pet lion, peacocks and a bird that had the colours of the rainbow.'

Aniket noticed that Dhanapati had not only mesmerized him with the tale but also his wife. She was looking at his dark glasses, fully enraptured. Her veil had fallen off. What a pretty young thing, Aniket thought to himself. She was the first woman whose face he had seen after setting foot on the island. How intently she heard the story.

Dhanapati stopped to catch his breath. 'Why did you stop, master?' Kunti asked.

'You have heard this story before.'

'When?'

'Think hard.'

'No, no,' she shook her head. 'No master, you never told me this story before.' She didn't realize that her veil had fallen off and the big government was looking at her face.

344

'You are my wife. How can you not know about Pedru saint?'

'I should know, I agree.'

'You knew it. Perhaps you are not able to recall.'

'Yes, the tale seems familiar. I think I heard something like this from my grandmother and now you are narrating the same story.'

Dhanapati seemed happy. His gaze was fixed behind the dark glasses.

He started murmuring again,

> He was a prince, with servants aplenty,
> With so much gold and riches, his coffers never got empty.

'That's normal for a prince,' Kunti said under her breath.

'He had servants to bathe him, comb his hair, dress him up and put him to sleep. In good time, he married a beautiful woman and had a bonny son. But he was not cut out for a family life.'

'Why?' Kunti was surprised. 'Such a palatial house, a family, riches and servants can make anyone happy.'

'One day, he left everything and went to the seashore. He found a small boat there and set sail, all alone.'

'Why did he go alone?' Kunti was surprised.

'He set sail on the Atlantic Ocean.'

'Why did he not take a helper? You need someone to clear the water from the boat.'

'He did not have a destination in mind. He just set sail with the sea below him and the starry sky above.'

> He sailed alone in the deep dark ocean,
> To remain awake, he needed no potion.

'Why was the poor prince alone?' Kunti was heartbroken.

'He wasn't alone. He had the water, the sky, the fish and other creatures for company. The waves spoke with him as he majestically crossed the waters.'

'My heart goes out to him,' Kunti wiped a tear.

'He was often reminded of home, his wife, son and parents and, of course, Lisboan.'

'What did he think of?'

'Of the houses, a broken bridge on which the vultures nested and, of course, the hundreds of pigeons that were found in Lisboan homes.'

'What happened next?'

'Once, when he was standing on the seashore, the sky became dark and there was lightning and thunder.'

'Then?' Kunti seemed to choke with tension.

'There was fog for seven days.'

'The sun did not come out?'

'No. The winter was so severe that the water of the ocean froze.'

'Then?'

'Pedru was so unhappy at Lisboan.'

'Then why did he think of his native place when he was so unhappy there?' Aniket could not stop himself from asking.

'After sailing, he missed the winter, the fog, the lightning above, the old broken bridge. They were so beautiful.'

'Did he return?'

'He hadn't quit to go back!'

'Then what did he do?'

'Two tortoises moved before his boat. He followed them. They crossed many waters and showed him the way. They were a pair. They would come here to unite and lay eggs. They had found out the route so that they could bring Pedru here one day.'

'Olive Ridley or Galapagos? Both cross the seas to travel long distances and reach these parts.'

'Yes, sir! You seem to know a lot!'

'They cross the Pacific and the Atlantic, and travel thousands of miles to reach islands here. After they mate, the male leaves while the female stays back to lay eggs.'

'I know this bit,' Kunti said.

Aniket Sen observed Kunti. He could guess what could happen on the island with such young, beautiful women around.

'Your veil has dropped,' he said softly.

'Oh my God! Master, the big government has seen my face!'

'How do you find him?'

'I don't know!'

'He should not see your face or body. Cover yourself well and keep the veil on.'

With the veil, there was no difference between her and a seventy-year-old-woman, Kunti thought, pulling it over the face. 'Master, please continue with your story.'

'Hope no one can see your face now.'

'No, master.' Kunti looked at Aniket once, smiled and then pulled her veil down. The big government had clean eyes. He felt shy to look up at her, she thought. Dhanapati had earlier said that, as Dhaneshwari, she could remain unveiled. He had lost his vision and did not want others to look at the women of the island. He made her announce this to others on the island.

'The story that you know of tortoises does not exactly match the two who showed Pedru the way. They were sent by Ma Mary.'

'Ma Mary and Ma Kamala,' Kunti said.

'Pedru rowed his boat, looking at the stars for direction and thought of the three years of drought at Lisboan.'

'What happened then?'

'Three years later, it rained.'

'What else did he remember?'

'The fact that he slept when others were awake.'

'Why did he do that?'

'He was reminded of the taste of tortoise flesh though he did not crave meat. Neither did he crave women. He often released them so that they could marry and settle down.'

'Tortoise meat tastes good and keeps people warm in winter,' Kunti muttered.

'Don't talk so irresponsibly, Kunti. Pedru would not have reached the island if those two divine tortoises hadn't shown him the way. You are Dhaneshwari now, talk more responsibly.'

'I am sorry, master. I have sinned. I forgot that Dhanapati is a giant tortoise.'

He sleeps a deep slumber, Dhanapati, my lord,
The island on his back, he is much adored.

The law of the land says that turtles and tortoises cannot be killed. There are so many species—Olive Ridley, Green Turtles, Hawksbill, Loggerhead, Leatherback, giant Galapagos . . . the last one is, of course, very, very rare.

'Are these their names? What about Dhanapati?'

'That too,' laughed Aniket.

Dhanapati listened to their conversation intently. 'Kunti, is your face veiled?'

Kunti lied. 'Yes, master.'

'Pedru the saint had ordered that women should be veiled on the island because their faces turned men on,' Dhanapati said.

Aniket lit a cigarette and observed Dhanapati closely. Was he really blind or did he act blind to keep his young wife in check? Why did Kunti lie? Was it because she knew for sure that the old man was blind? He was a giant, blind tortoise. Though he was blind, he wanted to keep the island under his control.

'Sir, we worship all tortoises because we believe that just like Pedru, they are saints too. They are all related to Dhanapati's family in some way or the other. In Lisboan, many people saw that the prince rode a tortoise and went into the deep, never to come back again.'

'Really?' Kunti asked.

'Don't you know that story?'

'No!'

'You have to think hard. Remember the story about how the people of Lisboan believe that one day, the prince will return riding the tortoise.'

'You mean Dhanapati?'

'Yes, you could say that.'

'Is he the one who is carrying the island on his back?'

'Where is saint Pedru?'

Dhanapati kept quiet. Aniket spoke up. 'Will you turn to Lisboan as saint Pedru now?'

'Big government, sir, you are so intelligent! You are our saviour, sir. Kunti, please touch his feet.'

Kunti smiled at him and then touched the ground near his feet with her forehead.

'The people of Lisboan are very sad, sir,' Dhanapati said.

'Why are they sad, master?' Kunti asked.

'After Pedru left Lisboan, a curse befell it. Crops and vegetables died.'

'Are their crops the same as ours?'

Aniket pulled out his mobile from his pocket to check if there were any missed calls. Not a single call had come since he had left Ghoradal and entered the Kalnagini river. He dialled a number and saw that there was no network. He looked around to see if there was any mobile tower in sight but found none. The towers in Ghoradal could not service the island. Aniket let out a sigh and looked up at the sky. Dhanapati started again.

'The curse on Lisboan was such that pigeons started dying, the feathers of seagulls floated overhead and dead sea fish could be found on the surface of the water.'

'Why did such a thing happen, master?'

'Sadhu Pedru went away, that's why.'

'Where did he go?'

'I told you, he went into the sea riding a giant tortoise.'

Aniket never thought that he would have to participate in this kind of a conversation one day. Such strange tales, but on the island they felt real.

'Even women started losing their beauty at Lisboan.'

'What happened next, master?'

'Their youth left them.'

'How did that happen?'

'They suddenly became old, their breasts sagged, their skin became rough and wrinkled, and they lost their lustrous hair.'

'Oh my God!'

'Even budding young women were not spared.'

'Saint Pedru had predicted this. Lisboan had become corrupt and majority of the people were involved in evil deeds. So, Pedru decided to leave his land and set sail on the waters. The women of Lisboan were full of lust. They were not satisfied with one partner and needed many men. They sinned and so they lost their youth. Their breasts and hips sagged in no time. Pedru's curse was on them.'

> Pedru went to sea taking all that was pure,
> Dhaneshwari's beauty was stunning for sure!

Twelve

There was gold in the soil, sir, do you know?
The women had youth, but lost it and how!

Dhaneshwari Kunti looked miserable. She found the misery of the people of Lisboan unacceptable. She looked helplessly at Dhanapati and the big government.

'How could Pedru leave Lisboan and go away? Why did such misfortune have to befall the people? Master, please tell me.'

'Dhaneshwari, this can happen.'

'Pedru went away just to give pain to the people of Lisboan?'

'Perhaps.'

'Then how can he be a saint?'

'When a saint leaves, bad times start. Don't you see how places are often affected by drought and famine? The skies dry up and, for years, there is no rain. The ground becomes so dry that deep cracks develop. Why do these things happen?'

'I don't know, tell me.'

'Pedru leaves, that is why.'

'What happens next?'

'All women lose their youth. They grow old and bend from the waist. Their breasts dry up and the body loses all juice.'

'How does a woman conceive?'

'She doesn't!'

'Then what about her hundred children?'

'She remains barren.'

'If this is what he does, then I cannot call Pedru a saint. He is nothing but a pirate. How can a saint give so much pain to people, big government sir?'

Aniket continued to feel strange. He was being called upon to be a witness to this outlandish conversation. One part of him felt that there was nothing wrong in what was going on. Perhaps, one day, he would get to know who the real Pedru was. It felt like the mythological churning of the ocean that brought up the elixir of life. Aniket was reminded of the story from the churning of the ocean when people waited for a saint to come and rescue them from all sorrow.

> I looked up with wonder at Pedru the saint,
> Blue eyes, fair skin, he hadn't any taint.

'Should I continue?' Aniket spoke up.

'Do you know the story, sir?' Dhanapati was surprised.

'I do.' Aniket lit a cigarette, trying to contain the excitement within.

'How do you know the story, big government?' Kunti asked. She was just as surprised.

'I have read it in books.'

'You mean this story is there in books? Has Pedru's story entered books already? Are the people of Lisboan aware of it?'

'I am sure all the people of the island are not aware of everything,' Aniket said.

'True, sir! Not everyone knows this Mahabharata,' Dhanapati agreed.

'But I am aware of one story.'

'Tell us, sir,' Kunti said, wrapping the loose end of her saree around her and pushed behind some of the curls that hung above her eyes. This was the first time that someone from Ghoradal had come to the island to tell a story. All this while, only Dhanapati was the storyteller. No one else knew the story of the island, the water, the sky and the tortoise. These were his own tales that he had inherited from Pedru. Pedru the saint, or was he a pirate.

As Aniket Sen prepared to tell the tale of Pedru, Malakar utilized that time to look for Batashi. He had to get her to agree. He would try to take her back with him on the motorboat that his boss would be using for the return journey. The trader was sitting at Ghoradal with dollars and rupees. Batashi could not escape the trader anyway, she would get caught if she tried to flee after Chait. He would tell her that she had been targeted by the trader and there was no way in which he could be distracted. Batashi did not know the trader well and Malakar would try his best to drive fear in her mind. She would not refuse him then.

Trader, trader, who is he really?
Foreign, Spanish, Burmese, not known clearly.

But where was he to look for Batashi? Everything had changed here. One came to the island to feast one's eyes on voluptuous women. They made one's winters warm. But that witch had changed it all. She was indeed trained in witchcraft from Kamrup-Kamakhya. She had got each one of them veiled. He could not make out who was passing by, whether it was Jamuna or Sabitri, Lakshmi or Parbati. Malakar was so frustrated that he felt like removing their veils and taking a look at each one's face to finally catch hold of Batashi. He could not do all that he wanted to do because his boss was present on the island. He sat sipping tea at a stall in Meena Bazaar.

'How did this happen?' he asked himself.

'What happened?' The stall owner stirred in sugar in the glassful of tea and asked.

'Such big veils,' Malakar said.

'That's normal. They have come here to set up families.'

'What will happen to them after a month?'

'Nothing! They will go back to Ghoradal and drop their veils.'

'Is this the new law of the island?'

'Yes, this is what Dhaneshwari has ordered.'

'Why should I come to the island anymore if I am unable to look at women?'

'Yes, those days are over,' the stall owner said.

'Nonsense! These women are all prostitutes, how can they start families?'

The stall owner, just like the others on the island, came there for six months of business. He too had a wife here. She had veiled herself and sat cooking inside. The stall owner sounded offended.

'What are you saying? I too have a family on the island!'

Malakar finished his tea and got up. Malakar saw someone's alta-smeared toe and ran after her. She was veiled but he thought that he was bang on target this time. But instead of Batashi, he turned out to be an old woman. Then, he realized that all women had alta-stained feet, shankha-pola and a red thread on their wrists. He went to Batashi's hut and found it locked. Where was she?

Feeling frustrated, he went and stood below a casuarina tree. He realized that Dhaneshwari had introduced a foolproof system. If, by a stroke of good luck he got hold of Batashi, he would be saved. But if he failed, he would have to go back empty-handed and lie to the trader.

Some fishing boats had come in. Fisherwomen were helping the men unload the fish from the boats. They were all veiled and no one could see their faces. Malakar was surprised. Could anyone do this kind of a job with the veil covering her face? One veiled woman walked past him, holding her basket of fish.

'Listen to me, did you see Batashi near the boats?' The woman just shook her head from side to side.

'Where is Batashi?'

She shook her head again.

'Tell her that Malakar Babu is looking for her. The inquiry is not over. The BDO sahib has come.'

The veiled woman shook her head again.

'Tell her that she cannot hide like this. The trader has bought her from the government and she needs to come with me. He is waiting for her at Ghoradal.'

She shook her head and moved on quickly. There was spring in her step but one could not make out whether she was old or young. Malakar shouted after her.

'Tell her that she cannot escape. Malakar has come for her and will not leave without her.'

Malakar placed his slippers on the sand and sat on them. He lit a cigarette and stared at the sea. Suddenly, a thought crossed his mind. The woman whom he addressed might have been Batashi! Why didn't he ask her to lift her veil?! The sea had receded; it was low tide. A beautiful breeze brushed against his cheeks but Malakar was in no mood to enjoy it. His mind was full of Batashi and the trouble that the rule of the veil had created on the island.

He thought of sharing the problem with the trader and taking his suggestion. The trader was a descendant of the Spanish and Burmese looters, so he might have a solution in mind, Malakar thought. Suddenly, Malakar felt drowsy. *When will the veils lift?*

The lord crossed the sea to come to them. He was a representative of God. How tall and handsome he was! Get people to serve the lord. Let the veils lift. All the women were put into the hold of the ship. Batashi cannot escape now. Malakar should buy all the women and then pick and choose the best.

Aniket Sen continued the story. The fishermen were at the dark sea but they could not move farther. They were scared of the dazzling light that went up and down with the waves, as if dancing in joy. Who or what was it? The fishermen decided to return and ask the wise man on the island. He was over hundred years old and knew the water like the palm of his hand. But even he did not have an explanation. He asked the fishermen to go back only in the morning. The mystery would be unravelled in daylight.

Dhanapati was never this surprised in his life. 'Whom did the fishermen see?'

'I think the stars of the sky had descended to the sea to drink water,' Kunti said.

'Who told you that?'

'You, my master.'

'When did I say this?'

'Who else will tell me?'

'That is true. Sir, who else but I can tell her this story?'

Dhaneshwari Kunti lifted her veil on her head a bit and tried to give a better explanation. 'When the rains don't come, the stars get thirsty and descend on the water to quench their thirst.'

> The stars in the sky die of thirst,
> I know which star comes down first.

'This is possible, but there are other stories too.'

'What I said is true. Batashi and I stood at the waterside and saw it with our own eyes once.'

'Let me tell you what happened,' Aniket Sen said. 'The fishermen stayed awake the whole night on the water and saw the lights dance, bobbing up and down.'

'They were bathing in the dark. It is so much fun to bathe in the dark in full tide. It is both scary and fun. Batashi Didi—I call her Batashi now because she is my subject—would bathe with me in high tide. Even in the peak of winter, we would bathe in the dark when no one was around.'

'You keep quiet, let the big government talk,' Dhanapati said. It is all coming back to me now. This is my tale but I am confused about whether I was on the island or in sea at that time. Was I the old, wise man that you are talking about? I am over a hundred years old too.'

'The old wise man had said that many stars had fallen from the sky,' Aniket continued his tale.

Dhanapati's dark eyes seemed to answer. He shook his head.

'The light of the old wise man's eyes had been blown out. He could not see,' Aniket continued.

'What are you saying, government sir!' Kunti shrieked.

'The old wise man listened to the fishermen intently. There was darkness all around. "The falling of so many stars from heaven will bring bad luck," he said. Some fishermen wanted to go out into the sea to find out how the stars could remain alight while bathing in water. "That is a sign of danger," the old man had said. "Let the night get over and then, you can go and find out," the old man advised.'

'Did the night pass safely?' Kunti's face was blue with fear and her bosom heaved. 'Government sir, will such a thing ever happen?'

'Such a thing had happened and might happen in the future too,' Aniket Sen replied.

'At dawn, the birds started chirping again. They had remained awake all night and stared out at sea, anticipating the worst. In the blue light of dawn, everyone saw a huge ship on the water. No one had seen a ship before. It had such a big mast and sail. There was a black flag. Some boats were coming towards the island.'

'Did they reach?' Dhanapati asked Aniket.

'Yes, they came, master. My old master sees what I see. He cannot see with his own eyes, government.'

Aniket continued to speak. 'The boat reached the shore and a white man jumped on to the island. He had blue eyes that flashed, blonde hair and a beard. His sword shone under the sun.'

'Is he coming again?' Dhanapati asked.

'He knelt on the ground with his knees folded and he looked up at the sky. "God, with your permission I take control of the land."'

'You mean someone will take control of this island in the future?' Dhanapati sounded distraught.

'He took control of the island, the men and the women too. He filled his ship with men. His people went in search of gold on the island. Some torched all homes. They started enjoying the women. They realized that they hadn't seen such youthful and healthy women in the past. Even the men were hardworking, they happily thought.'

'Where is the gold? Which gold, government?' Kunti was about to cry out aloud. Her voice shook.

'On the shore. There was gold dust in the sand. Did you know this, Dhanapati chief?'

'Never. Where is that sand?'

'They have taken it all.'

'Government, the women on the island are very helpless. The God above has given them youth. They need protection. Sir, please save them. People from other lands come here to loot them. I am sure government sir knows that.' Dhanapati appealed to Aniket and then fell silent.

Thirteen

When did they marry and when did she become a wife?
There are no rules sir, in island life.

After lunch, Dhanapati felt drowsy. He took Kunti by the hand and moved inside. 'Sir, you will not be able to return today,' he told Aniket. 'This government is not like the others, Kunti. He knows our story, he knows why the land of gold turned into a graveyard.'

'Yes, master. This government has come for inquiry but is not doing one. He is a real master, let him stay.'

Aniket sat underneath the neem tree in the courtyard and thought that it wasn't a bad proposition to stay on. He would not get a chance to come back soon. Perhaps only after the Ashwin, when the island would come back to life again. But where was Malakar? He was nowhere to be seen. Where was he having food?

'Don't worry, government sir, he must have found a nest for himself. No one goes hungry on the island, but the problem with Malakar Babu is that he extorts people,' Kunti said.

Dhanapati slept inside. Kunti sat on a small stool near Aniket, with her veil pulled on her head but short enough for her face to be seen. She looked at Aniket's face.

'Why don't you go and take some rest too?'

'Sahib, do you want to take rest? It is quite late now.'

'Yes, it is late now,' he replied. The sun had crossed Dhanapati's house and moved towards Agunmari Island, ready to leave for the day. Soon, the shadows of the evening would cover the courtyard. 'But let me sit here and enjoy the sights. If I sleep, I will miss all this.'

'My master would say the same but after he lost his eyes, he cannot stay awake for long.'

'He is old now.'

'Not much, sahib. Some tortoises live for thousands of years, moving about in the water.'

'I know of one that stays on land and is three hundred years old. He just sits in one place.'

'Where, sir?'

'In Kolkata.'

'I will go to Kolkata to see him, but how will my master see?'

'You can describe it to him.'

'That's not enough to appreciate such an old tortoise. What will happen to him, sir?'

Aniket saw that her face darkened with anxiety. 'There's nothing much to be done, Dhaneshwari. This is the rule of life. How long can someone live?'

'But he is the pirate Pedru's descendant. His life cannot be compared to others. Sometimes he continues sleeping for a long time and that scares me.'

'Try to learn everything from him, Dhaneshwari.'

'He has already given me all that he had—the island, the sky, the water, these fishermen and their wives . . . they are all my subjects now.'

Aniket listened to her as if in a trance. The girl seemed to be so happy with what she got from Dhanapati. She was really tense about the old man's failing health. Aniket felt that the story that he wove had now merged into the story of Dhanapati and his gifting of the island to Kunti. Dhanapati thought that he owned everything that one could lay their eyes on. The ancient tribes in the western islands also thought the same. Aniket's story had its roots in five hundred years of aggression, acquisition and torture. Dhanapati's story reminded Aniket about the myth surrounding Columbus on which the western world survived. So, he had added Columbus's story to Dhanapati's story while weaving a new one. The white man's aggression, Portuguese pirates or Spanish Armada, they were just different names to the same story of inhuman torture. 'Will you be able to hold on to what he gave you?' Aniket asked Kunti.

'I am learning from him step by step, sir.

'It is easy to get, but difficult to maintain what you get. Be careful.'

'True, sir! Look at the master today. He sleeps all day but once upon a time, he had so much strength and vigour. He ruled the seas and went up to Lisboan. Today, he has a sea of darkness in front of his eyes. Nothing is permanent, sir.'

'There are some things,' Aniket said. 'The island, the winds, the sea.'

'They are as old as Dhanapati.'

'Which Dhanapati, the tortoise?'

'He sleeps so much these days. I fear that he might go into the sea permanently.'

Aniket Sen looked up at the sky. Kunti wiped a tear from the corner of her eye. In these few hours, Dhanapati and Dhaneshwari seemed to have grown close to Aniket Sen. The new story of Pedru that they heard from Aniket made them feel that he was one of their kind.

'Sahib, please tell me the story. What happened next?'

'Where did I stop?'

'A Pedru alighted with a sword.'

'I told you all I knew.'

'Please tell us once more. Let me call everyone. Let them listen to Pedru's story.'

'But it should be Dhanapati who should be telling them. He is the chief and they respect him for that.'

'In your story, you mentioned about the old wise man who told the fishermen to wait and not to go the water in the dark. What was his name?'

Aniket thought for a while and then said, 'Dhanapati.'

'Then how can Pedru be called Dhanapati?'

'True. He cannot be called by that name.'

'Then the people of the island should know this truth.'

'You two can tell them that story.'

'You are the government, sahib, please tell them.'

'Government is not supposed to tell that story.'

'When the government says something, people trust him.'

'Do you trust the government?'

'Sahib, you are a government, isn't it?'

'As a government, I feel the government cannot be trusted.'

'Then what will happen, sahib?'

'You tell them that you are the descendants of the old, wise man and Pedru the pirate is an outsider. Tell them that you were born of the women who were looted by the pirates.'

Kunti was amazed by this explanation. There was respect and devotion written all over her face for Aniket. After a while, she murmured, 'I was always confused. How could Pedru be Dhanapati? My master is also equally confused. He cannot decide for sure whether Pedru was a good man or an evil one.'

> Was he a saint or a pirate was he?
> The pirate-saint story keeps puzzling me.

'I came here to tell you the story of Pedru.'

'Will the inquiry happen?'

'This is the inquiry.' Aniket laughed.

'Sir, I have not seen Malakar in a long while. I don't know what he is doing now and whether he has already started his inquiry on Batashi. She is a fisherman's wife. He will break her home.'

'I will tell Malakar not to come to the island anymore.'

'Shall I call everyone and tell them Pedru's story?'

'You must. Tell them how the pirates came and looted everything, not once but many times. They came for the gold and the women, and left the island high and dry.'

'My master will be so happy to hear this. He was so confused about Pedru that he went on changing the story every time. Pedru went after Ma Kamala! Can you imagine that? A person who had the audacity to chase a goddess will naturally have no mercy for women like us. No woman can escape his lust. I am protected by the master and so I am safe. Tell me, sahib, is the government related to the pirates?'

Aniket Sen kept quiet. He was part of the government too. He was the BDO and that identity brought him to the island. He couldn't deny that he was a government. He walked towards the sea. Women pulled their veils down further and scattered away. People seemed to be working silently on the island. At the shore, he finally saw Malakar. He was wearing a faded terri-cotton kurta, a dhoti and pump shoes. He had a headful of grey-black hair. Malakar had seen his boss too and started walking towards him.

'I have looked for her everywhere.'

'Whom?'

'The fisherwoman who is needed for the inquiry.'

'The inquiry is done.'

'Did Batashi come?'

'She was not needed.'

'We will have to get her statement, sir and her fingerprint on it. Otherwise she will deny everything later on.'

'Malakar Babu, we will not return today.'

Malakar looked excited. 'I told you earlier, sir, that one did not return from the island the same day. Night halt is a must.'

'You will stay with me.'

'I am your bodyguard, sir. I got late because I was looking for Batashi.'

'Did you have your food?'

'Yes, sir. That is not a problem on the island. People want to feed you and give you gifts if you are government. But one has to treat them like menials to keep them on track. Sir, you are unable to show your temper, I have noticed that.'

Aniket knew Malakar well. He would go back to Ghoradal and tell him not to return to the island again. People of the island disliked him. Aniket could make that out from what Kunti had already told him. 'Malakar Babu, please go to Dhanapati's house and sit in the verandah.'

'I will go with you, sahib. I am scared of his wife.'

'Why?'

'She is a witch trained in Kamrup. I don't want to face her alone.'

'What nonsense is this, Malakar Babu?'

'It is true. She told me herself.'

'With whom did she go to Kamrup?'

'That I don't know. These women float about here and there. This time she has come with Dhanapati, there is no guarantee that he will bring her next year.'

'How can that be! She is his wife?!'

'These women cannot be wives, sir. They are just living with these men. Just by putting vermillion on the forehead and wearing shankha-pola, one doesn't become a wife.'

'Don't forget that he has given all that he had to her.'

'What has he given?'

'This island.'

Malakar laughed. 'You are such a big officer, sir. You will go so far. How can you believe this rubbish! This island belongs to the government. Does Dhanapati have any paper to prove that it is his?'

'He has been holding this island for so many years. Does he have any tax receipt?'

'There are so many like him who encroach the footpaths of Kolkata. Do they become owners?'

Aniket had not thought on those lines. Malakar continued his argument. 'The land revenue officials have collected tax and given receipts against it. If the receipt says hundred rupees, they must have collected five hundred. But that cannot establish ownership.'

Aniket stayed quiet. Once, he tried to say that Dhanapati had control over the island for many years. He thought that the island, the sky and the water was his. He had given it all to Kunti. Naturally, she was his wife. Malakar started laughing a dirty laugh. 'Sir, why are you taking their side? Batashi did not show up knowing fully well that she was at fault and there were several allegations against her. She should have come and met the big government. He has taken the trouble to come to the island for the inquiry. Is this a joke?'

Malakar kept bringing up the issue of Batashi over and over again. Aniket had never seen Batashi but she was clearly central to this story. He just kept quiet to stop Malakar from laughing at him. Malakar went on talking about the six-monthly existence of these families and how the men lived with the women for six months to leave them at the end of the duration. 'Sir, unless you take strict action against this practice, diseases like AIDS, syphilis and gonorrhoea will spread. Who will take responsibility then? She had invited the police to her shanty. Otherwise why would he enter? Sir, you must be strict.'

Fourteen

The fish of the sea, the waves and the blue,
Who stole them sir, do you have a clue?

'Has Dhanapati woken up?'

'Why, sir?'

'I have something to tell him.'

'Shall I wake him up?' Kunti got up.

Malakar was sitting nearby looking very uneasy. He was visibly scared of Kunti. He could not trust this witch who had been trained at Kamrup. But he did not want to show that he was scared.

'Before you call Dhanapati, go and call that Batashi. She needs to give her thumb impression on the inquiry report that was conducted last time.'

'Malakar Babu, we know very well what your inquiry means. You cannot have any more inquiries with Batashi.'

Malakar seemed to coil back into his shell. He was scared that Kunti might reveal more than what she had already done. If she tried to accuse him of anything, he would simply deny her allegations, he thought. These women were not good and tried to trap men. It was difficult to escape from them. At least he had managed to do that in the past.

Kunti left. Aniket Sen turned towards Malakar. 'Tell me what the government can do about the island,' he asked.

'Dhanapati was looking for a lease, but he will have to pay a lot of money to us as *salami*, perhaps a few lakhs, to become a lessee of the island.'

'The government might decide not to take salami.'

'That is not within the powers of the BLRO. Perhaps you can forward a request to the district magistrate because you are the big sahib of Ghoradal. You might even request the SDO, but will that be right?'

'Why?'

'These are prostitutes, who have just learnt to veil themselves. Look at how obstinate they have become! The woman who is the cause of all trouble has the audacity not to turn up to give her thumb impression!'

'Don't speak like this, Malakar Babu. What is the harm in giving Dhanapati the right to look after the island?'

'Don't do it, sir. At least not before you ban women from coming to the island.'

Aniket Sen remained quiet. The blind Dhanapati had merged with the blind, old, wise man from 500 years ago. The Portuguese and Spanish looters set their feet on the island and started occupying everything. The old, wise man lost everything. Unable to handle his defeat and the insult that came with it, he left everything and went deep into the forest, never to come back again. It was said that he crossed the forest and the mountains and then swam the river to reach a place where the white men could not find him.

Aniket felt as if the Red Indian chief from five hundred years ago had crossed the river and the sea to come to this island. After a span of five hundred years, here he was, telling him how the white aggressors torched the houses and looted the women who ran for their lives, only to surrender to the beastly pirates.

'You are right, Dhanapati chief. You had seen it right.'

'When I close my eyes, it all comes rushing back to me. The pirates and the looters come back to me in my dreams.'

'Dhanapati, sit here. I will tell you the rest. The blind old man crossed the forests, mountains and seas to land up on an island that he named after himself. It came to be known as Dhanapati's Island. He did not know what the pirates did in the meantime.'

'They grabbed the women and stuffed the hold of the ship,'
Dhaneshwari Kunti said.

'They wiped all the gold and jewels from the face of the earth,'
Dhanapati added.

'The men were tied up and sent to a far-off land. They were,
perhaps, sent to Lisboan,' Kunti further added.

'Lisboan had lost all its glory. The mansions had broken down,
the palace was in ruins, the gardens were full of weeds, the cows had
no milk and the fields had no crops,' Dhanapati said.

'How do you know that?' Aniket wanted Dhanapati to say more.

'I saw it all in my dreams. Birds were without feathers, trees were
without fruits and barren land for miles and miles together. Pedru
sent big and strong men in his ships and then he sent voluptuous and
beautiful women, followed by gold and seeds. He sent it all from this
island. This island had it all.'

Aniket kept listening to him as if in a trance.

'Feathers were back on birds, the seeds grew into trees full of
fruits, the fields were no longer barren, the broken houses and roads
were rebuilt, cars started running, wine was brewed from grapes,
babies were born and mothers found it difficult to cope up, beautiful
young maidens got handsome and healthy husbands . . .'

'How did all this happen?'

'It was all done by Pedru's men.'

'What happened next, master?'

'The old man of the island saw how the pirates filled the ship
with women and how the men were tied up and transferred. They
were helpless. They were being taken to Lisboan. The men jumped
on the captive women who in turn jumped into the sea and were
eaten up by sharks.'

'How do you know all this, Dhanapati?' Malakar scolded, unable
to control his pent-up frustration anymore.

'Master cannot see with his eyes, but he dreams of these things,'
Kunti explained.

'Are you fooling me? Can anyone dream such things?'

'He is not like you! You can only dream about inquiry and nothing else,' Kunti snapped.

Malakar kept quiet. He couldn't think anymore. Was Kunti reading his mind? Why was Dhanapati saying such strange things? Was he also a wizard trained at Kamakhya? Why was he saying such strange things relentlessly?

'Malakar Babu, why do you dream about Batashi, Sabitri and other women of the island all the time?' Kunti looked accusingly at Malakar.

'Mind your language. The sahib is sitting here, don't you see that?'

Kunti went a step ahead. 'Tell me the difference between government and the pirates and looters.'

Malakar cringed. How did Kunti get to know the deep, dark secret about how he lusted after Batashi and how she came to him in his dreams? He had no choice but to turn his face to the other side to avoid looking at Kunti.

Aniket intervened. 'Let Malakar be. I will deal with him. Dhanapati, can you continue with your story?'

'As they worked in Lisboan, laying the rail lines or breaking big stones, the men and women who went from here, wept helplessly.'

'Was this place converted into a wasteland?' There was pain writ large on Kunti's face.

'Only the old men and women who were half-dead and diseased remained. They were driven away by Pedru and his men before they attacked the next village.'

'What happened next?' Aniket asked.

'Let me say.' Kunti butted in.

> Pedru took it all—the sea, sky and stars,
> All went to Lisboan, nothing was ours.

Aniket Sen could not talk for a while and then spoke up in a low tone. 'Not all went. It was not possible to take everyone. The hold of a ship is not big enough for that. Once, they tried to overload a ship and it sunk.'

'Poor souls!' Kunti wiped a tear.

'Perhaps, in death, they found their release.'

Aniket spoke in a low tone. 'Pedru and his men brought many diseases from their country. Malaria, syphilis, jaundice, smallpox. No one knew about these diseases here before that.'

'Oh my God!' Kunti's eyes were ready to pop out.

'They injected these diseases into women's bodies here,' Aniket continued.

'Yes, this is possible,' Kunti said thoughtfully.

'Sahib, can you give me this land legally, so that I can take care of it?' Dhanapati asked.

'Isn't the island, the water and the sky, already yours?' Malakar had, at last, got a chance to catch Dhanapati on the wrong foot.

'Yes, they were all mine.'

'Then when did you lose control?' Malakar laughed his dirty laugh.

'Pedru took it away, you just heard it!'

'Your Pedru is a saint, isn't it?'

'Malakar Babu, I forgot Pedru's real identity. This sahib reminded me. Malakar Babu, you had said so many times that you would help me get control of the island officially. You haven't done that yet.'

'That was the land revenue collector, not me.'

'Sahib government, please give us back all that we have lost. Please bring back everything that has gone from here to Lisboan.'

'What should I bring back?'

'Everything, sahib. The seeds, fruits, crops, men and women and happiness.'

'This island was mine. I saw the stars fall from the sky. I was scared and told the fishermen not to go out into the sea to find out what had happened. I knew what it could be. The next day, Pedru came with his men. Since then, he has been coming back again and again.'

Kunti joined her palms to plead before Aniket. 'He comes back for women, sahib.'

'Sahib government, I have given everything to Kunti, my wife, my child and grandchild. Now, I see Pedru has control over all that was mine. If the government does not allow me control over the island, how can I give it to Kunti? This island, the blue of the sea, the crabs, tortoises, the birds in the sky and the seagulls belonged to the old, wise man. Why should Kunti's children not play on the island and swing with the waves? Sahib government, it was all mine but Pedru took everything away. Please bring everything back from Pedru government. He took everything away to decorate his Lisboan.'

> Dhanapati lives, my master's life,
> His life is now in your hands, I say as his wife.

'Let me see what I can do.'

'Sahib, please save us. I am the master of the island but nothing is mine. The fishermen and women don't know anything about this. Please give us the lease of the island.'

'I will have to see what the law says. Malakar Babu, please note.'

'Sahib, Malakar will not give the right report.'

Malakar got up. 'Sir, let us leave. These women don't know that I have to do exactly as you tell me. Dhanapati chief, I did not know that you have lost sight. Can you cross your heart and tell me if I have never helped you in the past?'

Dhanapati fiddled with his hands. 'Sit down, Malakar Babu. How can I forget that after a dangerous storm during that Kartik night, when the island lost everything, you helped to bring relief. You were such a good person then, not so much a government as you are now. You had just joined your service then, do you remember?'

'He remembers,' Kunti said.

Fifteen

The clay and sand, go hand in hand,
With turmeric paste, the bride looks grand.

Malakar had returned with the BDO to Ghoradal. Constable Midde carried the news to the trader. 'I am sure Malakar has been able to do something for me on the island,' the trader said.

'Yes, sir, I am sure. '

The trader had automatically become Midde's 'sir'. It was only in the month of Kartik that this man had followed him to the island. After seeing Batashi, he had swooned over her. But a lot had changed since then. Midde had realized that Dasharath was no ordinary trader. He had one foot in Hong Kong, Singapore, Bangkok and Jakarta and spoke only about dollars. He bought and sold only in dollars and was about to introduce dollars to Ghoradal market. Soon, one would have to buy dollars with rupees and rice, dal, salt and oil with dollars. The times had started to change.

Vodka flew freely. It brought the constable to the trader every now and then. It created such fireworks in his brain. It brought back scenes of the 1350 famine that killed his father, grandfather, mother and grandmother. They seemed to stare at him from the depths of time. The trader was his Spanish master from the time of the famine. Midde sat with folded hands in front of the trader and swayed from side to side.

'Has Batashi come?'

'You should ask Malakar, sir.'

'Then what news have you brought for me?'

'Malakar has come back. Batashi has either come or hasn't come with him. There are only two options.'

'How can returning empty-handed be an option?'

'These are either or options, sir.' Midde sipped his vodka and reached out for the long cigarette that the trader had offered. There were some papers on the shelves from where the trader pulled out something. 'Government, in between fuelling yourself thus, please think of what you can do for me.'

'That's exactly why I have brought this news of Malakar's return to you.'

'Arrange to either take her thumb impression or forge it on these papers to make it official. Batashi will then be trapped.'

'What paper is that?'

'It is a sale deed that says that she has sold herself. Constable, mine is a powerful bloodline.'

> I come from the stock of the pirate Spaniard,
> The deed will bring what I have tried so hard.

'I didn't follow, sir.'

'We have been trading women for generations. We buy and sell through self-sale deeds. Government, come here, read this.'

'Is this a donation deed?'

'No, it is a self-sale deed.'

'What happens if one signs the deed?'

'One can sell oneself.'

Mangal Midde gaped at him in wide-eyed wonder. The trader no longer looked like a simple trader from the present. He looked like a foreign pirate, a Portuguese or a Spaniard. His eyes were red with rage and he stared hard at Midde.

'Once she signs here or puts her thumb impression, she will never be able to refuse.'

'With whom will she sign the deal?'

'Initially I thought that she would be sold off by you, government, and so I paid to you. But even after you sold her, she is not willing to come to me. But I have paid for her body; now I will not let her go.'

'Yes! Why shouldn't you stake a claim on her when I have already sold her to you?' Midde growled.

'So go and get her fingerprint or signature on the dotted lines of this deed for me. Batashi will then come under my control fully. We are used to taking control of women like this. Earlier, we would simply pack them into the hold of the ship and sell them in the markets of Arakan. From there, they would be sent off to Fashion TV. I will tighten my grip on her legally with the help of this signed deed. Listen to me as I read the deed to you.'

'First party: Mister Dasharath Singh, Nyaybhushan or Spaniard pirate.

Second party: Batashi Dasi, twenty-four years, wheatish complexion, full of youth, half-yearly fisherwoman, remaining half unknown, Dhanapati's Island or Island of the Pirates, district of the sea.

The second party is the seller and the first party is the buyer in this self-sale deed.

Second Party: I am a woman on the island at the peak of her youth, whose body has been measured by the surveyor and the statistics are as follows:

Height: Five feet and three inches.

Complexion: Wheatish or pre-sunset.

Eyes: Like a scared doe.

Arms: Like wild ivy.

Breasts: Like two ripe wood apples, about 36 inches.

Hips: Like the middle of a shapely boat, about 36 inches.

Waist: Proportionate, almost like the narrow tip of a boat.

That apart, a crown full of hair like a barn full of crops, depths of the eyes that match the high tides at sea and a flash of lightning frozen forever in the pupils of the two eyes.

I, Batashi Dasi, am signing this self-sale deed. I am a fisherwoman of six months. No one knows how I survive outside the island at the end of the six months without food, clothes and shelter. From the middle of Chait, my husband of six months forgets me and leaves me alone to my fate. From Chait till Ashwin, I belong to no one. The constable takes me just as the wagon breaker criminal does. I am there for anyone's asking but still cannot feed myself properly. An umbrella seller from Bangladesh promised to return but he didn't keep his word. Unable to continue like this any longer, I sign this sale deed and offer myself up for sale.

First person Dasharath Singh will take my responsibility from now on. In return, he will have the right to enjoy and exploit me in every way that he thinks fit. When I grow old, he will pity me and give me some money to help me survive. If I wish to free myself, I will pay more than a *maund* of turmeric to the first person, if he agrees, or else, I will give whatever he asks for. I accept and sign all these conditions and offer myself up for sale. Year 1412, Date 14, Poush.'

'Who drafted this deed?' Midde asked the trader.

'A barrister did it.'

'How did he manage?'

'I told him what to write.'

'How did you master such legal language?'

'It runs in the family. We have titles to show our legal prowess. We are Nyaybhushans since generations. My forefathers used to buy and sell women against deals that were fixed in maunds of turmeric.'

Dasharath spread out his feet and relished the look on Midde's face. 'If it were in those times, Midde, your Batashi would have been in the hold of my ship. There are hundreds of deeds in my house. Some deal with the sale of men and women while some deal with property and some with the sale of islands, sea, winds, mountains, day, night, full moon and what not.'

Midde's eyes were ready to pop out. 'Sahib, you are the lord of my life. Sahib, now I know who bought Kunjamala Dasi.'

'Who is she?'

'My grandmother's grandmother. She was sold off to a Nyaybhushan at the age of twelve because there was very little food in the family to feed her. Do you remember her?'

'You swine, don't you realize that you are talking rubbish?! You are drunk, you silly!'

'My lord, her mother could not feed her because the famine did not leave any food for anyone. She would cry for rice. Her youth had just blossomed like that of a budding flower.'

'Will you please stop now?'

'I think we also have such a deed in our house. No one had any turmeric to offer to release Kunjamala from Nyaybhushan. Her daughter, Mahamaya, too suffered the same fate. We were orphaned.'

'Shut up! I will never give you any foreign liquor ever. What kind of a government are you that you are still followed by memories of the famine and drought? What a wretched family background you have.'

My lord, trader of traders, Spaniard pirate, please release Kunjamala now.'

'She died an old hag on the streets somewhere. Her daughter Mahamaya was so beautiful that my grandfather bought her against her weight in gold. But she was so haughty that my grandfather could not control her. Finally, he sold her off in the Arakan.'

'Oh my God! My lord, why did you sell her?!'

'Get lost now. You need country liquor, you dog! You don't have the capacity to tolerate foreign liquor. Now take this deed and get it signed. If you manage to do that, I shall give you rupees or dollars or whatever you want.'

'Will I manage to do it, sahib?'

'You have to.'

'My lord, Spaniard, what if this government fails? Please give me the sale deeds of Kunjamala and Mahamaya. They will finally be released.'

'In that case, let me get into an agreement with you first. You have already taken two-and-a-half thousand rupees for Batashi, but she did not come.'

Midde kept murmuring, 'My grandmother's grandmother, mother, sister and all other women were taken away by the Spaniards during the famine. They would take starch from rice and lure the hungry women. They would twitch their tongues and call them the way one calls dogs . . .'

'Now stop your nonsense and write what I ask you to write on a piece of paper. "I am Mangalmoy Midde, government. In my presence, Batashi sold herself to Dasharath Singh. I have brought Batashi to Dasharath Singh and accepted my share of a maund of turmeric. This, I returned to Dasharath Singh to release the deeds of Kunjamala. I have helped release Kunjamala." Put your signature at the end.'

Midde started writing every word that the trader dictated to him. 'Today's vodka was the best—uncomparable.' Midde shivered in ecstasy. His salt-and-pepper hair stood on end. His flesh broke out in goosebumps. His nostrils flared up and his eyes were ready to come out of their sockets.

'If I fail to bring Batashi to you, I will give back to you all the turmeric that has been given to me and you will not have to return Kunjamala's sale deed . . .'Midde wrote.

'What if I fail to bring Batashi Bibi to you?'

'If you manage to take her thumb impression, she will be forced to come.'

'What if I fail to do that?'

'Then be prepared to repay two and a half maunds of turmeric.'

'What if I fail to gather that much turmeric?'

'What are you a government for, if you are unable to complete such a simple task?'

Mangal Midde looked helpless. 'Let me see what news Malakar has brought from the island.'

'You do your job, let Malakar do his.'

> Take your turmeric, bring me her sign,
> Free your Kunjamala, if Batashi becomes mine.

Two days later, he met Malakar. They sat at the tea stall under the
banyan tree as Midde related the entire episode. Malakar was tense.
He hadn't met the trader after returning to Ghoradal. He had already
spent the money that the trader had given him and it was impossible
to retrieve it from the depth of his stomach. This was not the first
time that he had taken money but failed to deliver. There were so
many people who had paid to him for jobs he promised but couldn't
accomplish. So, he had to take a transfer from Joynagar to avoid
facing his chasers. He had a bad habit of borrowing money and never
paying back his debtors.

'How will you collect the thumb impression?'

'From her left thumb.'

'What if you don't get that?'

'Why? Doesn't Batashi have thumbs? I thought she was complete
in every way.'

'Don't be stupid. I mean that to avoid trouble, why don't you
take a fake impression? Say the impression of your wife's thumb. The
trader won't be able to make out.'

'What if he asks for my wife then??!!'

'Don't be stupid. Your lathi-wielding job has made you stupid,
actually. I am talking of a fake thumb impression. Are you a kid? Take
an impression from anyone's thumb, I meant.'

'Will the deed still be valid?'

'Listen, the main thing is to get to Batashi.'

'Is that so difficult?'

'I have been keeping an eye on the riverbank daily so that I don't
miss her if she decides to leave the island and come back early. If I
don't manage to nab her, God knows what will happen to me.'

'I have also taken money from the trader,' Midde said.

'That doesn't matter.'

'What will happen if I fail?'

'Pay back with a maund of turmeric,' Malakar started laughing.

'Don't joke, Malakar Babu.'

'There's nothing to joke about. Yes, you had taken two and a half or three thousand rupees and sold Batashi to the trader. But is there any written proof about that? None. Let us not meet the trader anymore. The season is over. They should try and avoid getting caught now.'

Midde was sad. If he was able to get Batashi for the trader, he would have got a lot of dollars. In these hard times, such money was essential to survive. People like the trader kept his kitchen fire burning. Otherwise he would have had to sell off his family and himself like Kunjamala.

'Let's leave all that and chat now.'

'Okay.'

'Let me tell you what I saw on the island this time.'

'Tell me what you saw.'

'Batches of fishermen and women have started leaving the island and are coming back to Ghoradal. The women are all veiled and we cannot see their faces. What if Batashi was among those veiled women? What if she has managed to escape already?'

'Why aren't they returning together like they used to do in the past?'

'They are doing this to save Batashi. You cannot make out who's who underneath the veil. This is a scheme devised by that young wife of Dhanapati's.'

'Will she not come back next year?'

'That has to be seen.'

'So, my contract is broken?'

'Now look for a maund of turmeric.' Malakar stretched his legs. He lit a cigarette an offered one to Midde.

'What if the trader asks me to refund his money?'

'Arrange for turmeric and free Batashi.'

Midde felt relieved. He could not sell another Kunjamala. He was a small government, but a government after all. He looked out at the snaking Kalnagini and memories of that Kartik full moon kept rushing back to him. 'See you, Malakar Bhai.'

'Where are you going?'

'To where my eyes take me.'

Malakar smiled back. 'Go in search of turmeric, Midde. Batashi would have looked beautiful if someone smeared her with turmeric paste.'

'Do you love her?'

Malakar looked out into the river. The tide was high. He closed his eyes and could see the island in front of him. The fishermen and women, old Dhanapati and his young wife. The tortoise chief had woken up from his slumber and had started moving towards Ghoradal with the island on his back. Was it pirate Pedru's ship moving towards Ghoradal with the island and its people, complete with the sky and the flying birds? They swayed on the waves as they came towards Ghoradal.

Malakar hummed,

Dhanapati, Dhanapati, a trader was he,
Reached Ghoradal and said, help me.
One hand was held by Dhaneshwari,
The other was held by Batashishwari.

Part IV

One

Moonbeams pour into my broken home,
Who needs food under such a happy dome?

The fishermen return in Chaitra. They had started coming back to Ghoradal, their boats laden with goods and household items. For the next six months, they will stay at Ghoradal, Firingitala and Manasadanga. Not even once will the memories of the island come back to them. The men will forget the women with whom they had set up home for six months. There was a world of difference between land and water. One didn't talk of the life on water when one was on land.

The fishing boats had motors fitted to them. They had the power of seven horses. Whether the horses were five or seven didn't matter so much. That they were there was the most important point. Dhanapati called them water horses. He told stories about the fabled walrus in the deep sea. People were scared of going into the deep. If you met the sea horse, you had met death indeed. The horse would take you on its back for a tour of the sea. The journey was never-ending because the sea would never end and one sea would lead to another and yet another. Three parts of the earth were made up of sea and one part was land. The earth was the back of the tortoise and floating on sea.

It took the fishermen six to seven hours to reach Ghoradal on these horse-powered boats. In the older days, when there were no horse boats, one had to come by wooden boats and that took them at least twenty-two hours. A lot depended upon the east wind that was sent by Lord Jagannath from Puri.

'I just need to sleep for twenty-four hours now to get the island out of my mind,' Dhanapati said.

'Not possible for me, master,' replied Kunti.

'I have given it all to you. The island, the sea and the sky. They are yours now.'

'I am feeling so sad, master.'

'Why?'

'I have left my island unguarded.'

'You cannot move about with your earthly belongings, isn't it?'

Dhanapati's boat was spacious and colourful. It had a good seating arrangement. Dhanapati sat with his legs spread out, looking relaxed and happy. Kunti massaged his tired feet and he closed his blind eyes in pleasure. Kunti knew how to knead away pain. 'You are my mirror in which I see my happy face, Dhaneshwari.'

Kunti rested her head on Dhanapati's chest. 'Tell me that story.'

'Which one? I have exhausted my stock in the past six months. I have donated everything to you.'

'You haven't donated your stories! You have just given me the island, the sky, fish, sea, trees and everything else but the stories.'

'I have nothing left, Kunti. I have given everything to you, including my stories. The island, the sea, the birds and fish, the moon and sun are all witness to this.'

Dhanapati had given everything to Kunti and had called a meeting of the fishermen to declare this. Everything was hers and nothing remained with him now. If Kunti wished, she could stop Dhanapati from coming to the island from the next year and he would helplessly have to accept it. He had lost the light of his eyes. If Kunti decided to throw him into the deep, she could do that and he would have to accept that too. He would then transform into a tortoise and crawl into the water. Suddenly, Kunti became conscious of these thoughts and felt ashamed of herself. How could such thoughts come to her? She was immensely grateful to Dhanapati for choosing her and giving her a life. He was attracted by her beauty and made her his wife. Now, it was her duty to take care of him.

'You tell me new stories that are still untold. They are not mine yet.'

'Whatever I have is yours, the ones that I have given and those that are yet to be given. They are all yours and will remain yours.'

'I don't know how to spin tales. What will I tell the fishermen and their wives?'

'Tell them what I have told you all these days.'

'They know those stories.'

'They will forget them soon. These six months on the land will make them forget everything they know of the island. That's how things are.'

Kunti listened to Dhanapati in wide-eyed wonder. The old man's fingers ran over her face and neck and brushed against her breasts. Kunti kissed him on his forehead. 'Why do they forget everything?'

'Otherwise they will not be able to adjust to their old families.'

'Do they forget the island?'

'Yes, they do, Dhanapati murmured. Kunti just couldn't believe that. It showed on her face. The boat made its way noisily towards Ghoradal. The journey seemed to carry on endlessly. To Kunti, the world looked like a plate of water. The sun was up, and it was hot. There was no wind blowing. When the wind would start blowing, the sun's heat would make it mad and it would beat about the water, making waves.

'Unless they forget what happened on the island, they will never be able to live with their old families on land,' Dhanapati said. 'Gradually, they will wipe out all memories of the island. Even if stray thoughts come into the mind, they will brush them aside. They will return to their ancestors' house, wives, children, land with a few mango trees, coconut trees and small ponds near their homes . . . . This will keep them from thinking about the island and the wives they lived with over there. They will keep themselves busy by repairing their huts, clay cleaning them and re-laying the

straw and thatched bamboo roofs. Those who have some land
will start sowing paddy. They will return in Chait and calculate
how much they earned from the paddy they had sowed in
Agrahayan. They will buy new clothes for their wives and children.
The wives know that their husbands spend six months on the
island to go fishing and earn money. These six months, the wives
are starved of their husbands, and they think that their husbands
have also starved for them. But once in a while, dark thoughts of
their husbands lying with other women cross their minds. Did the
island have women who attracted their husbands to them? Were the
sea, sky, fish and island good enough to keep their men busy and
satisfied? They have heard vague stories of women on the island.
Are they true? Was the island the significant other in the lives of
their husbands?' Dhanapati had dozed off in the midst of explaining
things to Kunti.

She shook him up. 'Are you feeling sleepy?'

Dhanapati's voice had trailed off and he was deep in sleep. Kunti
woke him up. 'Let me think of what more I can tell you. I have
already given you all my stories too.'

'No, I don't believe that. Please tell me more stories.'

'The wives are suspicious but they remain quiet about it.'
Dhanapati picked up the strands of his story again. 'At least for these
six months, their husbands were theirs. Six months later, they have
to let them go. They have to go for business to earn money. Money
brings smiles, food and clothes. Men have to go out to earn and no
one in the family should stop them. They think their husbands have
spent these months yearning for them just as they yearned for their
husbands. They do not know if the men have strayed just as the men
did not know whether the women have been alone all this while.'

'Can they really forget their wives on the island?' Kunti
kept nagging.

'Yes.'

'Batashi is valuable on the island. On land, she has no value.'

'Hai Allah! What will happen to me?'

'Why do you fret? I don't have any family at Ghoradal. I will not forget you! My island is my only reality.'

'I will hang myself if you forget me.'

'I cannot forget you. It is not possible anymore.' Dhanapati laughed.

'Then why should the fishermen forget their wives from the island.'

'Their wives on land can make out that their husbands are in great health and their bodies glow with vigour. How can that be possible without the touch of a woman for six months? Were there women on the island? Never mind that. Those women didn't manage to keep the men back on the island, after all. Men need women; they are not used to fasting like women. Their wives at Ghoradal have a house and children, some land and its produce, cows and buffaloes. These are theirs and keep them going when the men were away. They try to forget their men during this time. Those who cannot do that have other routes to keep themselves happy.'

'You mean they look for men outside their marriage?' Kunti asked in a hushed voice.

'You don't have to pay attention to all this.'

Kunti was quiet. After a while, the heat and the breeze had a soporific effect on her and she started dozing alongside Dhanapati. He woke up after some time and started talking about the government. 'The government is in everything and yet in nothing. You cannot escape the government because he has his eyes on you. Government does everything and yet he has no work. Government is responsible for the running of the country but how can that be because he doesn't work much! Government does not bother about anything and yet everyone is under him.'

'Not this story, master.' Kunti was half asleep. 'Tell me the story of your travels on sea.'

'Those are long stories. I not only travelled on the sea but also on the rivers. That is because I was not a fisherman at that time. My grandfather and his father were rich traders.'

'Who is a trader? What is trade?'

'Buying and selling.'

'Like that trader?'

'He buys and sells women.'

'That too is trade, after all.'

'The pirates did that kind of trade.'

'Were you not a pirate?'

'No, I was Dhanapati Saudagar, a big trader of goods.'

'The fishermen are scared of you because they think that you are a descendant of pirate Pedru. If they get to know that you are a descendant of a trader, will they still be in awe of you?'

'How does that matter?'

'They need to fear the government. You are the government of the island.'

Dhanapati kept quiet. Kunti was right. People thought for long that he was the descendant of a pirate. Now, if they heard that his forefathers were traders, there could be a totally different reaction! They could turn suspicious and even belligerent. They would think that he was blind, old and weak since the blood of the pirates did not run in his veins. They were scared of Pedru the pirate and the stories of his swords and guns and how he tortured women before putting them into the hold of his ship. The story of the blind, old village chief who fled the island to escape Pedru, that the BDO had narrated, made Dhanapati believe in it. He imagined that he was the wise old village chief. He was a trader in his youth. Dhanapati started spinning a story.

'Master, please say something. Don't be quiet.'

'Have you heard the story of Chand Saudagar?'

'That is Ma Manasa's story.'

'I am a descendant of Chand Saudagar.'

'How is he related to Pedru?'

'They are not related. Pedru is from Lisboan, beyond the seven seas.'

While sailing on his boat towards Ghoradal, Dhanapati found a new story of his life to spin. This is the story that the BDO gave him.

He would now add branches and leaves to it. Pedru was a cruel pirate. He didn't have anything to do with Dhanapati. Pedru had come to loot the gold that Bengal once had and started by attacking the islands. The landmass at Ghoradal and the islands beyond it were made of gold but after Pedru looted them, they lost their sheen, leaving behind only clay and rocks. In his youth, he could associate with the power of Pedru but that didn't make him happy anymore. It gave him greater pleasure to think that he was a descendant of Chand Saudagar, the biggest trader that Bengal ever had. Lakhinder was Chand Saudagar's son. He was married to Beula. Beula floated on a boat on the waters of the sea.

'Which sea is that, master?'

'This one.'

'Where is heaven, master?'

'On Dhanapati's Island.'

'My island is so lonely now. There is no one to look after it. It lies alone in the midst of the seven seas.'

'Tortoise Dhanapati will look after it, don't worry. He will carry it on his back and travel from sea to sea.'

'What if he does not bring the island back?'

Dhanapati kept quiet. These thoughts often came to him and he brushed them aside. The island had to be in its place, else his empire would collapse. The island belonged to God and all things that belonged to Him were protected by Him. He listened to the waves as they softly hit his wooden boat. The sea would soon lead them into the mouth of the river and they would enter the waters of Kalnagini. The very name of the river proved that he belonged to the lineage of Chand Saudagar. There was a strong current in the river that made his boat go round and round for some time. He had drowned in this water twice and also managed to swim back to the shore. A long chain of thoughts kept him busy.

'Master, what would you buy and sell for a living?'

'Shankha-pola, betel nut and leaves, turmeric, coconut . . .'

'What else?'

'Rice and clothes.'

'How many boats did you have?'

'Tiya-thuti, Ratnamala, Shankhatali, Pankhiraj, Chandrapat . . .
so many of them.'

> My master sails on so many boats,
> Rice turns to gold and so he gloats.

Tears ran down Dhanapati's cheeks. Memories came rushing
back to him.

Two

The trader loves his betel nut,
Whether it's cut or uncut.

Dhaneshwari Kunti kept humming her tunes. Dhanapati was in a trance. He could visualize a giant boat laden with goods returning after a good season of buying and selling. Was it the famous Saptadinga of Chand Saudagar? It was known by seven names—Mayurpankhi, Madhukar, Sagarnati, Shankhachur, Chandrapal, Durgabar and Ranajoy. They went with turmeric and returned with gold that shone under the sun. It was a good season. The boats returned with riches after crossing the big sea and entered the river to reach land. The boats would cross Hathiagarh, Chatrabhog, Kaliadaha, Baruipur, Churaghat, Kalighat, Chitrapur, Betor, Ghushuri, Ariadaha, Kamarhati and Kotrang to reach Chand Saudagar's village.

> Ships full of gold sail to the land,
> Dhanapati trader sits on them grand.

Dhanapati's slumber broke and he started spinning his tale again. 'You could neither see the beginning nor the end of the water as you sailed on it. As the moon rose on the full moon night, the water turned into gold, making the sea look like a maiden.'

'Maiden? Woman?'

'Yes, a beautiful young woman who knew how to sing.'

'What song did she sing?'

'Songs that you sing.'

'Like me? She sang in the midst of the sea?'

'Yes, I remember how her songs would fill the air with fragrance. A lulling breeze blew. It was heavenly.'

'What happened next?'

'She was a mermaid and cast her spell on the boat. She led the boat away.'

'The boat followed the woman?'

'Yes, she had cast a spell on traders, fishermen and everyone else.'

'Don't tell me about that woman.'

Dhanapati smiled. 'Men were starving for women after living without them on the waters for so many months. They were naturally lured when she beckoned them.'

'She only helped to sink the boat, isn't it?'

'Yes.'

'What happened to the gold?'

'It sank too.'

'Women are treacherous.'

Dhanapati stayed quiet. This was part of the lore that he had heard in his youthful days on the sea. Kunti did not know how a man's mind worked, he thought. She should go to Khidirpur and see the market. This market served fishermen whose boats came to the dock. They would come up and judge every body part before selecting a woman. It was as natural as buying vegetables by running one's hand on them. Why had the trader come to look for women on the island? It was because he was a supplier of women to these markets.

'Master, I don't think there are women on the water. They should be there on land, isn't it? Land is where all the sin happens, not water. Tell me, master.'

'Mermaids are not just part of stories, they exist. They are part of the mysteries of the water that will remain unexplained forever. Once while crossing the water, I saw an island.'

'That is natural.'

'No, it isn't. That island was not there before. I knew every inch of the sea and that island was never there before. The fishermen wouldn't listen to me. They wanted to get on to that island.'

Kunti sat up. 'Tell me more about that island.'

'I don't remember.'

'Did you allow the boat to pull up at the shore?'

'I don't think so.'

'What was there on that island?'

'I don't know.'

Kunti looked disheartened. She rested her head on Dhanapati's chest. Her hot breath made the grey hair on Dhanapati's chest dance. 'I have become so incapable, wife. Everything is nearing an end now.'

'No, I will not let that happen.'

'I have given everything to you and now, I feel so spent.'

'Please sit up, master. I will first take you to a doctor who will see your eyes once we reach Ghoradal.'

Dhanapati sat up. He tried to spin another story, but could not. The Almighty was taking away everything, one by one. His manhood was gone as had the light of his eyes and now, even his talent of spinning stories relentlessly was leaving him too.

'Can you continue the story, Kunti?'

'Will I manage?' Kunti whispered.

'Your youth is unmatched. That should give you the strength.'

'Are you sure, master?'

Dhanapati kept thinking. 'With no land in sight, the boat sailed on. Do you understand, Kunti? It has to sail on.'

'Yes, let the water take control of the boat and let it sail on.'

'You are absolutely right, Kunti. This is how you add wings to your tale. Treat your story like one of the seven boats of Chand Saudagar. Let it be Madhukar. Let it sail on.'

'Yes, master.'

'Nothing can remain in one place, Kunti. Be it day, night or the moon. Everything has to move on.'

'I agree.'

'Just think of a new story and let the words flow.'

'Master, in that island you discovered, were there huts, trees, people?'

'What happened next, Kunti?'

'The houses were in ruins. They had been burnt.'

'Is that so?'

'Yes. The trader allowed the fishermen to pull up on the shore. They went around the island and found no one.'

'Why? What happened to the people?'

'The island is inhabited only for six months from Ashwin to Chait. Fishermen and women returned after Chait.'

'What happened next?'

'The trader and the fishermen did not know of this tradition. So, they kept thinking about why no one was there.'

'Did they find their answer?'

'One fisherman warned the rest. He thought it was dangerous to linger on and asked others to leave quickly. Another one thought about staying back to investigate.'

'What did Chand Saudagar say?'

'He felt powerless. He could not move till the fishermen agreed. He asked them to explore the island if they wanted to. He asked them to bring him anyone they found so that they could be taken away with them.'

Dhanapati listened intently. Was Kunti talking about his own island? Every year, while leaving the island this was what they did. All shanties made of bamboo sticks, jute bags and leaves were set on fire. Only his house remained intact because it was made of bricks. He had worked hard to build that house. Bricks and cement were brought from Ghoradal and labourers too. Naturally, he would never let anyone destroy that house. He was the only one returning to the island year after year. The fishermen and women changed every year. Not everyone who came this year, came back the next.

'Some fishermen asked, "Who set the huts on fire?"' Kunti picked up the strands of the story again.

'Who else but the ones who had lived there!'

'How will the trader and his fishermen know that? They naturally wondered at what they saw. Finally, they thought that someone has cast an evil spell on the island. A witch had cast her spell on the island, they concluded.'

'Why should a witch do that?'

'When a third person—man or woman—enters into a happily married life of a couple, homes burn. Didn't Batashi's home burn when the trader set his eyes on her? Didn't the inquiry destroy her peace of mind?'

'Continue your story of the trader without getting into the lives of people you know.'

'The trader and the fishermen went from one shanty to another to make sure that no one was left behind.'

'Did they find anyone?'

'Yes, one woman who was pregnant and had not left the island. They had not set her shanty on fire.'

'Was it real or was it an illusion?'

'It is quite possible that it was an illusion. But the fishermen saw that a beautiful pregnant woman sat there sucking on tamarind.'

'Please don't bring back Anna Bibi into this story. Do you think I would have managed to come back to the island if I set up home with Anna Bibi? I would not have remained Dhanapati then.'

'She could have been with you like I am with you now, master.'

'Don't bring her into the story, Kunti, and don't burn your heart. She was the wife of a moneyed man. That man couldn't satisfy her and so, she came to me. Can a pirate have a wife, home and hearth, children and land? Pirates do not lead regular family lives.'

'But you are not a pirate, master!'

Dhanapati sat up. He felt Kunti's hands and moved his hands up to reach her shoulder. He toned his voice down to avoid others from hearing what he said next. 'Listen Kunti, no matter what the BDO government says, I am indeed a descendant of that dangerous pirate Pedru who crossed the seven seas to reach Ghoradal. The BDO government called me the old, wise man of the island and I had agreed then to make him happy. It is not so.'

'Yes, you must be related to that pirate. Otherwise why would you choose a young girl like me?'

'You are the one who has cast her magic spell on me. You mesmerized me and pulled me to you. I got lost in your beautiful eyes that seemed to give me the light I lacked. You reminded me of my Anna.'

'Not again, master.'

'You stole the light of my eyes and made me blind so that I stop looking at other women.'

'Let us stop this discussion, master.'

'Women are the best gifts that God has created on earth for men. You can never have too much of them. Alas, my eyes cannot see you!'

'We must get your eyes checked and treated.'

You are the most intelligent woman I have ever come across, Kunti. You kissed my eyes and stole their light. Perhaps you wished that your old husband should turn blind.'

'Please don't continue like that, master. Let us understand that none of this is true.'

'You must have prayed that your pirate husband shouldn't look at anyone else.'

'Isn't that natural, master?'

'Is that why you made me blind?'

'There is poison deep inside you that is making you think like this. I have done nothing.'

Dhanapati remained quiet for a while. He could feel anger surge inside him. The heat of Chaitra was fuelled by the hot breeze and stormed within. As he neared Ghoradal, he could not tolerate his blindness anymore. If the island was his reality, Ghoradal was an alternate reality. He couldn't ignore it. His home at Ghoradal with its trees and ponds was all real. He just had to look out of this home into the never-ending greens like he looked out of his home on the island towards the endless waters. He could not deny the attraction of earthy Ghoradal. He could not accept the fact that he would not be able to see Ghoradal with his own eyes again and depend on Kunti to take him everywhere.

Kunti could feel the heat of his anger and tried her best to calm him down. 'Yes master, you are indeed a pirate. Your stories were so real that I could make out that you had lived the life that you described. Sometimes I felt that you were Pedru himself. You were given the boon by Ma Kamala. She had brought out the island, its sky, stars and sea for you.'

Kunti managed to calm the old man down. He reached out for her and pulled her onto his chest, moving his old hands all over her body and feeling his manhood making a comeback. 'The story is not complete yet, master,' Kunti whispered in half pleasure.

'Which one?'

'The one where the trader and the fishermen reached the island and started looking for those who had lived there before.

'Please don't bring Anna into that story. She should have known how to be a pirate's wife. If she did not manage to please the pirate, isn't it natural that the pirate would leave her and move on?'

Kunti kept quiet. She had to learn to spin her own tale. She was, after all, the owner of the island now, Dhaneshwari. She should have her own story to tell others. She should be able to spin interesting stories that would attract the fishermen and women to her. She had to rule the island well. She would have to come out of Dhanapati's shadow and create an identity for herself. Her old man would die soon, and by then, she should have her own story.

Three

Make you hay while the sun shines,
He who doesn't, riles and whines.

No one knew where Jamuna, Batashi and the others went after reaching Ghoradal. There were no limits to the endless land that stretched to the north, east and west. The high road led to the horizon. The trader, the constable and the clerk of the BDO office, Nabadwip Malakar, could only bang their heads against the wall. Who knew where the women had gone? They could have gone to Khidirpur, Watgunj, Metiabruz or Sonarpur or even Baruipur. The trader was purple with anger. He called the constable useless and said that the contract was cancelled.

'Let me try some old black magic to get their location,' Mangal Midde told the trader.

'Will it work?'

'Why not? My cousin Patit Paban Midde got his daughter back from Mumbai using this trick.'

'You may go and take a sacred oath in the name of Ma Vishalakshi,' Nabadwip Malakar suggested.

'Will that help?'

'Both Batashi and you will be saved from the tiger.'

'Are there tigers here, on land?'

'There are. There are crocodiles in the water too.'

'Yes, yes, you are right. The both of you . . .' the trader said, mimicking the style of the British masters. Both Midde and Malakar were impressed. This style of the masters never failed to get the desired result.

'We need to offer some prasad to Ma Vishalakshi and also pay hundred and one rupees to the priest.'

'Hope you will not ask for more after that.'

'The goddess has to be offered a red-bordered white saree and a new *gamcha* (cotton towel), so I need hundred and one rupees too,' Malakar said.

'For a black magic spell, I don't need more than hundred and one rupees, but I expect some more from you, if you are pleased with my work, finally.'

'You do what you want, black magic or not, I don't care. But make sure that I get that woman or I will file a case of cheating against both of you.'

Nabadwip Malakar was quick to reply. 'Please don't lose faith in us, sir.'

'I have used black magic to intercept smuggled goods in my area so many times, sahib,' Midde spoke up.

'India is the land of black magic, sir,' Malakar added.

The trader was lost in thought. If Batashi managed to come to Ghoradal and escape unnoticed, would black magic work at all? Malakar could read his thoughts.

'Your faith in us will bring her to you.'

'What do you mean?'

'I mean you will get her. Just have a little more patience.'

'What news of Kunti? The wife of that old tortoise. Can I get her?' There was frustration in the trader's voice now.

'She is still with him,' Malakar informed him.

'Should I go back then?'

'Please leave your mobile number with us. Let us complete the procedure to bring Batashi back. We will inform you the moment we get her.'

'What is the use of my coming here if I cannot return with at least one woman!?'

'Sir, I had given Batashi to you. You got her from the government already,' Midde tried to reason.

'But I didn't get control over her, isn't it?'

'This is a completely new procedure for me and I am taking time to adjust to it. I already told you that.'

'When did you tell me?' Suddenly, the tone of the trader's voice changed and he started speaking like a foreigner.

'I did, sir. Perhaps you have forgotten.'

'Don't try to cheat me. You had taken money and promised to give me that woman.'

'He he he . . .' Midde laughed.

'Shut up!' The trader did not hide his anger and shouted at the constable. 'How dare you laugh?'

'No, no, sir, the constable will not laugh.' Malakar tried to calm the trader.

'I will take you to court for taking money and not delivering the goods.'

The constable was totally deflated. He should not have come to the trader at all. The season was over and the fishermen and women had left the island. They came to Ghoradal in batches and left for their respective destinations. The constable came to see off the trader with Malakar with a promise to find Batashi. Midde thought that the trader would also leave and the matter would be pushed to the next season. But he had got himself into trouble now. The trader had realized that his money and vodka had been wasted. He would have to return empty-handed. Had he been successful in taking even one woman away, he would have started taking more in the future to be sold in markets. These days they were called sex-market products. Women would be paraded almost naked on a platform before their prices were fixed. They would even feature in expensive advertisements. Bookings would start thereafter. The island would become the main source of his supply chain. But nothing of that sort had happened.

'Both of you are governments. You took money and did not do my work. This is a crime, do you know that?'

The two remained silent. They allowed the trader let his steam off. He would eventually cool down and see reason. 'So what if she was a woman from the island with no guardians. She was a human being in flesh and blood. Could she be sold off so easily? This is not the age of the pirates where you can just huddle them off into the hold of a ship. This is the twenty-first century, the age of computers.'

'I have lost faith in you and your country now. I will not invest in industries here.'

'I understand, sir. I had given her to you, but you couldn't take her.'

'Shut up!' The trader shouted on top of his voice now. 'Your responsibility doesn't end there. You have to deliver the product as well.'

'We will complete the transaction in the next season, sir. You are right. The give-and-take ends only with delivery.' Malakar tried his best to patch up.

The trader remained silent for some time. He knew that he would have to come back to the island again. The place was a goldmine of women for him. No one owned these women. They were there for the taking and no one would want to find out where they had gone if they went missing. Everywhere else, if women went missing, the media would be alerted and relatives would go up to the ministers too. But there was no such risk on the island. These women had no parents, relatives or husbands who would miss them.

'Please have faith in us, sir.' Nabadwip Malakar tried his best to convince the trader. 'These women are raw and very aggressive. It will take some time to tame her. Once, to save her field from being taken away, a pregnant woman simply stood in front of the bayonet and got killed. There was mayhem after that.'

'The Tebhaga movement also happened on this side.'

'Yes, I am aware of that.'

'It was the women who fought in the forefront to reserve their rights on their paddy.'

'These are old stories.'

'But sir, they are facts all the same.'

'How do they relate to my business?'

'These women are descendants of those rebellious women. Haven't you heard of Ma Ahalya?'

'I respect those women. It is because of them that the world is such a beautiful place today.'

Both Nabadwip and Mangal were surprised. The trader continued to talk. 'Please install a statue of Ahalya Devi on the island. I will fund it. But, as far as my business goes, you need to make it profitable. The philosophy of my business is totally different. You leave your paddy and Ma Ahalya to history books.'

'We are just a constable and a clerk in the government, how will we understand all this?'

'You will have to, if you become part of my business. We are trying to sell this golden India to the world. This will bring us dollars.' Mangal Midde wondered of this was the same man he took to the island in the month of Agrahayan. He spoke so differently now. Like a master to his slaves. Midde's throat yearned for some vodka. Perhaps that would make it easier for him to understand what this man was saying.

The trader continued his lecture. 'Our neem and turmeric are in great demand across the globe. Soon, I will file a patent over these and my company will start owning all the neem trees and turmeric plants. You will lose the right to own a neem tree then. Do you understand? I have already set a price against all trees, cattle, humans, etc. These prices have been fed into the data of my computer. I just need to take a price list out of the computer. The business of buying and selling women is the best. The price is fixed according to their figure, age and face. You can check every bit before buying. In the olden times, there used to be markets for slaves. These days, there are sophisticated modern markets for buying and selling women. Do you follow now?'

'Yes, we do.' Malakar quickly said.

'We need women who are not owned by anyone. There is a demand for sex workers in the market and there is a lot of money that the market is willing to pay for them. Dollars and euros are waiting to be taken away. We shouldn't miss this opportunity.'

'Yes, sir, we agree.'

The trader lit a cigarette of a foreign make. He gave one each to Midde and Malakar. 'Just give me young women. I can operate on them and create a desirable figure, the kind that the market wants.'

Midde shivered. He yearned for some vodka. He couldn't believe what he had heard. A woman with heavy breasts could be shaped in a way that the breasts were reduced, those with small breasts could be plumped up, those with large hips could be sculpted, fat tummies could be flattened, etc. Soon, the trader started describing every inch of Batashi, and what needed to be added and what needed reduction.

Women were made perfect to be served up to men. The best offerings on earth were meant for men. Men's members were also repaired by his company, the trader said. This was done to help them get maximum pleasure out of women. 'Next time, I will bring a booklet of my company and you will have all the details. But before that, you will need to work out how I can lay my hands on the women of the island. Next time, I will pick up a dozen to start with. I will pay both of you beyond your expectations.'

Midde's eyes hurt, his throat went dry and his head reeled. There was no drought now, the pirates weren't around to loot people, then why should the women have to sell themselves and leave the island forever? Why did he ever meet the trader? It must have been an ill-fated moment. The trader was like a man-eater. He had tasted human blood and would never go back to hunt deer again.

Four

More dust than rice,
Stiffer interest hikes price.

After returning from the island, Batashi, Jamuna and the other women got busy planning for the next six months and forgot the island. That was the tradition. The police constable had returned hurt but he did not wish to rake up the issue again, so everything was forgotten. The officer in charge of the police station was also quiet. After the month of Chait, when the island became empty, the women were forgotten too.

The administration conveniently forgot everything as well. That was its nature. But Aniket Sen was a different kind of a person. He didn't forget what he had seen and felt on the island. That night on the island was one of the most memorable nights of his life. The district administration had asked him to send a detailed report. He had drawn it up bit by bit but hadn't sent it. He was in no hurry. He wanted the island to get free of people first. It was likely that the district administration would forget all about the report too once the island got empty.

Aniket called Malakar to get the latest news of the island.

'Has everyone left the island?'

'Yes, sir. I think so.'

'Not a single soul left, I hope?'

'Why should anyone stay back?'

'Batashi, the fisherwoman, had said that she would stay back on the island the whole year.'

'That is not possible, sir. After Bhadra, the island sinks.'

Aniket wanted to be sure about this. What if some people stayed back? How safe was that? One needed to know how many went and how many came back. At the end of Chait, it was necessary to go back and see if anyone was left behind. This was the administration's duty. The government was responsible for the well-being of the people. Aniket made up his mind to visit the island in the next season and take a count of the fishermen and women, boatmen, labourers and others on the island. He thought of setting up an office at the Ghoradal riverbank where a register would be kept.

'How about imposing a tax on them, sir?' Malakar suggested to Aniket.

'What kind of a tax?'

'They should pay a tax to the government for using the island for business and pleasure. That way, the government will have the right to give them permission.'

Aniket had been warned. He hadn't thought on those lines. If the government was allowed a foothold into their lives, it would try to control them. The police, BDO and panchayat would all try to stake their claim on the island. Dhanapati's power and prestige would both be reduced if this happened. That old man had given his island, sky and water to his young wife and had ten fishermen as witnesses when he did it. Would the administration be able to understand the depth and pathos of this?

'That old Dhanapati is fooling the government and minting money on that island. If you start getting involved in this business of the island, he will be shown his place.'

'Who told you it's government's land?'

'Everything belongs to the government, sir.'

'How did it become government's land?'

'I don't have that much knowledge but the law of the land says that everything under the sun, and the rivers, seas and land, belong to the government.'

'The island belongs to Dhanapati.'

'Not at all, sir! He has no document to prove ownership. He has no lease deed. He has just cooked up a story to fool everybody and make money. These people are like that; don't you see the encroachers on Public Works Department (PWD) land near the market?'

'It was Dhanapati who discovered the island. So, it is his.'

'That is what he claims. Does he have anyone else to second his claim?'

'No one disputes him either!'

'No one speaks in his favour too. People think that he is mad and avoid him. How can he own such a big island?! He has cooked up that story of getting patta from the Mughals.'

Aniket decided not to send the report. Initially, he had thought he would send it after people left the island at the end of the season. But presently, he felt that since there was no one on the island, it would be automatically forgotten. There was no need of reminding the administration about it by sending a letter. Let Dhanapati stay in peace with his island like the Red Indian chief or the old wise man of the village of ancient cultures. What if governments take a bow and people lead their lives without them? Aniket realized that despite being part of the government machinery, he was going against it. Aniket wanted the remains of an old civilization to survive and continue in one corner of the world. Let Dhanapati's Island live in its unique world of six months. He too would forget the island and its people from Chaitra to Ashwin.

Initially, he thought about finding out where Dhanapati lived—whether it was Firingitala or Manasatala. He thought of meeting Dhanapati and finding out more about life on the island. The man had lived a long life and had myriad experiences. It would be a fascinating story. The man was keeping alive a lost world. For six months, one went back to a time that existed thousands of years ago. Aniket had helped Dhanapati realize that he was not a descendant of the pirate Pedru but a village elder representing the people that the pirates had tortured. This was what had happened to the Red Indians. Dhanapati was like the Red Indian chief whose people were enslaved by the Spaniard pirate Columbus. But how did it matter if

Dhanapati believed that he carried the blood of pirates in his veins? The blood of so many nations had mixed with that of the Indians over the ages. It was possible that he was carrying the blood of pirates, otherwise why would he look so different from the rest?

One day, Malakar came up to him and asked, 'Sir, have you sent the report?'

'Which report?'

Malakar reminded him about the report related to the island.

'I forgot.'

'What have you forgotten, sir?'

'About the Island of Dhanapati.'

'How can that be possible?'

'It is a world of six months that doesn't exist now.'

Malakar laughed. 'I cannot believe what you are telling me, sir.'

'But I heard about the six-monthly island from you, Malakar Babu.'

'The island might be of six months, but our office is permanent, isn't it? The report should go.'

'Why do you think the report is important?'

'To stop illegal activities on the island.'

'We are not fully aware of what exactly happens on the island.'

'I cannot tell you everything that happens there but even you know that the constable and the trader were harassed by those people.'

'Let us forget the island for now. It is lying vacant with no inhabitants. The ancient tortoise is waking up slowly.'

Malakar was shaken up. It was good that the report had not gone out. If the administration stopped the fishermen and women from going to the island, the money that came to him from there would also stop. He had to go back and do the trader's work. He was ready to invest money, so why shouldn't his work get done?

'Forget the island for now, Malakar Babu.'

'Do you really believe in that story about the tortoise?'

'It is possible.'

'Sir, in this age of science?'

'Will science put an end to imagination?'

Malakar was totally confused. This BDO did not believe in God. He had returned a calendar that Malakar had brought for him with a picture of Ma Kali on it. He did not wear any rings. Malakar never saw him offering *pranaam* while passing by a temple or any place that the villagers considered holy. He was not scared of the gods or the ghosts that controlled the lives of the people around him. And yet, he was speaking of the tortoise that held the island on his back!

'Dhanapati consumes opium and cannabis and cooks up these tales. Do you believe in them?'

'How much do we know about the mysteries of the world, Malakar Babu?'

'But you don't believe in God, sir!'

'Who told you that?'

'You don't have any pictures of gods and goddesses in your room, sir.'

'I stay alone. Ma Kali scares me out of my wits.'

Malakar could not make out what the BDO was hinting at. 'Could anyone ever speak like that about a mother? Sir, everyone is used to that image of Goddess Kali.'

'Yes, she sticks her tongue out. I feel embarrassed about it. But how do you relate that to the island? It doesn't exist at this time of the year.'

'Who told you that, sir?'

'Dhanapati said that the island doesn't exist these six months and so, they go back only in Ashwin when the island can be traced again.'

'That's a false story. Let us take a boat to go and check.'

'It's all water now. We will not find the island.'

'I think that wife of his is a witch and has done some black magic on you.'

'Why do you think so?'

'She had learnt her black magic in Kamakhya. See how they have made you believe that the island has vanished now?'

'What if the tortoise has really woken up from his sleep?' Aniket tried to look as innocent as possible.

'No, no, sir, there is no tortoise. There is just silt and nothing else.'

'Dhanapati gives a different picture.'

Malakar had never been more surprised in his life. Had his sahib lost his balance? Did the evil couple really do something to him? How could an educated man, a BDO no less, talk like that?

'Other fishermen supported the story.'

'They just repeated what they heard from Dhanapati. This is not possible, sir.'

'Even the women—Batashi, Sabitri, Jamuna—said the same thing.'

'They are illiterate women. They repeated what they were told by the men.'

'Why did they worship the tortoise on the full moon night of Kartik?'

'Does that make the story real?'

'The old man said that it is a floating island on which he has sailed many seas.'

Malakar's eyes were ready to fall out of their sockets. Was this a dream? What had happened to his boss? He was saying that it was impossible to draw up a report of the island now because the island had vanished, not to come back before Ashwin. He felt pity for the BDO and was convinced that the man was in a trance. 'Let me leave, sahib. Please talk to the Assistant District Magistrate (ADM) and SDO and you will see how they laugh at the theory that you have started believing in.'

'They do not know the story of the old wise man of the island, or the Red Indian chief. How will they understand, Malakar Babu? Let the island remain where it wishes to be. Let us not get too many people involved in the story that is Ghoradal's own. The island will return at the right time, in the month of Ashwin. The tortoise will fall asleep then.'

Malakar left the place. He was stunned. His boss did not realize that even the illiterate constable would laugh at him.

Five

Look how the leaf floats without water,
Why does she laugh when I've fought with her?

'Jamuna Di, where will you go?' Batashi had asked her when returning to Ghoradal. It was still dark, a few hours from dawn. They wanted to avoid the constable, Malakar and the trader.

'I don't know, Batashi.'

'My brother's shanty at Bhangar was broken by the government.'

'I have nowhere to go. Dhanapati's island is my only destination, beyond which I am a vagabond. I feel so helpless, Batashi. Where will I go and who will I live with?'

'Our island will drown and, perhaps, move away over the next six months.'

'I don't believe in this story, Batashi. An island is not a ship to move away.'

'Kunti and old Dhanapati both said so.'

'They echo each other all the time.'

The darkness lightened up a bit. It was dawn. The river was calm and the speed of the boat had increased now. The boat was full of people returning from the island. No one spoke. The island lingered on their mind. Jamuna and Batashi whispered among themselves. Initially, the sound of the motor on the boat interfered with the peace of the place. But soon that continuous sound too became part of the silence of the river. The thudding noise floated away with the breeze over the water.

'Jamuna Di, come with me to Baruipur, Sonarpur or wherever I go. Let us stay together as two sisters.'

'Are you feeling scared?'

'Not scared but definitely tense.'

'Don't be scared of the inquiry anymore. The police won't trail you. If they had to, they would have done so by now.'

'Jamuna Di, can we go to our fishermen's homes and look for work as servants? We would just want food in return.'

'They won't know us here.'

'We assume that because we have never tried. We served them for six months, lived and slept with them too. How can they forget that?'

'They are forced to forget us because they have a family to keep here.'

'I cannot forget him, Jamuna Di.'

'We are women, Batashi. We cannot and do not forget. They are men who are born to forget.'

The sky was bluish red, and the first light of the morning was wiping off the stars, one by one. Batashi saw that there was just one star overhead and one more towards the east, the morning star, that was yet to disappear. 'If I could stay near him, he would have never forgotten me,' Batashi said.

'That will disrupt his family life in Ghoradal. Dhanapati's rule says that after reaching Ghoradal, if your fisherman went right, you had to go left.'

Batashi did not answer.

'I don't know where I will go, Batashi.'

'Let's stay together as two sisters.' Batashi repeated what she had said already.

'Once you cross Ghoradal, there is nothing more to fear, Batashi.'

'What if the trader finds me in Kolkata?'

'He won't.'

'What if the government catches me?'

'After you cross Ghoradal, its power ceases and another government takes over.'

'Jamuna Di, please come with me.'

'Will your umbrella seller come for you in Kolkata?'

'I am not too sure. I won't get to know before the month of Jashti.'

'That's not very long from now.' Jamuna let out a sigh. 'We will meet again in Ashwin after the big full moon.'

Batashi caught hold of Jamuna's hand. 'Let us go and serve that man from Bagerhat.'

'Not at all! He was your husband on the island.'

Batashi lowered her voice. 'Jamuna Di, why don't we get the same man on the island every year? The year before last, I lived in a shanty with two men and I looked after both of them, though I slept only with one. They shrugged me off after reaching Ghoradal.'

'That's what is expected of men.'

'Can we not be together, Jamuna Di? Together, we can work something out. Alone, I feel so lost. Neither of us has anyone to call her own.'

Jamuna looked at Batashi carefully. She was at the peak of her youth and very beautiful. It was also the cause of her agony. When she was young, people lusted after her too. She would have to take five men in a row on some nights, who would then leave her lying near the railway tracks. After that too, she would get up and try to walk and live. She had survived in the end. These days, no one lusted after her and it was safer. Look at that Batashi, she thought. How could she survive with a face and eyes that beautiful? Look at her breasts, they look so perfect. She was well-fed on the island and her body had filled out. She would have to suffer for that. Jamuna thought that if she went with Batashi, she would have to protect her from lustful men. But that made sense in the long run, she reasoned.

'Your umbrella seller will not accept you, if he sees you with me.'

'Don't worry about that. I will find someone for you too.'

'I have started hating men, Batashi. I don't like it anymore.'

'But we have to accept them to feed ourselves.'

'Let us work in people's homes or as labourers. Let us not look for men.'

Batashi was surprised. What was Jamuna Di saying! She didn't want to stay on the island as someone's partner anymore. She said she would stay on the island for a few months in the next season, working on her own. If she didn't like it, she would go back without staying the entire season.

Her fisherman husband Pitambar looked after her, not going out to fish in the sea when she was sick. When he was at sea, Jamuna would not sleep at night. And presently, she was saying that she would not live with men! What was wrong with her?

'Don't you want to stay again with your fisherman Pitambar?'

'He will not come again.'

'Why?'

'He says he is tired of saline water.'

'That saline water gives them their catch!'

'Perhaps he wants to fish in sweet water ponds now or do farming.'

'He told you so?'

'Yes, and he asked me not to go back to the island either.'

'How will you survive?'

'He didn't tell me that.'

'I hate men!' Batashi was angry now.

'You will grow to detest them, Batashi.'

'Go to his house and tell his wife that you are his other one.'

'He will pretend not to know me and might even get me arrested.'

'His wife gets him only for six months, just as you enjoy him for the other six. You have equal right over him.'

'I think I will come with you. We will stay together and work hard to earn.'

'Will you look for a man when my umbrella seller comes?'

'No. I think we should live without men.'

'You are right. We don't need men. But if we are without men, will the trader and the government come after us?'

'You were with a man. Did that stop the government and the trader from coming after you?'

'But still, I was saved because I was considered someone's wife on the island. On the island, I am a six-monthly wife. In Kolkata, I can be a twelve-monthly wife with my umbrella seller. For the past six months, even when I was lying with my fisherman, I thought of my umbrella seller. The trader asked me whether I belonged to Bangladesh. Yes, why not? My in-laws are there. The umbrella seller's first wife lives there. I am his other wife. I too have some rights on his house, land, farm and pond. So, in a way I am from Bangladesh.'

Jamuna listened to her quietly and let her mind travel away to someplace where she too would have right to a man's land, turmeric farm and pond. She too could be the second wife of her man.

'There's no food across the border, Jamuna Di.'

'Where's the food on our side?'

'His first wife starves there and I starve here.'

'Life is the same for women everywhere, Batashi.'

'The umbrella seller can take us to the other side but there is a government there that will soon find out that we are from India. The way we speak Bengali is different from theirs in Bangladesh.'

'We are not allowed there?'

'No. People of one country cannot live in another country.'

'I will never go back to the island. You are right, Batashi. Bangladesh is where our in-laws are from. It is better to go and stay there as the second wife. They have to accept me.'

'The government will not allow it.'

'Why won't it? It is my in-laws' house and I have a right to go there.'

'How will you avoid the government?'

'We can grease their palms.'

'Where is the money for the bribe?'

'Let our husbands pay.'

'Can you milk cows?'

'I will learn.'

'We will also have to learn the rules of a Muslim household.'

'Yes, we have to. But the umbrella seller does Lakshmi Puja on the big full moon night every year.'

Jamuna's eyes shone.

'It is true, Jamuna Di. They even pray to the Satya Pir before the puja.'

'Will you be able to offer namaz?'

'The umbrella seller taught me. He would read namaz early in the morning but said we didn't have the compulsion to read namaz.'

Suddenly, the two women were happy. They had spun a story for themselves and pretended to have an imaginary home. The story was like a grapevine that kept winding and let the women get lost in its foliage. They spoke of what the first wives of their husbands did at home and how they would gingerly start accepting them within the household. Soon, they were talking about getting their daughters married off—daughters they had never conceived. The two women basked in the warmth of their imagination. They didn't care about how much of it was real. They would reach Ghoradal and head for Kolkata. Then, the two sisters would go all out and look for their umbrella seller. Jamuna looked up at the sky and tried to spot clouds. The cloud would bring the umbrella seller to India. 'U-m-b-r-e-l-l-a . . . does anyone need an u-m-b-r-e-l-l-a . . .'

Six

I talk the day out,
My wife eats like a lout.

Dhanapati hadn't created a story for his life on the land. After reaching the land, his six-monthly life on water ended. It was quite a windy morning. The breeze from the water invaded the land. It reached the verandah and entered the rooms through every tiny crack in the doors and windows. Even the bed was not spared. However, it did not help spin a story. A few days were spent in cleaning the house and putting it in order. Dhanapati kept giving instructions every now and then.

Neighbours came in twos and threes to take a look at Kunti. They were inquisitive about the young wife that old Dhanapati had brought with him from the island. Kunti's looks surprised them. Kamala's mother, Bimala's mother, Jati Buri and everyone else was stunned by her beauty. Old Dhanapati lost his eyes and brought a beautiful pair with him instead, they said. They were surprised that Dhanapati had gifted the island to this young girl. He called the local jeweller and asked him to make a nose ring for his young wife. How beautiful she looked with it! Dhanapati's blind eyes could imagine how dazzling she would look with the ring tingling about her nose.

'I yearn to see you but cannot. Perhaps that is what God wants.'

'See me with your mind's eye, my master,' Kunti said. She had made eye drops with some herbs and put two drops in each eye. She knew that the light had been put off forever but there was no harm in trying. That would make the old man happy, at least.

416

The Ayurvedic doctor had told her that his eyes were gone forever. 'Nothing lasts forever, Dhanapati,' he had said after the visit.

What the doctor said left a deep imprint on the mind of the old man. 'Nothing is permanent, Kunti. One has to lose so that another one gains. Everything that I had was given to me by the two sisters—Ma Kamala and Ma Lakshmi. They have taken everything from me so that they can give them to you now. I haven't given anything to you. The goddesses have.'

It was a late Chait evening. The sky was full of stars. The south wind lashed against both of them. It blew away Kunti's veil and the part of the saree that covered her breasts.

'The island lies alone, master. Has Batashi come back? What if she stays back on the island alone?'

'Let us not talk about the island here.'

'The smell of the island comes in with the breeze. How can I forget the island?'

'Tell me that story that you had left incomplete that day.'

'The fishermen and others from Chand Saudagar's boat searched the island and came across a beautiful woman who was the only soul on the entire island.'

'Who was she?'

'It could either be Anna or Batashi. Anna could not come away because the moment she set foot at Ghoradal, her husband would have cut her up alive.'

Dhanapati did not stop her from bringing in Anna into the story. He seemed to be losing the will to oppose anything these days. Dhanapati returned to Ghoradal after many months, leaving Anna alone on the island. With Anna on his back, the tortoise floated from the Bay of Bengal to the Indian Ocean and then to the Atlantic. Lisboan lay beyond that. Dhanapati knew that the tortoise had crossed over to Lisboan with Anna Bibi. She gave birth to her baby there.

'How beautiful your tale is, master,' Kunti said in a hushed tone.

Dhanapati was surprised at the beauty of his own tale. *Why had he not thought of it earlier?* Anna had gone to Lisboan to give birth. She would go back every year to deliver healthy, fair and blue-eyed boys. They grew up listening to the story of their mother's motherland. Soon, they were big enough to take their own boat and sail towards that land, crossing the seven seas. The boat almost sank when they entered the Indian Ocean but they survived.

'My poor babies,' Kunti said as tears welled up in her eyes.

Their mother, Anna Bibi had told them to look for the place where Ma Kamala was worshipped. She would give them the boon of long life and prosperity, she had said. They should go to her altar to lie prostrate at her feet and offer their prayers. Otherwise they would be doomed.

'What happened next, master?'

'Wait for a while. Give me some water, my throat is parched. Dress a betel leaf for me.'

When she brought the betel leaf dressed with betel nuts and lime wrapped in, Dhanapati put it into Kunti's mouth and asked her to chew it leisurely.

'I will savour the taste as you chew it, Kunti. I have no teeth left.'

As she chewed the betel leaf, her mouth filled up with juice. 'Come, pour it into my mouth now,' the old man said.

She took her mouth close to his and did as asked. She shivered with joy as the old man sucked in the last dreg from her mouth. She was aroused. This did not happen on the island when she would grind the betel leaf and nuts for her old man. This man was indeed a pirate! How else could he arouse such a young girl? At his age, he should have just been a lump of flesh without any strength! It was probably because all descendants of Pedru were sent to Lisboan and raised by Anna Bibi there.

'If you hadn't come with me to the island this time, I would have lost everything.'

'Not at all, master.'

'My body would have become inactive. It would have lost all its strength. The island, its breeze, the water and the sky are all inside my body. My body carried the earth inside it.'

'Your body contains the earth!' Kunti repeated this several times, whispering to herself.

'My body would have given up and fallen like an uprooted tree had you not come back. Have you ever seen an uprooted banyan tree?'

'Yes, I have. You are indeed like a banyan tree, master. As grand as one, I must say.'

'Your youth and my lust for you have kept me alive.'

'So what if you are old? You are the best and I love you for it,' Kunti whispered in his ears.

'My body had become cold. You have heated it up. You are the medicine I needed. A potent potion.'

'I will bring your strength back, master.'

'Will you?!'

'Yes, I will, master. I promise you.'

'I am blind, Kunti.'

'I'll bring back your vision, master.'

'Are you telling me the truth?'

'I am, master. I swear by the light of my eyes. The stars are witness to what I say.'

'If I got back my strength, I would challenge the government and the trader.'

'Please take it easy, master.'

'Give me some magic potion from Kamrup-Kamakhya. Then, I will get back my strength. You will like it, Kunti.'

'I love you the way you are, master.'

'I will give you the magic medicine from Kamakhya. There is a dervish at Ghutiyari who knows that magic better than me. I will go to him.'

Dhanapati breathed in the evening breeze. He was feeling better. He yearned for a drink. But Kunti did not allow him to drink. She didn't mind him smoking cannabis and would dress innumerable betel leaves for him.

Kunti went close to Dhanapati and whispered in his ears. 'I can turn your tiny fish into a big, energetic one.'

Dhanapati shivered with joy. 'If you manage to do that, I will make a gold nose ring for you.'

'Pedru forgot what his mother had told him. Misfortune befell him.' Dhanapati picked up the strands of the story again.

Kunti realized that Dhanapati's head was giving up too. Anna Bibi was Dhanapati's wife. How could Pedru be her son? Dhanapati was Pedru's descendant. Pedru was ten generations before him. He had got it all mixed up. Was it delirium of some kind?

'How is that possible, master?'

'It is possible, Kunti. He was Pedru, I am Pedru too. Anna Bibi was my wife and his too. Ma Kamala and Anna Bibi merged into one. Pedru came out of her golden pot. One story runs into another, Kunti.'

'I too have a golden pot from which hundreds of my sons will be born,' Kunti whispered.

'Pedru Dhanapati went into the lotus forest and came face to face with the beautiful Ma Kamala. He was starving for women after so many days on water and did not realize that he could not loot her. Ma Kamala cursed him and made him unconscious. Later, she brought him out of her golden pot into the world again. Chand Saudagar's fishermen and boatmen found none other than Ma Kamala.'

Dhanapati had mixed up the whole thing, Kunti realized, as he went from one story to another. He had eloped with Anna Bibi, the rich man's wife, and made her pregnant. Then, he left her alone on the island. How had she become Ma Kamala? How could Anna Bibi go to Lisboan? That was Pedru's land. Again, how could she give birth to Pedru from her golden pot and become the owner of the island? No matter how bizarre it sounded, when Dhanapati told his story, it sounded real.

Dhanapati realized that Kunti wasn't believing much of what he was saying. 'Do not calculate time in these stories. There is nothing fixed about who came before and who came after, Kunti. Everything was possible. You cannot listen to this story if you try to fathom it with a calendar and a watch. The story of the island is timeless, with a million possibilities. There are many different truths in this world. While your light is real to you, my darkness is real to me!'

Kunti's eyes welled up as her heart went out to the old man. She looked up at the sky and prayed to the two sisters to help her bring light back to Dhanapati's eyes.

'Ma, give him back his strength.'

'I have told you my story. You tell me yours, Kunti. They are bound to be different.'

'I have no more stories left, master.'

'You have to continuously creating stories if you have to remain the mistress of the island. The fishermen will believe you only if are able to go on telling them new stories.'

'You are a giant, my master. You came out of the golden pot of Ma Kamala along with the island, sea and sky. Before that, there was nothing else in this world.'

'This is brilliant!' Dhanapati sounded happy.

'The world was dark before that. There was no light, no life, no breeze and no water.'

'What existed then?'

'Only darkness.'

'What kind of darkness?'

'Like the one that takes you under its grip when you are asleep. Not a ray of light anywhere. Then Ma Kamala started pouring light, land, water and breeze and along with them, you came out. You were the pirate, Pedru.'

'Why am I sinking in the dark, Kunti?'

'Just pray to Ma Kamala. She will bring you out of her pot again, refreshed and rejuvenated.'

'I can only remember your face, child.'

'Then recall my face to the best of your ability.'

'After coming out of the golden pot, whom did Pedru see first?'

'He saw me. Go to sleep now, master. I will wait for you forever. Let me put you to sleep now.'

Seven

They go and back they come,
See you in Ashwin, chum!

The trader came back again and again. He came towards the end of Baishakh and sent word to his two agents. When Malakar and Midde arrived, he asked whether they had made any progress.

'It's difficult to do much now in this off-season.'

'I have heard the story of a beautiful woman who had once stayed back on the island. She was left alone and could not come back to the mainland on her own. Her former husband sat at the riverbank every day with an axe so that he could kill her the moment she set her foot in Ghoradal.'

'You are talking about Anna Bibi, sir,' Malakar said.

'Is it true?'

'We have also heard the story, but did not witness the episode.'

'It's not about seeing alone. Hearing is just as important. What does a king do?'

'We are not kings, sir,' Malakar smiled.

'It is possible that Batashi would stay back on the island just like Anna Bibi. She knows that she has been sold already and the buyer was waiting on the mainland. She also knew that she had raised her hand at a cop. She would be scared of coming back to Ghoradal and would stay back on the island. Did you two see her arrive at Ghoradal?'

'No, sir.'

'Have you been on duty on the riverbank round the clock?'

'Yes, sir.'

'So, it's clear that she is still on the island.'

'But sir, she will die if she stays alone on the island.'

'What happened to Anna Bibi?'

Malakar nudged the constable.

'How would I know?'

'What does your police report say?'

'Her husband did not come to the police and tried to hush up the affair by dealing with it on his own. He feared that the episode would bring him disgrace. He was a strange man. He did not have the capacity to satisfy his wife, but he had a lot of money. He would spend his time fighting cases in the Alipore court, encroaching upon other people's land and making them his own. That way, he amassed a lot of land.'

'I am aware of this. I did a lot of background research.'

'Fearing that her husband might wait for her on the riverbank, Anna Bibi did not return from the island,' Midde said. That was many years ago. Perhaps before independence or it could have been during the drought. I wasn't born then.'

The trader listened to Mangal Midde and then said, 'Batashi must be there on the island. Let us go and check.'

'How is that possible?'

'Do an inquiry.'

'Not possible now, sir. The waves are high and turbulent. Boats will sink.'

'How can your BDO allow someone to sink and die on the island?'

'Sir, there is no one left on the island now. We would have known otherwise.'

'How would you know without going there?'

'The fishermen would have known and told us. It was the fishermen who brought news about Anna Bibi.'

'What happened to Dhanapati?'

'Nothing! There was no complaint against him at the police station.'

The trader remained quiet. It was clear to Midde and Malakar that the trader did not believe them. Batashi was the first one to escape unnoticed but they could not say that to the trader. Both Midde and Malakar were surprised that they did not see her and so could not nab her. But it was also true that they did not stand guard at the riverbank round the clock.

'How can you allow someone to drown to death?' The trader started again.

'No one is talking about her.'

'You should start!'

'No one is bothered about any particular woman here. There is greater supply than what is needed.'

'Batashi is not just any other woman.'

'I understand, sir. We will get her for you in the next season.'

'If you don't raise the matter with the BDO, I will.'

Malakar was quiet. He could not make out what was playing on the trader's mind. Why did he insist that Batashi was still on the island? Who had given him that information? He had gone to Nagpur or was it Mumbai? How did he get news of the island from there?

The trader had read their mind. 'Don't worry. I am giving you the right information. She hasn't come back.'

'Who gave you this news?'

'I have plenty of sources.'

'We would have known then.'

'I know how capable you two are. Just go and ask your BDO to act fast.'

'Why should it bother you if someone is still left on the island?'

'Don't forget that I have bought her and so, I own her.'

'Will you be able to tell the BDO what you just said?'

'If needed, yes.'

'Are you mad? Can you officially buy and sell people?'

'Yes, you can.'

'This is illegal.'

'Being a part of the government, why did you sell her?'

'There is no document to prove this. I verbally sold her to you and you will not be able to prove it.'

'Leave that to me. Just spread the news that one woman was still left on the island.'

'The BDO will get mad at us if he hears that we were involved in this kind of a sale.'

'You think he doesn't know?'

'How will he?'

'I will tell him that I recruited the woman for some work. Let him figure out what kind of work. You will just have to say that it is true.'

Mangal Midde and Malakar stood there and shook their heads. They had to listen to the trader. After all, he was spending a lot of money and had the right to behave like that.

Aniket was shocked when he heard the news. He had heard about the Anna Bibi episode. She had stayed back and was not found again. What if that got repeated during his tenure? Aniket was scared.

'Sir, everyone knows this.'

'Could it be a rumour?'

'Initially, I thought that it might be a rumour. But now I find that the constable and many others on the riverbank are talking about this.'

'Such a thing had happened many years ago . . .'

'It has been repeated again.'

The news spread like wildfire at Ghoradal and beyond. It spread and came back to Ghoradal like the waves of Kalnagini that lashed against the shore. Soon, people at Baruipur, Garia, Sonarpur, Bagha Jatin and Sealdah too started talking about the strange case. Aniket lost his sleep. Midde and Malakar heard the news echoing back to them from all sides. They had been successful.

The fishermen returning from Kalas Island had seen her while they were returning, a fisherman told the lathi-wielding Midde.

Some woodcutters repeated this too.

'Oh my God! How old is she?' Midde pretended not to know anything.

They said she was not more than twenty-one or twenty-two and was very beautiful.

The settlers on the island did not bring her back, a fisherman said. The settlers fought over her and since no one finally won her, they have left her there to die.

'They might be entirely wrong.'

Such tales started pouring in daily and finally reached Dhanapati and Kunti too, buoyed by the southerly breeze.

'This is not possible,' Dhanapati said.

'My grandson brought the news from the Ghoradal riverbank,' an old woman said.

'It's no longer my island.' Dhanapati's voice shook with emotion.

'No one is left on my island.'

'There are many islands around. She might have been taken to one of them and abandoned by evil-doers.'

'That is not possible,' Dhaneshwari said.

'Not in the modern times,' Dhanapati added.

'The sun and the moon were real in the ancient times as they are today. So, what used to happen in the past can happen now as well,' the old woman asserted.

'What will happen now, master?' Dhaneshwari asked the old man.

'This sounds like a repeat of Anna Bibi's story.'

'What should we do now?'

'Let us stay quiet and keep our eyes and ears open for more news.'

Some others added wings to the story and said that fishermen and traders had both seen Ma Kamala on her lotus throne on one of the islands.

Those fishermen were bringing back computers and TV sets in their boats. The boats sank after they witnessed Ma Kamala and all the computers and TV sets floated on the water.

Dhanapati sounded happy. 'This is how stories should be built. I had seen Ma Kamala so many years ago.'

'She is our subject, master. What should we do?'

'We cannot intercept anyone's fate, Kunti.'

'Master, we might get into trouble too. The police might come to us to inquire.'

'No one can do anything to me. I am a blind man. How will I know who came back and who did not!'

Eight

There's a tiger in front,
But there's money to hunt.

Aniket had heard of Anna Bibi from Dhanapati's wife, Kunti. She spoke about his youthful days and his prowess as a pirate. She said it as if she was present at the time when Dhanapati was a young man. She had claimed to be his wife from that time. She had also spoken about Ma Kamala having seen her. She told Aniket about how the fishermen saw the mysterious mermaid in the sea and how she led them away. She spoke like a fisherman who had been sailing at sea all her life. These days, Ghoradal was rife with Anna Bibi's story. One fisherwoman had stayed back alone on the island. Who had brought that news?

'The southerly breeze brings in news of the island, sir,' Malakar said.

'Let us investigate.'

'Let the police station do the inquiry, sir.'

'The police station did not want to take up the investigation because there was no specific complaint.'

'Soon the news was published in *Samudra Barta* newspaper. It was reported that this was a common occurrence in the islands around this place. It was common practice to send women to exile to these islands. Later, even their bones could not be found. Sometimes fishermen left women on the island to please the pirates. In this way, the fishermen were saved from being looted. Sometimes, these women managed to please the pirates and became their consorts, never to come back among common people again.

Aniket Sen met the officer in charge (OC) of the local police station. 'Do you think this is possible?'

'Yes, sir, quite possible.'

'So, you are aware of it?'

'Yes. Every two years, such news comes in. They are all bad women, sir. Let us not bother about them.'

Aniket was not sure about what he should do. If this was true, a part of the blame would come to him. He had gone to the island to inquire, but sent no report. But if this news about the pirates and the lone woman on the island was true, he had to share the blame too!

'I am writing to you. Start an inquiry on the basis of the news published in Samudra Barta,' Aniket told the OC.

'Let me arrange for a motorboat and send the sub-inspector and a constable. But I don't think they will find anything.'

'If she is there, why shouldn't they find her?'

'There are Bangladeshi, Burmese and Thai pirates on these waters. By now, they would have got her.'

'I feel you should go there yourself.'

'Let me handle that. I will write the inquiry report.'

If the OC was right, it would be difficult to find anyone on the island now, Aniket realized. Malakar too bought this argument. 'I know all this but I cannot tell you everything for the sake of propriety, sir. Women have to be offered to the pirates, otherwise they will never allow fishermen to go about fishing on these waters in peace.'

It was the trader who tutored Malakar into telling this story. Malakar sent this theory to the OC via the constable. When the OC himself started swearing by this story, the trader's job was done. People started talking about the pirates more and more. Just like one had read in the fables that the king of the jungle—the lion—had to be offered a prey every day, the pirates were offered women to keep them from attacking. Sometimes, the chief pirate didn't look for women. In that case, the lone woman on the island starved to death. Sometimes, they desperately got into the water to move towards the mainland but got eaten up by sharks and crocodiles. 'The constable had once gone to find out the truth, sir, and got beaten up. You are aware of that, sir.'

Ghoradal buzzed with different stories of pirates. The southerly breeze brought in these stories with the regularity of the waves. Soon people started saying that many of the fishermen who went to the island for six months were criminals who wanted to take shelter at the island because they were running away from the law. There were pirates among them too. The trader started coming every now and then and added to the story of the pirates. Malakar and Midde learnt them by heart and released them among the people of Ghoradal successfully. This season ended differently, they thought.

For so many years, they had been going to the island but never had anything like that happened, they thought. They thought that the island could be used only for extortion and the money could then be spent on their families. Dhanapati would tell them about pirate Pedru and traced his bloodline to himself and to Lisboan. It was from him that they had heard about Ma Kamala. All the stories about the island were told by Dhanapati. Malakar never thought that there could be any other story from any other source. It was the trader who wrote the first story and sent it to Samudra Barta through the constable. He had sent some gifts to the newspaper office too. The paper carried the news in all seriousness. The English and Bengali papers in Kolkata picked the story up from there. The trader faxed the story to some papers. He had even called up the reporters and editors and told them that this was 'breaking news'. He was given a lot of importance by the papers because he was a big businessman. In this world of give and take, the trader was suddenly a big and well-respected man.

The trader looked happy. He asked the constable to open a bottle of vodka. If all went as per plan, his work would get done easily.

The vodka made the constable speak up. 'Who told you about the pirates, sir?'

'Why?'

'I am the government and have been going to the island for years. I had never heard about them in the past,' the constable said.

'Have you seen Ma Kamala, government?'

'No. I have heard of her.'

'Let me tell you that the woman won't be found. She has been picked up by the pirates already.'

'Then how will we prove anything!'

'Her absence can be used to prove anything we want. If she had been found, it would be said that she was left back by mistake. Now, it can be said that the pirates got her and that the age of the pirates is not over yet.'

Mangal Midde was fully drunk now. 'Yes, sir, there are pirates on the sea and looters too. But who is saying so?'

'I am telling you.'

'But all the stories about the island should come from Dhanapati.'

'That old man who has a young wife and calls himself the owner of the island?'

'Yes, the old man is Dhanapati and his wife is Dhaneshwari.'

'F**k your Dhaneshwari.' The trader couldn't control himself. 'That old man has become blind, isn't it?'

'Yes.'

'Just place an old hag beside him and bring that young girl to me. I will buy her.'

'How much will you pay for her?'

'How much do you want?'

'What is the asking rate these days, sir?'

'She should fetch you a good price, especially if she is fourteen, fifteen or sixteen. Underage girls are the most expensive. Their body measurements are also important.'

'What does that mean?'

'It means I need the size of her breasts, waist, hips and thighs. I will have her measured again when I buy.'

'Who will measure? The surveyor?'

'You will see everything for yourselves after you bring her to me.'

The constable and Malakar sat there, too drunk to think or move. The trader's story seemed to swim on their minds. Why was he telling these stories? Only Dhanapati could tell stories. Dhanapati had become blind but he hadn't lost the capacity to spin tales! Every evening, he came up with different episodes and that kept the fishermen hooked to him. He carried the blood of pirate Pedru in his veins. Now, the trader had brought up another story of pirates hiding among fishermen. Could this be possible at all?!

'Just wait and see, you will not believe your eyes,' the trader promised them.

'But sir, what if all this is true?'

'Of course it is true.'

'What if a woman is still there on the island?'

'I am sure there is.'

'What if she was left there to feed the lions or the pirates?'

'That is exactly what has happened.'

'What if the lion did not touch her?'

'Then the lion that lives inside the pirate will consume her. The blood of the Dutch, Portuguese, Armenian and Burmese pirates runs in the veins of the pirates today. Then there are people like me, Dasharath Singh, who are lions as well. After devouring a woman and getting fed up with her flesh, I will supply her to the market.'

'Can a pirate look at his image inside the well and think he has a competitor and jump in?' Midde asked the trader. By then, he had almost lost his senses.

Wasn't this a story from Aesop's fables? The trader seemed to recognize the story. He was also intoxicated, though not as drunk as the other two. The story appealed to him. The shadow of another pirate excited him. He relished the idea of fighting over a woman. The constable was a bastard, the trader swore in his mind. Why was he spinning such a story? Was he trying to confuse him? This man was cunning. He had sold Batashi without delivering her and was now planning to take money again for bringing her to him.

'She is very clever, sir!'

'Nonsense! I just need her body, not her brain. Just get me the right measurements.'

'She might get us into a room and lock it from outside.'

'I don't care how intelligent she is. To me she is a product, just like oil, scent or soap. You have to bring that product to me because I have paid for it.'

Malakar realized that the trader would now get angry. He stepped in for the constable. 'Sir, he is totally drunk. Don't take him seriously. He will now start laughing or crying.'

'What will happen now?' The constable repeated his question. Nothing seemed to satisfy him.

'You are a government and should know what will happen, constable.' The trader was irritated.

'What if a woman is still left alone on the island?'

'She will get lost.'

'My grandmother lost her sister in the famine.'

Malakar tried to warn the constable. 'We have heard that story already. You don't have to repeat it.'

'Are we going through a famine now?'

'Yes, somewhat,' Malakar replied.

'It's a different kind of a famine. Women are no longer hungry for rice but for lipstick, bra-panty, cosmetics, cars, TV and whatnot. They are thirsting for money to buy these. So, they will readily come out on to the streets to sell themselves. They will come to traders like me. I will buy them and send them to foreign shores where they will be lost forever.'

Nine

How many ghats did the boat cross?
Did you manage to gather any moss?

The report from the police station said that there was no one on the island. The district administration had sent a paper cutting to the BDO and sought a report. Braving the high tides, the BDO would go to the island to inquire and send a report. Aniket wanted to start by first talking to Dhanapati. Malakar brought his boss to Dhanapati's house. The old man was sleeping. His wife, Dhaneshwari, sat outside the house and dressed paan while chatting with a neighbour. She was called Ganga. Kunti was telling her about the island and the tortoise. She was also telling her the story of Ma Kamala. As she had reached the part where the island, the sky, stars and the breeze were coming out of the golden pot of the goddess, she saw the two government officials coming towards her. The two women pulled their veils on their heads on seeing the men. Kunti recognized them. She knew why they had come.

'Sit, babu. Please sit. Sahib, my master is asleep. Let him wake up.'

'Wake him up, Dhaneshwari. We will just ask him a few questions and then let him go. You can put him to sleep then,' Malakar said.

'He gets very little sleep these days, Babu. Let him sleep.'

'How long will sahib sit here? He has no time to waste.'

'You can ask me, sahib. I am the owner of the island now. In any case, he is blind and can only hear, not see. I am the one who sees and decides everything.'

'Sahib, if you wish, you can talk to this woman. I will come back after a while.'

'That's good, actually. You might sit underneath the tree just outside the house. I have a lot to tell sahib.'

Malakar was scared of Kunti. He still believed that she could cast a spell on him. So, he moved away, lit a cigarette and sat under the tree.

'No, sahib, there was no one left on the island.'

'Are you sure?' Aniket took this woman seriously.

'It is not possible for anyone to stay there alone. You might go and inquire for yourself, sahib.'

'Can you read?'

'No, sahib.'

Aniket showed her the newspaper and explained to her where this story had come from. 'Sir, these are lies. My husband is a descendant of the pirates. We all know that. He has come from Pedru, the pirate. We know how Ma Kamala gave everything to my husband. He is responsible for our well-being. Why should he leave anyone behind for the water dacoits? He would have got them killed first. No, sahib, all these are lies floating about.'

Aniket realized that after Malakar moved away and her neighbour went away, leaving them alone, Kunti's veil fell off. She was as beautiful as the unbridled southerly breeze. Her hair was like a cloud hanging on her back from her crown. She had shampooed her hair and kept it loose. There was a bright red vermilion dot on her forehead. Vermilion also graced the middle parting of her hair. Her face was bright as sunshine. She wore a cross on her neck but all the signs of a Hindu married woman were present on her hands—shankha-pola-noa. She wore a black-and-red striped saree and her feet were red with alta. It seemed that she was just out of her five days of bondage and had bathed herself clean. Was she trying to send him a message?

Dhanapati was asleep and there was no one else to stop him! He could almost hear his heavy breath. The south wind lashed against both of them, creating an atmosphere of yearning. Kunti sat there chewing paan. Her mouth was full of its juice, drenching her lips.

'Do you want water, sahib?'

'No.'

'I thought you were thirsty.'

'No, I am not.'

'I know your throat his parched. It happens at such times,' Kunti hissed.

'What do you mean?'

'Nothing. Do you want a paan?'

'My master has no teeth, so I chew the paan for him first and then give him the juice. Do you want me to do that?' Kunti laughed.

'Wake you master up, Kunti.'

'He gets upset when he is awake. He is happy to be asleep because he can then see his island, Lisboan and me.'

'He won't meet me then?'

'You will meet him. Please stay here for a while, big government. I think of you all the time. Who gives you water and betel leaves? Who cooks rice and fish for you? Who picks the bones from fish for you?'

Aniket tried his best to control himself.

'Why have you dressed up so much today?'

'Who will I dress up for? My master is blind and it makes no difference to him whether I wear a good saree or bad, whether I put alta on my feet or not. He just asks me to put on some scent. But now I have no scent on me.'

'Why so?'

'A man who can see with his eyes doesn't need scent.'

'Did you know that I would come?'

'Isn't this the right time to come? When the master is asleep?' Kunti put up her two feet, red with alta, on him. Her nails were not painted but they seemed to be glowing pink with health.

'Remove your feet.'

'Why are you scared, government? You own everything. Though I own the island because my master has gifted it to me, he has told me to obey you because you are the owner of everything. He has said that there are several governments and they own everything. However, it is not possible to run everything alone so the government appoints people like us to run everything on its behalf. So, we are under you.' Kunti started gasping for breath.

Aniket looked at her and asked if she needed water. 'Drink some. It's needed in these times.'

'No, government, I am fine.' She didn't realize that her bosom was exposed and her saree was not in place. Her bosom heaved like a wave. Her face was full of sweat.

'Government, my master said that everything is yours. Even I am yours. I want it that way. I was sure that you would come to me. When I was bathing with soap and soda, the breeze brought me news that you are coming. So, I put the master to sleep.'

Aniket looked straight at her. Her body had filled out in these few days and was ready to be taken. How many nights could she spend with that old man?

'Your master is a pirate. He will kill you if he gets to know.'

'No, sahib. He won't do anything if government takes me. That's the right of the government. No one can do anything about that. The government has the right to sell anyone. That's why Batashi was sold.'

'I am not that kind of government.'

'You are bigger than all. You have the right to take me whenever you want. I will give you water and dressed betel leaves. I will give you sweets. Come to me.' She heaved and sweated as she spoke and then suddenly caught hold of Aniket's hand. After a while, she released his hand and entered a room. Aniket sat there for some time. Malakar had said that she was a witch and cast her spell on anyone she wanted. Was he getting under her spell? He got up and entered the room. It was dark.

'Where are you? What if Malakar comes back?'

'No one will come here now, government. Malakar is asleep underneath the tree. The whole world is asleep now. My magic has put them to sleep. Only you and I are awake. No one will come here, not even the birds and the breeze. I have stopped them from coming.'

She put her arms around Aniket and pulled him towards her.
'The day I saw you first, I knew that if anyone takes me, it has to
be you. I thirst for you government. Take me. After that, if you feel
like selling me off, do so or throw me into the water for crocodiles
to eat me up.'

Aniket shook with excitement. He didn't know what to do as
if he was in a trance. The room was steaming hot and, gradually,
he let Dhanapati's wife do what she pleased with him. She was like
a turbulent sea into which he slowly drowned. It was as if he could
smell saline water, fish and fungus.

'Can I kiss you, government? Take every inch of me, feel me and
let me feel you, my prince. My master arouses me and then without
doing anything more, he falls asleep. I remain awake and think of
you. I knew you would come to me one day. If you hadn't come
today, I would have told my master to take care of his island and his
house and I would have gone out to look for you.'

'Now stop.'

'Why did you come here?'

'To find out if anyone was left on the island.'

'Yes, there is one soul left.'

'Who?'

'Me. I have been left alone with an old, blind man who wishes to
sleep all day and night.'

Aniket shivered again. He realized that the darkness in the
room had reduced and he was lying on top of a beautiful woman,
as soft as the creamy layer of milk. Her breasts, stomach, thighs
and their intersection touched him everywhere and were within his
reach. He closed his eyes in inexplicable pleasure. Their bodies united
as did their sweat. As she accepted him inside her, she whispered,
'You have come here for me, government.'

'Yes.' Aniket was lost in pleasure. 'This is my first too,' he
managed to whisper back.

'You are my first, my Pedru. Take me as I am and complete me.'

'What if the pirate woke up?'

'Not before I wake him up.'

'Have you cast a spell on him to put him to sleep?'

'I have cast my spell and put the whole world to sleep. Just take me and given me a hundred sons. I will take them and go back to the island in the month of Falgun. They will cry for milk and I will suckle them.'

Aniket realized that he was thirsting for this physical union. He was aroused again. On seeing that, Kunti happily called him a pirate, capable of taking his woman again and again.

'I wish to have you in every birth, government. May you never desire anyone else in life. May I fill your thoughts all the time, government. You are my Pedru. You will fill me with whatever I desire.'

Aniket wanted to extricate himself but could not. He was enmeshed in Kunti and wanted to lose himself in her arms. He was happy. He never thought that such an afternoon could ever be born at Ghoradal. He never consciously thought about Kunti but it was true that he wanted to meet Dhanapati. Was it because deep inside he wanted to be near Kunti again? Did she lurk inside him while he had been unaware of it?

A spent Aniket now freed himself and drank water. He felt his breath gradually coming back to normalcy. Kunti's body looked as if it had dealt with a storm, a violent sea storm that uprooted trees on the soft sand. Her breasts were full of teeth marks, her thighs were full of nail marks, and she had been pierced. She got up and tried to pull her clothes about her. She had survived the storm.

Aniket came out of the room and onto the verandah. He was shocked. The blind old man sat at one end. Aniket made no noise but it seemed that Dhanapati had been alerted. Was it because he could sense the vibration of his footsteps?

'Who is it?'

Aniket froze. Kunti came out. 'It is me, master. I fell asleep. When did you wake up?'

Dhanapati looked like a tiger that had smelt prey. He was aware of the presence of a third person. Kunti signalled to Aniket to get down from the verandah. The moment he did that, Dhanapati turned his head. He knew. He felt the vibrations on the ground. He breathed in deep. He had sensed a presence.

'Who had come, Kunti?'

'Who will?'

'Haven't you bathed, Kunti?

'Why, master? Kunti came close to Dhanapati.'

'I can smell someone else's presence in your body.'

'Who can it be but you, master?' Kunti swiftly moved away.

Dhanapati did not reply. It was not clear whether he believed her.

Kunti crossed the courtyard and walked towards the pond behind the house. She wanted to wash off government's smell from her body. Dhanapati could not find out. She sank head down in the pond, taking off all her clothes. She yearned for Aniket again. He was her pirate and she was ready to be looted, again and again and again.

Ten

How did the boat cross over?
How will the man, this distance cover?

Dhanapati's Island floated on the back of the tortoise. The sky was full of dark, ominous clouds that seemed to rage like an angry bull. Sometimes, they reminded one of Dhanapati's wife's huge mass of hair, lying loose on her back. Monsoon was early this time. Aniket Sen yearned for Kunti. He had not gone back to Firingitala since that afternoon. Malakar did not mention the island or Dhaneshwari to him. He seemed to have forgotten everything. Did Kunti have a hand in this? He came out to find Malakar asleep under the tree. His driver too was asleep.

Malakar woke up from his sleep and asked, 'Sir, are you done?'

'Yes, I am done.'

When monsoon came, people forgot about the island. The administration too forgot all about it. This was natural because the administration always had current issues to deal with. The old files remained on the shelves, gathering dust. Aniket Sen took out his umbrella and walked to the Ghoradal riverbank one day, in search of some fresh hilsa. Looking at the turbulent water of the Kalnagini, he realized that six-and-a-half leagues away, the island would have vanished by now. The tortoise would have risen from its sleep and while carrying the island on its back, it would be moving from sea to sea.

One evening, when it was dark and thundered outside, Aniket felt that he too was Pedru's descendant. The blood of the pirate had

441

followed different routes to enter his veins too. Who knew if there was a connection or not? Otherwise why did he reach Dhanapati's wife that afternoon? How is it that everyone slept so that two of them could remain awake and enjoy each other? Aniket believed that Kunti possessed magical powers. If that was true, the other truth was that he was a pirate because no one else could reach sorceress Kunti.

There was a let up in the rains the subsequent morning. Aniket's mind was full of Kunti and what she might be doing at that time. As the day progressed, Kunti tightened her grip on him. Finally, he called Malakar and told him he wished to visit Dhanapati's house.

'Okay, sir. The roads are bad now. I will just go and find out if the dam has given away anywhere, making the roads inaccessible.'

'No one told me that the situation is so bad. I have plastic sheets, flattened rice and jaggery in my relief stock. Let us take these and go and find out how they are.'

'That will be good, sir. That's a beggar's village, actually. Dhanapati goes hungry in this season.'

'Who told you that?'

'I know this block like the palm of my hand, sir. You will find out for yourself how miserable they are now.'

'Why didn't you tell me?'

'The petitions will come to you soon. Panchayat pradhans will soon come to see you. You will get to know everything soon, sir.'

Aniket was going back to the village after more than a month. He had first visited it on 18 May and it was 24 June by the time he went again. The road to Firingitala was pucca but it had not been paved. There were huge craters to be negotiated and the drive was slow. The car swerved from side to side, almost like a boat. The driver and Malakar brought out the relief material. Thankfully, the ground was sandy and not mushy like clay. The sky was covered with dark clouds again by the time they reached Dhanapati's house. It looked like a broken boat. On his courtyard, there were bamboo poles from which ran colourful paper streamers. Dhanapati sat on his verandah wearing a colourful shirt. He wore a dark glass. There were gaps in the straw that covered the roof of his hut.

'We have come on the day when the village celebrates the pirates' festival, sahib!' Malakar sounded very excited.

'What festival is that?!' Aniket was surprised.

Dhanapati's wife came out. She couldn't believe her eyes. They welled up with tears of joy and sadness, each overtaking the other.

'Government has come on such a day! Has he come to find out what the festival is all about?'

'He wanted to visit you people to see how you are doing in the midst of the rains.'

Kunti addressed Dhanapati now. 'Master, the big government has come with plastic sheets, flattened rice and jaggery. We are lucky. Before the rains start, we can cover the roof with plastic.'

Aniket noticed that Kunti was wearing a shabby saree, had not oiled her hair and her sadness was apparent despite the fact that her face had lit up on seeing him unexpectedly.

'Come in, sahib. Come, Malakar Babu,' Dhanapati called out from where he was sitting. 'It is Chha Juan's festival today, sahib. Kunti give them dressed betel leaves, sweets and water.'

Kunti spread out a mat on the verandah for the two to sit on.

'What is this festival all about?' Aniket was inquisitive.

'People enjoy themselves all through the night—singing and dancing. This festival has come to us from the time of Pedru pirate and I am his descendant, as you know. Earlier, I would organize everything. But now, I am blind and old. My wife did what she could.'

'I am not too sure about the customs, sahib. I have heard about it from my master. I have dug in the bamboo poles and decorated them. Now, if the rains come, everything will get spoilt. But at least I will know I did my bit for the festival. I have also boiled milk and rice and made the festive dessert for my master. I will serve it to you as well.'

'Don't bother so much. Just water and batasha will do,' Aniket quickly said to ease her trouble.

'Leave that to me, sahib government.' She started bringing in the plastic and tarpaulin sheets. Aniket was surprised at her strength. Malakar quickly stepped in to help her. 'You leave these. I will do it. This is not women's work.'

'I am so impressed with you, Malakar Babu. You have changed. I think the big government has moulded you.'

'Pirates are good in water, just like babies on mothers' laps,' Malakar said.

Kunti laughed at the joke, though Aniket was not sure why. 'My master leads a sad life here. He is blind and can neither arrange for the festival nor can do much to repair this house. He fears that dacoits might come to loot us because everyone knows by now that he is blind. So, we lock ourselves inside when it gets dark. We don't have kerosene to light lamps and spend our evenings and nights in complete darkness. If government can give us kerosene, we can light lamps.'

'Sahib, I am scared of burning up cash. I have married a young girl. If Pedru leaves her to go to Lisboan, how will she live? I have asked her not to spend at all.'

Dhanapati looked like a sad and lonely king who had lost his kingdom. The power he wielded on the island did not exist on the mainland. His huge body was bent a little and he looked a sorry sight.

Kunti could read Aniket's mind. 'Though I lock myself in, don't think I feel scared, government. With the Pedru pirate beside me, there is nothing to feel scared about. Moreover, I am a witch from Kamrup-Kamakhya and people are scared of me.'

'This woman can put everyone to sleep,' Dhanapati agreed.

'That is how I am able to live here with you, all alone,' Kunti replied. 'Whoever comes near this house will start sleeping.'

'She belongs to Gilchhia,' Dhanapati said.

'Master, tell them the story of Chha Juan's festival. Let me get them water and batasha. This festival is celebrated in Lisboan, which is not far from Gilchhia.'

Kunti brought them batasha in enamelled bowls. She brought water in a pot and kept two enamelled glasses beside it. Malakar stuffed his mouth with batasha and drank some water.

'Nothing can be sweeter than this,' he said.

'Why, my hand?' Kunti joked a little.

Malakar controlled himself and did not give a befitting reply because his boss was present. But before going away, he decided to tell Kunti that it was he who brought the relief material, not his boss. How much did his boss know about the place? He would tell her that he would send kerosene soon. He would extract money for all these supplies from the couple when they were back on the island.

Kunti sat, covering herself well, and faced the two. 'I belong to Gilchhia. I am like the wind and remains suspended in the air only to touch the ground during Chha Juan's festival.'

'I don't like all these things that this woman says, sir. I feel eerie and sleepy. I want to stay away from this woman, sir. She can cast her spell on anyone. Look at all these things that she says! I am going and sitting in the car, sir!'

'Malakar, don't worry. I am there with you. She is just telling you a story from Portuguese folklore.

'No, no, sir! I know that they practise black magic and implement them on normal people during the festival. There was a boy who coughed blood and died. I want to stay away from these people, sir.' Malakar rushed out of the verandah on the courtyard and then beyond. Aniket knew he would go and sit in the car and smoke.

When Malakar left, Kunti's veil dropped and her saree moved to uncover a part of her blouse. Her eyes signalled at Aniket.

'Tell the story yourself, Dhaneshwari.'

'You had fought a witch, isn't it?'

'That was so long ago. These are Pedru's stories. I am giving these stories to my wife as my legacy, along with a gift of the island. Otherwise these stories will be lost in the sands of time, when I am no more.'

Aniket thought that Dhanapati was really that old, wise man of the village who had lost everything as Columbus stepped onto his land. If Dhanapati lost his island, he would lose much more than what one loses to death. Dhanapati added every event of his life to the lore that he wove continuously around his island. The day he met this girl from Gilchhia, he knew that he could leave everything to her and move to Lisboan. She was a sorceress and could cast her spell on everyone and everything. He hoped that her magic didn't get her into trouble one day.

Dhanapati stopped. He breathed in deeply. Kunti raised the water pot to his mouth and helped him drink slowly. Some fell on his clothes while he managed to drink some. She wiped his mouth with the loose end of her saree almost in the way a grandchild cares for her grandfather. The water gave him some peace. 'Sahib, the island now belongs to Dhaneshwari. She is the new mistress of the island. Please take care of her, sahib. Please ensure that the island remains hers. It is time for me to go to Lisboan.'

Eleven

Words flow everywhere,
If you know how to release them in the air.

Dhanapati sat immersed in his silence for a long time. Kunti moved her hand on his bare chest.

'Master, how long will you take to start speaking again?'

'It is your turn to speak now. You are the mistress of the island now.'

'Please tell me more about Gilchhia. I belong there. But I don't know much about it.'

It is not Gilchhia, it could be Gilacia, or am I getting confused too?'

'Doesn't make much of a difference, master. Tell me all that you know.'

'It is in Ispahan.'

'Who told you about it?'

'Pedru.'

Aniket spoke up. 'Where did you find Pedru?'

'I got the island from Pedru. Didn't I tell you that his ship had capsized, and he managed to save his life and come to the island?'

For centuries, the story of ships sinking in the midst of the sea have become part of the lore of so many countries. From Chand Saudagar to Pedru, there are so many survivors of shipwrecks. Aniket prepared himself for another round of stories.

'It was Chand Saudagar's ship that Pedru captured.' Dhanapati was active again.

'Okay, even if I accept that, where did you meet Pedru?' Aniket laughed.

Dhanapati lost track suddenly. Kunti became angry. 'Why should he meet Pedru? He is a descendant of Pedru!'

Dhanapati did not pay attention to what she said. 'I think I met him deep inside the sea. I have been floating on the sea for centuries. I have gone east, west, north and south and have stayed afloat on water, all my life. Water cannot be divided into countries. I know that there are police on the waters who say that the water is divided among countries, but I don't think that is possible. Water looks the same everywhere. While floating on the water, I met Pedru.'

'What happened thereafter?' Aniket was curious.

'I was young then and full of vigour. I had captured a woman from Chatgaon and brought her with me on my boat. I had a big one that was rowed by seven men. I tied her up and put her in the hold of the boat. Then I asked the boatmen to pull up on the shore of an island since we had finished all the drinking water and rice. It was here that Pedru came too. His ship was large and the hold had seven women. It was a moonlit night and that is when I first saw Pedru. He was a giant, very fair and had blue eyes. His thighs were like the pillars of a palace. I asked him what he would do with the seven women. He said that they were women from Gilacia who were not visible because they were under a magic spell. He broke the spell and turned them into women before taking them as captives to serve him. He broke the spell on Chha Juan's night, he told me.'

Aniket wondered at the limitless capacity of the blind old man to spin tales. He was indomitable and could spring a tale from just about anywhere and say it with a conviction that would force the listener to believe him. One lost one's sense of reasoning and logic when listening to Dhanapati and one forgot to question, even if one found that there were gaps in the stories he told.

Kunti looked uncomfortable. She was dying to butt in. 'Master, isn't Pedru your grandfather?'

'No, I am Pedru.' Dhanapati started moving his hand on his chest and spoke to himself. 'I think I am Pedru. I have forgotten so many links in this story in all these years.'

Then suddenly, he started addressing Aniket again. 'Pedru told me all about Galicia. He said it was in Ispahan. That country shared a border with his own country. He also said that at one time, they were all one country, connected by the limitless water. There was a time when both the countries were under water. Sahib, I think Pedru was talking about the great floods. You know about Noah's boat, sahib? I am talking about that time.'

'Tell me what happened in Galicia.'

'That's a land of magic. Almost every house had a magician. There were these seven women who were very proud of their beauty and would not entertain men at all. The magicians turned them into thin air.'

'This is greater than the magic that is practised at Kamakhya!' Kunti was shocked.

'Galicia is bigger than your Kamakhya. The magic of Galicia is bigger than that of Kamakhya. However, there is a possibility that Galicia and Kamakhya were connected with Lisboan and their magic was also connected. Everything is possible, sahib. Kamakhya was surrounded by mountains whereas Galicia and Lisboan were surrounded by the seas. So whatever it may be, whether it is Kamakhya or Galicia, that's not so important. What is important is that these seven women were turned into thin air for being boastful. No one could see them but they could see everyone.'

'Master, why didn't you share this wonderful story all this while?'

'I cannot remember everything all the time. Old stories keep coming back to me through a haze these days. I am blind and can only hear you, Kunti. Sometimes, when you talk, I am reminded of you. Sometimes, even when you talk, I cannot make out who is talking. This blindness has combined with my old age and has taken me to a state where I feel as if I am afloat with no one around me.'

Aniket felt that he had been transported to the island once again. Even after coming back from the island, Dhanapati mentally lived there and continuously spun stories that created an effect on all those who sat around him. Aniket had tried to participate in the spinning and told them that Columbus and Pedru were the same. Now, he realized that his bag of stories did not have this kind of creative variety. Dhanapati was the fountainhead of stories that had kept him alive. He did not require help or guidance like visitors who went to his island. Just as stories of the freedom struggle, land movement and the Tebhaga movement reached the island and became part of Dhanapati's body of stories, his stories too had got mixed with Dhanapati's like the water of Kalnagini got mixed with sea water, Aniket thought. One day, this story would reach the mainland and spread in all directions. One day, the stories would mesmerize people in the cities.

Kunti wanted Dhanapati to continue his story.

'Those women who had turned into air roamed about crying because they could not sleep with anyone and their youth was going waste. They can only be seen on Chha Juan's feast day and I saw one of them.'

'You saw her!' Kunti screamed.

'Either Pedru did or I did.'

'You are not Pedru.'

'I cannot remember everything well. It has been a long life. How will I remember everything? I think I am Pedru who turned into Dhanapati. There was no one before me. I captured the island. It is mine. The island and its waters are mine.'

'May it remain that way,' Aniket said.

'Yes, everything started with you, my master. Tell us more of your story,' Kunti tried to reassure the old man.

Dhanapati started again. 'I was stunned by her beauty. It was ethereal. Her youth was intact and it seemed that it would never wane. There was a fragrance around her, adding to the attraction. I forgot everything and moved towards her, despite knowing that it was dangerous to try to mate with a woman of Galicia.'

Kunti shrieked. 'Why did you, master?'

'Her beauty had cast a spell on me.'

'Was she more beautiful than your Dhaneshwari, master?'

'I hadn't seen Dhaneshwari then.'

'What about that beauty was so magical?'

'Her breasts were like ripe wood apples and her deep blue eyes reminded me of the sea.'

Kunti looked helplessly at Aniket who shook his head from side to side as if to reassure her that the woman from Galicia was not as beautiful as she was. Could a woman tolerate praise of another's beauty? Didn't Dhanapati realize that?

Dhanapati had become quiet. His eyes were transfixed in Aniket's direction. Did his sixth sense warn him about the exchange that Kunti had with Aniket? He suddenly spread out his hand as if looking for Kunti. She quickly pulled the veil on her head and moved close to him. As if to reassure him, she spoke up. 'What happened, master?'

Dhanapati let out a sigh. 'Though I could see her, she was not totally out of the magic spell. The closer I went, the more she started losing her beauty.'

'Oh my God!' Kunti sounded more relieved than shocked.

'When I was closest to her, her skin hung about her in wrinkles, her eyes were like those of a dead fish, her breasts had sagged and her teeth had fallen out. She started laughing the laugh of a witch. It was the result of black magic. I simply took out my sword and cut her into two. She died instantly. The magic broke and she came alive as a normal woman. Pedru took her away in his ship.'

'What happened next?'

'Pedru roamed the waters with her. Gradually, she started aging and losing her . . .'

'Was there another spell on her?'

'Yes, there was. This time, I took her from Pedru.'

'Are you Pedru?'

'I think I am, and I think I am not. I get confused, my wife. These days, everything seems so alike. But I was not her destination. She saw someone better than me, someone more handsome than I am, someone with better thighs and eyes, someone who was more intelligent, superior to Pedru or Dhanapati. The moment she left me for him, the spell started working and she lost her beauty.'

'But the magician wasn't there!'

'So what? I had saved her and given her everything. If my wife goes to another man, will the Almighty forgive her? He sees everything and I get to know everything. I am the descendant of the saint Pedru. The universe will not let such a sin happen under my nose. I will die and become a tortoise and float with the island on my back.'

Kunti started at Aniket. There was fear in her eyes. Why was the old man talking like that? She quickly pulled her saree and covered herself. 'You are right, master.'

'Magic never wanes. It remains strong.'

'Perhaps, master.'

'The woman who had to stay invisible throughout the year was saved by me. Now, if she forgets that, she will naturally suffer.'

'Yes, she must.'

'Women should be careful, Kunti. If they think that no one can see them, then they are wrong. They are always being watched.'

'I know.'

'The Almighty gives, but knows how to take away everything too.'

'Yes, master.'

'The one who gives can take away too.'

'Yes, master.'

Aniket Sen got up. The old man and Kunti kept talking. Aniket realized that the old man was still in control of everything and had given nothing. Pedru was taking his woman and sailing away. Where would he go now?

Twelve

Where have you come from, where do you stay?
I am back for six months, I have been away.

Soon the monsoons were over. The year was coming to an end.
The days had become short and the dark clouds had disappeared.
The sky was blue. Only the south wind had to stop now. The south
wind was the enemy of the island. It had remained an enemy since
the time of Pedru. At one time, the south wind blew throughout the
year. It didn't matter whether it was summer, monsoon or winter.
The wind had a lot of strength because there was no other wind
to compete with. It did not let the fishermen enter the sea. Boats
had to come back to the shore. Finally, the fishermen started their
fight against the south winds. Dhanapati was the leader of that fight.
He fought from the front keeping the fishermen behind him.

After monsoons ended, Dhanapati started his story of the south
winds. The whole of monsoon, he kept talking about the women
of Galicia. He kept repeating the same story over and over again.
He would forget what he had said the previous day and would add
or delete from the body of the story. But Kunti was certain about
one thing. Dhanapati was warning her through the stories. Kunti
suspected that the old man was not blind in reality. He just pretended
to be. He actually saw more than the others. She was scared of
him and the stories, combined with the miserable situation all around
because of the monsoon, made it difficult for Kunti to survive.
She realized that she was living under the thumb of the old man.

The big government, the BDO, had silently got up on the day of the Chha Juan festival, not to return to Firingitala for the entire duration of monsoon. He had left in the midst of the Galicia story. Malakar, however, brought relief again. The river embankment had given way and Firingitala was flooded. Dhanapati's house was on a raised platform, so it was safe from floods. Otherwise Kunti's life would have been all the more miserable. But she knew that she finally had the big government BDO sahib to fall back on. Though he did not come to see them, he kept a tab on what was happening in their lives. This gave her immense happiness. He had not forgotten her. When Dhanapati got to know this, he would start his story around Galicia all over again. He would go on repeating that Kunti's youth was not eternal and that it had to fade the moment she tried to be disobedient. Dhanapati would insist that someone or the other was keeping an eye on her and she could not escape those eyes.

After monsoon ended and the sky turned blue again from the end of Bhadra, Kunti became restless. Dhanapati too seemed ill at ease. Kunti was reminded of the island, the fishermen and women and the big government. One day, Dhanapati called Kunti and asked her to describe the changes to him.

'You are telling me that the sky has turned blue. I can feel the change in the breeze already. The sun is up too, isn't it? Let us go to the almond tree and see if it has started flowering. In Pedru's country, at this time of the year, everything gets covered with snow. One can see that colour on the island, the riverbank and the fields too.'

Kunti's eyes were wide with wonder. 'Snow falls from the sky?'

'Yes, Pedru told me that.'

'How strange that must be!'

'That is why the breeze from the north is so cold,' Dhanapati said.

'Then what happened next?'

Kunti wanted him to change the course of his story and go in another direction. She wanted to listen to as many stories as possible so that she had enough in her own stock when she went back to the island. She would tell the fishermen and women a new story every evening and gradually, they would start accepting her like they accepted Dhanapati. She would try to mix her own tales with the ones that Dhanapati had woven already. She wanted the fishermen to be in awe of her. A woman is no good unless men discussed her among themselves.

'You must remember two things. First, the south wind used to blow all day and night, making it impossible for fishermen to go fishing on the sea. Second, the north wind could not be born here because of lack of snow. Do you understand, my wife?'

'Please go on with your story, master.'

'On the island, by the river and on the fields, this is the time when the almond tree flowers.'

'I have never heard of this nut at all!'

'This nut is from Pedru's land. In that country, almond trees flower in spring.'

'But it is not springtime now. Spring will come in Chait, when it will be time to leave the island once more.'

'In Lisboan, spring starts after the monsoon.'

'Who told you?'

'Pedru. He told me that in Lisboan, it rained in winter and after that, spring came by, bringing flowers on almond trees.'

'God knows where that land is. I am a woman from Dhanapati's Island and my world remains confined to the island and to Ghoradal. But tell me more, master.'

'Only the north wind could counter the south wind. Fishermen who go to the sea know the value of these winds. The wrong wind can take a boat on a never-ending journey.'

'You have said this in the past, master.'

'The wrong wind tried to lead me in the wrong direction many times.'

'Then what happened to the south wind finally?'

Dhanapati kept quiet. Kunti realized that he was trying to think up a tale. Slowly, Dhanapati started weaving his tale again. He went back to the ancient times to bring out some unheard episode. He was trying his best, Kunti realized. She looked up at the sky that was full of stars. Had her master not been blind, he would tell her the names of so many stars now. He had roamed about on the sea and knew the stars well. Last Ashwin, when she first met Dhanapati, he had not become completely blind, although his vision had started blurring. It was with this failing vision that Dhanapati taught her how to identify the seven foreign brother stars and the north star. He told her how the stars saved the fishermen from getting lost when the south wind blew hard.

'In those days, the north wind did not blow over Ghoradal and the south wind blew throughout the day. It led Pedru to this land. After coming here, Pedru said that the south wind could be controlled only with the help of the flower from the almond tree. But that was not available on this land and so, Pedru had to go back to Lisboan to get the flower. However, the south wind wouldn't allow him!'

'What did he do, master?'

'Only once, if the north wind made its way here, it would be here to stay. "But where is the ice that could give it wings?" Pedru had said to Dhanapati. Once, even Lisboan suffered from this problem, so the king took flowers from the almond trees and sprinkled them everywhere. White flower-like specks of ice grew everywhere. The north wind got confused and thought that Lisboan had frozen and rushed in. Since then, the north wind and flowers of the almond tree came together in Lisboan.'

'It is so even now?'

'No. The almond flowers started dying from the shivering cold of the north wind and so, they started coming only in spring.'

'Then how does the north wind come now?'

'It is now a matter of habit for the north wind. So, it comes on time, even without the flowers of the almond tree.' Dhanapati tried his best to end the story but Kunti wouldn't let him do that.

'What signals the north wind now?'

'I don't know,' Dhanapati said.

'I think it is the flower of the Kans grass that brings the north breeze here, just like the flowers of the almond trees brought it to Lisboan. What the almond tree flowers are to Lisboan, the Kans grass flowers are to us,' Kunti reasoned.

'What a wonderful addition to my story!' Dhanapati held Kunti's hand in joy. 'Was it Pedru who made it possible for the flowers of the Kans grass to grow here?'

'Yes, quite possible.'

'Pedru helped the island blossom.'

'Yes, he did.'

'What else could he do?'

'He helped the stars blossom in the sky. I think he could help your eyes blossom too!'

Dhanapati fell silent. Pedru had brought the snow-like Kans grass flowers to the island and behind them came the north wind. It was time for the south wind to go away. Dhanapati yearned to go back.

'Kunti, get ready to go back to the island. Let us go there before the pujas.'

'But no one will reach the island then. It would be too early, master.'

'So what? It is our island and we need to reach first.'

Kunti was not sure whether that would be right. So, she kept quiet. Dhanapati continued to talk. 'Pedru has already brought the flowers and the stars on the sky. He will come to the island to bring the light back to my eyes. I need to go back there as soon as possible.'

'Do you think Pedru will really come?'

'I am sure.'

Kunti liked to listen to these stories. She got ready to spin her own stories now. She, however, did not believe that Pedru would come and cure Dhanapati's blindness. She knew that Pedru had taken good care of Dhanapati and brought him back when he was led astray by the naughty winds. This time, would he come to Dhanapati's rescue again? Kunti joined her palms to pay her respect to the Pedru she had never seen but believed in. She thought of the myriad forms of Pedru she knew—the devil, the saint, the pirate and the God. The Pedru that the big government spoke about was different from the Pedru of Dhanapati's story. Would Pedru really come and perform

some magic on Dhanapati's eyes? Kunti knew that was not possible
but Dhanapati had no choice but to believe in it. He wanted to go
back and wait for Pedru. Would he come out of the depths of the
water or would he cross the seven seas and come from Lisboan? If he
came, Dhanapati would start seeing again. He would also see how
beautiful Kunti was.

Kunti was certain that Pedru wouldn't come. It was not possible.
No one knew who Pedru was. How could such a character appear
from nowhere? Kunti laughed inwardly.

'Start packing up, Kunti. Call the boatman Jatan. He will arrange
for the journey. I will ask him to take some labourers who will repair
the house.'

'Yes, master. Don't worry.'

'There is no time to waste.'

'How will we stay alone on the island, master? The very thought
scares me.'

'Why? I will be there with you!'

'But you are blind, master!'

'I can see, Kunti. Don't worry at all. I am the last Pedru and till
the time I am alive, no other pirate can set foot on the island.'

'I am a woman.'

'You are Dhaneshwari, the owner of the island. People should be
in awe of you. Why should you be scared?'

'Let's not rush to go back there, master. There is still a lot of
time left.'

'No! We will go now. It is impossible to live safely here with a
young and beautiful wife around. The island is far safer.'

A shiver ran down Kunti's spine. Was Dhanapati aware? But that
was just one afternoon and then again, on the day of Chha Juan's
festival. She had not been with the government since then. She
mustered up enough courage and asked, 'Is anything wrong, master?'

'Pedru knows everything. He sees everything. Even when you
think that no one is around, Pedru is there, watching you. He tells me
everything. I am Dhanapati, but I am not sure if I am not Pedru too.'

Thirteen

Here's my appeal, listen government,
I have lots to tell you; you tell me when.

Kunti thought of informing the big government before going to the island. For the past two days, Dhanapati had nagged her about going back immediately. He believed that he would get his eyes back if he went back to the island.

Dhanapati looked so helpless when he appealed to Kunti that she could not ignore him any longer. He believed that Pedru was sitting at the island, waiting for him. Dhanapati said that Pedru waited with two eyes as a gift.

'We will go back to the island, master, but just wait for a few days. The news on the radio said that there was a cyclone coming in the sea.'

'That's on another part of the sea, on the southwest side near Jagannath Puri.'

Kunti thought of the appeal that she was thinking of making to the big government on behalf of the other fisherwomen. The appeal was that the government allow the women to stay back on the island for the remaining six months as well. She would stay back with old Dhanapati on the island. Only a small portion of the island was used up to build the huts and the market. The rest of the island remained empty. She would appeal to the government to allow the people of the island to farm there. That and fishing would be enough for them to lead a well-fed and happy life. That way, they would be able to lead a twelve-month life on the island. They wouldn't have to go back to Ghoradal at the end of the season. The traders would also think twice before buying and selling women from the island. Batashi was the only one who had protested. Otherwise, who kept count of the women who might have disappeared routinely from the island? Jamuna knew a lot. Old Dhanapati also knew everything but he wouldn't open his mouth. He was only interested in keeping the island to himself. How selfish was that! He didn't care what the small government and the traders did on the island.

Kunti wanted to first make her appeal to the big government and then leave Ghoradal to go to the island to set up home for the next six months. Could she leave the old man at Firingitala and go to Ghoradal to meet the big government? The old man wouldn't allow her to do that. He didn't want the six-monthly settlement to become permanent. That way, the island would lose its original character because it would belong equally to all those who lived there for twelve months. If they lived for twelve months, they would develop a right to the land.

The big government did not come back to Firingitala but Malakar did, one day. He was a changed man now, totally under the influence of his boss, the big government.

'It's time to go back to the island, Dhanapati and Dhaneshwari. Let there be no trouble this time,' Malakar said.

'There won't be.'

'Fighting the government is not good. That episode last year is already being treated as a black spot. Can a cop be beaten up?'

'It won't happen again.'

'I will not go to the island as frequently as I used to. My boss will not collect tax on the island. It is difficult to work with such people but I feel proud that I work under a man like that.'

Kunti pulled her veil above her head. 'Malakar Babu, do look after us. I am sorry for whatever mistake I had done previously.'

'You put me to sleep and kept my boss to yourself. Can you tell me why?'

'Let that be, Malakar Babu. I have an appeal to make to your sahib. We want to stay back on the island for twelve months.'

Malakar lit a cigarette. 'Does Dhanapati want that?'

Dhanapati sat at the verandah. His face was turned towards their direction.

'Come in, Malakar Babu. This year, we are planning to go back early.'

'That is why I have come to you, chief.'

'Please do come to the island, Malakar babu, like you used to. Let there be no change in the old ways. Let's forget what happened in the past. You will get what you used to get from us. We will go back to our old ways.'

'That's good.'

'Please tell the big government about our appeal.'

'Give it in writing.'

'I don't know how to write.'

'Shall I write it out for you?'

'Yes, Malakar Babu, that will be of great help. It is so difficult to switch homes every·year with this old blind man. It is difficult for me to set up home at Firingitala and then wind everything up after six months and move to the island to set up home there. Please have some compassion for us, Malakar Babu.'

Malakar nodded in agreement. Then, he threw his cigarette and brought out a paper and pen. Kunti's eyes shone with hope. It is women who built homes with every drop of their sweat and blood. After Chait, the men forgot everything that happened in these homes for six months, burnt them up, collected the money they earned for six months and left as if nothing had happened.

'Have you ever seen the faces of the women they leave behind?'

'Yes, I have seen.'

'What have you seen?'

'I was there once when people were getting ready to leave.'

'What did you see?'

'You are right. The women sat there and wept but the fishermen didn't care about them.'

'This is what my appeal is all about. Please end the misery of the women. Give them a home for twelve months. I am the owner of the island now and this is what I want. Only a woman can understand another's pain. Even my master didn't do anything about this. He didn't care. But I want things to change now, permanently. Please ensure that women's homes don't break.'

'The fishermen will come back, no matter what.'

'Some may, but if they get a home for twelve months, many won't.'

'If they don't come back to Ghoradal, who will take care of their families here?'

Kunti kept quiet. Malakar was right. She hadn't thought about the wives that the fishermen left behind at Ghoradal for six months. But she had to save the women of the island and that was her immediate task. 'I have to save my subjects on the island first, Malakar Babu. Only if they get a permanent home on the island will the women be safe from traders who come to buy them.'

Malakar sat down and started to write.

Respected BDO,
Ghoradal.

Dear Sir,

I am Dhaneshwari Dasi. I live under the care of Dhanapati Sardar, the owner of the island.

Malakar looked up at Kunti. She was looking at the words on the paper in great wonder. Malakar was not sure if he could describe Kunti as Dhanapati's wife. He had seen Dhanapati change his wives every year. He had lost count. Even Jamuna was his wife at one point of time, many years ago. How could such a young girl be Dhanapati's wife? Malakar was confused about what would be Kunti's official status and hence, 'under the care of' was the best option available.

'Why did you stop, Malakar Babu?'

'What should I write?'

'Let the big government know how cruel the men on the island have been to the women. Though you are a man, you should be sympathetic to the women on the island. Even my master has not been kind to women. But, being a woman, I cannot ignore their helplessness and their tears.

'What are you telling Malakar Babu?'

'He has come with jaggery and flattened rice again.'

'What is it about the island that you said just now? You are the owner of the island now. What are you talking about with him?'

'Nothing, chief. She is discussing her plans to go back quickly this time.'

'How much do I know, master, to be able to tell him? I know as much as you have told me. I just go on talking, as if by compulsion, master.'

Malakar got to writing again. He described Dhanapati as the master of both the island and the applicant.

'You write so well, Malakar Babu. Do write a good appeal for me.'

Malakar was happy. He was proud of his handwriting. Most people who wrote to the BDO came to him for getting their applications written. He started writing again.

'Sir, we get to stay on the island for six months. Then, we come back to Ghoradal and scatter in every direction, trying to find food and shelter for the next six months. We lead the life of vagabonds and go without food, mostly. Please allow us to stay for all twelve months on the island. This will save our lives. We will remain eternally grateful to you . . .'

Malakar stopped again. Was there any logic behind writing such a letter? The government had not asked them to either stay or go away from the island. Whether they stayed for six months or twelve was not the government's headache! They had decided this on their own. Why should the government peep into anyone's home to give or take away permission?

'Why are you making me write this letter?' Malakar asked Kunti. 'If you can stay on for twelve months, do so! Why are you bringing the government into this?!'

'Please speak softly, Malakar Babu. My master does not want me to write this letter. But this is my appeal on behalf of the women and it has to reach the big government.'

'But I am writing a meaningless letter, Dhaneshwari Dasi.'

'Just write that we want permission to stay for twelve months.'

'Why do you need permission to start your own family?'

'Write that we need a patta for the island in the name of Dhanapati and Dhaneshwari. We need proper papers to prove our ownership.'

Malakar realized the deeper meaning of the letter now and looked up at Kunti. He couldn't hide his expression of surprise mixed with admiration for the young, illiterate girl.

Kunti pulled her veil to cover her head properly. 'Give us the papers and we will give you a good tax every year. Be assured of that.'

'This is the job of the BLRO office.'

'That is also another government, isn't it? You will definitely be able to help us there. Won't you? Tell the big government that Dhaneshwari has appealed to him in writing. Let the government know that we won't come back from the island this time after Chait.'

'What will happen to this house?'

'Let it be there for now. Later, after the government gives us permission, I will sell it.'

'In the month of Bhadra, when the water is high, the island will be submerged. Will you still be able to live there?'

'We will try and stop the high tide.'

'My boss can help to create embankments. Shall I include that in the appeal?'

'Yes, Malakar Babu, please do.'

'Ok. I am including this.' He was surprised at his own behaviour. He had tried to sleep with this woman and now, the sorceress was making him write out an appeal on her behalf. He couldn't fathom what was going on.

Fourteen

He went back to where he belongs,
A sea in between, and many, many songs.

The report was sent to the district headquarters. It contained a brief history, a sketch map and the BDO's comments. Dhaneshwari Dasi's application was also attached to it and the entire file was sent to the office of the district magistrate. The SDO and ADM would take a look at the file before the DM did. It took time for the file to move from one room to the other. After sending the file, Aniket quietly waited. He had once gone to a meeting to the district headquarters. He thought the matter would come up for discussion. It didn't. Aniket didn't raise it. He wanted to, but didn't, finally. He could have. The appeal that Dhanapati's wife made had a developmental issue linked to it. The matter of the lease had to be initiated by the land department but it didn't begin and end there. The island had to be protected from the high tides after the month of Chaitra if people had to live there permanently. Embankments had to be built all around the island. Aniket had suggested this in his report. However, nothing seemed to move, even after the month of Ashwin. The pujas were over. The fishermen started moving towards the island.

Malakar came and told him. 'Sir, unless you poke them at the district headquarters, nothing will move.'

'You mean, no one will discuss the letter of appeal?'

'In a way it is good. Otherwise, we will have to do so much of running around to make this happen.'

'Malakar Babu, can you go and find out for me?'

465

Malakar went to the district headquarters one day. A surprise awaited him. Dasharath Singh came out of a grey foreign car. Malakar could not recognize him initially. His salt-and-pepper hair was now golden. He wore a suit and dark sunglasses and looked very fashionable. He hadn't looked like that on the island or in Ghoradal, Malakar thought. Was that because of the lack of electricity on the island? The lights at Ghoradal were not as bright as that of the city.

There was no mistaking Dasharath Singh. He had a file in his hand and a man, perhaps his employee, accompanied him. Malakar was right there in front of him but Dasharath ignored him as if he had never seen him.

'Trader, sahib!' Malakar tried to attract his attention but in vain. The trader completely ignored him and walked into the lift of the ten-storey building. The doors shut on Malakar's face. He stood there amazed and unable to react for a while. Dasharath Singh had not gone back to Ghoradal during the entire monsoon season. Was this the same man he had had vodka with at Shanti Nivas Hotel? Evening after evening, he had told them stories of dollars and how to earn them. Famine, drought, his Spanish connection and flourishing family business, the trader had said so much about the past to them. He was the one who showed them the self-sale deed and told them what the language of such deeds should be. But why did he choose to ignore Malakar now?

Malakar wondered how he would look for the trader in that ten-storeyed collectorate building. It had several blocks and it was easy to move from one block to another because they were all connected with passages. The abnormally tall Malakar paced up and down. He sweated heavily and that showed on the back of his kurta. He smoked continuously. Was the trader up to some other business now? They had many family businesses. They dealt in horses, jewels, oil, wood, ships and whatnot. Why did he still deal in women? There were such beautiful women all around him in the city. He could take any one he chose! Why did he have to hanker for

Batashi on Dhanapati's Island? Malakar thought that the trader must have forgotten about Batashi by now.

Suddenly, the trader's companion, who had gone up with him, came out of another lift. Malakar went up to him. 'Where is your sahib?'

'Which sahib?'

'The one who went upstairs with you!'

'He will meet all the bosses of the administration like the DM, ADM, SP, etc. He has several meetings to attend.'

'I know him,' Malakar said.

'The whole world knows him. Do you know how much money he has?' The man wore a blue shirt and black trousers. He asked Malakar for a cigarette.

'Is he getting enough business these days?'

'What are you saying! He is an industrialist!'

Malakar laughed. 'We know every inch of him. Mangal Midde, the constable knows him even better. On the island, they took off . . .' Malakar restrained himself from spilling more. There were secrets in every man's life. There was no point discussing them. He too had gone to the island and wanted to enjoy both Batashi and Dhanapati's wife but was forced to return empty-handed. Even his boss, Aniket Sen, had spent the whole afternoon with Dhanapati's wife, taking advantage of the fact that Malakar had fallen asleep. Otherwise he would have known more than he already knew. He read it in their faces.

'How big an industrialist is he?' Malakar asked.

'Very big.'

'How many businesses does he have?'

'Many.'

'Why has he come here?'

'He wants to set up some industries.'

Nabadwip realized that he wouldn't be able to extract anymore information from this man. But he wasn't one to give up so easily. So, he kept pacing up and down, with an eye on the trader's companion because he knew that Dasharath would ultimately go out of the place with that man. The man didn't seem to mind at all. After a while, Malakar asked the man who he was.

'I am sir's employee.'

'What did you do before that?'

'I was in the police but I lost my job and sir welcomed me into his business.'

'Why did you lose your job?'

'I got involved in a rape case.'

'Did you rape a woman?'

'I did. My name is Joseph Kundu.'

'Why did you commit such a crime?'

'It just happened. Haven't you ever raped anyone?'

'No, I haven't. So, you lost your job?'

'I did, but sir paid me double my earlier salary. Had I not raped that woman, I wouldn't have got this job.'

Malakar thought he was wasting too much time on this man. It was Dasharath Singh whom he wanted to trace. He had realized that the trader was a big man but what he saw now was beyond his imagination. How could such a man turn into a commoner and tour the island or put up at a cheap hotel like Shanti Nivas?! Malakar figured that the trader was so rich that he could buy a hundred women like Batashi. He realized his mistake then. He had underestimated the trader but now, it was too late to correct it. But was his name Dasharath Singh or was that a camouflage too?!

'What is your boss's name?'

'He has many names.'

'How is that possible?'

'Through affidavits. Now, give me one more cigarette.'

'Your boss smokes foreign cigarettes.' Malakar said this to the man to break the ice between them. One had to tap servants to extract information and Malakar knew this art well.

'Sahib doesn't smoke.'

'He does, I have seen him smoke.'

'You don't know him then.' The man laughed at Malakar.

'Your boss loves to drink vodka.'

'Rubbish! He doesn't drink.'

'You know nothing!' Malakar started laughing.

'Your sahib goes to Ghoradal.'

'Not at all! I would have known then. He doesn't go anywhere without me. There were four chargesheets against me but I killed four when in police custody. Sahib loves me.'

'Your sahib went to Dhanapati's Island from Ghoradal. Trust me.'

'Not at all! Sahib owns an island himself!'

'Where is it?'

'I don't exactly know. Sahib knows.'

'You know nothing. I know it all.' Malakar was happy that he had dumbed down the man.

'Impossible.'

'Your boss buys and sells women.'

'His is a multinational company and I don't know everything. He told me that he wanted to start a water business.'

'What kind of a business is that?'

'I don't know exactly but I heard my boss talk to his friends about it.'

'I really didn't know that he was such a big businessman. I thought he just bought and sold women.'

Malakar started pacing again. There was a plan that he drew up. This happened to him often. He just had to plan; the rest fell in place.

'Why has your sahib come here?'

'Only he knows that.'

'Then why do you shadow him all the time?'

'I am not interested in knowing what I am not supposed to know. I am always at his beck and call. He trusts me.'

'When will he come down?'

'I don't know. But he will give me a missed call when he is ready to come down. I will go up and escort him down. But why do you want to know all this?'

Malakar could not wait any longer. He left the man and took the lift to the ninth floor. There, he met an officer who was glad to see him.

'How are things in Ghoradal?' the officer asked.

'All well, sir. Just wanted to ask about a petition and an appeal from someone at Ghoradal. What is the status of that file now?'

After listening to details about the island, the officer started asking questions.

'Is that a very beautiful place?'

'Yes, you could say that.'

'Can I visit the island in winter?'

'You must.'

'The file is with the DM now, Malakar. Ask your BDO to come and see him.'

'You must help us in this. It's a genuine case. If the DM agrees, it will be done. I promise to collect tax for you on the island,' Malakar said.

Malakar realized that the officer did not want to tell him all. There was much more to this than what Malakar knew. Why did the DM call the BDO? He was worried now. It was quite late when he reached Ghoradal. Instead of going to the BDO's house, Malakar went to the riverbank and found Midde there.

'Where have you been, Malakar Bhai? Those two sluts, Jamuna and Batashi, went back to the island today. I did not stop them. They look like skeletons now. The trader wouldn't have liked them. Let them stay on the island for a few months. Only after that will their bodies flesh out.'

Fifteen

The breeze blows over the fermented rice,
My master adds salt and finds it nice.

Last time, the island was full of flowers of Kans grass. The whole island was white when they had set foot on the island. Her old master had told her that the white of the island was similar to the snow-covered white of Lisboan. The white of the flowers was the harbinger of winter on the island. The south wind would stop blowing and the north wind would take over. This was the season to fish and dry the catch. This was the time when the fishermen settled on the island.

Dhanapati kept talking to Kunti while she was busy setting up the house. Once in a while, she ran to the riverbank to see if the boats had come in. The shopkeepers would come in and set up the market and the fishermen would come in hordes to the island. No one had come. It was not time yet. The darkness all around held hands with thick silence and echoed from all over the island. Kunti felt scared. What if a pirate came and lifted her from the island? Old Dhanapati would not be able to do anything! He wanted to sleep right from early evening.

'What if no one comes to the island this year?'

'The fishermen and women will come when it is time.'

'What if the government stops them?'

'That won't happen, master. I have given a written appeal to the big government.'

'That was not the right thing to do.'

'Why?'

'Pedru got it for six months. He had not thought of twelve months. For the remaining six months, no one was supposed to stay on the island. Dhanapati tortoise comes to the island to sleep at that time.'

Kunti knew that these were just stories and could not be true. Dhanapati told her that if the fisherwomen started staying for six months, they would start asserting their rights on the land and even refuse to pay tax.

'What will you do then, Kunti?'

'No, master, they will still pay us. These poor women have no homes. Let them build their homes on the island.'

'Why are you taking such steps on your own? Why are you doing things without telling me? Do you think your master is totally blind? He can still see.' The angry Dhanapati seemed to freeze into darkness. His loneliness hung around him.

'I have not kept you in the dark.'

'Have I given you permission to go ahead?'

'Only a woman can think about another's pain.'

'That was not why Pedru got the island from Ma Kamala. Why did Pedru come here? He came here to loot women, not to build homes for them.'

'Those days are gone now, master. We have crossed the age of the pirates.'

'Nothing has changed.' Dhanapati again seemed to freeze into a dark stone.

'No, master. Those days are gone. If the fisherwomen are allowed to stay on the island, they will not remain as miserable as they have been all their lives, getting kicked from here to there for the next six months.'

Dhanapati kept quiet. Kunti tried her best to get him to see reason. Finally, he spoke up again.

'Can you stay here only with women? What if the men refused to stay for the next six months? Can women go fishing in the waters?'

'No, they won't. Only the men will go.'

'They won't come back, Kunti. Do you think they would like to live with old women? Those who will stay on will become old. Men come here to live with fresh and young women every time.'

'Oh, my God! Kunti was startled.' She had not thought on these lines at all!

'Listen, youth is all that a woman has and fishermen come here to enjoy that. Every year, they need new women. This island gives them an opportunity to choose anew every time. This year's mistake is not carried forward to the next. If fisherwomen stay here for twelve months, men will lose the freedom to choose and they will not come back to the island.'

Kunti's face was dark with anger now. She understood what Dhanapati, the pirate and looter, was trying to tell her. But she wouldn't let this opportunity go. She had appealed to the big government and was sure that she would get permission for the women to stay for all twelve months. Women would do farming on the island and grow vegetables. They could do a bit of fishing too. They didn't need men. They could survive on their own on the island. Dhanapati would not understand these things. He was Pedru's bloodline and only knew how to loot women. He thought he could only pin them down underneath him. Women could also lay on top.

Kunti shivered. She looked out into the dark. She realized that she was filled with desire for the big government. He would grant her permission to stay back on the island. Once she got patta over the island, she would rule the men with an iron hand. She would make Dhanapati powerless. He had lost his eyes already and now, he would lose everything else one by one and lay there like a lump of flesh. How dare he say that women were worth their youth! How did one assess the worth of men? What good was Dhanapati now? Could he satisfy his woman? How dare he leave the pregnant Anna Bibi on the island! What if she threw Dhanapati out into the sea now? Could he do much? Kunti's anger flashed in her two eyes. Her breath was quick and her bosom heaved. She was the owner of the island and the old, blind man could not scare her any more.

With the help of the big government, she would now establish her legal right on the island. Again, thoughts of the BDO filled her mind. She desired him deeply. Dhanapati and the BDO were both men. If Dhanapati thought that women were worth their youth, then even men were worth their youth. Dhanapati was past his worth and could be discarded now. The BDO could satisfy her and so, she desired him. There was nothing wrong with women desiring able men, if men only lusted after women and did not love them. She was filled with the thoughts of that afternoon when the BDO mauled her. She desired for more.

'Why are you quiet?'

'What should I say?'

'I will ask the government not to take your appeal seriously.'

'The government will just give me the patta. I will keep the women here. I will stay here too!'

'This is against the rule.'

'We will create a new rule.'

'That is not possible.'

'It is possible.'

'When I say no, it is final.'

'It is not. I am Dhaneshwari, the owner of the island. What I say is final.'

Dhanapati's blind eyes did not express the surprise that raged within. How did this slip of a girl learn to talk like this?

'I gave it to you, so you got it,' Dhanapati gathered his wits around him finally and said.

'You were forced to give it to me so that I stay with you. You are a blind old man. Who will stay with you and take care of you, master? You have become powerless and you have to accept that.' Kunti said this and waited for Dhanapati to react. She had become fearless now. She was suddenly happy that she could not be thumbed down by this man. She felt free. She felt as if she had already left the old man and the island behind.

'You are a traitor!'

Kunti did not answer.

Dhanapati hissed like a snake now. 'You were a beggar woman. I gave you food and shelter. Is this how you are paying me back?'

Kunti did not reply. She had quietened the rage within. She had said what was playing on her mind and that was necessary too. She would not let the old man hiss at her again. For ages, he had crushed women under his feet. It was now time for him to get crushed.

'You thought I am blind and so am unaware of what is going on?'

Kunti did not reply.

'I know what you did with the government that afternoon.'

Kunti laughed without making noise.

'I did not say anything to you. Do you know what Pedru's descendant should have done with you? Thrown you into the deep sea for the crocodiles and sharks to feed on.'

'Why didn't you do that?'

'Because he is government . . . government . . .' Dhanapati started gasping for breath. He was angry but had lost the strength to shout.

'You are no one to shout at me. I am the owner of this island, water and sky. I take pity on you these days, master. I keep you with me out of that pity I have for you.'

'How can you say this, Kunti? I gave you everything; is this how you will repay me now?' There was fear in Dhanapati's voice.

'You belong to Pedru's family, isn't it?'

'Yes, the pirate who came from Lisboan. The very mention of the pirate gave him back his self-confidence.'

'How did Pedru get the island?'

'He won it.'

'He looted it, isn't it?'

'Yes, you can call it loot if you wish. His ship came to the shore and all the people on the island fell at his feet, looking at his huge physique. He towered over them. He was so strong that he could take five women, one after the other.'

'So Pedru took everything that lay in front of his eyes, isn't it?'

'Yes, you are right.'

'So these things didn't originally belong to him, isn't that so?'

'No, they didn't. He came from Lisboan to take it all.'

'You got it from Pedru, right?'

'How many times do I repeat this?'

'So please understand that all this was not yours originally. They belonged to us, the people of this land. You are giving back what you looted from us. Remember the story that the big government told us?'

Dhanapati tried to understand what the girl was saying. How did she learn to talk so much? It was only after she got the island from him did she muster up so much courage, Dhanapati thought.

'That big government is a bastard. I would have finished him that day itself. I didn't do anything because he is government. The government is all powerful. He can do anything. If he demands one has to give up his wife as well. Otherwise do you think a pirate will tolerate any outsider laying his hands on his wife?'

'Government did not force me into the act. I tricked him into coming into the room with me. I like the government; he is so youthful.'

'You are a shameless woman.'

'I don't care about that. I have nothing to keep from my government.' Kunti found immense pleasure in saying this. Dhanapati growled like a caged tiger. But what could he do? He was just a blind old man. But he was not prepared to surrender so easily. He had not spun his stories about the island, Pedru and the tortoise for nothing!

'Let the fishermen come back. I will take it all back from you.'

'How will you do that?'

'The fishermen know that I am everything and you are nothing. They will accept what I say.'

'Behave yourself, master. You are old and blind, and you need me to take care of you. Don't equate me with Anna Bibi whom you left alone on the island. She was a woman you wronged. You could do that because you were young and powerful. Today, you can no longer show that power. The situation has changed now for you.'

The old blind man got up and walked about, stamping his feet in anger. 'I am Pedru's descendant. I am the owner of the island.

Don't think you will take everything away from me so easily. I have
decided to take away everything from you. You will spoil the empire
I built over so many years.'

Kunti was firm in her resolve. She kept quiet because she had
made her stand clear to Dhanapati. If he supported her in her mission
of making the island a permanent home for the fisherwomen, it was
fine. Otherwise she would have to devise other ways of making her
plan successful. She would bring the government to the island again
and again. She would get children from him. Her children would
roam about on the island and become her strength. The old blind
man would never be able to give her children.

'You are a bad woman. I picked you up from the streets and gave
you everything. Now you are cheating me.'

'You looted the island from people like us. Now we have
taken it back from you. This is the reality you have to accept.
The situation has changed for you forever. Oh! Jamuna Mashi and
Batashi Di are coming towards us. They are back! Master, don't utter
a word of what has happened to them. That is for your own good.'

The two women looked like skeletons. Jamuna looked worse
than Batashi. Just skin and a few bones jutting out here and there.
'Where were you all these days?' Kunti went out to receive them.

'We were in hell.'

'Whom should we address? The old master or you, Kunti?'
Batashi asked.

'Tell me everything.' Kunti lifted the veil on her head.

'We will stay together in a hut on the island, we don't need men.'

'Only the two of you! Why?'

'We are fed up with men. They just use us. We will work hard
and earn for ourselves,' Jamuna said. 'Dhanapati and Dhaneshwari
just need to allow us to.

The old blind man sat there saying nothing. Why on earth did
he have to bring a sorceress as a wife? She had looted everything from
him and thrown him into the deep sea.

Sixteen

Is she yours, under the same roof?
What goes in her mind, who has proof?

A few days later, Aniket went to meet the DM. Pujas were over. This was also a routine visit. It was ten in the morning. He entered the DM's bungalow alone. The trees, the lawn and the bungalow were silent, as if asleep. Did they all lower their heads because the seat of power was nearby? There was a bird singing somewhere. Aniket realized that the bird too had chosen to sit on a tree outside the boundaries of this powerhouse.

Aniket pushed open the door to enter the DM's office. It was massive and the DM sat towards the end of it. Every time, the room seemed to grow bigger than before. It might become like the limitless sea one day.

'Sir . . . sir . . . yes . . . yes, sir.' The DM was on the phone. He pointed towards a chair and indicated that Aniket sit on it. He was obviously speaking to someone more powerful than him, Aniket realized. The conversation ended soon and the DM smiled at Aniket.

'So, Sen, how have you been? How were your pujas?'

'Shubho Bijoya, sir! I was at Ghoradal during the pujas.'

'You mean, you didn't go home?'

'I wanted to see the pujas here.'

'Tell me about the books you read recently.'

'I was reading about Portuguese travellers in Bengal. The book is called *Banga Brittanta* and I found it very interesting, sir.'

'Tell me more about the book.'

'Sebastian Manrik, Dom Joao, Duarte Barbosa, Joao de Barros and Caesar Frederik were all Portuguese men who came to Bengal for trade or for spreading Christianity. *Banga Brittanta* is a collection of their accounts and what they saw in the Bengal they explored.'

'Interesting.'

'Yes, sir! There are graphic details and you get transported to that time and place.'

'I like your interest in books, Sen.'

'What else will I do, sir? I stay alone.'

'Why do you stay alone? You can always come over! You are a bachelor, right?'

'Yes, sir.'

'So, is it just books you read or do you have any other hobby?'

'I am also spending a lot of time getting to know the place.' Aniket was a bit surprised at the way the DM was behaving with him. This was unusual. The DM was extremely class conscious and never did anything to come down to the level of the junior officers. He loved to maintain a distance and never laughed or joked with them, leave alone getting into discussions about politics, art or culture. But this time, he was definitely making an exception for Aniket.

The DM stared at the blue velvet underneath the heavy glass on his table. He had suddenly stopped talking. 'Sir, there are many descendants of Portuguese travellers and even pirates who live in Ghoradal. They either go fishing in the sea for a living or till their land.'

'It was not clear if the DM was paying any attention to what Aniket said.'

'There are some who remember the names of their Portuguese ancestors from seven generations ago!'

'Is that so?' The DM was surprised.

'I have forwarded a petition to you from a woman called Dhaneshwari Dasi, who has prayed for the long-term lease of an island. She had given the prayer in writing to me but it was addressed to you.'

'Yes, wasn't it the island where some trouble had broken out last time?'

'Correct, sir! Dhaneshwari's husband says that he is of Portuguese descent. A very interesting man.'

'Have you been to that island?'

'Once, sir.'

'Are the women into prostitution?'

'No, sir! Fishermen go and set up home there for six months to fish. The season starts in Ashwin and ends in Chaitra.'

'Is free mixing allowed on the island?'

'I am not aware, sir.'

'Then what inquiry have you done?'

'Sir, this is beyond the inquiry. The fishermen go there for six months . . . .' The DM signalled to Aniket to stop. His mobile phone rang and he spoke so softly that Aniket couldn't make out what the DM was saying. Aniket kept looking at the high ceiling, the white walls, the photograph of the DM with the chief minister, the lawns beyond the window and the river beyond the boundary wall. *But why was everything so quiet? Was there no one around?*

The DM finished talking on the phone after some time.

'We need to conduct a survey of the island.'

'Sir?'

'Your Dhanapati's Island needs to be surveyed. Who is Dhanapati?'

Aniket explained that Dhanapati was a descendant of a Portuguese pirate called Pedru. He went on to talk about the tortoise of the same name and the belief that surrounded the name.' The DM laughed out aloud. 'Horrible! Do you believe in all this?'

'These are part of the lore that surrounds the island. A bit of it is true and the rest is imagination.'

'Not totally false?'

'No, sir. Rural people everywhere live with their lore.' Aniket tried his best to make the DM understand the importance of folk tales that finally get interpolated into the main body of the country's cultural texts and traditions. 'So what? What do we need to do about that?' The DM sounded fed up now.

Aniket realized that the DM was not interested in what he was saying. Why was he called then? It was clear that he had an agenda but what was it, Aniket wondered.

'We need to stop fishermen from going to the island. It has become a den of prostitution and soon, there might be an outbreak of venereal diseases. Can you imagine how dangerous that could be, Sen?'

'It's not exactly this, sir.'

'Why are you trying to screen the truth from me?'

'Why should I do that, sir? What is my interest in doing so?'

'Stop the women from going there. Then, the men will then not go there automatically.'

'I am confused, sir.'

'Sen, let's face it. The detective report that has come to me says that the island gets converted into a red-light area for six months.'

Aniket kept quiet. The DM was saying that Aniket should have sent a report about how the police was beaten up on the island. Why didn't Aniket submit the inquiry report? Women were smuggled out of the place and sent off to the flesh market. It was natural that Dhanapati was also involved. The police were heckled when they got wind of this and tried to stop a girl who was getting sold on the island.

'This is not true, sir. It is primarily a fishing island and women go there in search of work.'

'Sen, what is this? You are deliberately trying to hide something from me. The detective report clearly says that the island is a den of prostitution for six months and young girls are regularly sold off from there, never to be found again. The island is infested with pimps who auction women and send them to foreign shores. Arab Sheikhs pay a lot of money to lay their hands on such young, helpless and illiterate girls who accept everything silently.'

Aniket could make out that the DM was repeating what had been written in the newspapers a fortnight ago. There was nothing new in what he was saying. Most of what was there in the detective report was not true. But it was difficult for Aniket to counter the highest officer in the district who had already made up his mind against the islanders. The DM had clearly said that Aniket was deliberately hiding something and that that was also the reason why he had not sent the report. This was damaging for Aniket's reputation and career. His head reeled.

'The constable and the pimp were both heckled, sir, when they tried to smuggle a girl out of the land.'

'So, you are admitting that pimps are at work on the island, right?'

'Sir, it is primarily a fishing island and people go there to earn. It is not a brothel. The island was discovered by this man Dhanapati whose forefathers were pirates.'

'Listen, Sen, you are getting unnecessarily emotional because you are young and yet to get accustomed to the ways in which a mature government officer works. This island has been formed due to alluvial deposits. It has come out of the sea and is definitely owned by the government.'

'Yes, sir.'

'Dhanapati collects money from those who go to the island to live and work.'

'That is because he thinks that the island is his.'

'Get this out of his head. Prevent people from going to the island this time.'

'They have already gone there, sir. Usually, they go after the Kojagori Lakshmi Puja. But this time, they have gone before the pujas, sir. Dhanapati is blind. He went ahead of the others.'

'Have you sent them there?'

'I am feeling insulted, sir! I have no connection with this island.' Aniket got up.

'Come, come, sit down. I didn't mean to hurt you. I just said that you are still very emotional about villagers, their songs and culture. Sen, they are not so innocent. Writers have traditionally been very sympathetic towards villagers. It is their profession to spin stories and make them unnecessarily emotional. You are getting influenced by such stories. This Dhanapati was a crooked man. The detective

report about the place is very bad. We have to stop them from going
to the island.'

'Dhanapati is a blind man, sir.'

'Then someone else must be controlling his business for him.'

'People have already reached the island for the season, sir.'

'Bring them back. Let the government decide what it wishes to
do with the island.'

'Sir, the island is an ideal place for fishing. It should be used
throughout the year. During the hilsa season, it is not in use. We must
use it then.'

The DM shook his head. 'That cannot be done. Bring them back.'

'Sir, the six-monthly life on the island is an age-old tradition.'

'No, no. We cannot allow prostitution on the island. How
can you turn a blind eye towards buying and selling? The matter
has reached the highest levels of administration. We cannot ignore
it anymore. Please follow my orders on this. I will give you all the
support you need to remove them from the island. You will have the
police with you; you will get funds and also a few tough hands who
can be useful while evacuating the people.

'But sir . . .'

'Nothing more . . . please follow my orders.'

We are going wrong somewhere, sir.'

'We are not. They have been looting government property for
years. We will stop it forever now. Everything under the sun belongs
to the government and that is the logic we will use while evacuating
them. Sen, no more arguments please. Else you will bring trouble
onto yourself.'

Aniket felt sad. His head felt heavy. He thought of the blind
Dhanapati who grew old in the belief that the island and its sky were
his, just as the water was. He had given everything to his wife. The
DM wanted it back now. The biggest government, the DM, wouldn't
allow them to stay on the island.

Seventeen

Don't let your water pot float away,
There's no water here, but it sinks to stay.

Dhanapati's Island sloped into the sea on its southeastern side. The sea came up to the island from that side every full and new moon. During the monsoons, the island started sinking from that very side. But in winter, there was less water so the island did not get submerged even on that side. The saline water left a lot of salt on the island. There were some freshwater ponds that Dhanapati had dug on the island but they would get mixed with saline water because of the submergence. Embankments had therefore been created to protect the ponds. Aniket Sen had collected a lot of details for preparing his report. He got a draughtsman to draw a sketch map of the island too. He had recommended such embankments on all sides of the island so that people could live there throughout the year. They could even do some farming. The sandy soil was ideal for growing watermelon, pumpkin and nuts. Sunflowers could also be grown and, if the people put in some effort, paddy and wheat too. Fishing would remain the main livelihood. The island could turn into a fishing port over time.

The report had come back with comments from the DM. The comment ignored these ideas that Aniket had put forth. The DM had, instead, instructed that no one should be allowed on the island because it would soon become a disease bed. It would be difficult to save people once that happened, the DM had written.

Nabadwip Malakar sat opposite Aniket. He seemed to have guessed that Aniket was unhappy since he had come back from meeting the DM.

'Sir, should I go to the island? Is there something that I can do?'

'Have people left for the island?'

'Many have, many are still going.'

Aniket told everything to Malakar. 'I knew this would be the outcome. Those women should have realized that if the government wants, they should not resist. See what they have finally got themselves into!'

'What do you mean?' Aniket frowned.

Malakar opened up to Aniket and told him about how the constable had sold Batashi to the trader.

'Why didn't you tell me earlier!?'

'I would have mentioned it in my report!'

'The constable sold her but that could not be considered a sale. The trader wanted to buy but it remained incomplete because the woman protested and created a scene. The trader got angry and twisted the whole thing into an anti-island story and fed it to the government. It is true that a few women would vanish from the island every year.'

'Were you aware of that?'

'These women belong to no one. They live contented lives with their temporary husbands in make-believe families. So, if one or two women vanish, people just ignore it. The supply is much more than the demand, sir.'

'Are you saying that the DM is right?'

'He has been tutored by the trader. Let me tell you one thing, sir. People who are into smuggling women have the support of the government, sir.'

'How is that possible?'

'Sir, the constable, OC, the revenue collector and even you and I are all involved in this.'

'Do you know what you are saying?'

'If the trader comes and makes us dream of dollars, can the government ignore it?'

Aniket looked out at the advancing darkness of the Ashwin evening. The office was empty. Malakar sat across him, joining the dots. Everything was gradually becoming clear to him. Aniket shivered slightly.

'This needs investigation. It is bad indeed.'

'No one will admit to the crime, sir. No one will tell you how many women have vanished. How will you search for the truth in the dark?'

'Are you sure these things happen?'

'Yes, sir. There are traders involved in this but no one makes any noise.'

'I hope you are not making any mistake.'

'There is not an iota of lie in this. However, there has been no official complaint all these years.'

'How did it reach the DM this time?'

'It was deliberately done.'

'By whom?'

'The man who tried his best to get her and even paid for her but could not lay his hands on Batashi.'

'The constable needs to be nabbed first.'

'Sir, he is very greedy. He has always facilitated such smuggling because he was paid in return. He thinks he is the government and so, he has the right to earn extra money. He is otherwise quite simple; cries every time he gets drunk.'

'He has misused his powers.'

'That is how the government shows off power to the fishermen and women. Otherwise, they will not be in awe of him.'

'You should have told me all this before, Malakar Babu.'

'We are all government, sir. Malakar is a government and BDO is also government. We are all misusing our powers. Otherwise how is it possible that old Dhanapati was in one room and his wife slept with the government in another?'

A shiver ran down Aniket's spine. Malakar stared at him. Aniket lowered his head.

'Sir, year after year, I have brought young women from the island to be supplied to the big officers who came on tour to Ghoradal. The officers left the young women half dead because they unleashed their lust on them. I had to take so many to the hospital.'

'I am scared, Malakar Babu.'

'One girl consumed poison after the big officer left. The then BDO and I were in deep trouble. Thankfully, she didn't die. The BDO got transferred thereafter.'

'Stop, Malakar Babu.'

'Please permit me to smoke, sir.'

'Give me one too.'

'Nothing would have happened had Batashi agreed to go. Then it would have been Sabitri's turn. Perhaps that young wife of Dhanapati would have gone too. But things would not have come to such a pass. The DM wouldn't have got involved.'

'How did the trader stand to gain?'

'He is a cunning man. He hasn't gone to the DM for nothing!'

Aniket asked Malakar about the trader. 'Sir, he is like a chameleon. He looks different each time—while on the island, while drinking vodka at the Ghoradal hotel and while meeting the DM. It's the same man in three different guises. He went to Batashi with Mangal Midde's help but she didn't entertain him. When he tried harder, she simply locked the two in. Midde wields a lathi and wears the uniform, but he doesn't have the personality of a policeman. Naturally, Batashi did not take him seriously and overpowered him. The trader returned hurt but promised not to forget the insult soon. He had to take revenge. After all, the trader's family has been in this business for many generations and he knows all the tricks of the trade. Those have helped him become a millionaire. Batashi's attitude has proved to be very costly for the islanders. Now, no one will be able to go back.'

'What will happen now, Malakar Babu?'

'You are a government, you will have to do the work that a government is supposed to do.

'How will I do that? They want to stay there for twelve months!'

'That will not be possible now, sir.'

'I won't be able to evacuate them.'

'We will have to do it, sir. At any cost. Give me some people who can go with me to the island. Let me announce this on a loudspeaker first.'

'You will be assaulted.'

'No, sir. Malakar knows how to save himself.'

'Those poor people had prayed to me to allow them to stay for twelve months. How can I let them down?'

'This is part of your duty as government, sir. You cannot avoid it.'

'I feel so sorry for them.'

'No, sir, don't be. You are a big government, don't let such thoughts make you weak. You are a big government, that is why Dhanapati's wife slept with you. She didn't choose the constable or me.'

'Don't say all this so loudly, Malakar. How do you know so much?'

'That day, I knew that my government had come of age. I felt so proud that you could make her sleep with you. She is no ordinary woman.'

Aniket hung his head. He thought that there was no difference between him and the likes of the constable, Malakar or the OC of the local police station. The pride with which he held his head high had dissolved completely. Malakar was right. Kunti had surrendered to him because he was big government and powerful. Didn't she say so at the time of their union? If the government desired, no one said no, she had said.

'You will have to ask them to vacate, sir.'

'Will they listen?'

'I don't really know, sir. For so many years, they have been going back to that island. They know no other life. How will Dhanapati and his wife survive away from the island? The women totally depend upon the money they earn on the island.'

'Look at this letter. The island will be turned into a resort.' Aniket held out a letter for Malakar to see.

'A multinational company, Greenwood, wants to set up the resort. That is what the letter says, sir.'

'Yes, they will beautify the island, add some make-believe hillocks, etc. Tourists will come here to enjoy themselves.'

'Sir, I know who this could be. It is trader Dasharath Singh.'

'The whole place will gradually turn into a centre for sex tourism. Women of all kinds will be supplied to tourists on the resort. There are some countries like Thailand who have taken sex tourism to another level altogether. We will need the police and military together to vacate the island.'

Malakar looked sad. 'At this rate, the importance of the government in the eyes of the people will also wane.'

'Dhanapati made a grave mistake by not giving up Batashi to the trader. She could be put to sleep and then carried out of the island. Even tigers are put to sleep and smuggled out. That sorceress changed everything.' Malakar cursed her. Can she now put her magic into action and protect the island from the government? 'We are government servants; we will have to do as we are told,' he said aloud.

The Greenwood company was coming in, on the pretext of afforestation and saving the environment. In return, they would build a resort. The complaint that had reached the government added that the fishermen and women destroyed the greenery of the island. This was over and above the original complaint of young women being smuggled out from the island. Aniket looked out of the window into the darkness outside. He could see the island, he thought. Dhanapati was telling his favourite story of Ma Kamala and her golden pot from where the island had come out, along with pirate Pedru. Saint Pedru had come from Lisbon. Aniket wanted to write these stories down so that they didn't get lost forever. The evacuation would wipe the stories out too. The saline water would wash everything away. The golden pot would float away into the deep sea.

Eighteen

One who seals the fate of the sea and isle,
May he have the final say, till the last mile.

There were meetings at Ghoradal and the district headquarters simultaneously. All officers of Ghoradal were present in both. The big officers from the headquarters had visited Ghoradal to explain how the evacuation had to be carried out.

In the first few days, there would be announcements on the island using loudspeakers. People would be asked to vacate the island because the environment had to be protected and the island was being taken over for afforestation and planned development. After that, leaflets would be distributed that would mention a deadline by which everyone had to leave. Those who continued to stay on would be threatened with dire consequences. The next stage would be to physically lift them out of the island and send them packing. The island had to be evacuated at all costs. People of the Greenwood Company were also part of the advisory committee that oversaw the evacuation.

Mangal Midde met Malakar and told him that the trader had come. He was at the hotel and had called the two of them.

'Now what? He is getting the island.'

'I am not sure, Malakar Babu, if people will really leave the island.

'There is no choice there, Midde. They will have to.'

'My instinct says that they won't leave so easily.'

'Who will have the courage to face lathis and bullets?'

Mangal Midde looked out at the dark. 'Things will change now. There will be special boats to go to the island throughout the year. Those women will get what they wanted.'

'Yes, they will be in great demand. We will supply them to the hotels and earn a huge commission.'

'Is this how the government will be expected to help the project?'

'Don't be rigid about what we should or should not done.'

'It will not be easy to vacate the island. They will refuse.'

'The company will send goons to rape women. There will be gang rapes. The women will not be able to hold on.'

'How do you know so much?'

'It's easy. Just keep your eyes and ears open.'

'Let's go and meet the trader. He has called us.

So, the two government officials headed towards Shanti Nivas Hotel. They found the trader exercising in his hotel room. They sat there and watched him till he finished. After that, the trader wiped himself, put on a T-shirt and came and sat with them. In the meantime, Malakar tried to confirm if he had indeed seen the trader that day at the district headquarters.

'Sir, who owns Greenwood Company?'

'We do.'

'Will it create a forest on the island?'

'Yes, and also hotels and a resort. We will promote tourism.'

The trader was talking to Malakar. Midde butted in. 'Nothing will happen, sir. It will be impossible to vacate the island.'

'What do you mean?'

'Two-and-a-half thousand is a paltry amount.'

The trader laughed. 'There will be a permanent arrangement now. Plus, you will have commissions to earn too.'

Midde looked sullen. The trader started pouring out vodka for them, rang the bell and asked for chicken pakoras. Midde ate and drank and then spoke again. 'It will be impossible, sir.'

'What do you mean?'

'It will not be possible, sir.'

'Don't worry about your two-and-a half-thousand. You will get more and that too, on a monthly basis. You will just have to tell us which woman has to be picked up from where; homes where are starving and need help, etc. There will be a huge demand for women. You two will go to the island, stay there for two days and then come back.'

Midde's eyes were clouded. 'Not possible, sir.'

'Shut up!'

'No one will leave the island, sir.'

The trader laughed. 'They will. You can bet on that.'

'They have nothing to lose. They will not budge. Midde took out a bidi from his pocket and started smoking.'

'We will force them out.'

'No, sir. They will not move.'

'Who told you that?'

'I am saying so. They will stay there permanently. I am the government's man. I know.'

'Government has given the island to me.'

'No matter who gives it to you, they won't budge.'

'Listen, we are experts in evacuation. We have been evacuating people for ages. In my Hispanic days, I have evacuated people and now, in my Greenwood days, I will continue to do so.'

'You can try but you will not be successful.'

'Listen, just because I spent time with you and desired a woman from that island doesn't make me a small man. I own a big company which has the power to do a lot of things.'

'What can you do?'

'I can even overthrow a government.'

'Is that so?' Malakar was intrigued now.

'Do your research. Find out what we did in Chile, Iraq and Africa. I need the island.'

'You will fail this time,' Midde said.

'We will organize gang rapes and torch their houses. Police will give us protection.'

'They are used to getting raped.'

'This time will be different.'

'No, sir. Ask Malakar Da. They are not scared of getting raped.'

'Yes, he is right.' Malakar joined Midde.

'Okay, leave it,' the trader said.

'Why? Do you accept that it is impossible to vacate the island?'

'No. Let's bet on it. I am saying that evacuation will be complete and before that the women will be raped.'

'I am saying you will not be able to evacuate them.' Midde was firm on his stance.

'Malakar?'

'I will wait to see how things go and then bet.'

'I will win,' Midde said.

'No. I will. The trader was firm.'

'If you lose, how much will you pay me?' Midde wanted the trader to commit.

'How much will you give me for losing?'

'I will sell myself to you. I will be your slave for life.'

'Malakar?'

'I will wait before getting involved. Such planned rape will bring bad publicity. Please avoid it, sir.'

'You are yet to fathom my strength. We have been silently removing women from the island. Has anything happened?'

'They weren't proved, that's why.'

'This time too, there will be no proof.'

'What about the statements that the women will give?'

'You have to cross hurdles if you have to achieve something, Malakar.'

'Tell me how much I will get.'

'You mean if you win the bet? Hundred dollars.'

'Not enough, sir.'

'Thousand dollars.'

'Too little.'

'You are an old man. How much do you think your price can be!'

Malakar got up and went to the verandah. It was dark outside. The days had become shorter. There was a dry and cold breeze. Malakar wondered which side he should be betting on. How was Midde so sure of his stand? Was he getting information from the island? Had he discussed this with Midde before coming to meet the trader, he too would have been able to decide on the bet.

'Malakar Bhai . . .' Midde called from inside.

'Coming.' But he did not go in in a hurry. The trader and the constable were excitedly talking about the bet. The trader said that once he had bet on a man who was swept away by the sea. He had bet that the man would come back. His body came back after a few days and he won five hundred dollars. This time, too, he would win the bet.

After a long time, Midde and Malakar came out of the hotel. They were both drunk.

'You shouldn't have participated in the bet, Midde bhai.'

'No, there is nothing wrong in it.'

'You will turn into a slave.'

'I am already one. That is why he will make me supply women and control me all the time. Can I disobey him, even now?'

'He has promised to bring back the forest on the island and develop it.'

'True. We will supply food for the wild animals.'

'Don't become emotional.'

'I am absolutely sure about the outcome and so I have placed my bet.'

Malakar and Midde walked out into the dark. Malakar had realized that Midde was cleverer than him. He had been roughed up by the women on the island but had still bet in their favour. He had guts. Malakar, on the other hand, was neither here nor there.

Nineteen

The old master counts his days; government please come,
I thirst for you, spend time with me, even if it is just some . . .

Just before the full moon of Kartik, Malakar went to the island with loudspeakers and a van rickshaw on which he would move around. Midde and three other constables went with him.

The fishermen were still coming in batches to the island. Many had begun building their homes. New faces got added to the existing population. Malakar saw that the women did not have their veils over their heads. *What had happened to Dhaneshwari's new rule? Was this an indication that they were going back to Dhanapati's regime? Was this being deliberately done to help the pimps pick up a few women now and then?* Perhaps Dhaneshwari had realized that she had to keep the government happy if she had to live in peace on the island. It was also possible that it was getting difficult to go about one's work with the veil on. Perhaps Dhaneshwari was in a combative mode and was waiting to confront the traders. Last time, Batashi had squared them up.

'How beautiful it was earlier when we used to come along with the fishermen and collect taxes. They respected us so much.'

'If they did, why did they beat you up?'

'That was the trader's mistake and so, he was roughed up. He went on luring her with snow powder, clothes and what not. He spoke to her about delicious food that he would give her. But she refused to budge. We did not realize that yesterday's women are different from today.'

'Had you conducted things differently last time, we would not have suffered this time, Midde Bhai.'

The constable rotated his lathi as he walked with Malakar, who moved with big strides. People looked at them as they walked. They were known faces among the people. Every year, they came to collect their share and fleece the islanders. However, they had never come to the island together. The folks on the island, though, did not have the time to think about these two.

They reached Dhanapati's house and called from outside. 'Dhana chief . . . Dhaneshwari . . . we have come.'

'Who is it?' Dhaneshwari came out from the kitchen. The old man said something from inside. It was ten in the morning. Kunti was surprised to see them together.

'Why have you come together? We have not yet collected any money to give you. It's too early. Many people are yet to come. We cannot entertain you two now.'

'Where is the old man?'

'He is inside. He got hurt yesterday while stepping on to the courtyard from the verandah. He is old and is gradually giving up.' Kunti made it clear that they had to talk to her.

'We need to see him.'

'Talk to me. I am the new owner of the island, you know that. Buli Ma, bring chairs for these two visitors or roll out a mat underneath the neem tree.'

Malakar paced up and down. Midde stood at a distance looking uncomfortable. He realized that it was his mistake that has brought so much trouble to the island. Now, they had come to Dhanapati's house to read out the death note. Midde blamed the trader for everything. Had he not lusted after Batashi, things would not have come to this. Midde had helped to sell off women from the island in the past. However, that was all done with consent or with false promises of marriage. It had never been as complicated as this.

Buli Ma had laid out the mat for them to sit. Malakar lit his cigarette.

'I love the island, Dhaneshwari. It makes me happy.'

'What happened to my appeal?'

'Call Dhanapati. Let me talk to him.'

'Wait a bit. He will come out. When will the big government come here?'

'He doesn't have time to come to the island.'

'Tell him that Dhaneshwari called him.'

'He has to look after Ghoradal and go to the headquarters to meet the DM too. He has no time!'

'Just tell him that Dhaneshwari wishes to see him. What happened to the application?'

'Give us some sweets and water first! You are bombarding us with questions from the moment we have set foot in your house!'

Dhaneshwari gave some instructions to Buli Ma. Then she addressed the two men again. 'Constable Sahib, have you come to the island to buy and sell again? Forget all that you did during Dhanapati's time. The regime has changed now, and Dhaneshwari has asked all women to keep a knife hidden in their saree knot at the waist.'

The constable did not reply. He was very sad. He couldn't believe that the island would not be the same again and he would not be able to come and collect money. This was the best season of the year for him when he could earn extra by sending some women off with the pimps or traders. Midde could not believe that Dhanapati's stories about Pedru and Lisboan would come to an end. Greenwood Company was going to take over from the original people of the island and decide everything. The constable hung his head in shame.

'Dhanapati is calling you from inside. Go fetch him,' Malakar said.

'I will bring him out when it would be time for him to bathe.'

'Why is he inside?'

'He was out in the morning to visit the toilet and brush. Now he is resting inside.'

'Bring him out.'

'Not now. He just sits in the verandah and shouts. That is not good for his image. He is a descendant of the pirates who stomped the seas, looting women and torching houses. He was a very dangerous man who had captured the island and ran it for years. Today, he is nothing but a lump of flesh, unable to handle himself without help. He just sits in the verandah and shouts. So, I keep him inside, mostly.'

'There is something very urgent and we need to speak to him for that.'

'Tell me. I don't want to expose him to people right now.'

'He was alright even in the month of Bhadra. What happened to him in these couple of months?'

'He is deteriorating fast and cannot come out by himself now. You can tell me what you have to. But remember no one will come for any inquiry anymore.'

Malakar had batasha and water that Buli Ma brought for them. 'Can you give me some paan?'

'What about my application? Constable sahib, can you please move away for a bit? I want to talk to Malakar Bhai alone.'

The constable sprang up. He was happy to be away from Dhaneshwari. He just couldn't fathom how Malakar would broach the evacuation with Kunti. The trader had convinced everyone that the island was forested and that the fishermen had destroyed the forest over the years. He had promised to first bring back the forest and then build hotels and resorts to promote tourism on the island. The constable thought that he was to be blamed for this. Had he not been involved in trying to sell Batashi, the islanders wouldn't have been in trouble. He was primarily responsible for this disaster, Midde told himself while walking towards the sea.

'Tell the big government that I have called him. He will definitely come.'

'I will tell him, but you must remember that he is my boss and I will feel uncomfortable.

'I will write a letter to him. You can carry it for me. Can you please write what I ask you to?'

'Okay. Now can you please call your master?'

'I told you he is immobile now and cannot be brought out in front of people.'

'He needs to know something.'

'It doesn't matter whether he knows or doesn't. I am the owner of the island now and you can tell me whatever you wish to.'

Dhanapati cried out for Buli Ma from inside. He wanted to come out. His wife wouldn't bring him out but the maid could. 'See how he has become! He doesn't let me be in peace, that old man,' Dhaneshwari said.

'Never mind. Bring him out.'

'No, no one will see him in that state.'

'One does grow old, Dhaneshwari.'

'Pirates don't grow old. They turn into tortoises and go down into the sea.'

'Who told you that?'

'I know.'

'You have created this in your mind.'

'Possible. I carry on Dhanapati's tradition now. Pirates don't die a normal death like other men. They have lived their whole life raging about in the sea. At the end of their lives, they transform into tortoises and go down into the water.'

Malakar was surprised at the transformation of this girl. She spoke with so much confidence. Dhanapati hadn't tutored her. She had learnt everything on her own. She went up to the verandah and screamed at old Dhanapati inside. 'Shut up and try to sleep, master. You were a dangerous pirate. Why have you turned into a pitiable rag, suddenly? I don't want anyone to see you in this state. If you don't stop nagging, I will stop giving you food. No rice for you, old man, if you don't obey. I will not take you to the toilet either.'

Dhanapati was silent now. Dhaneshwari came back victorious. Malakar looked at her in wonder. She was beautiful and her body had filled out in the right proportions. She had near-perfect hips and breasts. They rose like mounds from under her saree. Wasn't it natural for his boss to fall for her? But Aniket was a good man. Otherwise, he would have taken the sap out of her. There was no one she called her own and Dhanapati was immobile. The big government could use her as he wished. But he did not.

'He will come.'

'I worship him,' Kunti said. She pulled her veil over her head and covered herself well with the loose end of her saree.

'What do you want me to write?'

'Write that I spend sleepless nights without him.' Kunti lowered her eyes and turned red. 'Tell him that even when the old man dies, I will stay on the island and wait for him. He can come anytime he wants.'

'What else?'

'Close your eyes and ears as I say this. Write that I send him love and kisses. Write that there is much more that I wish to say but cannot. He has to come to me to hear all that I have to say.'

'I will write and take your thumb impression on the paper.'

Malakar realized that there was no use hiding anything from her. 'The government has decreed that the island has to be vacated.'

'What are you saying, Malakar Babu?!' Dhaneshwari cried out in disbelief. 'Are you joking? We are preparing to stay for twelve months!'

'That won't be possible. Everyone will leave.'

Dhaneshwari was angry like a serpent now. 'Who told you all this?'

'Your government.'

'That's not possible! You are a devil! You are making up a story.' She pounced on Malakar and tore his clothes. 'I know how to kill you, you devil.'

'Leave me, Dhaneshwari. I haven't done anything. I have just come here to read the order that the government has given.'

'Shut up you bastard! Have you forgotten what happened to you people last time?'

Malakar moved away. He couldn't face her now. She was hissing like a serpent, ready to sting. Look at what she had done to Dhanapati! He walked towards the seashore and saw Midde at a distance. He would finish his lunch and then move around announcing the evacuation on a loudspeaker. He was scared now. What if the islanders retaliated the moment they announced the evacuation?

Twenty

We are birds of the same feather,
If you trap us, we'll get together!

Both Malakar and the constable realized that the moment they announced the evacuation order, the island would get heated up and there would be adverse reactions. Dhaneshwari's anger had rattled Malakar.

'Go back, Malakar Babu. Ask the big government what he has done about my appeal. We will not pay you a paisa anymore. We will stay back for twelve months. Do whatever you can do to stop us.' Dhaneshwari threw a challenge at Malakar.

The constable was reminded of what the trader said. He had threatened to use goons to rape women. He had to come to the island to see Dhaneshwari's anger and face her. If the trader thought that it would be easy to drive people out of the island, he was wrong. He had to face Dhaneshwari and then decide for himself.

'I told you, didn't I?'

'What had you said, Midde?'

'No one will leave.'

'We are yet to announce it.'

'You saw how Dhaneshwari reacted.'

'What can a lone woman do?'

'Have you seen how she has broken Dhanapati's fangs? The fierce pirate just licks his wounds these days.'

'That's because he is old.'

'When did he become old? She has made him old by casting a spell on him. First, she took away his eyes and then his abilities, one by one. She is a dangerous woman and can finish off the trader too!'

The two decided not to go around with a loudspeaker on the island because they might be attacked by the angry islanders. Instead, they planned to stay put on the motorized launch in which they had come from Ghoradal and announce from there. When the loudspeaker crackled and they just tried to test whether it was working, people on the island stood up to listen.

Malakar went on testing the mic. Midde stood there and watched the quiet water during low tide. The water was low and so, the launch boat had anchored at a distance. The constable's mind was full of remorse. What if the evacuation happened and this was the last time that he was looking at the island and its people? Malakar suddenly stopped testing the mic and played a popular folk song.

The people on the island were surprised. Why had they tested the mic and not started the meeting? Nevertheless, they loved the song that was being played.

'Malakar Bhai, when will you announce?'

'Not immediately, constable.' The launch was stuck in the mud because of the low tide. If I announce now, they might come and attack us. 'Let the high tide come and lift the launch. After announcing, we will simply speed away.'

'You have a double-barrelled gun with you, Malakar Bhai.'

'I don't want the situation to go out of hand. My duty is to make the announcement. Kunti already knows, the others will also get to know soon.'

It was evening. Although it wasn't winter yet, evening got chilly. The moon rose from the east. It seemed to come out of the water. Midde thought that for just two-and-a-half-thousand rupees, he had spoilt this moonrise. He raised his hand and sent prayers to the moon god. His eyes welled up and his heart went out to the people of the island whom he had wronged. High tide had started. The launch boat was shaking from side to side.

Malakar switched off the song that was playing and prepared to address the islanders who had gathered on the coast. 'I have come here to announce on behalf of the government . . .'

Malakar took a deep breath and cleared his throat but got deflated on looking at the hundreds of islanders who had gathered on the opposite side. He asked Midde to make the announcement.

'I have bet on the other side, so I cannot announce, Malakar Da.'

'I have known these people for so long and have eaten their food. How will I announce?' Malakar was feeling helpless. Then, he mustered all the strength he had and said, 'Brothers, we will not be able to stay on the island anymore.'

'Why? Have you been transferred? Who will come in your place?'

The two could not hear what the islanders were saying. But the people could hear them. Malakar cleared his throat again. 'Brothers, we will not come back again.'

'Why? Won't you come back to extort us?'

The tide was steadily progressing. The moonlight shone on the people of the island. A thin blanket of fog seemed to embrace the moonlight. Malakar tried his best to speak out again.

'We will never be back again, friends.'

The crowd on the other side grew impatient. They had realized that Malakar and the constable had not taken pains to come on a launch with a loudspeaker just to say just that. Jamuna and Batashi stood there in the crowd. They hadn't taken any male partners this time. Pitambar, Jamuna's partner from the previous season, had taken another woman when he could not find her. Ganesh had stayed out, fearing that the police might come for Batashi after what she had done.

'I cannot make out what he is trying to say. He is just beating around the bush.'

'No, no, I think he has been transferred. It is a government job after all,' another woman said.

'It's high tide now. Why don't you come to the island with your launch boat and talk to us?'

Malakar tested the mic again. He couldn't shake off his clumsiness and make the announcement clearly. 'The government has asked me to tell you that I will not come to the island anymore.'

'Bastards. Don't come if you don't have to. Why are you wasting our time and yours?' Someone from the crowd said this and looked around for support. How did it matter whether they came to the island or not!

'Listen all of you. You will have to listen to the government. If you don't, you will not be spared. The highest government—the DM or district magistrate—has said that the island, the water and the stars in the sky . . .' Malakar stopped to catch his breath. '. . . they all belong to the government.'

'They belong to God,' Midde butted in.

'You are right, but what is God's also belongs to the government because the government looks after it.'

The people on the island kept listening to the conversation between the two that floated to them through the mic. Why were the two speaking in such contradictory terms?

'The island belongs to Dhaneshwari Dasi. It was Dhanapati's before that and, before that, it belonged to Pedru who got it from Ma Kamala.' Malakar knew everything and yet he said that everything belonged to the government!

'Listen to me, friends, whether the island once belonged to Pedru or Ma Kamala is another matter. It now belongs to the government. So, you can make out that God and government are one and the same.' Malakar said this as if he could make out what was going on in the islanders' minds. 'We have been asked by the government to tell you that we will not come back to the island.'

'That doesn't concern us,' an islander said.

'Come to the island. Bring your launch in.'

'We are pained by this. We sympathize with you but one will have to listen to the government.'

Batashi stood close to Jamuna. After a while, she nudged Jamuna. 'What is that man saying? Why should we feel bad if the two governments stopped coming to the island? It should make us happy, isn't it?'

'Listen, friends. The government is all-powerful. It doesn't listen to people like us. That is because it has our interest in mind. It is called public interest.'

'So what?'

'No one will be able to come to the island again,' Malakar finally blurted out. 'Do you follow? The government has taken over the island and will not allow anyone to come to the island.'

'What will the government take?' Many islanders asked in unison, still unable to fathom what Malakar had just said.

Malakar asked the boatman to lift the anchor. He prepared to make the final announcement. 'By the coming new moon, the island should be vacated. I have been instructed by the government to inform you. If you do not vacate the island on your own, the government will forcefully throw you out. We will not come back to the island either. Please ensure that you leave the island by the new moon. The government is not prepared to listen to any excuses and will use force, if necessary. I have left some leaflets at the tea stall. Please read them carefully and prepare to vacate the island.'

The launch blew its whistle and prepared to leave. Malakar and Midde could hear the roar of the islanders behind them. They pelted stones at the launch. Some tried to get into their boats to chase it. It picked up speed and soon got lost in the foggy darkness of the vast waters. People on the island fell silent. *Had they heard it right? Where were the leaflets?!*

Twenty-One

See them float away, the waters surge,
The tortoise takes them, as the wives urge.

It was the Kartik full moon night once again; the night on which this story started. Many moons ago, on this night, Pedru Dhanapati had gone into the sea and took the island on his back.

Deep underneath sleeps the great Dhanapati,
From Lisboan came the pirate haughty.

Jamuna hummed her tune. The launch had vanished into the darkness immediately after Malakar made the announcement. It took a few moments for the rattled villagers to understand what had happened.

'Where are the leaflets?' someone finally asked.

They got hold of the leaflets and ran towards Dhanapati's house. Dhaneshwari sat alone in the verandah. She had heard the crackle of the microphone. The north wind brought some words to her and she could piece them together.

Buli Ma lit a lantern and placed it in the verandah when people started gathering at Dhanapati's house. He had been sedated with medicines, otherwise he kept irritating Kunti from inside the room. She was not sure if the announcement was true. Could the big government, the BDO, do such a thing? Could he order them out of the island? Did he not know how helpless they would become?

Had he forgotten their lonely afternoon when everyone else slept but them? Did Kunti not teach him how to make love? If he had forgotten everything, then there is no magic in Kunti's body and she was not prepared to accept that.

After someone read out the leaflet in the light of the lantern, people started wailing. 'Dhanapati, Dhaneshwari . . . please save us from this disaster!' they cried in unison. 'When the government takes something, it doesn't listen to anybody. It has been taking village after village around our native places.'

'Let Dhaneshwari do something.'

'You had promised us food and shelter for twelve months.'

'What has your big government done?' Buli Ma joined the others now.

'Shut up, all of you. We don't have to go immediately. Give me time to think. Tomorrow, let's conduct the puja of the tortoise underneath the Malabar ebony tree. We'll seek help from him.'

The Malabar ebony tree looked just the same. There was no change there. The puja had supposedly been started years ago by Pedru himself. This was the place where the trader and the constable sat last time. Much had happened since then. Last year, Dhanapati was a strong man and controlled everything. Kunti was his child-wife. This time, she sat on Dhanapati's chair. The shadow of the evening was reflected on the water. The moon shone in it. There was no change in the way the moon shone on this day since the ownership of the island changed hands.

Dhanapati and Dhaneshwari belong to Lisboan,
Ma Kamala gave them all they own.

'Jamuna, will all this happen next year again?' Dhaneshwari let out a sigh.

'Come! You hold the private part of Dhanapati. You should be knowing how it looks, better than others!' Jamuna joked.

Sabitri, Lakshmi, Saraswati, Natu and Batu chuckled on hearing what Jamuna said.

> The water shakes and Dhanapati comes,
> He is aroused in both his homes.

Dhaneshwari came down. No men were involved in the puja this time. The women had decided that they would do all within their power to please the government. They had no other place to dry the catch that the men had brought in. They would give all that the government wanted. They would not resist if he wanted to have a woman to serve him.

Dhaneshwari did not agree. The women would stay on the island for twelve months. They would not be kicked around like dogs. 'This is Ma Kamala's island. She gave it to Pedru Dhanapati. Now I have got it. Let us pray to Ma Kamala and Ma Mary. They will protect us. The island will remain ours.'

The previous night, the men seemed to give up. They did not want to fight the government because according to them, it was futile. They wanted to seek compensation from the government and leave the island for good. They would find jobs in trawlers instead.

The women listened quietly and did not reply. After the men left, the women asked Kunti to call Dhanapati. 'We need his advice now,' they said.

'His time is over. He will not talk anymore. I am the owner of the island and I will take a call.'

'Will you manage? You are just a woman like us! Listen, we might have to surrender to the government and go to him to satisfy his urge. He can call any of us and we will have to go to him. Why should we resist? We belong to the government just like the island does. Do you know that the government can arrest any of us, including you and put us behind bars?'

'I have told the big government, BDO sahib,' Dhaneshwari said.

'He was the one who sent the leaflets, isn't it?'

'No, it wasn't him.'

'You are mistaken. You don't know how tough the government can be. Call Dhanapati.'

'He is preparing to go down into the sea and leave for Lisboan.'

'Times have changed, Dhaneshwari. Let us offer ourselves to the government.'

'Stop! Not a word more. No one will go to the government. Dhanapati had allowed this, but could he save the island?!

The men did not understand why the women should not offer themselves to the government as and when they were called. If they could live with different men for six months every year, why shouldn't they go to please the government? They decided to go to Ghoradal and find out more. They would be happy to get some compensation.

The women had made a model of the giant tortoise the way they had been doing for the past several years. They had fashioned breasts on his body and his private part looked like a trunk. Dhaneshwari made the trunk and unknowingly started fondling it, her mind full of that afternoon's lovemaking.

> The Kartik full moon night takes her back,
> The afternoon love of which there is lack.

Soon, her blood surged and she grew excited. Her breath was quick and short. She was ready to offer herself to the government again. *Where was he?* Her master had seen them that afternoon. He didn't need eyes to see them together. He had perceived the heat of their togetherness.

> Government, my government, do you remember me at all?
> My master is blind but his eyes see our call.

'They won't do it. No one can remove Dhaneshwari from her seat.' Kunti said with a resolve that surprised the other women.

That afternoon, the government had removed her clothes one by one. He savoured every bit of what he saw. Kunti kept saying that she needed to stay on the island for twelve months. He agreed. That way, they could find each other easily.

'Yes, you will stay there and wait for me, always.' He had promised her that. Then, he put his finger on her mouth and asked her to be quiet. But Kunti carried on.

'Will you give me a hundred babies?'

That was when Dhanapati woke up from his sleep and called out for Dhaneshwari. Her words got carried to him through the porous walls made of bamboo sticks.

How could he forget his promise and ask them to evacuate the island! Dhaneshwari grew angry and felt that her body was getting pumped up.

'Government takes everything he wants,' Jamuna tried to emphasize her point again.

'It won't happen, Jamuna.'

'They have been taking village after village.'

'I will not let the government take our island. I will fight.'

Batashi and Jamuna had realized that Kunti would start her story again. She had inherited this legacy from Dhanapati. This was the tradition of the island. Dhaneshwari was continuing it.

'I left Lisboan because of the government there. I came here and took control of the island. Now, there is government here, I will move elsewhere.'

'Is that true?'

'I came from Lisboan when the government started torturing my people. The saint Pedru rode a tortoise to escape the government. I will also go elsewhere with you women. My Dhanapati is getting ready to go into the water. He will turn into a tortoise and start his journey.'

'Wake him up,' Jamuna urged.

'How do we do that? Batashi asked.

'Do it the way women arouse men. Kiss his manhood. Tap it. He will wake up.'

'That is how my umbrella seller would get aroused,' Batashi said.

'It's not just him . . .' Jamuna said.

'The private part of the tortoise looks like that of my umbrella seller,' Batashi whispered into Jamuna's ears.

'Dhanapati's was also like that when he was young.'

'Bring your man into your mind. Imagine that it is he who sleeps. I am bringing my government into my mind. When your man rises, Dhanapati will rise too.'

> Kartik full moon night, moon washes all,
> Dhanapati answers to Dhaneshwari's call.

'We will go to a place where there is no government.'

Yes, take us there.'

'We will go to a Lisboan where there is fragrance of flowers in the breeze . . . where there is white snow that gets reflected in the colour of the white flowers. We will not go to the Lisboan that is cursed and where feathers of birds fall off.'

'We will go to a place where women are worshipped by men and government does not demand to sleep with them.'

'Will we get a man for twelve months there?'

'Yes, we will. Even the big government cheated me. He said we would get to stay on the island for twelve months. During those times, men become weak and say what the women want them to say. The old master was blind but got to hear everything.'

'Shame on the government,' Batashi said.

'Let us wake Dhanapati up,' Kunti hissed. 'Remove all your clothes and wake him up. Touch him with your breasts, hips and lips. Kiss him everywhere. He will wake up.'

> Dhanapati, Dhanapati, take us there,
> Where there is no fear, in your care.

'What if he really wakes up?'

'Let him wake up and take the island away on his back. The government takes everything it wants, I know that. It has been taking village after village, leaving people homeless. My mother and father were left on the streets. The government took their home, their land and everything they had, to build towns, bridges and mills. Even the tree under which my father and mother sat was cut down. They found no shelter anywhere. The government has forgotten his promise. He finished his job and forgot me. He threw me in a garbage dump.' Kunti kept beating her bare chest and entreated Dhanapati to wake up and take them away to a land where there was peace and love. 'Take my body . . . see how youthful I am. Wake up, take us away,' she cried helplessly. The other women did the same.

Naked women kept repeating their plea. They went into a trance trying to wake the tortoise up. There was no other way to save the island but to wake him up so that he could float away with the island on his back.

Deep in the night, Dhanapati woke up. The women realized to their joy that the island was floating like a ship and moving forward. The sea surged all around them and Pedru's ship—the island—whistled aloud.

This might have been true. Dhanapati's story might have come true. There was so much in this world that was pure imagination in the beginning but turned out to be true later. Aniket Sen stood on the riverbank at Ghoradal and prayed that the team of policemen that had left that morning to take control of the island, don't find it there. The women had floated away along with their island. He imagined that the team would find just water at the spot where the river met the sea. The island had vanished. Many in the administration would ask if the island was just a figment of someone's imagination. *Had it really existed at the spot?*

Let the story of Dhanapati's Island remain as elusive and magical as the island itself. Let Dhaneshwari create her own story in her own island. Let those stories get carried to the mainland by the breeze. Let her stories lash on to the mainland along with the waves and get scattered from land to land.